The WAITING HOUSE

A NOVEL IN STORIES

LISETTE BRODEY

SABERLEE BOOKS

Published by:

Saberlee Books
Los Angeles, CA
United States of America

Copy editing: D.L. Savvides, Kenneth Brodey
Cover illustration & design: Shykia Bell

ISBN-13: 978-1-7340894-4-8 (paperback)
ISBN-13: 978-1-7340894-3-1 (e-book)

To Sheri A. Wilkinson,

Thank you for being such a supportive friend in so many ways …
for so many years.

"If you are not long, I will wait for you all my life."

— Oscar Wilde

ACKNOWLEDGMENTS

To D.L. Savvides for coming to my rescue and being such a wonderful editor;

To Kenneth Brodey for his superb preliminary edits and brotherly support;

To Shykia Bell who worked so hard to create this beautiful cover art for me;

To Lisa Wentworth for being such an amazing friend over the past eleven years, and doing so much to support the writing and production of this novel … and always believing another book will follow;

To Charles Roth for his endless love and support over the many years;

To all of the following people who lent a hand with my research:
Dara Brodey, John Daly, Laura Daly, Lone Nyboe Jensen, Ricardo Motta, Nica Hernandez; Cynthia and Mike Pecoraro, and Sue-Ellen Wellfonder;

To Deborah Nam-Krane for being an invaluable beta reader and friend;

To Stephanie Bauerlein, Shykia Bell, Kenneth Brodey, Dody Cox, PattiAnn Cutter, Dionne Lister, and Sheri A. Wilkinson for their ongoing support and kindness;

And to Kathleen Harryman for creating such beautiful animated and promotional graphics for me;

There are so many people who have supported me in so many ways. I wish it were possible to thank each and every one of you. I hope you all know who you are. And last, but not least, thank you to my fellow authors for your support, advice, inspiration, and friendship. You all mean so much to me.

SABERLEE BOOKS BY LISETTE BRODEY

Crooked Moon
Squalor, New Mexico
Molly Hacker Is Too Picky!
Mystical High (Book 1, The Desert Series)
Desert Star (Book 2, The Desert Series)
Drawn Apart (Book 3, The Desert Series)
Barrie Hill Reunion
Hotel Obscure: A Collection of Short Stories
Love, Look Away
The Sum of our Sorrows
The Waiting House: A Novel in Stories

The WAITING HOUSE

A NOVEL IN STORIES

Chapter One: CONRAD

I am the man.

I am the grand master of this architectural relic of a bygone era. Truth? I'd prefer to claim these walls are the ancient ruins of a grand society long extinguished ... perhaps something akin to the Roman Forum. But this imposing erection, this bastard child of misappropriated funds and offensively garish taste, was never the hub of anything worthy. Nothing governmental or respectable ever happened here ...and yes, I am well aware those two words do not often hold hands when they're out together in public. Let me put this another way: you will never find goings-on from this establishment in any history book. This cluster of rooms, all differing in size and status, has no significance in the world.

Built in 1942, courtesy of Nathaniel Noca's inheritance (two-thirds stolen from his siblings), his dream of owning a hotel for those who wanted to live the authentic Hollywood life became a reality. Ironic, I think, as the very meaning of an authentic "Hollywood life" was to exist in a mirage ... to feel cherished and superior, to toss decorum to the wind, and to feign affection for the adoring crowds before seeking refuge from them. Here, one engaged in wanton recklessness and aberrant sexual behavior while simultaneously working to get their names in and out of the very same publications. It was a daunting, befuddling, and never-ending task for those inclined (or forced by the powers that be) to give a damn.

With no ethics to guide him, the felonious Nathaniel, a failed doctor, along with hotel guests, most of whom were more skilled at balancing their escapes from virtue than he, plunged into a never-ending bacchanal. He dined on debauchery and sipped on sacrilege. Beautiful women rotated in his orbit solely as a means to satisfy the desires of his flesh and work off his ever-present rancor. There was only one woman, a long-standing resident (yes, she did often sit), Ava Elisabeth, to whom he gave his heart ... only she did not wish to have it. Then, after many years, she gave her love to a Parisian doctor, a hotel guest of only a month or so, and left to marry him and build a new life across the seas.

His anger at its peak, Nathaniel burst from his bubble of delusion, raging against the world. He had not only lost the object of his unwanted affection, but also learned that his mostly ill-gotten fortune no longer bulged from his pockets ... and what used to bulge from between them was hopelessly flaccid. Official cause of death: auto-defenestration from Ava Elisabeth's just-vacated eighth-floor penthouse suite. Only there was nothing sweet about it. He was mercilessly mocked and shamed ... so savagely, I would say, that even in his state of un-aliveness, he felt every stone cast in his direction and the spit from every nasty word spewed on his face.

His next of kin, Ruth and Victor, the siblings who were still attempting reclamation of what he had stolen from them years ago, were granted ownership of the hotel. Quietly slipping into the background, they hired me (as "grand master"), among others, to resuscitate these weary lodgings from near death.

Nathaniel was granted one last wish: for the "death suite" never to be occupied by anyone again unless Ava Elisabeth returned. His siblings agreed, most especially because they were terrified of the postscript in his last message to the world ... "I shall haunt this space without remorse if it is occupied by the wrong person."

History lesson over. Today, this fifty-one-room structure, once a place to rent for a night or to live indefinitely, is now an apartment house. Each unit boasts a unique ensemble of faded Hollywood Regency furniture, appealing to those with a desire to avoid a stale world where the ordinary thrives and often reproduces. But it is far more than the dated décor that lures them here.

I will not offer the legal name of this residence. Nor will I give you the address. There is no physical room at the inn. It is pregnant with souls who wait … some for things they can name … others who only know something is missing. Thus, with questionable faith, they must wait for it. Length of time: indeterminate.

This is The Waiting House. And I am Conrad Daniel Beauregard Shintz: overseer, landlord, possessing the gift of near-perfect omniscience and a laudable judge of residents. I know little else about myself, for my memories are gone. My superb intuition speaks to me, however, and informs me that my amnesia is due to unspeakable trauma. When Nathaniel's siblings, Ruth and Victor, offered me employment, I did not tell them I am unable to remember myself. Rather, I fabricated a very normal past, replete with the most relevant of experience, and confidently expressed a desire to obtain a position I felt entitled to be mine.

As is now evident, my charm and aplomb swayed them. I am here, having offered decades of service, still fixated upon the notion that my gift of omniscience is at fatal odds with my long-standing amnesia. While I know not from whence I came, like the now-extinguished Nathaniel, I am hopelessly in love with Ava Elisabeth. However, as she is old and mired in a state of moral dereliction, literally, she cannot see me. She is the living, breathing key to my wretched heart. Nathaniel's slavish obsession with her may be partially responsible for her incessant greed and coveting of expensive trinkets at the expense of others. Losing her, no doubt, was truly the reason he chose to auto-defenestrate from the space she occupied. (Coward!) Alas, there was always more money to be found, but never another Ava Elisabeth.

Traumatized as a young woman, she carried her pain with her, which, no doubt, was perhaps an even greater factor in the decisions she has made. Unlike Ava Elisabeth, I am one of the lucky ones who don't remember their youth. That is what I tell myself. Perhaps I should be more merciful toward the woman I love. I am so ravaged and torn.

She is not the only one who cannot see me, but I single her out because her blindness pains me so. Now, it is time, with discretion of course, for me to offer glimpses into the mad-brained and extraordinarily strange existence of all who wait here. I shall begin with my beloved, expanding upon what I have already disclosed.

Chapter Two: AVA ELISABETH

Love does not age. Not when it is so deep that upon first sight, one feels tethered to the soul of another being. Nor when that soul's imprudent desires cause unbearable and irreparable destruction to those unfortunate enough to feel fortunate in possessing such grand love for said being.

Not enough years can ever pass to sever the ties that constrain so tightly that they overwhelm with desolation.

Ava Elisabeth was one of the earliest guests in this structure's original incarnation. The young, exotic, dark-haired beauty, barely of legal age, was of such well-formed allure, that she was heartily welcomed. Her ability to pay from her own coffers never mattered as Nathaniel, the owner, was deeply obsessed with her, thus craved her presence far more than her money. He struggled to maintain a somewhat professional decorum, thereby ever so slightly toning down his untamed libido.

Thus, how he would despair when those more handsome, of great wealth and fame (hungered for by harried housewives and libido-driven mortals of any age or sex), would fancy Ava Elisabeth. This failed man of medicine, whose field of endeavor was obtained only so that he would not be stricken from his father's will, hated those who succeeded in corralling the young goddess. Having to bear witness to it often drove him to wanton behavior better left in the dust-covered annals of unabashed shame, along with the harlots he paid and the beauteous women he spoiled.

I refer to these beings as a cluster of desperadoes, though, as I have confessed, I, too—like my predecessor whom I condemn—know what it is like to love Ava Elisabeth. I share now something of her humble beginnings. First: an overview. Then: details.

Ava Elisabeth arrived here after escaping from the safe haven of her youth. After six years in this formidable edifice, she moved to Paris, where she lived for many decades. It was upon her return here, much later in life, that I was to know her. Let me draw upon my gift of omniscience to provide detail.

On the eleventh day of the eleventh month of 1942, the U.S. Congress lowered the draft age from twenty-one to eighteen. As a result, the heartbeat of Ava Elisabeth's young life, somewhere not far from the cornfields where they frolicked, was shortly thereafter sent off to war. Romantic notions of his return fluttered above victory gardens and scrap drives as she carried on with her assigned tasks, side by side with numerous men and women of all ages. Cheerfully enough, the young beauty, as instructed, also wore a brave face and dutifully pledged allegiance to every morale-building exercise suggested to her and others who waited, with buoyant expectations, for the return of their loved ones too.

On the day that Ava Elisabeth received the distressing news, by way of the telegram sent to his family, her illusions and her heart shattered simultaneously. The rest of her life would irrevocably change, bearing sparse resemblance to any existence she had thus far known and to the reality that would become her colorful, intricately woven, yet tortured future.

A week after the gut-wrenching communiqué, once everyone had deeply settled for the night, Ava Elisabeth pulled the vulcanized fiber suitcase from the dark reaches of her closet, and into it, she packed as much as it would hold. Under her bed, where she had stored it for safe-keeping, was his canvas-and-leather duffel bag (with two of his flannel shirts still tucked away inside) that she filled with her more personal belongings. (And yes, she took his shirts.) She was content with what she could carry, but in her haste, she neglected to wrap and carry the porcelain bisque angel that her grandmother had given her on her thirteenth birthday. Standing by a birdbath, a dove on her shoulder and one in the water, the angel, Grandma Rice promised, would always look after her. Loving the angel and her paternal grandmother, Ava Elisabeth treasured the ethereal figurine, never forgiving herself for leaving it in her past.

In the still of the star-filled night, her beloved's older brother parked his 1938 blue Ford pickup truck at the foot of the dirt gravel drive and walked toward the house to meet her. Firmly taking the two bags in hand, leaving his ne'er-to-be sister-in-law to carry only her handbag and makeup case, he quickened his pace and led the way to the truck. Once inside, he spirited her to the nearest Greyhound station, art deco on the outside and a few assorted souls decorating the waiting room. Chivalrous to the core, and honoring his late brother's sacrifice, he waited with the young beauty until morning broke through the night sky's slumber, bringing with it the bus that would carry her far away. As per her instructions, five days later, he mailed her family a letter from the local post office, letting them know that while her love was forever, it might be prudent for them to expect never to see her again.

Seven months after the young Miss Rice stepped off the Greyhound bus at her destination, she came to the hotel, met Nathaniel, and moved into the eighth-floor suite. Immediately, he hired a designer to upgrade the bedroom so it would be like none other in the hotel. Behind the bed, from the ceiling, there hung a crown canopy with sheer silver curtains. The headboard—gray satin silver fabric—fashioned as rays of sunlight, with a long satin pillow beneath it, created the most elegant setting, complete with the finest bedding, for the young beauty to lay her head and her taunting and curvaceous body.

To complete the renovation, the wallpaper was changed. A sparse wildflower motif turned the entire room, along with the plants and flowers (mostly artificial), into an extraordinary garden of nature's finest and most exotic delights. A twice-weekly bouquet of fresh flowers was delivered without fail.

The living room boasted exquisite lacquered and oversized furniture, a three-paneled brass-ornamented mirror on one wall, art and sconces on the others, and an impressive array of glass knickknacks from cities worldwide. The chandelier that hung was a ten-branch cut glass monstrosity replete with matching beads and dangling crystals.

What Nathaniel could not purchase with his mostly ill-gotten fortune and undistinguished vocation as a medical professional was her love. This I have said before. The following, I have not: everything he bought to create her paradise belonged to him. There were so many strings attached that one might have thought the young beauty a marionette. But she was not. And thus, though he tried, he was not a marionettist. Every move she made most willfully was born from her mind alone.

For six years, she lived in a glossy, glittering stupor. In the eyes of others, she was envied and alternately scorned. Always occupied, she tended the gardens, walked the canine guests, smiled invitingly from behind the reception desk, spoke in dulcet tones to the hotel's telephone callers, and performed as hostess for the many private functions held in the ballrooms and smaller spaces.

Nathaniel greatly benefitted from the efforts she put forth to respectfully earn her keep, but he was insatiable. And though he bathed in lascivious waters with those he could not name, he fumed at the baubles routinely given to her by adoring suitors. He seethed as others were bestowed with the pleasures she would never allow him.

As time raced by, leaving the hands of his clock in a permanent blur, he viewed her as coquettish, greedy, and overindulged, yet still, he could not shake his intense and unfading obsession with her. With money ill-spent, he would try to out-bauble the gift givers, silently cursing her for not loving him as he wished, most especially aware that unlike everything in her suite, the baubles were hers to keep. To control his worst impulses, he fornicated with fury, thrusting his angry manhood into the weary orifices of women whose faces he could not and did not wish to see. Rage: pounding, incessant, humiliating rage, which, as I have just illustrated, spread to every fiber of his pathological being.

On an October day in 1949, the skies at their very bluest, he learned Ava Elisabeth had departed without warning or an in-person good-bye. A note of farewell, written on the finest Crane's stationery, was all she left for him. Taking every last bauble with her, she left to marry the Frenchman I spoke of before. And this great fool, Nathaniel Noca, ever bereft of the only woman he loved, as all now know, took the only thing he had left: his life.

Incognizant of his earthly departure, she arrived in France, where a residence in the eighteenth arrondissement, a third-floor apartment, was presented to her. It was there and then that she learned that her betrothed was actually still wading in connubial waters.

She was beside herself with outrage when she learned of the deception, but when he, the doctor of falsification, Henri *le menteur,* argued with frenzied desperation that she never would have come had she known, and that their love would have been forever destroyed, she relented. And oh, how she hated herself for yielding, but this larger-than-life Frenchman, far superior to the faux doctor she left behind, opened her life and mind in ways that no man had ever done. And here she was in Paris, the City of Lights, embraced by a nascent enthusiasm she could not contain. Surrounded by seven dormer windows, split between three sides, in a small self-contained unit, she agreed to wait until it was "comfortable" for him to dissolve his long-suffering union with the daughter of a dying surgeon of notable lineage.

Though her new home was modest, it appealed to her. It was

not far from Montmartre, where she joyfully explored the cobbled streets during the day. Usually, at night, with Henri on her arm, she hobnobbed with the Paris elite, comprised of existentialists, artists, writers, politicians, the rich, the brilliantly eccentric and of most anyone who ascribed to be any of the popular pretentions *du jour.* Or in this case, *de la nuit.* Frequently, her nighttime companions fit into many categories at once … though none would recognize themselves as such. People can be so blind.

One day, missing the garden environment of the suite she abandoned, and the home of her youth, she found work with a Montmartre florist and gaily spent her days mingling with tourists and locals alike. Often, on her lunch break, she would walk up the hill to the Sacré Coeur basilica and light a candle for the first and never-forgotten love of her life. After she had said a prayer and spoken silent words to him, she would then leave the church and look out at the awe-inspiring, unencumbered view of Paris. It thrilled her so, especially as she imagined what gaiety awaited her that evening, though the camaraderie of her "*amis de la nuit*" both enthralled and exhausted her. But she was happy in company of the undeserving reprobate she had let take possession of her heart, only to stick her in a converted attic apartment, allowing her to never cease wondering what life might have been if her true love had returned from the war … or perhaps, if she had made other choices.

Henri's "dying" father-in-law lived for another fourteen years before giving up the ghost with a condition entirely different from the one Ava Elisabeth was told he suffered from. Then, and oh so conveniently, just when Henri was finally free to leave his wife, Madame *le menteuse* developed an unknown cancer, making it "*impossible*" for him to walk away, lest be scorned by all who knew him.

Livid, no longer possessing any forgiveness for Henri's egregious deception, Mlle. Rice, as the locals called her, began asking around for a new home. Upon learning this, and desperate to keep her where she was (and in his vile clutches!), Henri took a generous portion his of wife's inheritance from her recently departed father, bought the building, and handed the deed of ownership over to his mistress. As I have alluded to Ava Elisabeth's greed, this is a prime example. She happily took the property bestowed upon her, collected rents from the two apartments below her, and after two years, decided that she no longer owed Henri the pleasure of her company. Tired of the nocturnal "intellectuati" that she fraternized with, and now having a social circle entirely of her own making, she bid him farewell.

He, now being on the receiving end of deception, threatened her as only rich people know how to do, but Ava Elisabeth knew his secrets, his friends, and most of all, that his "dying" wife would not have appreciated the adultery, the spending of her money, nor the exaggerated reports of her imminent demise.

In 1964, at the age of forty, Ava Elisabeth was on her own, quite well off, and able to do as she pleased. When the second-floor tenants moved out, she moved in and turned her third-floor apartment into an art studio. She hired an artist friend to help her run it, and, when time permitted, to help develop her natural artistic gifts. Soon, she had a small but exclusive studio. For years, it was a hub for her eclectic circle of friends, and she was particularly pleased when the young men would pose in the nude, offering a leg up to her burgeoning life-drawing skills. Her forte, however, was landscape, but nude models offered explicit perks that trees and fields of flowers were (and still are) unable to provide. (Scandalous!)

When she tired of her life-drawing escapades, she hired a second person to run her studio, enabling her to freely come and go. For the next twenty-five years, she had three long-term relationships. The last one, which spanned ten years, ended only when her paramour died. Heartbroken, unable to look anywhere without seeing him in empty spaces sans mournful traces, she sold the building and made the decision to come full circle and return to her former home. I do not believe even she understood why, but her desire was compelling.

Though I had seen many photos, that day in 1990 was first time I saw the glorious Ava Elisabeth in the flesh. Nathaniel's sister, Ruth Tellert, now in her seventies, had picked her up at the airport and brought her, dare I say it, home.

This enchanting specimen of a woman, once with flowing dark hair, now had flowing silver hair, mixed with the dark hair that still grew. Her figure was every bit as voluptuous as it had once been, and she found no reason to avoid the low-cut necklines she had favored decades before. Her chestnut-brown eyes bore a hole through my heart, taunting it. Her plump lips, perfectly coated with blood-red lipstick, kissed the air as she spoke. Though I had never seen her before, she was even more beguiling than my imagination had allowed me to believe she would be.

When I heard her speak to Ruth, her smoldering tones enveloped my soul, giving me every reason to believe I might lose consciousness, but I did not. Even though the baubles she wore offered a painful reminder of every man who had loved her, I could not turn away. I could only stare, and even when she looked in my direction, it was not the face one makes when she is pretending not to see. It is the face of looking upon nothingness: me. Oh, how cursed I felt, though perhaps I was blessed that her penetrating eyes would never see how Father Time had ravaged me so. I knew then I would love her … always a bit more than I would resent her.

Shortly after that day, I learned she had no guilt (only pity) that her abrupt departure some forty-one years ago had resulted in Nathaniel Noca's wretched auto-defenestration. Unsurprised to learn that the suite had remained uninhabited for all of the years, she ordered a complete remodeling, having no wish to live in a "time capsule," then occupied the space next door until the original unit was habitable. In fact, with her vast accumulation of wealth, she purchased the unit so that it could never be taken from her.

In the year 2000, Victor Noca having died, and Ruth Tellert, a diminishing, yet still sharp eight-five-year-old woman, sold the property to a new owner, (an exotic vision in her early thirties), Darah D. Gregnut, who transformed the premises into an apartment house. From her first day as ruler of the roost, Darah did not charge me with any duties, so I carried on with my previous function … that of chief inspector and grand master.

In the twenty years since Ava Elisabeth's return, while she has grown older, she has somehow managed to be every bit as alluring, even though her eyesight has begun to fail her and the lines on her face, albeit not too many, have deepened. For all of these years, she has been as effervescent as I envision her to have been in Paris. And while her presence no longer graces the French city, rarely has a season passed without visitors from Paris and assorted other locales.

Always dressed impeccably, full to bursting with trinkets and baubles, trophies of the many men who have lusted for and with her, Ava Elisabeth is noticed by all. I would be remiss not to add that there is a pervading sadness that accompanies her, though if one does not possess the depth to see beyond her come-hither smiles, one would not notice it. One has to love her, as deeply as I do, to know the sadness exists.

Perhaps Darah, her frequent companion, understands this. Eight years ago, she gifted a Persian kitten to her, a creature of white fluff with a face that appears annoyed and disgusted, yet who is endowed with the most endearing personality.

Even when it comes to cats, Ava Elisabeth must always have the best. The cat wears a rhinestone collar, and, as I often muse, looks every bit as mercenary as the breathtaking woman who owns her. I shall tame my conflicted soul some day. For now, I move on.

Here, in the present day, one can listen to Ava Elisabeth speak, then judge for oneself.

"Mickey," she says to the cat on her lap. "No man in my life loves me as you do."

I want to scream and tell her how wrong she is. That I, Conrad Daniel Beauregard Shintz, love her more than any man ever could, but damn her, she gives the honor to a cat. I am slightly horrified and more than moderately enraged. But endowed with great fortitude, I shall calm myself and soldier on.

Wearing champagne-colored silk-satin loungewear, she blends with the furniture as if she is gracing a magazine cover, posing like royalty on her loveseat. With a button-tufted backrest, tapered wood legs, elegantly carved arms and trim, and adorned with pink and silver pillows, of tassels and shimmer, the small sofa's deep velvet cushions offer the comfort and luxury that she craves. It is her oxygen, I dare say. It is at a right angle from the matching couch, but she prefers the intimacy of the smaller piece when only one guest is present. On days that she is expecting company or no company at all, she often sits on her chaise lounge by the window. What she sees, however, is not outside. I'm certain of that. I desperately wish to know what commands her attention so.

The cat purrs.

"It's getting quite late. Do you know what time Darah is coming by?" With two fingers, she brushes hair from her forehead, showing off the jeweled rings and diamond tennis bracelet given to her by lovers. Such a flagrant exhibition of her greed.

The cat looks toward the front door as if to say "Soon."

"I'm patient." She strokes the cat and lets a delightful laugh escape her lips. "Except when I'm not, I suppose." She cocks her head and turns it to meet Mickey's eyes. "We all have our moments, don't we? Even you, *mon petit chou.*"

As if to agree, the feline nuzzles her forearm.

Ava Elisabeth's eyes sweep the room but focus on nothing in particular. Her faint smile reverses as she continues talking to the cat.

"There are so many beautiful treasures in this room, and while I am still able to identify them, and to remember where every single one came from, I can no longer see anything with great detail. With much in life, we don't always appreciate an existence until it begins to fade … or until it's gone." She feels wretched and displays her emotion with a sigh. "I've endured so many losses. The very worst, Mickey, are the ones that rob us of good-bye. No matter how many times you speak to a departed soul, nothing ever takes the place of having been there … before or during one's transition. It's so very painful." She pauses to allow a distressing thought in. "If I do have to say good-bye to you, sweetheart, and I hope that won't be so for a long time, even with my declining health, I promise you, we will have our moment. And never to worry, Darah will always look after you. And one day, we will be reunited."

The cat appears to understand. Perhaps I am just transferring my emotion to the creature lucky enough to be upon her lap feeling the tender touch of her fingertips as they caress him.

"I do hope Darah gets here soon. I expected her a good fifteen minutes ago. Something is weighing on me." She looks down at Mickey and laughs. "Not you. Something much heavier that I don't think you would understand, *mon petit chou.*"

A knock is heard at the door. (I should note that while all units have doorbells, Ava Elisabeth's does not. When she was eighteen, the news of her boyfriend's tragic death was delivered after the ringing of her family's doorbell, and thus, the sound of them has traumatized her ever since.) As she always does, Darah lets herself in. She is smartly dressed in a black pants suit with a pressed white blouse underneath. Her dark hair pinned up in a fashionable messy look on her head, is held in place by a tortoiseshell comb with cubic zirconia studs. I notice she is wearing a pendant belonging to Ava Elisabeth. It must have been given to her, though it is hard for me to imagine my beloved parting with anything of significance. My goodness. Even the gold bangles on her arm were gifts from Ava Elisabeth's long-ago Parisian lovers.

With grace, Darah places her shoulder bag, and a small tote she is carrying, onto a chair to the right of the door. A smile lights up her face, one that perhaps even rivals Ava Elisabeth's. She walks over and sits on the loveseat next to her. "Sorry I'm late. I had the craziest guest ever." She pauses. "Well, maybe not *ever*. My regular concierge, Stephanie, asked a rather desperate-looking guest if she could help him. When she heard him say 'I feel awful,' of course, she told him where to find the nearest doctor. She couldn't figure out why her suggestion went over like a lead balloon or why he was screaming at her. Apparently, he was looking for a 'falafel,' and she thought he'd said 'feel awful.'" Darah flicks her hands in the air, palms up, toward heaven. "It would be rather funny if the guy hadn't gone so crazy on her. A sane person might even have laughed."

Ava Elisabeth responds with a sly smile. "And what did he get, dearest, a doctor or a sandwich?"

Darah laughs. "Neither. Only the force of the two cops who hauled his ass out of the lobby for disturbing the peace."

As Ava Elisabeth participates in a respite from her despair by way of a laugh, Mickey jumps from her lap and runs over to his miniature brass bed and promptly, after three full rotations, goes to sleep.

"He was tired. But he can rest now that you're here." Ava Elisabeth squeezes Darah's hand.

Her visage morphing from mirth to consternation, Darah appears alarmed. "You said something was on your mind ... something heavy ... are you ready to talk about it?"

Ava Elisabeth's eyes travel the room as they soak in the details of what they can still see. "As the oft-quoted yet unknown sources are often known to say, 'there is no time like the present.'"

"Talk to me," Darah says.

"I haven't offered you anything to eat or drink."

"I know where the kitchen is. I'm fine." She pauses. "But I'm not so sure that you are."

Letting a long sigh travel between them, my dearest begins her speech. "Darah, there's no one I trust more than you. I'll go one step further: there's no one I've ever trusted more then you … only one person I've trusted as much as you."

Darah looks quizzically at her. "Please, tell me what's on your mind."

Another sigh. "Well, when I first lived here, from 1943 until 1949, this elegant, yet Uriah-Heep-filled structure, was truly no more than your garden-variety den of iniquity. And on good days, it was actually respectable. Simply put, my darling, it was life with all of its warts. Occasionally, dressed in its Sunday best, I'd say that it represented life, well, Hollywood life, but really, just life."

Nodding in recognition, Darah's eyes reveal her understanding. "Ruth schooled me on the history … and the reputation. She wanted me to know exactly what I was getting into before I took over the reins. And in the many years I've owned this place, I can't say she steered me wrong."

Picking up the small crystal ball off the coffee table in front of her, Ava Elisabeth peers into it, offering the onlooker the idea that she expects to receive an answer. She looks into Darah's eyes. "My darling, if you think I'm a bit daft, or even worse than daft, you must tell me. Just promise, no matter what, that you won't 'play along' to placate me. My God, I would despise that."

Taking the crystal ball from her hands, Darah gently lays it on the table and takes Ava Elisabeth's hands in hers. "I'm listening. And yes, I have a clear picture of this place in its heyday. But you want to say something about it *now*, don't you?"

"I do."

"Which is …"

"This is not the same place it was back when, Darah. And I

don't mean because society outside of these walls has changed. Before I elaborate, I must tell you, this suite is haunted."

Taking one hand away, Darah places it over her round, luscious lips, then lets it drop. "Ruth told me that her brother threatened to haunt this place after he jumped out of the window. Do you think it's him? Nathaniel Noca?" She removes her hand and clasps it once more over Ava Elisabeth's.

Without even a second to ponder the question, it is answered. "No, I'd recognize that lecherous man in any form he presented himself. I'd be able to feel his eyes undressing me at every turn as his pants bulged in sync with his randy stare." She pauses to expel a sigh of disgust. "I'm quite sure of it, my sweet. No, it is not him. It is a much gentler spirit. And perhaps I misspoke when I used the word 'haunts.' I think that 'visits' is far more befitting."

Confused, Darah looks at her. "I understand. And I don't doubt you. But how does that tie in with what you said about this place many years ago. I'm not entirely following."

Ava Elisabeth laughs uncomfortably, banishing the awkward moment with a quick and fleeting smile. Letting go of Darah's hands, she squeezes her own together. (The emerald ring from her deceptive paramour, Henri, burns my eyes as it mocks me.) "My dear, you have owned this place for many years now. While you are far too young to have known it in its infancy, you must be able to see that we no longer have the need to exist in verisimilitude. Rather, we eat, sleep, and breathe in a faux reality of our own making." She looks up at the Parisian floral crystal chandelier. "Tell me what you see."

"A vintage waterfall chandelier." Darah looks curiously at her. "Isn't that what you see?"

My dearest is disturbed and must hide her inner discord. "At present, only streams of light that look as if they are flowing downward. I cannot see much detail in the chandelier at all. My vision is fading, so it isn't really that odd if our perceptions were different."

"No." Darah has an evolving hesitation in her voice. "And this isn't about lighting fixtures. If I know nothing else … I know that."

Ava Elisabeth abruptly stands, but finding the act dizzying, she sits again, with Darah's quick assistance. She has decided to speak no more on the subject; that is clear. "I'm not sure what I'm saying. I'm very tired."

Eyeing Ava Elisabeth's loungewear, which usually doubles for nightwear, Darah exudes sweet sympathy. She looks at the matching couch. "Do you want to lie down for a bit? Better yet, why don't you let me help you prepare for bed? I think a good night's sleep would do you good."

Ava Elisabeth squeezes her hand again. "Will you, please? I don't see so well anymore. Last night I nearly walked into the wall." Noticing Darah's alarm, she hastens to lighten the mood. "But I escaped my brush with death; I live to tell the tale."

Ten minutes later, my darling rests comfortably in her bed, her head sinking into the top pillow. As her eyelids flutter, Darah turns off the bedside lamp and checks to make sure that the three pink scallop-shell night-lights, leading the way to the bathroom (and inside it), are in working order.

Darah walks to the chair beside the front door and picks up the tote. I am expecting her to pick up both bags and leave, but that is not what is happening. Pulling a wrapped item out of the tote, Darah retraces her steps into Ava Elisabeth's bedroom. Unwrapping what I presume is a gift, (too far away for my eyes to identify) she places it on a dresser and speaks in low tones that I cannot hear. Then, as I once again expect her to leave, she walks over to Ava Elisabeth's bed and whispers something else in her ear.

Finally, taking the now-empty tote and her shoulder bag, Darah is ready to depart as I first expected her to do.

I am shaken to the core. This is the first time I can recall not being able to see and hear all that my inquisitive nature demands to know. I must get some sleep and try to clear my head of Ava Elisabeth. Tomorrow, I shall visit another floor. Perhaps the fourth. There are some interesting creatures residing there.

Chapter Three: LEE AND ELLIE

I have always enjoyed an odd attraction to the west corner apartment on the fourth floor. Its grand windows, including two that intersect at 90-degree angles, please me. They are, however, replete with distinct graphic treatments that would tire me to describe and exhaust my creative juices. I am unable to comment on the view outside. Not because beauty is in the eye of the beholder, but rather, because we all see what we wish ... or need ... to see.

In the category of defying description, hanging on an opposite wall would be the garishly framed grotesque portrait of Gloria Swanson as Norma Desmond. She is, perhaps, waiting for her close-up, but I, for one, never want to get close enough to verify.

Wait. Reset. Back to one. I am unable to continue without a brief commentary on the revolting "beholder" cliché that I utilized to make a simple point. While we can agree that "beholders" have divergent opinions, we may not agree on which "beholders" are to be believed. Suffice it to say that, for the sake of my continuing narrative, my opinion of what *I* behold will hereby be deemed as undeniable truth. That was easy enough. Moving on ...

Ellie and Lee, the young couple who live here, vacillate between bickering and mouth-to-mouth (or genital-to-genital) combat. It is rare that they enjoy any kind of in-between. Why is this so? I will attempt to explain.

The maternal unit of Ellie is a supermarket cashier; the paternal unit a union machinist who belongs to a lodge where they serve iceberg lettuce and Russian dressing.

Lee's units, two overpaid attorneys who pretentiously self-identify as a "power couple," were not pleased when their barrister spawn not only began dating, but also had the audacity to marry a young woman of appalling social status: a manicurist who believed her station had been elevated … merely by exchanging the act of cutting dead cuticles with the styling of proletariat hair. She is judged on little else, and constant pressure, mostly of the passive-aggressive kind, is put upon Lee to uncouple and "realize his full potential." And therein lies the foundation for much of the unpleasantness between them.

As a distraction from their own problems, Ellie and Lee enjoy speculating about an older couple living in the east corner apartment whose names they don't even know. Discussing what they perceive to be OPI (other people's issues), has been their most successful way to temporarily detach from their own inconvenient reality.

Something is happening now. I shall narrate.

Lee, returning home from work, too weary to take the stairs, departs Darth (his pet name for the elevator). He is reenergized to see the old man standing against the hallway wall, his well-loved clothing caressing the honeycomb wallpaper as he slides to the ground. Thud! Or perhaps crack! Does it matter? There, oblivious to the perhaps-broken bone, he sits. It is obvious, Lee surmises, that the man cannot bear to return to the missus. She must harangue him at every opportunity. Perhaps, she puts too much garlic in his mashed potatoes so that it will emerge from his pores and thus serve as a natural repellant to other women.

Lee rethinks his conjecture. No, in his natural state, the man is far too weary to be attractive to anyone … not even himself. Garlic-oozing pores would be superfluous. Is it possible that he has not tried to enjoy life and that his sad stature reflects *his* failed efforts, not those of his wife's?

Before I continue, I must interject. Darth's original name (and gender) was that of Lee's wife, Ellie. While "Ellie Vator" amused *him*, it did not please *her*, and he was requested to "lose *it* or lose me." Lee protested briefly, then changed the contraption's gender and moniker to Darth. I would be imprecise if I tried to estimate whether the human female or the transportation machine has more ups and downs. Not wishing to loiter in the lobby of wayward thoughts, I return to my original narrative.

A neighbor, walking toward Darth, doesn't even acknowledge the old man on the floor to his right. Because, for this dwelling, Lee must surmise, spontaneous seating may not be perceived to be out of place … if it is perceived at all.

The old man looks like hell, but clearly will survive. Deciding to emulate the neighbor and deny the offer of a helping hand, Lee adjusts the strap on his right shoulder as it dips from the weight of his fancy leather satchel. He strolls to his front door, turns the key, and walks into his abode. Without stopping to look around, he drops his satchel onto one of the odd-green vintage wingback chairs (he despises them with great passion), then settles in the leopard-patterned chaise (with deep-button tufting and brass-nail head trim) he adores. How it understands his body's need to curve just so. Relaxing, he fails to make the usual apology to his satchel for resting it upon a fixture of such nauseating taste. Grabbing a faux-fur pillow, he hugs it to his chest, smiling as the gold tassels tickle the underside of his chin. He is reminded of Ellie stroking him in the same spot as he once caressed the beloved kitty of his youth. But after the verbal brawl of the night before, he is reticent to allow any carnal pleasures to travel south.

"Oh, happy day. Mr. Superior comes home to his white-trash wife," Ellie says as she walks into the living room, licking a touch of melted butter from her middle finger. "I thought you might be dining with Dadsy and Mumsie at one of those oat-cuisine places where the plates look like they were prepared in an avatar."

"Haute not oat. And aviaries enclose birds. Not avatars." As Lee corrects her, the fight seemingly drains from him.

"Yeah, that," she says, now rubbing her index and middle fingers along the windowsill to assess the dust situation. "The high-class aviary-slash-greasy spoon where they try to max out your credit card for capturing that 'a-bird-shit-green-polka-dots look on your plate. Except the customers are so rich, that never happens." She feels a need to clarify. "The maxing-out part."

"I'm sorry you feel so judged and inferior. And really, you don't have to prove your worth to me or keep the sarcasm going twenty-four seven. Come on, Ell, don't blame me for what my parents do ... or where they eat."

Ellie bites her lip to keep away the tears. "Your parents definitely think they're better than me ... and too many days, it feels like you think the same way. Your mother thinks I'm low-rent garbage just because I don't eat the same food as they do."

"That's crazy. Come on, Ellie. State your point of view, but don't exaggerate."

"Who's exaggerating? That one time I ran into her, she went on and on about how wonderful the food is at their chosen eateries ... and that if you never went to eat with them ... your palate wouldn't appreciate anything beyond spaghetti and meatballs. So, yeah, Lee, excuse me if I mock that crap they pay the big bucks for." She slaps her palms together, and the dust and butter on her fingers become one. "Because they mock me all the time, and I get much-needed satisfaction giving it right back ... even if they never hear me."

"Forget about them. They're just restaurant snobs."

"No, it's a lot more than that. They're everything snobs. And getting back to their chosen vittles—I get that it's some kind of food art—but that green color ... I think it's how gan*grene* got its name." She laughs as he smirks in acknowledgment.

"So, you hate *that* particular shade of green, but yet you love these chartreuse-y olive chairs?" Lee nods to indicate the wingbacks with caned sides. He does his best impersonation of an aggressive salesman. "Want some despair in your chair? Fear for your rear?"

"Stop, you. They're retro coolness. I've grown to love them. A smart decision since we rented a furnished place and can't toss anything."

"Not allowed. It's right there in the lease."

"Your choice, Lee. And I know why. You didn't want to invest in anything that might tie us together."

Lee yawns and rubs his eyes. "Cut it, Ellie. I married you. That's a wee bit more permanent than buying furniture."

"Not when Dadsy is a divorce lawyer who'd be happier than a pig in shit to take your case." She puts a hand out to silence him. "And before you tell me you don't want to fight, I don't either. Last night took everything out of me. Imagine being married to someone who you love with all your heart, only to know you'll never be good enough for his family. And you know what makes it worse? To know that person loves you but *still* can't figure out if you're worth the trouble. And can't tell his parents, for once and for all, to butt out." She seethes. "So, Mister 'I'll placate both sides,' I'm sick of waiting to find out if I'm good enough for the long haul. If you can stomach me for more than two years. Or if you'll have the cojones to ever get off the fence."

"Ellie …"

"No, I'm talking. And you know what's really pathetic? You can't even say for sure because you're waiting to find out if you're going to be disinherited. Or made partner someday."

Lee, still lying on the chaise, sighs and looks at the ceiling. "If I never inherit a dime, I'll be quite well-off."

Collapsing into the wingback *without* a satchel, she stares at him. "There. See? You said it: '*I'll* be quite well-off.' Not *we*. Just you. No wonder you can't look at me. I'd like to think you were looking up to God for answers, but no, just at an eight-armed chandelier that looks like an electric octopus." She bristles. "Yeah, *you'll* be well-off."

"Don't nitpick my vocabulary." He thinks for a moment. "And

maybe *I* worry you'll be tired of *me* when the gold dust rubs off."

She leans forward with a growl. "I'm not a gold-digger!"

"I didn't mean that, Ellie. I meant maybe I won't be good enough for *you*. I hate it when you mangle my words."

Expelling her disgust, she flicks away his admonishment with both hands. "No, no. The girl from the wrong side of the tracks should never mangle the words of the boy born with the silver fork in his mouth."

He turns to analyze her body language because he understands her taste in aphrodisiacs. "You know its 'spoon.' But you said 'fork' on purpose ... because that's exactly what you want to do."

And then they shag. Right there on the leopard chaise. No narrative or dialogue missing from this story. It's as simple as turning a switch on or off with these two.

No need for graphic commentary, either. I can only say that it was quite intense ... as it usually is after a contentious night and a follow-up mini-bicker. Ah, Minnie Bicker. She was a guest here once. A film actress who always played the schoolteacher or maiden aunt. Brain, do not distract me now.

Hours have passed. Stark naked, they sit on the peach-colored crushed-velvet davenport and eat the dinner Ellie has so lovingly prepared. Eating in the raw never fails to stimulate them. They do sit on towels, showing some mercy to Dave N. Port, Lee's sobriquet for the couch.

Dinner is laid out on the mid-century Hollywood Regency coffee table before them. Sprouting from the gaudy gold-colored base are brass palm fronds, holding the large round glass top in place. The table may be vulgar to some, but 'twas once all the rage. And so, it stays, refusing to be banished into obsolescence, waiting to rage again. Conrad relates.

Feigning nonchalance, Ellie reaches for the Tabasco sauce, letting one of her nipples make ever-so-brief contact with her Green

Beans Almondine. She knows what it does to Lee when his two favorite pleasures touch. Faster than an ejector button, he blasts off, thankful that his member is not *dis*membered during the high-speed launch. Within seconds, much to Dave N. Port's distress, they go at it again.

Conrad tends to other business.

An hour and a half passes; they crawl into bed.

"Tonight was *so* much nicer than last night," Ellie says, running her index finger between his lips. "We should always remember why we're together and forget the other stuff."

He licks her finger before responding. "We should."

Ellie's eyes sparkle. "I saw the old woman today. She looks like she's aged ten years since I saw her last week. Poor thing didn't even bother to comb her hair, which on some days is incredibly well styled."

"Depression." He now runs his finger between *her* lips. "I wasn't going to say anything, but before I came home, I watched the old man slide right down the hallway wall onto the floor. At least I noticed him. Another neighbor just walked right on by."

"Oh my."

"I know I should have helped him up, but it's not like he was crying out in pain. And he didn't even know I was there, so yeah, I wasn't going to humiliate the guy. Plus, he seemed content to just sit there for a while." He looks embarrassed. "See, maybe I'm not as well-bred as you think."

"You're well-bred and I'm white freakin' Wonder bread. But damn we make one hell of a sandwich." She runs her finger over his philtrum. "I don't know why we have these little indentations under our noses, but they're groovy."

"We must need them for something. They're a metaphor for life really. You know, how something can be right under our nose and we fail to recognize it."

Ellie giggles. "Or remember what it's called. And be able to pronounce it."

"We don't even know the names of the old couple. It doesn't stop us from talking about them."

"Nope." She thinks. "So, when I saw her earlier, even from a distance, I got this feeling that her eyelids were crusty."

He laughs. "You didn't buy those contacts with telescopes in them, did you?"

She swats his arm. "As if, babes. But seriously, I just felt it in my gut."

"Crusty eyelids in your gut?"

"Gross. How is it that you repeat pretty much exactly what I say and make it sound completely different?"

Conrad observes that the "witty banter" intensifies when they are most uncomfortable with one another.

He shrugs. "Legal training. It comes in handy. Especially if you want to rattle a witness in court."

Or your wife at home. Ellie continues, "One thing I've noticed … if one of them looks good, they both look good. When she looks shabby, well, according to you, he slides down walls and stuff." She yawns. "I'm tired. I wanna sleep. No more forking, but if you wanna spoon, I'd love that."

"Me too," he says as he wiggles into position. "I wonder if they spoon."

"They definitely don't fork …," Ellie mumbles as she begins to drift off.

They awake in the morning … euphoric and still feeling the merging of their nether regions. If not for obligations outside the home, they'd go at it again, as they often do. But they both have imperative needs to hurry, and all of twenty minutes pass when Lee is the first one out the door, heading toward Darth, still thinking about Ellie's O-shaped mouth on his … I am being too crass.

Blissful, yet not unaware, Lee opens his eyes with hackneyed surprise when he sees the old man almost skipping down the hall, talking to no one at all. "I've got pep in my step! Yep! Yep! Yep!"

"Looks like you had a body transplant," Lee says aloud as he steps onto Darth, convinced the old man is too far away to hear him. "I swear you broke your back last night." Lee looks down in shame as he realizes what that says about him for not offering help.

The man is now only yards away. "I've got get-up-and-go, which is far superior to having *to* 'get up and go' all through the night."

Lee wants to respond, but the man, appearing happily self-absorbed, makes no eye contact. Before Lee can decide either way, Darth closes his doors.

"I guess he's taking the stairs," Lee mumbles to himself. "Like I should have done."

Yes indeed. But Lee rarely does much of anything in an anti-meridiem post-coital haze.

An hour later, her hair and makeup ready to greet the day, Ellie strides through the lobby. Stunned, she stops to see the old couple jitterbugging to "Rock Around the Clock." The woman appears to have shed thirty pounds and twenty years overnight. Her gray hair, now dark red, is neatly coiffed in a back-bun style. Their matching smiles exude a joy Ellie has yet to discover.

"So freakin' weird," she says to herself. "And in a week, I'll bet she'll look as bad as she did the other night."

The music changes. "I Only Have Eyes for You" plays, and the old woman rubs her breasts against his chest, licking her glossed-red lips as she does so.

He smiles, touching one breast as if he's fine tuning an old radio.

"I think you've already got the right station, buddy," she says as she looks at them. "Seriously, people? Can't you see I'm watching you?" She glances through the sparsely populated lobby, surprised that nobody else shares her fascination.

The old man has a goofy grin on his face as they turn, grab hands, and run toward the stairwell.

"And I thought you were too old," she says. "And after all these years, you'd think she'd have found classier methods of seduction. Can't believe he goes for that."

She stands there for several minutes, having forgotten that she has a salon to open. "He's probably already inside her. Holy crap. Wait'll I tell Lee." She walks toward the front doors. "Bet it's a full-pronged fork too."

Night falls. Both having endured long days, Lee agrees to pick up a pizza on his way home. Ellie, having set the dining table, complete with two full glasses of wine, thus spares Dave the displeasure of posteriors, clad or unclad, on his crushed velvet cushions.

Ellie opens the box and stares at the pizza in horror. "What the ever-lovin' eff is on what has to be your half of the pizza?"

"Pesto and anchovies."

"You were trying to emulate the aviary food … and maybe the fish market, weren't you?"

A guilty smile passes his lips. "A little unpredictability is good for our marriage, don't you think?" He tastes the wine and nods his approval.

"As long as I get the pepperoni-and-mushrooms half." She lifts a triangle out of pizza from the box. "Oh, God. I forgot to tell you about what I saw this morning … with *them*."

Lee looks at her with interest. "Can't wait to hear. On my end, I can report that he was in one happy mood when I left. And you'd never have known this was the same old geezer who slid down a wall last night."

"Tell me about it! By the time I did my hair and make-up, I left about forty minutes after you did. Her look had drastically changed. Not a freakin' hair out of place … and it was dyed Country Copper. I know … I use the same shade on a couple of clients.

"They were dancing the buggerjig in the lobby, and then they slowed it way down when the music changed. She was rubbing against him like some dive-bar stripper." Subconsciously, Ellie strokes the stem of her wine glass, which tantalizes Lee. "Next thing I know, they're heading toward the stairwell."

"You mean they took the stairs?" He stares at her hand until she stops stimulating the stemware. "They didn't wait for Darth?"

"Oh, hell no, babes." Ellie picks up the shaker of crushed hot peppers and sprinkles the flakes all over the pizza. "I'm surprised they even got their apartment door shut. Betcha they power-napped for a while, then went full-steam ahead into an all-nighter."

Lee finishes chewing his pizza as he lays the half-eaten slice on the plate. A devilish twinkle appears in his eyes. "You know, I think it's time we stepped up our surveillance game. How about after we finish eating, we go down the hall and see what we can hear." He pauses. "Wait. That sounds weird. *Hear* what we can hear?"

"I was going to comment on that, but since you didn't correct my 'buggerjig,' I went easy on you."

"You said that on purpose? You know it's 'jitterbug?'"

"Of course I do. Just testing you. To see if my working-class background would get on your nerves tonight."

"You don't need to test me, Ell. Life has a way of doing that without any help."

"Yeah, I know. And it's not like I want to go back to fighting. Conflict rears its ugly head way too much already. I don't need to help light a fire under its fat ass."

"No, you don't." Lee picks up his slice and takes a large bite.

Ellie takes a sip of her Merlot and rests her glass. "After all this time, we don't even know the old couple's names. I looked on the mailboxes, and whatever had been there was so faded, I couldn't read it."

"Maybe there's a name on the door." Lee says this with a visibly full mouth of food, antithetical to the manners he'd been raised with.

"People don't put their names on apartment doors here."

Mercifully, he finishes the masticated food. "We should check in the lobby again. Maybe I'll be able to see the name."

Desperate to show that she possesses class, Ellie waits until *her* masticated food is swallowed, deciding, unlike her spouse on a temporary refinement sabbatical, not to display it like clothes whipping about in a washer, as had he. "What, like your eyes work better than mine?"

"Humor me, honey. We'll just check. Okay? Then we're coming back upstairs and putting our ear to the door. I'll do it if you want. You can be my lookout."

She thinks. "Maybe we should bring a magazine with us. We can always say it got delivered by mistake if we get caught. And we're returning it."

"Because we're such perfect neighbors. Good thinking."

And with that, they finish their meal in silence, wheels turning, both eager to move onto the exciting post-prandial caper they've planned.

In my attempt to exclude tedium from this narrative, I should explain that whether it's up or down ... whether *they* are up and down in their relationship, their obsession with the older couple never seems to waver. To demonstrate this, one evening, as Ellie was calling Lee names not fit to repeat, she found cause to mention an earlier sighting of the older woman scrubbing the lobby's marble floors. Based on that visual alone, she concluded that perhaps the female octogenarian now lived alone and was working off the rent, as it sadly must be in arrears. After Lee offered welcome commentary, Ellie returned to her verbal fusillade of grievances—all relating to his parental units. This gloomy conversational pattern has replicated itself for nearly two years ... since they settled here. While they wait for happiness that exceeds intermittent status, their anxiety only perpetuates the discord between them.

After finishing dinner and stacking the dishes in the sink, with anticipation (and a travel magazine under Lee's arm), they head for the lobby.

Guiding his index finger over the small labels on each mailbox, Lee's finger stops on 401. "Really, Ell, you couldn't see this?"

Fascinated, Ellie looks at the names underneath his finger. "Eleanor and Leonard L. Glass. No way! This was *not* here before. Like I said, it was too faded to read. "Their names," she exclaims. "They're—"

Just as Ellie had witnessed the couple do that morning, Lee grabs her hand and whisks her to the stairwell, not even stopping to see if Darth was free. Curiosity is a powerful motivator.

Once on the fourth floor again, Ellie and Lee walk down the hallway with the guilt of two who have just robbed a bank … or worse. (Perhaps a teller was shot!) Skittish, yet filled with invigorating expectation, they walk slowly, nearly reaching a brand of climax they'd yet to experience in their carnal explorations.

Now at the door, in perfect synchronicity, they turn to look down the hall. It is empty. While Ellie continues to serve as lookout, Lee finds a spot to listen. Hearing nothing, he slides his ear around the door. Quite the sight.

"They can't possibly be out," Lee whispers. "It's only eight-thirty. I know some old people go to sleep early … but not this early."

"It's weird. Keep listening."

Lee puts his ear to the door again. "I'm telling you, Ell. Crickets."

"You know," she says, a devilish smile commandeering her lips, "when I saw them this morning, like I said, they were in such a hurry to get it on, I wouldn't be surprised if they never locked the door behind them." She pauses to plot. "I mean, your hand could slip, and if it happened to open a door …"

He replies with a grin, grasps the door handle, and turns it with expectation of failure. To their surprise, the door opens, and the apartment welcomes them inside with a whoosh. Nothingness greets them and wraps its arms around them, hugging them gently to let them know it is not a dream.

"There's nothing here," Ellie says. "I mean …"

"Nothing."

With wide-open mouths, they both stare into the stark blank space. Conrad cannot help but visualize a swarm of flies heading for the newly created orifices.

"The only thing here is *that*." Ellie points to an Italian brass shield mirror on the wall. It is the only object in the room. "Would go kind of nice with our coffee table."

"No way." Lee is firm. "Not touching that thing. Something is very wrong here."

"Let's look in the mirror. Maybe it's two-way glass, and they're hiding behind it."

"Ell, that's insane."

"Like you said before about checking the mailbox again: humor me."

"Fair enough." Lee walks beyond her until they are side by side in front of the mirror. They probably will not figure out that the middle initial of "L" and the last name of Glass, together, form "looking glass."

They stare. First, ever so faintly, their own images, looking back at them as reflections do, appear.

"How the hell does a mirror wait before it reflects?" Lee asks. "It's not like it's some coin-operated thingy and we just popped a few quarters in the slot."

Before Ellie can respond, the images grow stronger until they are exactly as one would expect any image to be. Then, their true-to-life images begin to morph before their eyes, aging five years with every five seconds that pass.

"Eleanor and Leonard," Ellie cries. "Old-fashioned versions of *our* names."

They hold hands.

"Oh my God, Lee. No wonder we couldn't stop watching them. No wonder we were so fascinated. They are us, and we are they."

She finishes her sentence, and the older couple, no longer a reflection, look at them and nod. Ever so slightly, the couple smiles. They alternate between the healthy and unhealthy versions of themselves, then wave good-bye as their images fade. Once they are gone, a message fogs up on the glass. "Mirror, mirror, on the wall … judge not others, or you will fall …"

In the time it takes for Ellie and Lee to exchange looks, the writing and the mirror are gone.

"What the hell are you doing in my apartment?" A burly man in a blue blazer, a sky-blue pin-striped shirt, and pressed designer jeans leans toward them with a reddened face. "Did you break in to stare at the art? Or just to steal it? Druggies?"

They look around to see a well-furnished apartment, rife with more custom furniture and accessories than their own rental. It is filled with indicators that many more than two currently occupy the space. Several glasses of wine, a tray of partially consumed hors d'oeuvres, and a stack of magazines atop a round tufted fuchsia ottoman complete the scene.

The man looks at the magazine in Lee's hand. "Might as well add yours to the pile. Stupidest damn excuse for breaking into an apartment I've ever heard, but you nitwits all think the same."

"Uh, how long have you lived here?" Lee asks, his breathing labored.

"Ten years and two months. Is that a good answer, Mr. Cat Burglar?" He looks at Ellie. "Mrs. Art Thief?"

"We weren't here to steal," Lee says. "My wife and I had a few too many glasses of wine at dinner. We live at the opposite end of the hall, in the mirror apartment. I think we got confused and somehow got turned around."

The man points to his face. "See my expression? Clue: it's angry. But what does it say?"

"Bullshit? Get the fuck out of here?" Ellie murmurs.

"Almost."

"Get the fuck out of here, or I'll kill you?"

"Bingo!" The man chortles. "Bye, bye y'all." He walks behind Ellie and Lee, slamming the door behind them, narrowly missing their respective cabooses.

Alone, in the hallway, Ellie turns to her husband. "You know, now that I think about it, every time we had a horrible fight, she looked terrible."

"Yeah," Lee chokes out. "When I saw him slide down the wall, we'd had the worst blow-out the night before. Whatever we saw in them ... always reflected ourselves. When we were happy, they looked years younger ... healthy, radiant almost."

"Now we know why they never seemed to see us."

"We need to start living a better life, baby."

"We do." Ellie sniffles.

"What are we waiting for?" He takes her hand. "Let's go home." They walk down the hallway and reenter their apartment.

"Why do you think that guy told us to add our magazines to the stack?" Ellie sits on Dave and pats the space next to her for Lee.

He obliges. "It's like he was expecting us. As if bringing a magazine to break into that place is a regular thing."

"He had to have meant something else. Because if he didn't, then that means other people are having the same experience as we are."

His visage illuminates. "Precisely why the neighbor didn't see the old man slide. He only existed for me. Now I feel even worse for ignoring him."

"I think he was giving you a message."

"What's that, Ell?"

"To help ourselves. Because if we don't, we won't be good to anyone. Now I know why I was the only one in the lobby to see them dancing and carrying on. I think that was a message to me that I shouldn't judge, because one day, that could be or will be me."

Lee twists his wedding ring. "This all makes sense, but at the same time, it's too phantasmagorical, you know? And I swear, if I was the only one having this experience, I'd think maybe you sprinkled hallucinogens on top of the pizza." He thinks. "Did you doctor the hot pepper flakes? Truth."

"Get real, babes. What kind of hallucinogen gives two people an identical trip?"

"You get real. Would that be any stranger or any more improbable than what just happened?"

"What happened?"

"Funny." A droll smile rests comfortably on his face.

Ellie looks at him oddly. "Seriously, what are you even talking about?"

He stands and begins pacing a short figure eight. "This is not the time to fuck with me, Ell. We were just talking about it. You were just talking about it. We were there. In apartment-fucking 401. Corner east."

"Huh?"

"I know you think you're being hysterically funny ... denying everything mid-conversation ... or maybe this is payback for whatever crap I've dished out to you, but now isn't the time. I'm in full-freak mode right at the moment, and I need to discuss *what* happened and *why* it happened."

"Oooookay. Well, we had pizza for dinner because we both worked late. You ordered it and picked it up on your way home.

Standard stuff. Are you mad that I made comments about the pesto and anchovies? Because that was seriously no biggie."

Grabbing his hair, Lee, poor dear, is now visibly unhinged and tugs away. Good thing his hair is his own or he'd be holding it in his sweaty hands by now. He takes several breaths, exhales, then resumes his seat. He plunks down on Dave so hard that the long-suffering davenport whimpers. Lee cannot hear it.

Ellie, unsure how to identify the soft cry that floats into her ears, shakes off the strangeness.

Panting like an overheated dog, Lee looks into her eyes. "Had your fun? Can you get real with me now?"

"You know what?" Ellie's voice grows louder, her patience clearly diminishing. "You're fucking with *me*. And if you're not, then maybe you need a brain screwdriver or something ... because things are loose in there. Screws, nuts, bolts ... and God only knows what else. Maybe someone left a wrench in there when you were constructed in Mumsie's womb."

"You're taking this way too far now. Joke's over. No loose hardware in my brain. I need to know what just happened. Hear me, Ell?" A silent ohm chant calms his frazzled nerves as he hopes that Ellie will be more willing to participate in his inquiry. "Do you think the universe was giving us guidance? Was that entire experience what our marriage has been waiting for?"

"We'll always be waiting for guidance," Ellie tells him. "It's out there for everyone, I think. Only some people aren't paying attention."

"So, you're admitting what happened in the old folks' apartment just now?"

Her face goes blank. "Say what? How would I know what happened in their apartment? We haven't left this apartment since you brought the pizza home. And I think we need to stop stalking those people ... and talking about them. Sheesh, Lee, they could be us one day, you know?"

Conrad shall not taunt by narrating any more of their circuitous dialogue. Nobody has that kind of time to waste.

Indeed, they were both right in their own ways. They had their own illusions. We need not take the same road to reach the same destination. Yet, some unfortunate souls, even with an occasional lesson learned, will always dwell in the house of the waiting.

Chapter Four: POODLEY

Most of us know this much: life is bizarre, yet it goes on.

I cannot absent myself from the fourth floor before pulling back the privacy curtain and continuing my narrative. Where to begin?

It is early evening and our friend Lee is returning home from work, his brain still spinning from the previous night's events. Exiting Darth, he is bewildered to see yet another man (this one in his late sixties) sitting on the floor, his back against the hallway wall, forlorn and defeated.

As Lee stuffs his brain with conjecture, adamant that he will never "fall for the same mirage twice," he walks past the work-shirt-and-loose-jean-wearing, gray-haired man who is wiping a tear from his whiskered cheek.

"Hey, there. Can you help a neighbor?"

Lee is startled to hear a voice, not to mention seeing two dark blue eyes stare at him. "Are you real?"

The man takes an ever-so-brief moment to ponder the idiocy of Lee's inquiry. "Nope, I'm a department store mannequin on the run. Got tired of having my limbs snapped off like twigs when they stuffed me in a storage room after Christmas. Turned into a flesh-and-blood man ... Pinocchio-like and all ... and made a run for it. And here I am. Sittin' on the damn floor, like an old fool, telling you my tale of woe." He blows a loud breath from the right side of his mouth. "Am I *real?*" The disgust in his voice is delightfully clear. "What kind of foolhardy games you playin'? You never seen me before? Because I damn sure see you ... all the time ... carryin' that briefcase like a shoulder bag. Your wife, she's real nice. Name's Ellie."

"Your name is Ellie? That's a coincidence because—"

"Oh, for cryin' out loud! My name is Kenny Seymour. Live on this floor. I was talking about your wife's name. I think that's pretty clear."

Lee appears only a smidge embarrassed. (He deserves far more shame.) "Sorry. It's a long story."

Kenny shifts uncomfortably on the floor. "One I'm sure I don't need to hear. You gonna help me up or not?"

Lee closes and opens his eyes, trying to break whatever trance he imagines himself in. Still suspicious, he extends a hand and yanks Kenny off the floor. Feeling the grip of human flesh, he is startled. "Wow, I thought you'd be translucent or something."

Kenny, now standing, takes a moment to brush off his clothing. "You on drugs?"

Lee offers an exasperated sigh. "That's two times in less than twenty-four hours I've been asked that."

"Hmph. Good reason for that. Don't ya think?"

"I think it's weird that twice in twenty-four hours I've seen a neighbor … or what I thought was one … sitting on this hallway floor. Only I actually watched the first guy slide down the wall."

"Let me guess." Kenny cleared his throat. "Ya didn't help him up."

Lee taps his brilliant legal mind, avoids the question, and asks one of his own. "So why did you fall?"

"Because I'm tired … and a bit shaky, I guess. My wife disappeared nearly two years ago. My Martha. Every bit the beauty … just like your wife, Ellie." He sighs. "I swear my Martha is around somewhere. Just waitin' for me to find her, come hell or high water. So, every day, I go searchin' for her. Ain't never gonna give up, neither. I must walk five, six miles every time. Overdid it today, I think. Got off the elevator there, started walking to my place, and just like that, I slid to the floor. Like someone had buttered the wall."

"And you're toast, so it was a match made in heaven." Lee laughs, pleased with himself.

Kenny presents with a contemptuous formation of his facial features. "You think it's funny that my wife is long missing and I pound the pavements every day looking in every damn nook and cranny for her." His eyes meet Lee's. "I'm a tired and lonely man. And that's funny to you?"

"Oh. No. I guess not."

"Today even had a dog feel sorry for me. Black-and-gray-poodle-y thing. It followed me all the way to the lobby, but I didn't let it in. Didn't want it to get trapped and not be able to find its way home. Think it just wanted to make sure I got home all right. I've seen the dog before. And that pooch got more manners than you do."

"Guess it wouldn't take much." Forlorn, Lee, now playing the I'm-pathetic-I-suck card, looks down at the floor. Before he can finish his piteous act, the elevator door opens, and the "poodle-y" dog walks off, following a woman who is carrying a bag of hot take-out food.

"Ah, guess it belongs to someone here after all." Kenny gives Lee a hard look and starts to walk away, his back to Lee as he speaks. "Thanks for helping me up, but I'm gonna tell you: you're a first-class kook."

Lee starts to protest, but Kenny is already inside his apartment, the door closed behind him.

Weary, Kenny grabs a beer out of an old teal ColdSpot fridge, then takes a seat on the Hollywood Regency upholstered chair, looking solemnly at its counterpart, a curved sectional sofa, taupe, with a matching embossed butterfly design and gold tassel fringe around the perimeter. "Martha always called you Goldilocks ... that sleek blonde hair of yours brushing against the rug. Me, I'm wondering if them there ugly butterflies carved in your 'pholstery ain't gonna get up and fly away." He mutters to himself. "Wish they would." Kenny cracks the tab on his beer. "Better shut up, or I'll be sounding like that darn kook who helped me off the floor." He looks at the bouquet-of-roses print in the scalloped frame that Martha loved. "Never much for flower art, but my eyes are soaking you in because she ain't here to do it."

A knock on the door surprises Kenny, and a bit of beer splashes out of the can and lands on his nose like rain. Oh, my, I do feel a song coming on: "Rudolph the red-nosed rain-beer, had a shiny little hose. They always said poor Rudolph, would sprinkle some where'er he goes." I shall insert a pause here. And now, fully satisfied, I return to my narrative: "Who the Sam Hill is that?" Kenny calls out. He rests the can on the bronze bamboo end table to his right. "Hold your horses! I'm coming." He rises and drags himself to the door, letting out a tiny moan as he opens it.

"Hi, Dad."

"Willie. What in the blazes are you doing here? Didn't expect you today."

Pushing his shoulder-length blond hair out of his face, Willie, tall and rugged, engaging his legs in a purposeful walk, plops onto the loveseat. He eyes the open beer. "Got one of those for me?"

After a small yet appropriate grunt, Kenny walks to the kitchen and takes a beer out of the ColdSpot. Saying nothing, he returns to the living room and hands it to his son before resuming his seat. "Spill it, Willie. Not the beer. Whatever reason you've cooked up to come spy on me again."

Willie plays coy. "Isn't spying something you do in secret?"

"Don't get fancy with your words just because you work for some magazine. Thing is, son, you're here to find out what I'm up to. Wouldn't be surprised if you're a wantin' to put me in a damn home."

Willie, in a heavily ponderous act, pulls on his lower lip then lets it go. Conrad is unaware of any benefit to the action, other than the stalling of time. Then, with his middle finger and thumb, Willie gathers the skin on his forehead.

"For cryin' out loud, son. You come here for me to watch you play with your face like it's modelin' clay? What happened? Someone tried to rearrange it for you and you gotta check to make sure everything's where it should be? Well? Is that it?"

Willie cracks the can open, straightens, and takes a sip. "Sorry to disappoint you. Nobody punched me in the face. Just burning off some nervous energy." He bites his lip. "I'll get to the point. See, a couple of coworkers of mine were in a coffee shop, and they said this man came in with a photo of a woman named Martha and asked everyone in the place if they'd seen her. Geez, Dad. You can't keep doing this. You've already scoured this town for Mom a hundred times. You know what Einstein's definition of insanity is? Doing the same thing over and over again and expecting different results."

Kenny laughs. "Smart man, that Albert. So why aren't you listening to him?"

"What? I'm talking about you."

"How many times have you come here to tell me to stop looking for your mother? And how many times have I told you I'm going to do what I damn well please?"

"Yeah, but …"

"Ah, but nothin'. You're doing the same thing over and over and you're expecting different results. Tell me you ain't."

Willie, in an attempt to put the kibosh on sound reasoning, moves on with his conversation. "When did you start talking like some old farmer who forgot how to use the English language? As I recall, you took great pains so that I didn't talk the way you do now. I know you grew up in a rural area, but—"

"Listen here, son. If my past life creeps back into the one I got now, then so be it. And farmers are good people. Smart, hardworkin' people. So don't be knockin' them or lookin' down on anyone from your high-and-mighty throne. Plenty of city folk talk the same way.

Hear me? Not to mention your grandfather spoke with a whole lot more of what I'm speaking now, and he was a good, decent man. Take your case of the snobs somewhere else. As for the great pains I took for you to fit in, well, glad they had a positive outcome. Speaking of them pains, you're giving me one in the butt."

Willie groans. "Okay, Dad. Since you don't want to hear the same thing over and over, I'm going to confess something to you. And I'm sorry if it's hurtful, but I've got to get through to you." Willie inhales deeply to inflate his chest like a very important man. "Mom told me years ago … that one day, when the time was right … she had plans to just up and leave for some tropical paradise. A secret location somewhere in the world. And maybe she'd come back, and maybe she wouldn't." Willie looks for incredulity on Kenny's face and sees none. "As you might have noticed, we don't live anywhere near a tropical paradise. So, showing Mom's photo to everyone in town, a thousand times over, isn't going to help anything. Even if coconut trees sprout from the sidewalks, and the west side of the street morphs into a stretch of sparkling white sand, she's not here."

"Insta-beach. Just add water and stir." He remembers. *Insta-bitch. Just add a martini and stir.*

"Not funny." Willie finishes his beer with a very long and crass über-sip, then crushes the can in his hands … a confident confirmation of his manliness. He stands and walks into the kitchen to dispose of that which he has crushed, promptly helping himself to a second crushable beverage. As he walks back into the living room, he spies a pink depression glass bowl on the low table next to the artificial ficus tree. He picks it up. "Ah, it's a bowl of sea glass. Mom loves these. I think it's the feel of the beads through her fingers. I remember she used to buy the ones with holes and string them together when I was young." He puts the bowl back on the table and returns to the sofa. "I'm surprised she didn't take these with her. But then again, why would she?"

"I don't really think much about her possessions. Only about your mother herself." Kenny stands and walks over to look out of the nearest window. "We had a good life, most of the time, and it's stripped raw without her." He turns to face Willie. "And that, my son, is why I sound like an 'old farmer' to you. Without your mother, I found it easier to slip back to the time before I met her."

Having no patience for his father's memories, Willie bulldozes ahead with his rehearsed speech. "Dad. I know it sounds frightening." He alters his face in what he believes to be a 'compassionate look.' "Having given it a great deal of thought, I really believe that talking to a professional would make a world of difference for you. Now, I've done some research, and I've dug up the names of a few therapists ...."

"Sorry you wasted your time diggin'. But you can put 'em back in the hole where you found 'em, cover 'em up, and retire your shovel." Kenny shakes off his vexation. "Y'aint hearin' a word I'm saying, Willie. You're so programmed to deliver the same message that all you can do is spit it out by rote. Well, I've heard it all before. Kenny Seymour is tired. And he ain't buyin' what you're sellin'." He looks out the window again.

Willie shrugs. "Sorry, but that language ... the way you talk now ... it makes me sick. It would make Mom sick. If she ever came back, you'd be so immersed in talking that way, you wouldn't be able to retrieve your old self."

"Kenny spins around to face him, a scowl painted on his visage. "This *is* my old self, boy." He walks over to pick up a dusty-rose chenille throw blanket that is draped over a chair. "Whenever Martha was cold, I'd wrap this around her and rub her upper arms. It brought her so much comfort."

"Yeah, so much comfort that she had to leave."

Now, poor Kenny is stunned. Such cruelty from his offspring was not anticipated. He puts the blanket back on the chair. "Time to leave, Willie. I've had my fill of ya."

"Dad, that came out the wrong way."

Kenny stands there, fighting back tears, barely able to raise his voice to repeat the command. "Leave, Willie!" He returns to his chair and sinks into it with concerning despair.

Defeated, and realizing that he has utterly failed at his mission, Willie rises and walks to the door. He opens it, and the black-and-gray "poodle-y" dog comes running into the place.

Willie looks down at the animal. "You might as well adopt this dog, Dad. I was talking to one of your neighbors. She said the dog comes by all the time but doesn't belong to anyone. Hey, it might be the cure for what ails you."

Kenny turns and slaps his thighs. "Come here, poodle-y one." He looks up to see Willie watching them. "You … good-bye. Get out."

"Maybe that dog can get through to you better than I can," Willie says under his breath as he closes the door behind him.

Once the door is solidly shut, the dog jumps up on Kenny's lap, licks his face, and puts one paw on each shoulder.

"Now this is real love. Don't get anything like this from my son. Just a bunch of grief. At least you won't tell me what to do." He scratches the dog's head as two big brown eyes look at him. "You wanna live here with me?" He checks the dog's neck for a collar. "I hear you're homeless, Poodley. Well, no more then. I'm adopting you right here and now." An important thought enters Kenny's mind. "Guess if you're gonna live here, I should know your gender. You don't mind if I peek at your underside, I hope."

Kenny, who has never performed this precise task, feels a bit odd. But nonetheless, he checks. "Doesn't look like you've got the same plumbing I do, so I think we've got that settled. You don't mind being called 'Poodley,' do you, girl?"

The dog licks his face, jumps off his lap, and begins to check out the apartment.

"I should tell you … we rented this unit furnished. This Hollywood stuff was quite the craze back in the day. Looks like an old magazine shot now, but that's the way the owner lady keeps it. I know it's out of place and I don't care. *I'm* out of place. My Martha got a kick out of all this. Said it made her feel like a starlet in a time when the world was more glamorous. That's why we took it."

Poodley paws at the fringe on the curved sectional.

"That's Goldilocks. I thought I'd tell you that as seeing by the looks of it, you two are gonna be friends."

The dog rubs her nose along the row of gold tassels, sneezing when she gets to the end.

Kenny howls with laughter. "Now you gone and did that, Poodley. You made yourself sneeze. Tickled the heck out of your nose there." He thinks. "I'm getting hungry. Lord knows when you last ate."

The dog whimpers.

"So, you *are* hungry?"

More whimpers.

"Tell you what. You wait right here and I'll go out and buy the best dog food money can buy. Treats too."

Poodley shakes her body, much like a dog who has been unwillingly soaked and is desperate to dry off.

"You're not hungry?"

The dog emits a low growl and runs to the kitchen, then back to Kenny.

He stands. "I'll be damned if you ain't trying to tell me somethin' or other. I just don't know what it is. Like I said, I'm going out to buy the best dog food I can. You're a skinny one. Doesn't look like you've been eating regularly."

Poodley runs to the teal-colored ColdSpot, stands on her hind legs, and paws at the door.

"If I was a betting man, I'd wager that you want something to eat from this fridge. Maybe you can smell right through this thing.

You dogs have some mighty powerful schnozzolas. Am I getting warmer?"

The dog whimpers, then back on all fours, turns excited circles on the teal-and-white checkered floor.

"Well, let's see. I got a ham and cheese sandwich on rye. Was going to take it with me this morning and I plum forgot." He opens the door and takes the sandwich, tucked in a small plastic bag, from the shelf. "You want this?"

Poodley, highly animated, runs into the living room and hops up on the sofa, her eyes never leaving the sandwich in his hands.

"How 'boutin I just sit next to you and feed you like you're a lady of leisure?" He frowns. "Just remembered … put some French Dijon mustard on this delicacy. Might not be to your liking. Might upset your inside plumbing."

Whimpering and licking her lips, the dog appears to anticipate the food with even greater yearning. Taking a seat next to her, Kenny breaks off the first piece. Within seconds, Poodley has scarfed down the food, eagerly eyeing the next bite. A short moment of time elapses.

"Well, I'll be. Took you less than a minute to chow that down. And you look as hungry as you did before. You stay here, girl. I'm gonna see what else I can find for you. Bet you'll need a bowl of water too."

Kenny, back in the kitchen, reaches into the cabinet and pulls out a pink plastic bowl. He turns on the tap, lets the water run cool, and then fills it up. No longer his forlorn, aggrieved self, he walks into the living room where Poodley has not moved. He puts the bowl on the floor, but the dog only looks at him, in an odd, quizzical fashion, I may add.

"Now I know that mustard had to make you thirsty."

The dogs paws the empty spot in front of her, then repeats the action.

"You want to drink off the loveseat? Okay, then." He sighs.

"Martha'd kill me if she knew I was allowing this, but she's not here." He picks the bowl up and places it on the upholstered cushion. Within seconds, the dog laps up a good deal of the water, then looks at him with wide anticipatory eyes.

"Oh yeah, I promised you another treat. I know just the thing."

In no time at all, Kenny goes back to the kitchen and returns with a matching bowl, this one filled with vanilla bean ice cream and two cookies. The dog, having left the couch, is playing with the bowl of sea glass on the low table, batting the beads about with her paws. Seeing Kenny, she runs back to the loveseat and jumps back in place.

"I think you're gonna like this, Poodley." Moving the water bowl to the side, he places the dessert bowl in front of the dog. His mood has elevated to a level he has not known in years. He rubs his cheek, mindful that he needs a shave. Before he can say another word, the dog is going to town on the sweets.

"I see you like those cookies. Lorna Doones. Martha's favorite. She's got a novel by the same name." He nods to indicate a mahogany bookcase filled with literature. "I think Martha read the book three times at last count. By some fella named Blackmore. A romance written in the eighteen-hundreds, set in England. Liked the book so much she bought the cookies, not that one has a darn thing to do with the other. You might like me to read to you sometime."

Poodley, who was using her tongue with great 'lappiness,' stops to look at him, then finishes the bowl … or rather its contents, if the literal is required here.

"You sure were hungry." His vibrant enthusiasm settles a speck. "You know, Poodley, it's been two years now, and I'm a lonely man, so I haven't really talked about this to anyone. But as much as I miss my wife, well, I suspect absence has made my heart grow a bit fonder than it was. Martha wasn't the best partner. In retrospect, I'm afraid it was all about pleasin' *her.* Can't really think of much she did for me. Still loved her, though. My name is Kenny, by the way."

The dog looks away, then lowers her eyes and looks up at him.

"I think you're feelin' my pain. See, I didn't tell Willie this, when he was trouncin' on my linguistic habits, but Martha looked down on my family and me for talkin' this way. I changed my ways when I took a fancy to her and kept them ways up best I could. When she left, I went back to what felt natural for me. And you know, it felt good. I could just *talk* … didn't have to think about every darned thing before it came out of my mouth." He picks up the empty bowl and places the water bowl inside of it. "I kind of felt free. But then I started missing her something fierce." He stands and walks the bowls into the kitchen. He places the water bowl in a corner of the room, washes the other one, and then, after setting it in the dish drainer, returns to the dog.

By this time, Poodley is lying down on the sofa, her head resting on the cushion.

"Making yourself comfy. That's good. I'll leave this space for you and sit in my chair. By the way, when ya need some more water, it's in the kitchen." Kenny, feeling a bit lighter from his partial confession, offers more. "I'll tell you the rest of my story, girl. See, even though I look for Martha every day, I don't expect to find her. Not around here. No, it's just nice meeting folks. And when I happen upon someone with a heart, who gives me a bit of their time, well, that's swell."

For the next hour, Kenny unburdens himself with the complex saga of his meeting and subsequent marriage to Martha. The dog alternates between looking directly at him and looking away. After all, nobody can maintain steady eye contact; it is quite intimidating.

After excusing himself for two trips to the "loo" during the unburdening, Kenny looks at Poodley, aghast that he has forgotten that dogs have the same needs as humans. "I'm sorry, girl. You must have some business to do, and here I'm gabbing away like the old fool that I am. You must need to go for a walk somethin' fierce." He pauses to think. "Just don't have no collar, harness, leash, or whatever else I need for ya. Oh yeah, some plastic bags to pick up your offerings." He laughs uncomfortably. "Sorry, Poodley, haven't had a dog since I lived on a farm. Had three growing up. Martha didn't like 'em one bit. Thought they were dirty and tracked in all the nasty the outside world has to offer. Yup, one of many pleasures I gave up on her account.

"Bad way to look at things, I know. Should have known right then, when she gave me that ultimatum: 'No dogs, no Martha,' that she wasn't the woman for me. But when you're smitten, well, you toss all logic to the ill winds. And that's what I did. I know, I probably don't seem like the kind of man she'd go for, but she found me 'rugged and sexy,' or so she said. We had fun back in the day." He sighs. "Don't worry, I'm not gonna keep repeatin' my tale of woe. Only needed to say it once. Get it off my chest."

He stands. "I'm gonna hook two ties together and fashion some kind of leash for you. Tomorrow, I can get a proper one. Better make a list of everything you're gonna need. Only the best dog food for you."

Poodley growls.

"Now ain't that some strange reaction," Kenny muses to himself as he heads into his bedroom to assemble a makeshift leash. Grabbing Martha's seashell scarf, he walks back into the living room.

"Look what I got here," Kenny says, standing before the dog. "Martha's favorite scarf. Guess she forgot to take it. I reckon it will be a suitable collar for tonight, and these here neckties of mine will make a fine leash." He sees the dog is shivering. "Oh, geez. You must really have to go."

Just as our boy Kenny is about to loop the scarf around Poodley's neck, the dog leaps from the sofa and runs to the bathroom. Dumbfounded, Kenny can only ponder the strange event before he hears the door shut. "What in the Sam Hill?" And yes, Kenny is still standing when the sound of a flushing toilet propels him back square in his chair.

Poodley wanders back into the living room, jumps up on the chair where the chenille throw rests, puts it in her mouth, and walks back to the sofa. With her right paw, she adeptly arranges the small blanket to her liking, nuzzles her way partially underneath it, then rests her head and goes off to sleep.

"Well, doggone it. I'll be a monkey's uncle." Kenny stares in disbelief. "Heavens to Murgatroyd. Butter my butt and call me a biscuit. Then bugger me dead. I ain't never have believed it …."

TWO DAYS LATER

Poodley, now with a pink rhinestone collar around her neck, a pink-and-gray-plaid harness, and a pink rope leash hooked to it, steps out into the hallway and looks both ways as if she is crossing the street.

Seemingly on cue, Ellie and Lee exit their unit while the elevator doors open, expelling Willie onto the fourth floor in the same manner a cat coughs up a hairball. Oh, perhaps I'm being hyperbolic. And what if I am. But that is how Kenny sees it.

Lee whispers to Ellie. "It's happening again. This is the other old man I was telling you about. First, he looks like he's at death's door and slides down the wall. Now, here he is, looking like the weight of the world has been taken off his shoulders … and check it out, he's got a dog."

"Babes, I've seen this man several times before. He's as real as we are."

"Willie!" Kenny says. "What are you doing here?"

"It's Saturday, Dad. The same day I come to see you every week, remember?" Willie walks toward his father.

"Sure I do. It's just that you were here the other day, so I figured today might not be necessary."

Lee nudges Ellie and whispers again. "Just pretend to be looking for something in your purse. Something important. We need an excuse to stand here and listen."

"Really, Lee. Is this necessary?

"I really hope you can find the tickets," Lee says loudly. "You better check every inch in there."

Ellie whispers now. "I've already done every inch of you. Still not satisfied?" She winks. "Need an encore?"

Lee goes out of his mind when Ellie titillates him in public. This is no exception. Now he must stand behind her to obscure his happiness.

Willie smiles at Kenny and slaps his upper right shoulder. "Dad, I can't tell you how happy I am that you took my advice and adopted this dog. She's a real cutie." He rubs the dog's neck. "And word has it you've stopped looking for Mom. You're already looking worlds better now that you're not walking the streets all day long. I'm glad you've finally accepted the fact that you're never going to find her."

"Don't have to," Kenny says. "She found me."

"You mean she called you?" His jaw drops like a broken elevator speeding toward the bottom floor, then shakes his head in disbelief. "Really? I don't think 'found' is the right word, since you still live in the place that she left you in."

"I'll give you that all right."

"So, tell me. When did she call? Is she in town? No way she came by, did she? Or did word get back to her that you've been scouring the town for the past couple of years. Where is she?"

Kenny looks down at Poodley. "Right here. At the end of this leash. Don't have any idea how it happened, but it did. Willie, this here is your mother!"

The extraordinary shock of Kenny's statement causes Willie to whack his own forehead with the mighty force of brawn and bluster, to fall against the wall, and alas … slide helplessly to the ground.

Having heard the exchange between father and son, Ellie's eyelids flutter and she turns to face Lee, whose augmentation is no more. "Your mother can be a full-on bitch, well, she is, but you never looked at a female dog and called her 'Mom.'

Kenny realizes Ellie and Lee have been watching his interaction with Willie. He takes a moment to fix his gaze on them but has no words.

Lee laughs, then directs his voice to Kenny. "And you called *me* a kook? So, um, maybe you or your wife, at the end of that leash, might want to help him up." He roars with laughter as Ellie's elbow jabs him in the ribs. He ceases to laugh, but a nervous chuckle escapes his lips like a defiant postscript. Lee now addresses his wife. "See what I'm saying, Ell. Three times now, some form of a man slides down the hallway wall. Don't even try to tell me that's normal, because it's not."

With a large vein protruding from his forehead, Willie stands. "Who the hell are you?" He lumbers over to Lee. "And what business is this of yours? And who are you calling a 'form of a man?' You think I'm some kind of pussy because I fell? And just for the record, this dog is *not* my mother. My father is clearly dealing with some form of dementia. I fail to see the humor."

"He's a kook," Kenny tells Willie, staring at Lee. "The kookiest kook in all the land."

Embarrassed, Willie plods on. "But even with dementia, he's right about you. Only I'd find a better name than 'kook.' Since you're making reference to my mother, who is not here, I might add, maybe I'd call you something that starts with the same word. You like that, you mother …"

A tad intimidated, Lee takes a step back while Ellie watches curiously.

Willie returns to Kenny's side. "Dad, I'll get straight to the point. This is very awkward, and I know you're going to fight me on this." He fiddles with the keys in his pocket. "But I need to have you evaluated."

"Not going to happen. I'm fully in my right mind."

Making a miserable attempt at patience and empathy, Willie speaks again. "It's not a bad thing, Dad. Just a simple evaluation so I'll know how to better help you. So we'll all know."

With his free hand, Kenny sticks a middle finger in his son's face. "How's 'boutin you evaluate this? What d'ya think this means, Willie?"

Ellie turns to Lee. "Still think they're not real?"

"All part of the mirage," Lee says. "Just more realistic this time. I'm telling you; they're hallucinations. Only now, you're admitting you see them too." He thinks. "And don't try to change up on me again and pretend you didn't see any of this."

Overhearing Lee, Willie is having a pesky time of choosing who he wishes to deal with first. He settles on shooting Lee a poison eye dart but attends to his father. "Dad, let's face reality here. Mom left you. She's off on an island somewhere." He looks at Poodley. "This dog ... is *not* my mother."

Kenny's gaze morphs into a powerful and challenging stare. "Let me ask you this, son? Did your mother leave *me* or did she leave *you?*"

Affronted by the question, Willie stiffens. "She left *you.*"

"But y'ain't heard from her, have ya?"

Willie appears rattled. "Well, no, but ..."

"But what? If she left her husband, there'd be no reason not to call her son, would there be?" Kenny waits a long theatrical beat. "Unless she's a *dog* now and can't make no damn phone calls!"

"Who's the kook?" Lee yells.

Elie looks quizzically at her husband. "Babes, if he's a mirage, how can he be a kook? And that's rude."

"Take it from me, Ell. There's no law saying you can't be a kook and a mirage at the same time. Rudeness is a moot point."

"I ain't no damn kook," Kenny yells back. "And I ain't no damn mirage. And if you think I'm one, then that makes you an even bigger kook for calling me one. So, there you go, you kook-aracha." Kenny does a small folkdance as he sings. *"La Cucaracha, la cucaracha. Yo no puedo caminar."* He stops and stares Lee down. "Case closed."

Ellie giggles. "He told *your* lawyer ass off. And he's got a point. C'mon, babes. Let's go."

As the elevator doors open, mercifully swallowing Ellie and Lee whole as they step inside, Kenny turns his attention back to Willie. "Now, I'm gonna take Poodley here for a walk."

With great relief, Willie sighs. "I see you call her Poodley … and not Martha. That's good, Dad … because she's *not* Mom."

"Listen, son, I know this sounds strange to you. But this dog here does everything your mother did. Even uses the toilet. I ain't takin' her on no walk to do her business, just to get some fresh air. She eats the same food as your mother, sits where your mother used to sit, and boy, does she love her chenille blanket."

Willie steps in front of his father to keep him from leaving. "Okay, Dad. I can see why your loneliness has brought you to such a nutty conclusion. But it means nothing. Of course, the dog eats what Mom ate. Most dogs prefer what humans consume. And so what if she likes the same spot on the sofa? And what dog doesn't like a soft blanket?"

"First time I had her home," Kenny says, "I caught her playin' with your mother's sea glass. Not too much later, she goes down the hall, straight into the bathroom, shuts the door, and does her business. Few minutes later, I hear the toilet flush, and she comes back on out."

"How did the dog open the bathroom door again, huh?"

"Stood on her hind legs and turned the knob, I s'pose. Wasn't in there with her. Never am. We're not in the damn Twilight Zone, son. I never said she walks through solid wood. You listening to me or drifting off into some fantasy world?"

"Dad, I get that you've been grieving since she left. And I think you've forgotten that Mom wasn't so good to you. You weren't very happy together. In fact, she could be downright mean when she'd had a martini or two. You've put her so high on some imaginary pedestal that it's messed with your mind and your memories." Willie, now feeling empowered, happy he's not being interrupted, soldiers on. "You know what? I'm just gonna come out and say it so maybe you'll remember how things really were. It's time to put an end to this nonsense. Dad: Mom was a fucking bitch!"

No sooner had the words oozed out of his mouth and slid down his gray Oxford shirt, when the dog walks over to him, stands on her hind legs, slaps him with her right paw, then, down again on all fours, sinks her teeth into his ankle.

"Ow!" Willie jumps. (Quite high, I might add.) "What the actual fuck?"

Kenny smiles. "Like I said to the kook. Case closed." He looks at Poodley. "Come on now, girl. Let's go for that walk."

Chapter Five: MOTHER REDUX

Some days, this lobby has the solemnity of a funeral home. Today, for whatever reason, it has the bustling spirit of an old-time department store or a busy city street at Christmas. Everyone strides with purposeful steps ... even the lonely hearts who aimlessly wander have a smattering of luck in keeping up the pretense that someone is waiting for them. This, of course, is an ephemeral mirage, for the owners of barely beating hearts have neither the energy nor the acting skills to indefinitely perpetuate their charades. I am feeling kindly in the moment, so yes, I briefly laud their efforts ... even if the outcome is destined to be woeful.

These lonely hearts I speak about ... they wait ... and they hope ... because there is nothing else to do. Many labor under the delusion that a part well played will become reality ... a state of being that is highly overrated.

Shoes of every kind click, smack, and slide on these imported Italian marble floors, leaving the residue from where they last visited ... real or imagined.

In the large lobby, inside the recessed wall, Darah stands at the concierge's desk, going over some paperwork. Hearing the clearing of a throat, she looks up. "Millicent! What the ...?"

The dark-haired woman, whose dyed locks appear to be sprayed into place so as to keep them from making a run for it, adjusts the navy-blue-and-red scarf that was lashed to the mast (her scrawny neck). She makes some sort of harumphing sound that I surmise to be a grunt of superiority. Then, raising her chin, the haughty one deigns to respond. "Lovely greeting. It's been six years since we've seen one another … or spoken … and this is how you say hello. And to you, I am 'Mother,' so don't call me Millicent again."

Darah tidies the stack of papers in her hands, lays them on the counter, and nods to Stephanie, the concierge, as she walks around the desk. "Let's move somewhere more private, shall we?"

Millicent follows Darah to the small sitting area, atop a square cream-colored Persian rug, in the center of the large room. "I feel like a horse being led to its stable."

"Well, hay then," Darah mumbles to herself.

"I know you didn't just make an equine joke under your breath."

"Neighhhhh …."

Darah stops at a couch that occupies one quarter of the sitting area. "Would you care to take a seat? Or do you just want to stand like always? Whichever way you feel more stable." Clearly amusing herself, Darah turns her head while her smile takes a final bow and leaves the stage.

"I shall *sit*." Millicent does so as she looks up at her daughter. "And you shall take a seat by my side." Oh, dear, her head is looking quite explosion-friendly at the moment.

Darah abides, taking care to leave a fair amount of space between them.

"I was here last week, and that concierge person behind the desk, Stephanie somebody, said you flew off somewhere. I can't remember the imprecise destination she reluctantly offered after a great deal of prodding, but I believe it was some place where they grow crops."

Her patience diminishing all too quickly, Darah's face morphs into tortured tedium. "You and I stopped speaking well over six years ago. I don't see that I need to explain anything to you … *Mother* … much less where I choose to travel."

"You abandoned me."

"Oh, no. Not even close. I told you that if you didn't stop judging, trying to control, and criticizing every last thing I do, I was going to say good-bye. I warned you so many times." Darah rages internally.

Millicent's words are preceded with a high-flown huff. "I assumed your comment to be hyperbolic, Darah. Because it never dawned on me that you could be so cruel as to abandon your mother forever. I'm only looking out for your welfare. I'm not treating you any differently from the way my own mother treated me."

Darah tenses but admirably maintains control. "That's fascinating. Considering you said that you were raised as a prop to help her to 'more properly assimilate' with the in-crowd."

Millicent's mouth drops open. "Yes. But I *never* said that to *you.*"

"Oh my God. Does that even matter?" Darah's eyes go dark. "No. You didn't. But I heard you all the same. You said that your mother didn't have you until she was thirty-five, after several miscarriages, and the only reason she kept trying was to keep up with the people in her social circle. Have children and brag about them. Oh, and she hated the fact that when other kids were accomplishing things and having expensive birthday parties, you had the audacity to still be a baby, thus still denying her the inclusion she craved." She pauses to deflate a bit. "Your words. I don't speak like that."

Millicent sneers at her daughter. "Okay. You're right. About all of it. Your grandmother was insanely awful. Your grandfather as well. Happy? So, here's my problem, Darah. If you clearly know all of this, why don't you have any compassion for me? If you understand why I'm the way I am, why did you so heartlessly walk away?"

Biting her bottom lip, Darah creates deep grooves while she contemplates how to respond. "If you're so unhappy, if you understand what having a miserable childhood did to you, then *why the hell* did you perpetrate an even worse one on me? Never once did you encourage me to find my passion in life. No, not you. Never. You wanted me to be properly educated only to get married and live a traditional life that would satisfy the image you wanted your uptight friends to have of *you*. I was *your* fucking prop."

Another high-flown huff, this one tinged with shock, is expelled from Millicent, this time by forcing air through her nose. "Language! I was fine with you getting a college degree. I thought you'd settle into a good job, perhaps meet a nice man at work, and eventually quit to marry and have babies while he brought home the bacon. Then, down the line, you might have taken a part-time job or done volunteer work after your children had grown. But what did you do, Darah? You zoomed around the world with some insatiable need to 'experience other cultures' while you threw opportunity in the garbage, purchased this oversized museum piece, and for the grand finale, let your child-bearing years pass."

"And I invited you to this 'oversized museum piece' so many times over the years, and you adamantly refused. Now, for some reason I've yet to ascertain, when you're no longer welcome, you show up."

Millicent prattles on. "I shudder to imagine why you decided to spend every last penny you had. I know your grandfather was generous to you, but he'd be horrified to see that you've squandered his last gift on some homage to an obsolescent lifestyle." Eyeballing her daughter, Millicent has an addendum. "That sapphire pendant around your neck, with the gold leaves wrapping it … those come quite dear. And those gold bangles … which I recognize as Tiffany's … come with a pretty little price tag as well. Who paid for them? A man? Or have you stooped low enough as to purchase them for yourself. Perhaps you *didn't* spend every last penny on this antique dwelling for deviants." She scans the room. "This establishment is akin to one giant round hole filled with square pegs."

Darah's mouth opens to speak, but the maternal unit's snit has not ended.

"I knew a woman who moved here with her husband. Martha Seymour. She was rather pathetic. Always tried to act like they had more money than they did while her husband acted as if they had less, if you can imagine the absurdity of *that* charade." She lowers her voice and does not see Kenny approaching Darah with Poodley on the leash. "Once, at Buffy Bruce's birthday, everyone was absolutely tittering to see that Martha was wearing panty hose with runs in *both legs*! Indeed, quite the metaphor for who the woman she is, and how apropos that she moved *here*."

"Hi, Kenny!" Darah says. "And hello, Miss Poodley."

The dog, who usually greets Darah, sits in front of the seated Millicent and stares at her stockinged legs below the hem of her gray dress.

The words, "What a rude and mangy mutt," trip carelessly off Millicent's tongue.

Raising one paw, Poodley lays it against Millicent's right leg, stares at her, then claws the stockings until they are shredded.

"Ouch! That hurts. I'm being mauled to death by a shaggy street mongrel. Stop this creature, Darah. Now!" Millicent looks down. "This four-legged thing has drawn blood, not to mention the destruction of my nylons."

Then with the other paw, Poodley repeats the process on the left leg. Millicent shrieks in horror again … then, more quietly, sputters like an engine that won't start.

Panicked, Kenny looks at Darah, relieved to see her laughing eyes and smiling face. He looks at the aggrieved one and sees she is trying to vaporize him with a hard stare.

"And *this*, Kenny Seymour, is why one gets a purebred … or at the very least, trains their mutt. Get this unruly animal away from me. As I recall, Martha doesn't care for dogs. Not even purebreds. Why is it that you even own this pooch?"

"Not that's it's any of your business, but, well, Martha's gone and done changed somethin' fierce. In fact, I can say for sure you wouldn't even recognize her. She ain't nothing like she used to be; I'll say that much."

"Something to be grateful for! As for you—"

"I don't think she liked you much neither." Kenny scratches Poodley on the neck. "I think she said you were a 'climber who kept missin' the steps and fallin' on her ass.'"

An unknown substance I wish not to identify angrily dislodges from Millicent's throat, making an unpleasant sound as it does. "A more apt description of herself. And your grammar is as atrocious as the mongrel by your side."

Poodley growls.

"Get that beast out of my space." She turns to Darah. "And just why the hell aren't you doing anything about this?"

"We'd best be going," Kenny says. "See you soon, Miss Darah."

"Bye, Kenny. Bye, Poodley." She looks blankly at her mother, then at her legs. "Oh, gee, you have a case of the runs."

"A tasteless joke I will do us both the favor of ignoring. Can we get back to our conversation?" Millicent looks down at her tattered hose and shivers.

"The part where you were mocking Martha Seymour? Or the part where you were spewing contempt at my life choices?"

Tugging at her hose, in a failed attempt to twist the runs to the back of her legs, Millicent plods on. Disgust on her angry visage, she scans the lobby. "Why have you dedicated your life to this dinosaur, populated with nobody worthy ... only misfits searching for something they'll never find."

"How dare you judge people you've never met or seen?"

"I've seen all I need to see. When I was here the last time, some man had the audacity to mistake me for someone named Miss Aggen before telling me that the reports of my illness were greatly exaggerated. Oh, yes, and he wanted to know why I wasn't wearing a hat. I told him he was mistaking me for someone else, and he insisted he wasn't. I'm quite sure I resemble no one in this abode."

"You know," Darah says, "now that you mention it, you actually look quite like her. The poor woman is quite ill at the moment, so no, she wouldn't be stomping around the lobby causing a ruckus like you've been doing. As for the hat remark, she's never seen without one. They're her trademark of sorts. I think she feels almost naked without one." She exhales in exasperation. "As I was saying, you have no basis whatsoever to judge the people who live here."

"Oh, the hell I don't. This place, as the chosen residence of the Seymours alone, tells me all I need to know." (Insert yet another harumph here.) "Look at your life, Darah. You don't even have a husband to ignore you when you clean the house and make dinner for him." Her voice gets louder. "You have no child to worry about. Not even one who doesn't speak to you, except to mock you when you tuck an olive branch under your arm and summon the courage to come see her. You don't even have fading memories of life with your only child to cling to. You have no real friends to talk behind your back and purposely forget to invite you to parties."

"This is satire, right?"

"It certainly is not."

Darah's eyeballs somersault in their sockets. "Did you even hear what you just said?"

"I know exactly what I just said."

As residents walk by and offer greetings, Darah smiles. She turns to her mother. "To make sure I understand you correctly: despite knowing why I cut you out of my life, you've returned after more than six years to hurl the same garbage at me and to insult my life while you simultaneously tell me how miserable *you* are with the life you wanted me to have? Is that correct? Did you even hear yourself? What kind of sadistic monster are you, anyway?"

"I'm not a m-monster …."

"Oh, the hell you're not. Listen to yourself. You want me to have a husband so he can ignore you like my father ignores you? I'll give you this: your husband is not a nice man. It's why I don't speak to *him*, either. Yet, you'd like me to find his clone and settle down? Misery loves company, right? If not that, then what?"

Opening the palms of her hands, Millicent drops her face into them and begins to sob. "My stockings are a mess; I suppose I *should* have a matching face."

Without emotion, Darah only stares. She already knows, after years of failed attempts, that consoling or commiserating with her mother will solve nothing. It will only give her mother renewed power to attempt control. There will be no comforting arm embracing Millicent's shoulder. No "There, there, Mother."

After several minutes of her finest performance art, Millicent looks at Darah. "How can you be so cold?"

"I'm not. I've tried for years … in ways you never recognized. Just now, I asked you a question, and you started weeping to avoid answering it."

An older woman, walking by, notices that Millicent is crying. She reaches into her purse, pulls out a tissue, and smiles as she hands it to her.

Millicent, barely uttering a thank-you, waits until she is a good distance away before tossing the tissue at Darah. "God only knows where this thing has been."

"And God forbid you should notice that a stranger took time to offer a kindness to you. And that's why we've been and will remain estranged."

Wiping her tears with the underside of her wrists, Millicent watches Darah stuff the offering into her pocket. "Are we estranged because I won't use a product of questionable hygiene from a stranger?" She huffs. "I taught you better than to put that germy thing in your clothing."

"I'm the owner. I don't litter here or anywhere else. The tissue is clean, you dried your tears with your hands, and, like always, you're deflecting."

"Oh, I'll answer your question, Darah. I'm not as evasive as you think. I just had a swell of emotion, as human beings will do. And in my swell, I got so overwrought with emotion that I forgot I carry my own tissues." Her eyes sweep the large lobby to ward off onlookers as she draws a calming breath. "Yes, I'm sure it does appear that I'm trying to push a lifestyle on you that was pushed on me … and that hasn't worked out. I don't know why it hasn't, nor do I understand why I've always felt like a fish out of water. But despite my failed life, I see so many who have absolutely wonderful lives. Children, grandchildren, homes filled with cheer and friends clinking glasses. These happy women offer their many talents to charity and yes, some to paid endeavors. And they feel satisfied on every level. I can't help but to still want those things."

Darah glances over at Stephanie to ensure there is no immediate need for her return. "So, you want me to step in and live the life that failed you … so you can vicariously repair whatever went wrong? Because the life you want for me isn't the one I want for myself. But you already know that. The biggest irony here is that you don't even want that life for yourself. Maybe those women are happy because they actually want the lives they live. And hello … that's why you're not … because you don't and never did. I guess you never heard the expression, 'If it don't fit, don't force it ….'"

Finally, at a loss for words, Millicent drops her head to ponder the weight of her daughter's statement. "No, I don't want that life. Your point is well taken, and you're correct. And yes, I am *that* broken." She looks up. "Who has any idea why?"

Darah gulps. "I might."

"Really?" Millicent looks quizzically at her. "I was speaking rhetorically, but you answered me as if you have some theory about my mindset. One that has surely eluded my consciousness. What aren't you telling me?"

Repositioning herself in her seat, Darah is weighed down by a heavy decision and lets her burden reflect in her eyes. "Well … it …"

Before Darah can speak another syllable, Millicent has rediscovered her anger. "If you know anything about me that I should know, if you understand why my life has been so painful, not that I can imagine how that's remotely possible, then it is utterly unconscionable of you to have kept it from me, and it is utterly repugnant that you have abandoned me knowing there's a reason for my misery. Absolutely loathsome."

Darah exhales. "Thank you."

"For what?"

"For reminding me who you are and why I've made the decisions I have. My God, to think I was just about to—"

"To what? You were just about to *what?* Tell me why I've been so unhappy my entire life? How would you know? Did your grandparents confide in you as to why they treated me so horribly? Is that it? Did your grandmother tell you I was some kind of demon child and deserved it? Was she punishing me for something? She's dead, and I can't ask her. Or my miserable father. Therefore, if you know something, then you need to tell me."

The fingers on Darah's right hand squeeze the fingers on her left, until she feels pain, while she ponders how to respond.

"I'm waiting."

"What you said about theories," Darah says. "I think you were punished because she had you so late in life, not in her early twenties like all of the women in her social circle. Of course, you can't help when you were born, but resentment is not always rational. If anyone should know that, it's you."

Millicent notices a woman staring at her ripped hose. She

grimaces, forcing the woman to quickly walk away. "I am being stared at. All because you allow mutts in this place. Shame on you. That horrid woman probably thinks I'm homeless."

Clenching her hands, Darah grinds her fists together. "You're the worst kind of snob. And it's impossible to be nice to you … because despite what's happened to you in your life, you're a cruel woman with little if no empathy for others. And maybe that's why I surround myself with people who are nothing like you."

"I've been a victim all of my life!" She snarls as she simultaneously suppresses tears. "And all you can do is insult me."

Darah's head tilts back, and she stares up at the massive gold chandelier she may be wishing would drop onto her mother's head. After receiving what may have been a divine transmission via the garish light fixture, she returns her attention to Millicent. "Do you really think that your misery hasn't hugely impacted my life? Do you think your victimhood ends with you? Some people give their children secondhand clothes because it's all they have; you stuck your only child with secondhand misery … because I suppose it's all *you* have. If anything, I'd think you'd want to save me from your own life. But no, you want me to *live* your life. To marry a man who will ignore me … just wow, Millicent. That's all I've got because I'm really trying to hold in every word I'd like to say to your face." She pauses … the pain in her eyes is too much to bear. Now, she looks at her mother. "If only you were a nice person … if only … everything would be so different."

"What?" Millicent's cold yet sad eyes look at her, then into the lobby area. "You wouldn't have adopted that old woman as your mother and let her replace me?"

Darah has no words.

"Oh, you didn't think I asked around about you the first time I was here. I took advantage of your absence to find out every little piece of information I could. I know she sits out by the gardens every day. And that she tended them as a young woman."

Following her mother's eyes, Darah sees Ava Elisabeth walking through the lobby. With only minimal exaggeration, I might say she flies off the couch and runs to her.

"Hello, dearest. I'm on my way to La Place de Montmartre. *Pour un verre du Côte du Rhône.* Would you like to join me?"

Darah's face falls, and Ava Elisabeth's frail hands cup her cheeks. "No worries, sweet Darah. I know we're not in Paris. Some days, I miss it terribly and I let myself forget … or more delightfully put … to remember."

Not entirely convinced the lapse was purposeful, Darah is happy the fearful moment has ended, but a new one has begun as she follows Ava Elisabeth's eyes to her mother, seething on the couch. At such a time as this, I'm quite sure Darah is grateful to Poodley for putting her mother in a position to stay put. But the intense gaze between her mother and Ava Elisabeth unnerves her.

"I cannot see so well, Darah. But I know that angry eyes are powerful enough to be felt even from behind. Is that your mother? The one who has treated you with such scorn all of these years? From everything you've shared with me, and from the way her eyes rip into my soul, I can't imagine she is anyone else."

"Yes. That's her."

"She's quite jealous of our friendship. That makes me sad."

Darah glances at her angry mother, then returns her full attention to Ava Elisabeth, whom I must say, is an absolute vision in her cinnamon-colored crushed-velour dress. If only she didn't taunt me so with her souvenirs of every man she's bed over four score years.

Just as Darah is about to speak, she sees her mother, rising like a phoenix from the ashes, intent on confrontation.

Taking her beloved friend by the arm, Darah, with no time to ask permission, swiftly walks Ava Elisabeth behind the concierge desk and gives a strict order to Stephanie. Seconds later, she disappears with her beautiful captive. I shall follow.

Gently, behind a closed and locked door, Darah asks Ava Elisabeth to have a seat on the deep-blue velvet sofa. She speaks softly as she sits beside her. "I'm so sorry to have rushed you in here without any explanation. We've been friends for a very long time, and I think you know, this kind of thing isn't in my playbook."

"You want to protect me from the unfortunate behavior you've known all your life. I understand that. I'm fine with however you see fit to handle things." She rubs her hand over the tufted fabric. "Oh, how I do love this piece." She turns more serious. "But Darah, my darling, you must also know that I hold my own and have done so my entire life."

Yes. She indeed has. She has collected baubles and favors from more men than she has years. Even when she agreed to live the semi-shadowed life that Henri created for her … she did exactly as she pleased.

Stephanie's voice is now quite loud. "You're not allowed back here! I've told you that several times. If you don't leave, I'll have to call the police. Oh, no. I guess I won't; I see our security guard is already on it." She speaks more quietly now. "Please, Mrs. Gregnut, don't make a scene."

Darah and Ava Elisabeth listen to Millicent's strong protestations as they watch the door handle rattle.

"I'm so sorry, Darah," Stephanie says through the door. "I really tried."

"You have locked your mother out of your life for the last time, Darah, And that damnable old woman can go to hell for taking my place."

With despair, Darah speaks to Ava Elisabeth. "She doesn't understand that nobody in the world with an ounce of kindness in them would ever want to take her place."

Ava Elisabeth nods. "No. They would not. You haven't exaggerated your characterizations … not that I believed you had. I'm just so sorry that you've both lived with such misery. It pains me so."

"Ma'am, I'm going to have to escort you out of here," a male voice says.

"And I'll punch your plebian lights out and sue you for assault, you, you paunchy prick!"

Darah stands and offers Ava Elisabeth a hand. "Never heard her go there before. Come on. There's a secret door in here for a reason. I'll take you wherever you want to go."

"You are so kind to me," Ava Elisabeth says as Darah opens the bookcase and holds open the door.

"You make it easy. You always have."

Now pounding on the door to an empty room, Millicent continues to scream. "You can avoid me all you like. I'll wait here forever if I need to. You'll see."

There is no response, and two men in blue arrive and circumspectly approach the subject.

Millicent gives the knob a last rattle. "Your father has left me, Darah. For some slut. I have no one. I'm completely alone in the world. I know you'll come around. You're far more compassionate than I've ever been. You'll change your mind. I'll see to it. Somehow. I've waited my entire life for love. Any kind of love. I won't stop now." She turns to the policemen. "There's no need for any offensive procedures you may have in mind. I have an urgent need for the ladies' room." She pushes them aside, and they do not protest. "Let me go!"

Elsewhere, feeling peace, Darah lets her mind settle as she and Ava Elisabeth sit by the open window at a nearby restaurant. Without needing to say a word, they clink wineglasses. Then, beautiful Ava Elisabeth looks out the window. She smiles at all the activity on La Place de Montmartre. As tourists eagerly swivel round racks of postcards, artists display their colorful works, and strangers ask one another to snap photos, the cheerful commotion of the busy street swells in her heart. *Quelle journée parfaite!*

Chapter Six: SAD SANTA

If a room could cry, it would be this one.

The sole resident, Alejandro Castillo, sits in a worn mustard-yellow club chair that is every bit as unfortunate and as disconsolate as he. The chair's cushion, misshapen and discolored, has flattened so much over the years that Alejandro saw it worthy to put an old pillow underneath to add a bit of comfort. That simple act, which would be of little consequence to most, enhanced his life. There is a matching chair by its side, with a slightly better cushion but no living being to occupy it. Perhaps a séance would reveal if anyone does.

In his early seventies, he is still quite handsome, though he has never had the funds nor the desire to be dapper. His long white-gray hair touches his shoulders, and his mustache and beard are neatly trimmed. Despite seeing few people, he takes care with his appearance, even putting a thin touch of petroleum jelly on his face to soften the skin.

A man who has worked as hard as Alejandro should be entitled to a grander station in life to reflect his fine character and years of dedication to the well-being of others. Yet, Alejandro often feels undeserving to even have the space that he does.

When he was fifteen, his hard-working father died in a factory accident, devastating the family and leaving his wife and children to survive on the inadequate compensation they received, along with her wages as a seamstress. Alejandro, desperate to contribute, illogical guilt over his father's death eating away at him, was eager to leave school, but his mother would not allow it. When he was sixteen, she agreed to his working a part-time job and helping in any way that he could.

After graduating high school, he cared for his mother, two brothers, and his sister by depriving himself of everything but a roof over his head. When his mother remarried and his siblings were finally self-sufficient, Alejandro found love and married beautiful Sophia. He was now thirty, and she was twenty-six. Within a year, she gave birth to their son. Six months later, the child died from an unknown cause, and Sophia, despite his every effort to console her, went mad. Her family, revealing that she had suffered from mental illness all her life, committed her to a gloomy state-run hospital and insisted that Alejandro immediately file for divorce. Reluctantly, with their insistence he go live a happy life, he dissolved the marriage and extinguished all that he had in the blink of an eye ... even the hope that she would one day recover.

Several years later, he ran into Sophia on the street. She was radiant yet filled with rage and hurt thinking Alejandro had cut and run because their son had died and she'd had a lapse of sanity. She cursed him as passersby gaped and sniggered. Alejandro pleaded with her to hear him out, but she refused. Her angry words broke him ... there in public view for all to see and hear.

I know this much: she had never suffered any chronic mental illness, only the one breakdown under tragic circumstances. Her affluent family, who had actually sent her to a top-tier mental health facility, had used the consequences of the child's death to orchestrate the divorce, thereby "putting her back on the market," hoping and plotting for some wealthy man to acquire her as if she were livestock or some Wall-Street-type commodity. Alejandro never forgave himself for being so trusting and capitulating to her family's brutal lies. He was diminished, not only in her eyes, but in his own.

Today, his memories of Sophia and the child still haunt him. This is a man who accepts responsibility for everything in his midst ... and it cripples him. No, it is not the kind of infirmity for which one requires a cane or medication. Alejandro is keen to dismiss all that casts light on his goodness while embracing that which he perceives as failure or regret. It is sad, though not uncommon for when one embraces negativity, it hugs back even tighter. Many feel at peace when held firm because it is such a familiar feeling to them and therefore welcomed. I shall continue his story.

A year after his chance meeting with Sophia, Alejandro came to work at this establishment as a maintenance worker. Though reticent to love again, he fell for a chambermaid from Latin America.

When she had first come to this country, long before Alejandro, she spoke no English. Only eighteen when she got the job, on her first day, while making a bed, a co-worker asked her name. Misunderstanding the question, she replied "sheets" as she held a set in her hands. Later that day, when a bi-lingual colleague explained why her answer had elicited a hearty giggle, she laughed herself silly and insisted on being called "Sheets" from that moment on. Over the years, she worked hard to learn English. A favorite among guests and staff, years later, she was promoted to supervisor of housekeeping. To reveal her given name would be to tarnish a legend. I shall not.

The apartment where Alejandro lives, at the end of the second-floor hallway, was originally one of four inhabited by hotel employees who, for a variety of reasons, required an overnight stay after a double shift, or, perhaps, when finding themselves in an enhanced condition not suitable for travel. I've no doubt they all have their ghosts, but three souls, on two separate occasions, perished in this very space. The other three rooms, to my knowledge, are death-free and slightly larger.

This is the least-expensive and shabbiest of rooms. The only renovation here has been to knock out an adjacent supply closet, once used by chambermaids, thus allowing the addition of a small kitchen area. Two years ago, when Darah ordered a fresh coat of paint for the place, Alejandro only reluctantly agreed, feeling it wasn't deserved. (What to do with this man!)

He sits at the small square table in the kitchen area. It has a plastic top in mother-of-pearl yellow and the remainder of it is chrome. He sits in one of two matching chairs to read his newspaper so he can spread it out. Today, he is opening a package that arrived from his sister, Alyshia. He is curious; it is neither Christmas nor his birthday. As his eyes meet the gift, the tears stream. It is a small wooden-framed illustration of Santa Claus. The iconic figure is dressed in a candy-cane baseball uniform, a Santa hat, and holds a bat as if he's stepping to the plate. Alejandro reads the accompanying note:

Mi querido hermano:

I know how much you love baseball. When I was a little girl, I thought you would be a professional player one day. Then Papi died, and you gave up everything for our family. I can never thank you enough for your love and sacrifice. I just wish you had kept more of the fruits of your labor for yourself.

When I saw this vintage treasure in an antique store, I had to buy it for you. There is no Santa who could give a gift as special as you've given to all of us. I don't know why you stopped being Santa at Christmas, but I know you can't talk about it. It haunts me. You loved the children, and they loved you back. The department store manager told me you were the best Santa they ever had. I don't want to pry, but I still wonder why you left the job.

I hope this gift brings love, not pain. Also, I must tell you, another is on its way. I can only say that I pray it will help you to know and accept what a difference you've made to so many. I hope I haven't overstepped. I just want you to see yourself as others do. I wish we didn't live so far away.

Con mucho amor de tu hermana devota.
Aly

He looks around the room. I know what he is doing: imagining where he would hang the illustration, if only he could take a respite from self-castigation. There are many possibilities, but he spies the perfect place: over the single bed where he sleeps, which is directly across from where he rests his posterior. From that spot, he would see it all the time. But he is so undeserving.

Two days pass, and Alejandro still contemplates hanging the picture. He vacillates in a chasm where pleasure and pain are interchangeable. He wishes to write and thank his sister, but not knowing what else is to come, he opts to wait. He is filled with dread. What else could she have sent? Why does she torture him with her love?

He sits at the table and lets the illustration consume his thoughts. It is exquisitely painted and framed: the embodiment of two things so important in his life, given to him by someone so special. Watching him stare at the gift is akin to seeing two people with deep love for one another in pain and unable to communicate. They rack their brains, desperate to find an elusive path to acceptance ... and to clarity. But none comes.

There is a knock at the door. It is neither angry nor timid. It is a confident knock. The last time anyone knocked at the door was two years ago when Alejandro allowed it to be painted. Who could be there?

A dark-skinned man, neatly dressed, with a broad smile, greets Alejandro. "Hello, you don't know me. My name is Nicholas Santi, and I've been searching for you for years. I finally met someone who knows your sister, Alyshia, and I was able to phone her and share my story. After we spoke for some time, she offered me your address. I must add, she seemed quite eager for us to speak. Would it be an imposition if I asked to come inside?"

Alejandro must make a decision on the spot. Something he has not been used to doing for a very long time. "Yes. Okay. Please, come in." He gestures toward the matching club chair with the better cushion. "Would you like to sit?"

"I would. I've come a long way."

"I-I don't know what to offer you. I'm not prepared for guests. At the moment, a glass of orange juice or water is all I have." He looks angry with himself. "Not very hospitable of me. I'm sorry."

Still smiling, Nicholas sits. "There's no need for an apology. Besides, you weren't expecting me. You know, I would love a small glass of orange juice. Vitamin C keeps me healthy. Someone once told me if I drink it every day, I'll live forever." He laughs. "Not sure I want to do so, but I'll chance immortality."

Alejandro nods and walks over to the mini-fridge. He pours two small glasses of juice, finishing what is left in the carton, and gives the larger portion to Nicholas.

"I can see the apprehension in your eyes, Alejandro. I'm sure if a strange man came to visit me, one who had gone to so much trouble to find me, I'd wish to dispense with any small talk and get to the point of his visit." He takes a sip of juice. "I see we have something in common; I prefer mine with pulp as well." He thinks. "Hmm. That *was* small talk, wasn't it?"

"I'm glad you like the juice."

"You wouldn't remember me, but I remember you so very well. We met when I was six. I sat on your lap. You were the first and only Santa Claus I ever saw."

Alejandro's eyes pop with surprise before his shoulders slump. "This sounds insane … even to me, but now that you mention it, I do remember you." His brow creases as he thinks. "Maybe it's the old soul that looks at me through your dark eyes. It seems almost impossible … being so long ago, but yes. I just wish the recognition made more sense to me. I can't think of one other child I would know today."

"It's not as surprising as you might think. I had a feeling you might."

His voice weakens, but he is able to speak. "You were living with an aunt and uncle. You had come from Turkey after both of your parents died. Is that right?"

Nicholas finishes his juice and places the glass on the small side table between the chairs. "Do you mind?"

"No, not at all." Alejandro's mind is racing, and his eyes are filled with fear as he sets his glass down as well.

"Yes, I was born in Turkey. My father was from Mexico and came to Demre, on the Mediterranean coast, to study their history and archaeology. There, he met my mother, a student from Istanbul, who was also in Demre for a similar purpose. They bonded instantly and married after six months. As the story goes, they would have married in two weeks, but as to not frighten their families, they waited." He laughs. "I was born a year later, and I'm told we lived a happy life until …." He goes quiet for a moment. "I have a faint memory of us together, by the sea, and only two photos. Even after so many years, it is painful to talk about, but I must tell you: my parents died tragically when I was still young, and I was sent a very long distance to live with my father's brother and his wife."

"I remember." Alejandro is unable to meet his eyes. "I've dreaded this day forever. I'm so sorry. That afternoon preys on me. And it should. I was so wrong …."

Nicholas sits back in his chair, trying to process these odd words. "I think perhaps you might be merging my story with someone else's. While you have the historical aspects correct, I can't imagine you'd have anything to apologize for. You changed my life. I think I would have grown up to be a very different man, angry and embittered, if our paths had never crossed. I consider the day we met to be the most serendipitous and luckiest day of my life." He expels several breaths before continuing. "I had to track you down, to find you again before ... to thank you for a life-changing experience."

"Oh, no." Alejandro is defiant. He cannot conceive of praise when he is so dastardly and scorn-worthy. "I-I can't imagine, Mr. Santi. I, uh, think it's probably you who've mixed things up ... or merged stories ... to use your words. What you just said ... you couldn't possibly be speaking about me."

"I'm very sure I have the right man."

For one who has always been loath to emote in the presence of anyone, Alejandro bursts into tears while the near-stranger looks on. Catching sight of a box of tissues by the bed, Nicholas gets up to retrieve them, setting them on the small table next to the empty juice glasses.

Alejandro grabs one and blows his nose, then continues as the tears course down his cheek into his beard. "There's nothing to thank me for."

Reaching over and touching his hand, Nicholas tries to calm him. "May I take the liberty of asking you to indulge me? Let me tell my story, and then, if I have the wrong man, I'll leave immediately. But I'm quite certain that I don't."

Alejandro runs his fingers through his long white hair. "If you must. I'm sure I deserve it."

Steeling himself, Nicholas begins. "I not only lost my parents, but I watched them die. They were on an expedition ... and had taken me with them ...well, there's no point in sharing more than that." He studies Alejandro's weeping face. "Clearly, we are both upset. After the tragic accident, by the kindness of those who worked with and loved my parents, funds were raised to send me to live with my aunt and uncle, my only living relatives who wanted me. They are fine people, but back then, they had very little. Still, they took me into their one-bedroom apartment and put a bed in the corner of the living room. They did everything they could to make me feel loved and special. I was just five.

"That Christmas, they bought me a few small items from the thrift store and tagged them from Santa. I loved them. There were four wooden soldiers and a green plastic car with shiny wheels. I was excited to learn the doors actually opened. When I returned to kindergarten in January, I brought the toys with me. It was then that life's cruel ways hit me again. The other children mocked my joy, flaunting all kinds of fancy gadgets and toys that put mine to shame. But the most horrible revelation was that my green car had been given to charity by a classmate's mother when he lost interest in it. The boy accused my aunt and uncle of having dug through their trash. I still remember the moment when the teacher heard what was going on. Before she admonished my classmates, she cast a sad look at me. I understood it immediately. It meant the other children were right. Santa hated me.

"That was only the beginning. As the year went on, they noticed my secondhand clothing. When the teacher wasn't looking, they'd call me 'poor boy' and spice their insults with racial epithets, that now, as an adult, I know came from the collective mouth of their parents."

"How very awful," Alejandro says. "Hearing your story, yes, you're the child I met that day, but—"

Nicholas takes a tissue and dabs his eyes. "I'm afraid I need one of these as well." He pauses. This appears more difficult than he imagined. "It wasn't long after that I learned all about Santa Claus … from my classmates … and I came to understand why he left such drastically different gifts. I didn't want to hurt my aunt and uncle, who thought I still believed, so the following Christmas, when they had a bit more money, I allowed my aunt to take me to the department store to meet—"

"Me." Alejandro gulps.

"Yes. I was too old to see Santa, but I was angry, and you were just there, with the same beard you have now, smiling and ho-ho-ho-ing me. I can't possibly recall my exact rationale as a child, only that I wanted to make you pay for all of the taunting and ridicule I'd endured. I think, when I sat on your lap, I told you I knew you were fake."

"Yes. You said I was a big, fat fake and a liar. You punched my stomach and said even my fat was fake. You tried to pull my beard off but quickly saw that was for real when I winced in pain."

"Did I? So sorry. I'd forgotten that part. Can you tell me what else you remember?"

The tears, which had momentarily stopped rolling, began anew. "You said I got money for lying to little kids, asking them what they wanted, then letting their family give them cheap stuff while other kids got 'the best toys ever.'"

"I barely recall that. How terrible I was." Now Nicholas looks away for a moment. Reclaiming his gaze, he looks at Alejandro. "What else?"

"That it was a stupid lie … and mean too, you said, that Santa comes down chimneys because homes like yours didn't even have chimneys. And then you asked me again why I lied to children to get money."

"Isn't it funny? I don't even remember that part." Nicholas casts his eyes downward for a moment. "Now, I am a bit clearer on why our memories are so contrasting."

Alejandro feels emboldened to continue. "What you didn't know about me … is that I'd already done terrible things, and hearing such harsh words from a young boy, direct from his heart, solidified, in no uncertain terms, the bitter truth that I should never play Santa again."

Nicholas looks at him curiously. "You can tell me to get out if

I'm being too invasive, but what do you mean, you'd done 'terrible things?'"

Shame fills Alejandro's eyes. "When I was a teen, I begged my father for a Rawlings Mickey Mantle baseball glove. Mantle played three positions and was a switch hitter. I wanted to emulate him. And I was good … very good … and I thought the glove could be my lucky charm to send me to the major leagues one day."

"And your father didn't agree?"

Too distraught to grab a tissue, Alejandro wipes his tears on his sleeve. "Oh no, he agreed. He was very proud of my athletic prowess. So much so that he took an extra shift to make the money to buy the glove for me." He sniffles as fresh tears fall. "That's the shift where he was crushed at the factory."

Tears well in Nicholas's eyes. "Oh, my. We have more of a bond than I ever imagined."

"That was only the beginning." Alejandro, his voice fully restored and needing to release years of pent-up guilt, rambles on. "I worked so hard to care for my family. When I was thirty-two, I married my Sophia … an angel on earth. We weren't married long when she had a baby, a son, and he died from that horrible thing called SIDS … Sudden Infant Death Syndrome. She had a breakdown, but her family told me it was much more … that she'd always been mentally ill but had skillfully hidden it from me. And they said the doctors had told them she was too far gone to ever recover. They pressured me night and day to divorce her. I didn't want to do." He raises his voice. "I loved her with everything I am. But they convinced me it was hopeless." He slows his erratic breathing. "I thought I was being punished for killing my father, and God was telling me I didn't deserve a wife or a son. And that because of my sins, Sophia would waste away in an institution." He pauses. "Her parents had forbidden her to tell me how wealthy they were. I was never invited to their home. They were afraid I'd take her money." He temporarily finds traces of his righteous indignation. "Taking someone's money is the very last thing I would *ever* do." He calms. "While her breakdown was real, it was temporary. And when the door opened for her parents … even a little, they walked in and broke us up. I should never have acquiesced." He sobs. "I saw her years later. They'd told her terrible lies as well. But she was so convinced I'd betrayed her … that I never got to offer my side."

With great solemnity, Nicholas slowly shakes his head. "I see that wealth … and the lack of it … also bonds us."

Alejandro is not prepared to stop there. "I should have known not to marry her, but the love I had … still have, truthfully, is overwhelming. After my father's death, after my son's death and losing my wife, after meeting you … it was clear that I carried a curse and needed to separate from society." He weeps. "But I am human … or so I think. I came to this place … when it was still a grand hotel. I took a job on the maintenance crew and fell for a chambermaid who called herself 'Sheets.'" He looks around the room, as if he expects her to appear. "She was as delightful as her name. I adored her. Not in the way I loved my Sophia, but she was a gem. One night, we were in this very room, two hotel employees sharing a bottle of wine, when she asked me to run down to the gift shop and pick up some antacid tablets. She said the chipotle peppers in our Mexican dinner had given her heartburn." He stops cold and says nothing for several moments. "When I got back to this room, she was gone. Dead. Heart attack. I shouldn't have taken her word that it was heartburn. If only I'd called for help, maybe she'd still be alive."

"That's dreadful. I'm sorry, Alejandro. So much pain in your life."

"A year later, two bellhops overdosed in here. The death of Sheets probably called to them."

"And you choose to live here … where three people have died?"

"I deserve it. Don't you think?"

Nicholas lowers his head. "No, not at all. Ill fortune doesn't make a man bad."

"Well, I heard 'ill fortune' speak quite loudly to me. He told me I had earned him. So, now, I live a quiet life and try to spare everyone I can from knowing me. My brothers, for the most part, have given up on me, wisely so, but my sister, she's some kind of persistent."

"May I tell you the rest of my story? The part *I* remember?"

"Knock yourself out." Alejandro lets his head fall against the chair in defeat.

"Well, I suppose, it was after the business you described, where I made you feel terrible for playing Santa Claus. I wanted to humiliate you in any way I could." He looks sick to his stomach at the remembrance. "I asked you why Santa liked rich kids better and gave them all the good stuff, while kids like me got cheap toys so rich kids could make fun of them." He nods. "Oh, yes, I wanted you, a random department-store Santa Claus, to pay for my misery." He looks into Alejandro's eyes. "And you know what you told me? You said that poor kids get the best gifts of all. They learn to be strong. In words a child could understand, you told me that kids with less money never let toys define them. And that when they're growing up … and once they're grown, they know how to stand on their own. They can go out into the world with all of their smarts and live their best lives and help those who need it." He sighs. "And that the rich kids think they're getting the good stuff, but really, it's the poor kids. They learn all the important things you never learn in school." He stifles a cry. "And then you whispered to me that it was our secret, and when I grew up to be a successful man, I should come back and tell you."

Alejandro looks blankly at him. It as if Nicholas is talking about someone else entirely. "I barely remember that part."

"You have been so down so long, my friend. You have twisted

your beautiful soul into someone you no longer recognize." Nicholas stands and plants himself in front of Alejandro. "After that day, by some miracle, I realized you had taken my anger and channeled it into a passion to succeed, to grow up and be proud. For years now, my aunt and uncle have lived a most comfortable life, in a beautiful home with a garden. It is everything they've ever wanted. As for me, I have my own manufacturing company, up north, and my wife and I couldn't be happier. Our children our happy. If I hadn't met you, well, who knows. I'm glad you were my Santa." He stops to reflect. "It feels good to put smiles on young faces, doesn't it?"

"It did … but then …"

Nicholas shivers. "Never did I imagine that at the very same time you gave me a life, I somehow took yours away." Nicholas's countenance grows even more serious. "Hear me. All of the things that have happened, Alejandro, they weren't your fault. Who knows why the world turns as it does? Life is not fair, and even Santa Claus can't change that."

"No, he can't."

"I've got to get going." Nicholas smiles and puts his arms out. "How about a hug for an old friend."

Poor Alejandro. He stands, but not having felt the touch of another human being in so many years, can barely comply as he tries to let the sage words soak in.

Nicholas does not wait. He puts him arms around Alejandro and squeezes him. "Thank you for the most wonderful gift you have given me."

"It's hard to imagine that I—"

"Please … do me a favor. After I leave, perhaps you might take a walk outside. Feel the sun on your face or go down into the lobby and meet the eyes of those who smile at you. You are not cursed, my friend. No, you are a blessing. A rare and true blessing indeed." Nicholas lets go, takes a good look at Alejandro's bewildered face, and speaks only a few words more. "Start slowly if you must. But hear me when I say the world awaits you. Good-bye, my friend."

Alejandro has barely choked out a good-bye, when Nicholas has left. Walking over to the table, he picks up the gift from his sister and smiles at the image for the first time. Gathering up the little courage he can muster, he goes to his front door, and with nowhere in particular to go, he walks into the hallway.

Just as he is coming out of his room, a twenty-something-year-old woman is exiting her apartment with a young boy by her side. Immediately, Alejandro is transported back in time and now remembers what he said to Nicholas. Every word is clear. The boy looks up at him. "Are you Santa Claus?"

"Oh, you mean because I have white hair and a white beard."

"Yeah. You have to be because you look exactly like him. So, are you?"

"Once upon a time I was."

"Cool. But how come you're not dressed like him?"

"You're asking a lot of questions, Timmy," the woman says to him. She looks at Alejandro. "Sorry."

"There's no problem. You must be his mother."

"Actually, no. I'm his babysitter. His mom works here, and he spends time in my apartment, asking me nonstop questions until she's done for the day. It's so much fun." She laughs. "Today, I'm thinking he asked me about two hundred and fifty-two."

Timmy laughs. "I did not."

"Oh yeah you did, kiddo." She extends her hand to Alejandro. "Hi, I'm Gina. Your neighbor. And this is Timmy."

"Hi, Timmy."

"I'm going to my friend Gracie's birthday party. She lives on the fourth floor. We're gonna walk up the stairs because Gina thinks exercise is good."

"She's right. I know I don't get enough of it."

Timmy jumps up and down. "You know what would be so awesome. If you walked me to the party. I wanna show my friends that I know Santa."

"Well … if that's what you'd like. I'll give it a try."

"Do you have your Santa clothes?"

"I'm sorry," Gina says to Alejandro. "Timmy, that's too much to ask."

"I've got my hat," Alejandro replies, surprising himself. "What if I get that and put it on? Will you wait for me? It's right inside my closet."

"Sure!"

"I'll be back in a moment. But I'm only going to walk you and Gina to the party. I can't come in with you. Is that a deal?"

"Okay."

Alejandro rushes to his apartment door, hurries inside, and within moments returns wearing a Santa hat. "How's this?"

"I knew it was you. I knew it. I knew it. I knew it."

"He's very clever," Gina says with a grin.

The three of them head to the stairwell. Alejandro, more out of shape than he wants to believe, is feeling the strain of the climb. Finally, reaching the fourth floor, he catches most of his breath and walks the boy and his babysitter to the designated apartment door. "I'm afraid I won't be able to say hello; I just realized I have to be somewhere."

Gina sees he is struggling. "Are you okay? I'm just going to say hello and then I'll be going back to my place. I can walk with you."

"Oh, I'm fine. You take time with your hellos. Timmy, enjoy the party."

Timmy rings the doorbell. "I sure wish you could meet my friends."

"Another time, okay?"

"Thanks for everything," Gina says as she escorts Timmy into the party. "So glad we finally met." She winks. "Thanks for wearing the hat. It meant a lot to Timmy. And to me too."

As Alejandro walks away, he realizes that it has been a very long time since he's walked up two flights of stairs, and the strain has left him quite winded. He is of no mind to take the stairs, afraid he might take a tumble down them, and walks to the elevator. Just as the doors open, he feels weak, then leans against the wall before sliding to the floor.

By now, it is clear that this is Lee's clue to depart Darth. Yes, just in time to witness Alejandro's humiliating slide downward.

In typical Lee fashion, he stares at Alejandro. He sees a flesh-and-blood man, but he will not acknowledge that yet again, an older man is in peril and requires assistance. Alejandro, reverting back to the mindset of one undeserving, says nothing as the two men stare oddly at one another.

Within a minute, Gina, seeing him on the floor, runs to his side. She turns to Lee, about to chastise him for his cruelty, but turns back to Alejandro. "Are you all right?"

He nods and reaches for her extended hand.

Once he is standing, Gina smiles, then snickers at Lee who continues to stare. Biting her tongue, she turns back to her neighbor. "Steady on your feet?"

Embarrassed, Alejandro nods again.

"Come on, Santa," she says with a smile. "We've got to get you back to the North Pole."

Taking one last gape, Lee runs down the hall toward his apartment. "Ellie!"

Alejandro is now inside his apartment again. He feels as if it was all a dream, and he's back where he started. Only something is different. He looks on the wall over his bed, and the gift from his sister Alyshia is exactly where he envisioned it hanging. Sitting on the table, he can't believe his eyes. It is the baseball glove he wanted as a child that his father never got to give him.

"This is impossible," he says softly. "How could this be?"

There is a knock on the door. At first, he assumes Gina must want to tell him something else, but then he intuits that it cannot be her. It is someone connected to these gifts ... perhaps to Nicholas Santi. He must have returned for some reason. He will explain. All will make sense.

Fortifying himself, he walks to the door, pauses, then opens it. He is unable to process what he sees. Such a beautiful woman she is still. Older, as is he, but as lovely as the day he married her. She has the same radiant smile he fell in love with. "Sophia. I can't believe ..."

She lifts her head and raises herself to kiss his lips.

"Sophia," he repeats, as he pulls her in and closes the door.

Somewhere, Nicholas Santi is smiling.

Chapter Seven: THE COLORS OF REMEMBRANCE

Millicent gulps as she rings the bell at the sixth-floor apartment.

A well-built African-American man, in dark gray jeans and a long-sleeved black T-shirt, answers the door. "Oh, hello. Can I help you?" He appears momentarily confused. "Sorry. I didn't know Ms. Aggen was expecting anyone …." He takes a closer look. "Or that she had a sister. Don't know how I missed that. Need to keep my eyes on the road when I'm driving. Or maybe I missed it because I was." He laughs.

Millicent, having removed her torn hose, hopes the man will not notice her bare legs, even though only a little of them is actually showing. "I'm sorry. I'm Millicent Gregnut. The owner, Darah Gregnut, is my daughter. I've come to see Miss Aggen, though clearly, my timing is all wrong. And no, we're not related, though I've heard there's a resemblance."

"Sure is." He gives Millicent a once over.

Millicent offers a nervous shimmy as his eyes take her in. Clearly, no man has looked at her for a very long time. Especially one decades younger with such clear muscular definition.

"So, you haven't met."

"No."

"But she knows who you are?"

"I'm afraid that's a no as well." She can't seem to meet his eyes. Paying a call on a stranger makes *her* the stranger — a branding that doesn't suit her uptight sensibilities.

"I see." He scratches his head. "Actually, if she is up for a visit, this may be a good time. I'm Drake, her companion. I'm leaving, and

I don't think she's quite ready to be alone. But Ms. Aggen'll have the final word on that, of course. So, if it's a go, as I suspect it might be … there you have it … perfect timing."

Millicent sighs. "I think you're the first person to ever tell me *that.*" She gulps. "That I had perfect timing." She is desperate to air a grievance about Darah but realizes it will make a bad first impression.

"Come in," he says, moving out of the doorway. "I take it that she won't know why you're here … seeing how she doesn't know you exist."

Millicent's unease squeezes her like a sweater that's shrunk in the dryer. "No, she won't. It's just that when my daughter told me we looked alike, I had to see for myself." She laughs nervously. "As a matter of fact, I was mistaken for Ms. Aggen the other day."

"Hmm. I see. Well, as far as I know, she's never been mistaken for you." Drake studies her face. "I wouldn't presume you two for twins, but yeah, there's a definite resemblance." He nods toward a dark blue kidney-shaped sofa. "If you'll wait here …."

Millicent sits and immediately clutches one of the two round pillows as a nervous child would cleave to a teddy bear. "Certainly."

As Drake goes into the bedroom, Millicent soaks in everything she can, from the nearby mid-century blue-lacquered rocking chair, to the more traditional Hollywood Regency furniture in keeping with the rest of the room. Most of it, she notices, is some shade of blue, while the green carpet, nearly the color of grass, looks almost like a freshly cut lawn. A sun-shaped wrought-iron copper-yellow mirror hangs nearby, and Millicent wonders if it is tired from shining all day.

Although only three minutes have elapsed, they feel like thirty to her. She despises being discussed in the next room. Perhaps Drake noticed her bare legs and thinks she is a low-class fraud. The mere thought makes her stomach flip. Would that be a reason for Miss Aggen to decline her visit? One would hope that Millicent possesses the sagacity to recognize when said wisdom has momentarily left the building.

Now, she hears weeping from the bedroom. Has her visit brought the poor woman to tears? She contemplates making a run for it, but having already identified herself as Darah's mother, she can't do so anonymously. Even worse, they would surely think she absconded with some precious bric-a-brac, and Drake would have to help Miss Aggen take inventory to discover that nothing has been pilfered. (Unless she actually decides to abscond with something.) And, what if Darah hears about her visit, which she surely would. (The hell she would have to pay.) No. The die is already cast. She will have to remain and endure whatever punishment she is about to receive. Part and parcel of her miserable life. I do think this woman forgets that she alone made the decision to ring the doorbell. Listening to her tortured thoughts, one might believe a stranger took her finger and pressed it to the doorbell against her will, then fled.

The sobbing now turns into a torturous wail, yet she, Millicent Gregnut, is more concerned about how *she* feels than the stranger in the other room shedding the actual tears. Such egocentricity I cannot abide.

Again, she contemplates leaving, but going full circle with the same logic, she stays put.

Seven minutes later, Millicent, enervated by the burden of her trifling ruminations, pastes a smile on as she sees Drake walk out of the bedroom, his arm around the enfeebled Miss Aggen. Her tears have dried, but she is clearly distressed. She wears a thin tortoiseshell headband in her white hair and a modest green dress, not too dissimilar from her own style. Immediately, Millicent stands.

Drake gestures toward the sofa. "Maybe you'd be more comfortable here, Ms. Aggen … rather than the usual spot."

She nods in disagreement as she walks to her rocker with the laminate arms and wide blue cushions. "This will do just fine." Before she sits, she extends a hand to Millicent, and they shake. "Hello. I'm

Lone Aggen. My first name … it's Danish, as was my mother. And I hear you are Darah's mother."

"I'm Millicent Gregnut. She is my daughter. Yes." (I cannot help but notice the egocentric rephrasing of the familial tie.)

Lone takes a seat on the rocking chair as Drake eases her into it. "And you've come to visit me because we share a resemblance."

(If I didn't have a compulsion to narrate the goings-on, I would rest for a while and laugh until my sides split open. Millicent, now seated again, clearly feels humiliated and foolish. The lines on her face deepen before Lone can finish the question. What a sight she is.)

Millicent squirms. "Well, yes. I've never been told I resemble anyone. I look nothing like my parents, and Darah only favors her father. So, when I heard—"

"It's a fine reason to meet." Lone sniffles. "I'm just in a terrible state because today is the last day I'll have my wonderful companion, Drake." She looks at him with a sad smile. "He's been offered a superb job at a nearby hospital, and while that makes me ecstatic, I can't bear to think of daily life without him."

"If only I could be two places at once," Drake says, his affection for the older woman clearly genuine. "But I'm not going far; I'll be here to visit as often as I can. I'll turn up again like a bad penny. You know that, Ms. Aggen. And now those tears are flowing like the Mississippi River. I'll get you a tissue or two."

"No need," Millicent blurts out. "I carry them in my pocket."

"That'll do," Drake says.

Without thinking, Millicent reaches into her pocket, and to her horror, pulls out the torn pantyhose she had shoved in there during her visit to the ladies' room. A single tissue clings to the fistful of nylon.

"Oh, mercy me," Drake mumbles to himself. "I'll be back in a jif." He hurries into the other room.

Now, the water from Lone's faucet stops as Millicent's begins to flow. "I've never been so embarrassed in my entire life. I was sitting in the lobby when a dreadful mutt ripped my hose. Before I came here to meet you, I went to the ladies' room and removed them. Normally, on a different kind of day than I've had, I would go out and buy a new pair before paying you a visit, but—"

"We all have bad days. And there's no reason to explain a thing." Lone smiles.

"This has been a terrible day," Millicent moans. "And not a good one for you, either." (She only thinks to add that at the last second.)

"Perhaps we can comfort one another."

Drake, tissues in hand, returns from the bedroom and is pleased to see that Lone has stopped crying. He acknowledges Millicent, who turns red in his presence.

"I suppose you're leaving now," Lone says to him.

"I am. Date with my sweetheart." He laughs. "My *other* sweetheart. Before you know it, I'll be back for a visit. You'll see." He hands her the tissues. "I've nabbed a few of these for myself. Think I'm going to need them."

Lone stands and throws her arms around him, squeezing as tightly as she can. "Oh, Drake! My dearest Drake."

"I'm going to miss the heck outta you," he says. "Nothing easy about this on my end. Hope you know that, sweet lady."

They exchange many more words of love and admiration for one another as he prepares to go.

Millicent, longing to be so loved, feels completely out of place and squirms again in her seat until he is gone. Now her playing field is more level.

"I should offer you something," Lone says. "Tea and biscuits, perhaps?"

"Oh, no. You stay put. I don't need anything. I already feel like a ridiculous imposition."

"Not at all." She clears her throat. (I believe intentionally so to thwart the awkwardness.) So, you've come to see our resemblance. Aside from your brown hair and my white hair, what do you think?"

"I think we could pass for sisters ... or for one another if someone didn't know us too well. We're nearly the same height, but yes, the hair is different. And you have that mole above your lip."

"I do. Tell me more, Millicent. About why you're here."

"Oh, it's just what I said."

"I don't want to contradict you so early in our acquaintanceship, however long or short it may turn out to be, but somehow I don't think curiosity was your sole motivation. Maybe I've lived too long and I'm overly cynical, but I suspect there's more to this visit."

Millicent wants to lie, but she knows she will lose Lone's trust forever. "I do have another reason. And while the first one is embarrassing; the real one is shameful."

"Were you hoping to rob a bank? Disguised as me? Perhaps have me arrested while you live the life of Riley?"

"Gracious, no!" The affronted one stands. "I should go."

"Please sit. I was only teasing." (But was she?)

Millicent sits back down on the edge of her seat.

"Why don't you just tell me?" Lone says. "Then I'll share something about myself."

"Well ...." Millicent edges back a bit, quite aware that she will fall on her derriere should she retain that position. (Oh, that would be delightful.) "I told you that Darah is my daughter. What I didn't share is that we've been estranged for over six years, and I've just seen her today for the first time. And she wants nothing to do with me. Furthermore, my husband has left me. I'm a mere shadow of the woman I once was. I thought if we became friends, I'd have a reason to come here for a visit ... and catch an occasional glimpse of my daughter."

"Oh, dear. How Stella Dallasian!"

"You mean that movie, *Stella Dallas*, where the woman has to watch her daughter marry through the window?"

"Yes, that one. From nineteen thirty-seven, I believe."

Someone is flustered. "I think I should leave. And I promise never to come back." (It would be perfect should Millicent touch her forehead with the back of her hand and look upward to the heavens with a beleaguered sigh … but she fails to satisfy.)

"Millicent. I'm sorry. That movie just popped into my head and, yes, I tend to be outspoken at times. Not rude, just honest. And while candor is on the menu, I'll add this: if you're estranged from Darah, don't you think it would exacerbate the pain for both of you — to see one another from afar? Because I think it would be unbearable."

"Well, as you and I resemble one another, I was hoping she would think that I was you."

"But she recognized you today as yourself, yes?"

"Of course, I'm her mother. But, keep in mind I was standing right in front of her. However, at a distance, walking through the lobby, she might not … especially thinking she's rid herself of me for good."

"My goodness." Lone shakes off her frustration. "Did you hear a word I just said? Are you looking to heap more pain on your plate like a big scoop of mashed potatoes? I'm in a great deal of pain myself now, after saying good-bye to Drake."

"Oh, I guess you are. It's just that after the time I had today, I'm feeling utterly rejected. And mashed potatoes are never on my menu."

"And people who don't understand metaphors are never seated at my table."

Millicent looks away in shame. "I'm so sorry. I don't know where my good sense is. I'm just so alone. First, Darah, then my so-called friends, and now my husband."

Lone looks angered. (As she should. After all, it is Millicent who invaded her space, not the other way around.) "And, for all intents and purposes, I'm all by myself as well. In fact, I've come to believe that my given name is prophetic: Lone Aggen … alone again."

Millicent puts her hand over her mouth in shock. "Indeed. It never occurred to me. Is this your original surname?"

"It is. I've always been a rebel, so when I married, I kept my own name."

"How long were you married?" (She is happy to change the subject after being so foolish.)

"For forty-six years and two months. My Nigel was a wildlife biologist, who was born in England and who came here for school. We never had children because it wasn't possible to travel with him to remote areas of the world with him and raise a family. And I wanted a life with him more than anything.

"Out of necessity, at age thirty, he learned to fly a plane. Our adventures were plentiful and breathtaking." Her mind goes back in time. Even Millicent can see she is somewhere else. "Such beautiful memories that we shared in the sky, gliding above some of the most spectacular places on this planet."

Millicent looks around. "As soon as I came in here, I couldn't help but notice that you've decorated with a great deal of blue. Like the sky. And that your mirror is like the sun and the carpet like the grass."

"And the moon hangs in my bedroom," Lone adds. "With a few stars. They're the colors of remembrance; they were my life for so long before I became ill and was unable to go out anymore."

"How do you get your groceries and such? How will you do that now that Drake is gone?"

"Oh, Drake was only my companion. I have people who help me with groceries and other things. I'm too poorly right now to do them myself. But I'm getting better." She smiles. "I suppose what I miss the most about going out is wearing my extraordinary collection of hats. My signature accoutrement, as my friend Oliver often teases. But of course, I only wear one at a time."

"How wonderful. I'd love to see them." Millicent stands. "Do you mind if I pour myself some water. What can I get you?"

"There's a pitcher of cucumber-and-lime-infused water in the fridge that Drake always makes … made for me. Oh my." She sighs. "One more thing to miss. Though I suppose I can do it for myself. But I can't replace my dear friend. Anyway, yes, I'd like a glass. Pour yourself one if you'd like. I think you'll prefer it to tap water. It's divine. I'm happy to share. There are clean glasses in the drainer to the left of the sink."

Millicent notices the cobalt-blue tiles that make up the splash guard, interspersed with painted tiles of beautiful scenery. The glasses she takes from the drainer are tinted blue. The warmth of color surprises her with a squeeze of comfort. She prepares the glasses of water and returns to the living room.

"Thank you." Lone delicately takes the drink from her hands.

"You're welcome." Millicent resumes her seat. "I noticed some beautiful painted tiles. They all appear to be views from high in the sky. Are they your handiwork?" (Now, she's laying it on thick.)

"They are. Tile and vase painting was something I did long ago to make money for people in the villages we visited. I sold the tiles in small galleries and craft markets all over the world. I enjoyed it so much, and it kept me busy while Nigel was doing his nighttime work. I wrote poetry as well. But just for me."

"You never tried to publish it?"

"It wasn't meant for other people. My poetry, like the colors that surround me, are all meant to remind me of the seconds in my life. Not so much the days, not the years, but the seconds, the moments, those little pieces of time that we lose or let go of without realizing how they maintain our sanity."

"Oh." Millicent tastes the water, and the new flavor pleases her. "I never thought about seconds. I think more about years ... all the ones that have passed with such burdensome consequence." (And there she goes. Off to the races with her woebegone tale.)

Lone leans forward. "Honesty time again. Perhaps, as we resemble one another physically, you might do yourself a favor to adopt some of my coping skills. Hear me, Millicent; I say this in the kindest way. Yes, appreciating the significance of seconds, good and bad, can bring back the details of otherwise blurred memories."

"Oh. I don't think about seconds. What do they matter? I never—"

"In one second, the scent of a friendly flower ... or welcoming honeysuckle, can lift a heart and bring back the memory of a joyous time or place. In one second, the smile of a stranger meeting our own can form a unique connection." Lone smiles. "Seconds can protect us too. In one second, a shiver up my spine can warn me to be on my guard, just as the chill from an ominous wind can do." She pauses. "And in one second, I can admire the swirl of a cloud before I blink and it changes form. In one second, a crack of thunder can tell the tale of the raging skies, and I can cry, for a second, knowing my pain will be smothered by nature's booming voice. One second is all I need to remember the gut-wrenching pain of my forever loss, but also to feel the joy it brought me. In one second, I can feel the weight of my burdens, and then, because I know I would be better off, let them go."

"I see." (She sees nothing.)

"With life being so fleeting, I've learned to fall in love with the slivers of time ... both the good and the bad. I need to remember where I've been. Some days, when it all seems gloomy, I remind myself that moments of love and beauty are often sandwiched between terrors."

"Yes." Millicent slides over to the end of the sofa and places her glass on a coaster that sits on the end table. Her tone has become more authoritative, and poor Lone, without meaning to, has hit the ball into Millicent's park. "Life is a series of terrors indeed; I have an entire list of them from today alone. First, when my daughter—"

"Did you not find meeting me … meeting Drake … to be pleasurable?"

"Well, of course it is. But no doubt, when I leave your fine company, another terror will find me."

"I see." Lone smiles. "They'll just chase you down the street and around the corner, won't they?"

"I didn't say it like that. I only stated that terrors have no problem darkening my path."

"Well, sometimes they do, and usually they don't. But I know this: when you look for them, or expect them, you're far more likely to stumble upon them. I believe it's called the Law of Attraction."

"I suppose you have a point," Millicent says in a pathetic attempt to change the subject. "Am I wrong in assuming Nigel has passed away?"

"No. Sadly, you're not. He died in a fiery plane crash in South America. I was there with him but not on the plane that day. His colleagues begged me not to visit the crash site, but I had to go or I would have never allowed myself to believe he was gone. There was so much blood. It was everywhere. Bright red among the deep green of the forest. He was barely recognizable. Some brave soul removed Nigel's wedding ring and gave it to me. I sobbed, took one last look, and left." Lone holds up a chain on her neck where she keeps his ring.

"How did you end up here?"

"Because I needed the comfort of a dear friend who reached out to me after hearing what happened. Having nowhere to go, I made this place my home, where I wait, having no idea what fate has in store for me. Neither do my doctors."

Millicent wants to ask more probing questions, but she senses that it would not be in her best interest. "You know, Lone. I was just thinking. With Drake no longer here every day, perhaps you'd like the two of us to spend time together. I can do all sorts of things for you. I don't expect to take his place, but I could save you from having to make new arrangements." She thinks. "How silly of me. Of course you've made other arrangements. But maybe I could visit regularly."

Skepticism sits boldly on Lone's face. (For many reasons.) "Well, the people who shop for me were going to pick up some more hours, but it might work to have things stay as they are, if you would like to be a companion of sorts." She thinks again. "Perhaps we can give it a trial run and see how it works out ... for both of us. No promises."

"That's wonderful, Lone." She thinks. "Now, if you don't mind, I'd simply love to see your hats."

THE NEXT DAY

My darling Ava Elisabeth sits on the white wicker patio sofa under the large pink-and green-striped umbrella and smiles at the bright colors of the flowers that her eyes allow her to see. Her mind drifts back to her younger years when she so dutifully tended the victory gardens back home and these very same hotel gardens ... both with such love, reverence, and devotion. While the plants and flowers have grown anew, to Ava Elisabeth, the gardens are still the paradise of her youth. The walkway in front of her has been repaved, but the palm trees are the same, with perhaps, a few additions.

Every afternoon, when my darling retreats here to commune with nature (and her past), she wonders if the trees remember her. (I am certain they do.) She loves large pots with colorful mixed succulents. She remembers the gardener who taught her how to care for them, schooling her on the dangers of too much water, or, during a heat wave, too much sun.

To either side of her, she admires the pots of redhead coleus and the Silver Falls Dichondra that hang down, just like her beautiful locks. Her once-brown hair, now silver with strands of her original color, yearns to be free … just like the plants … and to flow in the breeze. I am quite sure she is remembering her days in Montmartre, working for the florist when she grew lonely for her garden suite of long ago.

While some residents walk around in the distance, Ava Elisabeth cannot miss the woman in the bright-red dress walking toward her on the path, the lush greenery framing her on either side. A navy-blue pillbox hat, decorated with rhinestones and a netted veil wrapped around it, covers part of her forehead. The woman sits in the wicker chair to my darling's right. The hat is not a color most ladies would choose to wear with a red dress and matching shoes unless desirous of emulating some patriotic garden statue.

The bright-red lipstick matches, and the mole above her lip is prominent. Shoulder-length white hair, though appearing a bit crooked, serves as a hat stand of sorts.

Ava Elisabeth, usually the first to offer a greeting, looks at the stranger with great curiosity and says nothing.

"Hello. You're Ava Elisabeth, yes? I've heard so many delightful things about you."

"Really?"

"Of course. Why wouldn't I? Oh, where are my manners. My name is Lone Aggen. My mother was Danish … hence the name."

"Lone. Yes. When I lived in Paris, I knew a lovely woman with that name."

Ava Elisabeth reaches for a small jade Buddha statue sitting on the round glass-top wicker table in front of her and begins to fondle it.

"What do you have there?"

Displeased by the intrusive question, my beauty pauses for many seconds, then unfortunately, gives a response that is undeserved. "One of my lovers bought this for me on a trip to the Far East. (Again. How she torments me.) I lived in Paris at the time, as I did for many years of my life. Anyway, I often keep it nearby. While I can't see the details as I once did, I remember the touch … of precious items such as this one … of people … and of all that surrounds me." The corners of her mouth turn down, but not for long. "Often when we lose one sense, or a part of one, our other senses grow stronger. So, this Buddha brings me almost as much comfort as my cat, Mickey, but I don't dare bring him outside to roam free."

"I see."

"You're not saying a lot, but there's quite a purposeful quality to your voice. I'm quite sure you're not sitting in that chair by accident. Someone must have told you I'm here most afternoons. What is it that I can do for you?"

"Well, I-I heard you're very good friends with my … with the owner, Darah D. Gregnut, and as my companion has just left me for greener pastures, I thought I might like to get to know her. I know she spends a great deal of time with you … and I hope, against all reason and logic, that you won't resent me for asking for just a teeny bit of it. I know she owns this hotel and is very busy, but I thought maybe, if she comes to visit you, I could be there as well. Or maybe she'd just spend some time alone with me. If you asked her to do so."

Ava Elisabeth puts the Buddha down carefully. She stiffens as she responds. "Darah is a grown woman. I neither schedule nor dictate her time. As you say, she's very busy. A friend … certainly not a professional companion. And you also have to know this is wholly inappropriate … most especially to invite yourself to join us during our precious time together."

"I'm just so lonely. I have an incurable case of the blues, I'm afraid." (Of the reds, *I* should say.)

Goodness. I wasn't expecting this. Now, Ava Elisabeth looks as if she might cry. She turns to the imposter, who, I might add, is wearing fresh hose today. "I'm sorry. Have you always been so lonely?"

"Oh, yes." Millicent finally has the willing ear the real Lone would not give her. "I've always been horribly alone. It's probably why my mother gave me this name. She knew I'd be 'Lone Aggen.'"

My darling exhales. "Why is that? Didn't you grow up in a loving family?"

Deciding to tell her own story, and not Lone's (which she barely knows), Millicent plods on. "My mother didn't give birth to me until she was nearly thirty-six. And the only reason she had me ... was because it was the thing to do. Just like the women who emulated Jackie Kennedy by wearing pillbox hats, like the one on my head, I was a prop for my mother who wished to emulate the women in her social circle. She would have had a sibling prop, which would have perhaps left me far less miserable, but she had no genuine interest and wasn't going to try again at thirty-six. It was only by some miracle she finally conceived." The tears flow. "After all, if you don't really want the first child you have, why in the world try for a second? Her job was done. In addition to having a child ... just to 'fit in,' I suppose she also needed to prove, more than anything else, that she wasn't barren."

Ava Elisabeth picks up the glass of lemonade she had all but forgotten about and takes a sip. "I see. And do you have children?"

"I have a daughter, but she despises me."

"Why is that, dearest?"

"I'm afraid I may have treated her as my own mother treated me. I never set out to do that, of course, but there may have been a couple of small incidents, which she's blown absurdly out of proportion, not to mention having punished me terribly for being the damaged woman I am. No doubt she has told people horrible lies about me."

"Do *you* ever lie?"

The paragon of virtue takes a moment to think. "Certainly not. Having suffered at the hands of my parents ... especially my father who had no affection for me ... I have made it my purpose in life to be truthful and kind ... to my child and to strangers alike."

"Uh, huh." My darling places the glass back onto the coaster on the table. "There are secrets we keep ... and there are bold-faced lies. I don't know if one is any more acceptable than the other, but I try to stay away from blatant lies. They never resolve what pains us."

Uncomfortable with an inconvenient principle clobbering her on the head, Millicent points to a cloud. "That rather looks like a flower. A daisy, I'd say."

"I can no longer make out shapes of things so far away. But I'm glad it pleases you."

"I won't ask again to interfere in your friendship with Miss Gregnut. But it would please me to hear about it. Please, won't you allow me to indulge in fantasy and imagine she's my daughter?"

My darling is quite troubled. "It pains me to the core to know you've been so unhappy. I promise, I shall pray for you. But no, I'm not going to talk about Darah or any other friends of mine. It's wrong. Very wrong. Don't you understand how extraordinarily inappropriate it is of you to even ask?"

"I suppose it is. But I'm so alone." She looks almost accusingly at my beloved. "You've known true love, I hear." Anger coats her words. "So much of it."

"I've had great heartache that I will carry with me forever ... and maybe beyond. Perhaps, pain greater than what you've known. But that isn't something we should compare or gauge. And it most certainly isn't a burden to rest on a stranger's shoulders, or more importantly, your daughter's or your own. Blame and self-pity will make you even lonelier. As will intentional dishonesty."

Millicent shoots up like a burnt piece of toast. "Every word I've said to you today is the truth. Every single word."

Dropping her head, Ava Elisabeth is flustered. "I'm sorry dearest; I can't help you. But more than anything, I wish I could."

"Nonsense. Why am I not surprised," Millicent snaps, glowering at the most beautiful face in the world, then turns on her heels and stomps away.

TWO HOURS LATER

After having taken time to cool her rage, Millicent, still in costume, reenters the establishment, walking quickly toward the elevator, so as not to be seen by Darah, wherever she might be.

Once on the sixth floor, she steps off the elevator and looks both ways. With no one in sight, she grabs the hat and white wig and stuffs them into a black zip-up tote she is carrying. Reaching into her pocket, she grabs a tissue and wipes off the bright-red lipstick and faux mole. Quickly reapplying a shade more to her liking, she walks to Lone's apartment.

"Come in," Lone says, hearing the doorbell.

Feeling no better after her failed ruse, Millicent forces a smile and walks in to find Lone in the same rocking chair.

"And how are you today?" Millicent asks with absurd gaiety.

"Well, I'm not off my rocker." Lone laughs but is clearly uncomfortable. "I'll reckon there's many people who assume I am … and perhaps take advantage of that."

Ignoring the comment, Millicent helps herself to a seat on the blue kidney-shaped sofa. "Isn't it funny? I was looking at this sofa yesterday, and I couldn't help but wonder who ever saw a kidney and decided it was so worthy of reproduction. Kidney-shaped pools, sofas, desks, and even washing basins. I said to myself, 'Millicent, whatever is the allure of this shape? But all I could come up with was that it's different. I suppose everything has its fifteen minutes ... its day in the sun, so to speak."

Lone tenses as she looks at her.

"I've been babbling, haven't I? Well, no more of that. I'm here to begin my first day of our trial run, and what I hope will be a long friendship."

Lone, who has been rocking to calm herself, stops the motion with a firm foot to the floor. "There will be no association, Millicent, no friendship ... something you know nothing about."

"You haven't even given me a chance!" the aggrieved one protests.

"Oh, I have. Everything in my gut said no, but I wanted this to work. *That* ... I want you to take with you. I truly did want this to work."

"But you've lost your friend. You need me."

Lone shakes her head in furious disagreement. "Oh no. Drake is still my dear friend. I just won't see him every day. But I'm happy for his gain. As for best friends, I've had one for decades. When Nigel was doing work in the French Alps, he took me to Paris to stay for a while, as he was on an expedition that would have been too grueling for me." Still shaky and clearly distressed, Lone continues. "You commented on my tile painting. Well, my inspiration was nourished in this beautiful art studio I found near Montmartre in the eighteenth arrondissement. And the lovely woman who owned it, became my lifelong friend. She was the one who comforted me, years later, when my Nigel was killed." Lone raises her voice. "Please come out, dear."

Nearly choking on her own saliva, Millicent gulps as Ava Elisabeth comes out of the bedroom and takes a seat on the sofa near Lone. She says nothing, but the aggrieved one feels as if my darling's eyeballs are searing her flesh.

Despite her wretched discomfort, Lone remains as calm as she can as she looks at Millicent. "First, I would like you to return my hat. No doubt you have it on your person."

Fumbling furiously, the pilferer reaches into the zipped tote bag, takes out the hat, and places it on the table in front of my darling. The cheap white wig falls to the floor.

Lone points to the faux white tresses. "That thing is yours. You can dispose of it as you see fit or use it for another charade. That's up to you. As for that mole you painted, the next time you attempt to disguise yourself, as it has been reported to me, you might wish to get the size of the mole and the side of the face that it's on … correct."

Vesuvius erupts, and the tears flow like lava. "I'm so sorry. I wanted access to my daughter." She shoots venomous eye darts at my beauty. "This woman, this stranger, has taken my place for multitudinous years. I needed to understand what she has that I don't. It's so unfair. Darah worships her and despises me … her blood mother. When I went into labor, I refused all drugs so I could see her come into this world. It was ghastly. The worst possible pain … and that's all I've had ever since. But I wasn't going to miss the birth of my daughter for anything. I wanted to give her everything my mother never gave me."

Lone speaks softly. "I'm genuinely sorry for your pain, but I don't want to hear your sad story, Millicent. There's nothing you could say to ever make me trust you again. Please go."

Ava Elisabeth only watches.

"You horrible woman!" Millicent shouts to my beloved. "Now I know where Darah's gotten all of that fancy jewelry she wears. You've given it to her. You bribe her with everything you can. You've stolen my child! You have no idea what it's like to have a child ripped from you."

Tears fall from my beloved's eyes, but she still says nothing.

"Millicent," Lone says. "One last thing. That dress you're wearing … those shoes … that red that is the color of blood, and not life-saving blood, but the draining of it. And, like the blues and green that surround us ... it is also a color of remembrance. I look at you and I see my Nigel lying in a pool of blood, his limbs going every which way, his face nearly unrecognizable. You wear the color that traumatizes me ... and you have the gall to do so as you pretend to be me."

"I'm sorry; I didn't know."

"But your subterfuge would have been acceptable wearing the correct colors?" She tries to steady herself. "You do know that what you were doing was criminal, yes?" She doesn't wait for a response. "Leave."

Millicent scowls at Ava Elisabeth. "You brutal old woman. You haven't had the courage to say one word to me."

My darling chooses to speak. "It was brave of you to forgo medication to welcome your child into the world."

"You're mocking me!" Millicent screams. She runs to the door. "I hate you both."

Lone looks sorrowfully at her friend as the door slams shut. "What odd last words you offered to her."

My darling says nothing.

"You've always had the wherewithal to be kind to those who don't deserve it, yet you're anything but shy when a strong admonition is necessary. I'm never quite sure how you will react, but you always do so with grace, no matter your words. I always hoped one day to mirror you, Avie, but it doesn't look like that will happen in this lifetime. Certainly not today." Lone smiles. "As well as I've known you over these years, you still are, and always will be, an enigma to me ... and a truly beautiful one ... but really, you were way too kind to that awful woman."

Chapter Eight: THE NINTH FLOOR

There are some mystifying anomalies here. The most glaring is what I perceive to be a unit on the ninth floor in a structure where only eight were built. I have only just stumbled upon its existence. Disconcerting to say the least. Regrettably, my powers of omniscience do not function here, as if I am some low-grade communication device unable to attract a signal. Therefore, being outside of my omniscient range, I know nothing else beyond what my visual and auditory senses allow. This troubles me profoundly, and I resent any similarity to the essence of other mortal beings.

To tell the most complete story, I shall share what I do know. This appears to be the sole unit on this phantasmagorical ninth floor, though I have no tools to estimate its size. Unlike every other room in this building, this one appears nearly empty. Also, unlike the other spaces, this one is not furnished in any discernable style, and to my eyes, what I *can* see is somewhat out of focus.

Those who inhabit this space do not receive mail, pay rent, or have any known ways of contacting the outside world. There are neither stairs nor elevators that can access this floor. Additionally, I have no powers to ascertain the names of the three figures that I am observing, so I shall simply number them.

One, a fifty-something-year-old man wearing a plaid shirt, plays solitaire atop a plain white table.

Two, a female in her mid-twenties, has stylishly coiffed and heavily lacquered red hair. Bold makeup choices overpower her delicate features. She wears a long-sleeved apple-red dress sporting a large, incongruous ruffle at the neckline, which most assuredly wonders what it is doing there as it simultaneously strategizes a fast escape. Sitting in a stiff-back chair, Two turns her head in measured motions, lifeguard style, as if monitoring the activity in her midst. I must point out, as there is almost nothing happening, the futility of her actions is especially preposterous.

Lastly, slumped on a nondescript couch, in the manner of a stone-cold drunk or one who is ceasing to exist, Three, an older man with several days' growth on his face, is the life of this surreal jamboree. (Who loosed the sarcasm?) Now, if *I* could be seen, that title would pass with indubitable honors to me. Only I would not be Four. I am Conrad Daniel Beauregard Shintz ... and I would never be diminished to the lowly status of a numbered existence.

Wait. I do believe their mouths are moving. What could they possibly be saying?

Three, still splayed on the couch, groans before he speaks. "I'm so tired. I can't move a muscle."

Ah, but he is moving the orbicularis oris and lateral pterygoid muscles to discharge this contradictory statement.

"If you're too tired to move ... then don't," One says, slapping a five of hearts on top of a six of spades. "It's pretty simple. Lie there and get sunburned. Bake like Aunt Nellie's overdone carrot cake."

"It's a lovely day," Two says.

One halts the slapping of cards to address her. (No, she is not an envelope.) "Who asked *you*, doll? Just sit there and look pretty." He looks at the ceiling. "Besides, it's no longer a lovely day; can't you see the sky is about to open?"

"I'm so tired," Three says again.

"Well, at least you don't have to worry about sunburn anymore," One says.

"I never did," Three tells him. "We're inside, you nutjob."

"Ahoy, mateys! All aboard the SS Nutjob. This is your captain speaking." A queen of spades covers One's king of diamonds.

"I wish I had a boyfriend," Two says.

One glances in her direction. "Well, you sure don't want this drowsy deadbeat slumped on the couch. Rip Van Winkle here is about to sleep for a hundred years. Or die. Every last bit of toothpaste has come out of his tube. He's nearly a goner."

"Not so," Three says. "I'll be fine. Just need my batteries recharged."

One holds a jack of clubs in his hand, eyeing it sternly. "You think you know all the trades, do you? Doesn't matter to you that you're a master of none. Hit the road. You're not the exclusive club you think you are. Therefore, I won't be joining you. Even if you come apart."

Three groans. His eyelids flutter as he fights to stay awake. "Cray cray …"

"I feel like having a party," Two says. "Who wants to have a good time with me?"

"You're not my type," One says. "I don't like forward dolls who offer themselves like party favors, or worse yet … just tease." He looks around. "Getting kind of dark here. There's a strong wind picking up." He moves his head in a circular motion as he blows air while his right hand wildly destroys the card game. "My, my. Thar she blew! Life on the open plains isn't for the faint of heart. Might need a trip to the saloon seeing how that gale wreaked all of this damage. Liquid consolation to ease my woes. Ah, that wind, thar she blows. Where she goes next, nobody knows."

"Cray …" Three is too tired to finish his insult.

"I feel like dancing," Two says.

One bursts out laughing and nods in Three's direction. "He'd be a drag on the dance floor. And even if he wasn't fading before our eyes, he only knows one dance: the jerk."

"Cray …"

"I like it when people say nice things to me." Two's eyelashes bat three times.

One makes a face as he deals a new game of solitaire. "I like it when the neighbors plow my driveway after it snows and the milkman leaves an extra quart. And the *puta* across the street forgets to pull her shades down. But we don't always get what we want, doll."

"Cr ..."

A booming voice, belonging to someone unseen, says, "Package delivery." A massive vertical box appears on the floor, not far from Two.

One stands, raises his left arm and crooks it at the elbow as his bent wrist directs his hand to his head. His left arm, lowered, also of crooked elbow, has a bend leading his other hand away from his body. I believe he is with song. "King Tut. He's here for slut. King Tut. He's here in his crypt. Her dress is unzipped. She's gonna get whipped. King Tut, he's here for the slut ..."

"C ..." Three croaks out.

Two stands. Before attending to the box, she walks over to One, pulls an ace out of her sleeve and hands it to him.

Smiling, he slides it into the deck. What a transformative moment. "Thanks!" he says. "Just like you to help me out. It's hell not playing with a full deck. Any way I can return the favor? How about if I help you open your delivery there?"

"Thank you for being nice to me," Two says, leading the way back.

One reaches into his pocket for a Swiss army knife and walks over to the box. "Just a small slit where it's sealed here and you'll be good to go." He gently slices through the taped crevice, allowing easy access to what is inside. Smiling, he walks over to the couch. "Hey, my friend, looks like you need some help."

Three, now barely showing any form of function, can only open his eyes in slow motion to respond. One opens two buttons on Three's shirt. Then, reaching between the last seat cushion and the arm of the couch, he pulls out a long cord with a charger at the end, and plugs it into the port in Three's chest.

Like magic, Three sits up and smiles. "Thank you. I think I came pretty close to certain death there for a moment."

"You called it," One says. "Your batteries just needed recharging. I think you'll live. Give it a couple of hours. A full charge and you'll be A-okay."

Three offers a thumbs-up as One heads back to his table.

Two, batting her eyelids three times, opens the box to discover a man, still and strangely similar to herself, staring with a fixed expression.

"Hey," One says, rushing to Two's side. "Let me get rid of this cardboard so you can enjoy your new friend." Grabbing the large pieces, he walks away and stashes them into a corner. As One returns to his table, they disappear.

Two stands and bats her eyelids at the male figure before her. Extending her right arm, she pulls a ring on a string that is attached to his neck.

"Hello," he says. "I am happy to be here."

With his right arm, he pulls an identical ring on her neck.

"Hello, my name is Dolly. It's nice to meet you. What is your name?"

"It says 'Pete' on the label," One yells to her. "Call him Pete. Hope he can think outside the box."

"Is your name Pete?"

"RePete," he says. "I am happy to be here."

"I am happy to be here. Hello, my name is Dolly. It's nice to meet you. What's your name?"

"RePete." He smiles. "I like you. I have been recycled from Pete."

Two's head turns sharply. "I feel like a party. Who wants to have a good time with me?"

"I am happy to be here." He winks.

"It's a lovely day. I wish I had a boyfriend."

"I like you. I have been recycled from Pete. I am RePete."

"It's a lovely day. I wish I had a boyfriend."

"Think you got one now, Dolly. I reckon you two were made for each other ... literally. Same factory and all." One slaps an eight of spades onto a nine of diamonds.

"I wish I had a girlfriend."

"I feel like dancing."

"I like you. Let's dance."

"It's a beautiful day."

And on they go, with their banal, repetitious, and limited phrases, pre-programmed to exist without rancor or regret, happy to hear the unvaried utterances and never losing their smiles. One, happy to be sane again, continues with his game. Three sits charging on the couch, reading a magazine that appears to have blank pages.

The scene is sad, yet happy. This is someone's blueprint for how we should all exist ... by using the simple means we may have to help one another ... to save one another ... simply by what we possess, by what we are able to do ... that others cannot. These souls, whether made of flesh, plastic, or something in-between, will exist in this self-perpetuating bubble, unaware that their world is any stranger than that of others. As I cogitate on the matter, I wonder: might these extant life forces on the ninth floor, perhaps, be the sanest of all ... or perhaps quite the opposite? I have yet to find out and likely never will. I only want my omniscience back and contend that this clear-minded thinking is a vexing disruption to my sense of reality. If this scene is indeed a metaphor for how humanity might thrive, I wish to exempt myself immediately.

Wait. Something is different with Two. Ah, the ruffle on the neckline of her red dress is gone. A successful escape. If only I could be so lucky.

Chapter Nine: OF PINK AND PRINCES

Carolyn, one of the most peculiar residents here, who has resided on the fourth floor for decades, is of questionable sanity … and age. Despite the passage of time, her appearance is still that of a young woman in her twenties. My fading gift of omniscience does not allow me further insight, so I shall have to sleuth it out. Being a dedicated soldier in the cataloging of souls past and present … that is all right with me. And thus, I plod on.

It requires no scholar to see that Carolyn likes pink and members of its immediate and extended family. While the furniture in her unit is in keeping with the ubiquitous style of this establishment, she clearly has acquired as much pink as the universe sees fit to grant her. She sits upon a rose-colored loveseat with tapered wood legs and carved arms. The trim on this precious seatery is a garish rose-gold glittery kind of monstrosity that warns of a personality that is enmeshed in romantic delusions of the highest form. Six pillows, four of them heart shaped, only punctuate this spot-on assessment. One of the hearts has a plush arrow through it. Uncultivated stuffery!

Nearby, there is a shockingly bright-pink credenza against the wall. Only the brass fixtures and legs are spared from the brash color. On top of this where-are-my-sunglasses horror sit various framed photos of the same man. I do not think I need to reveal what color frames his photos are in.

Lastly, because I cannot stomach much more, I will simply reveal that a plethora of art deco mid-century pottery flamingos dot the circumference of the room. I am surprised the room is not filled with ceramic mounds underneath every one of these skinny-legged birds.

Sitting on the loveseat, with a fluffy fake (yes, pink) cat by her side, Carolyn, also with pink hair, watches TV on what appears to be a set from 1960 … which, oddly, still works. It is my impression that current technology would render this impossible (without some technological adjustments), but nonetheless, I am wholly uninterested in the finer details. I have only visited this unit once before yet can unequivocally state that the young lady was enjoying the very same show she watches now. The hunky blond man on the screen, shock of all shocks, is the same one whose image sits framed on the credenza. Closer inspection tells me that nearly every photo, except for a signed headshot, was cut out of a magazine. Oh, how pathetic.

I have just learned something new. Carolyn is not alone.

Trish, a kind-looking woman in her fifties, emerges from the dining area around the corner as the show ends. I have no doubt she was instructed to wear a particular color of scrubs. In her hands, she carries a small tray upon which sits a croissant sandwich with four pickle slices and a glass of dare I guess — strawberry milk. (It is rendered this way by a powdered substance that pours from a vintage container. Thankfully, the ghastly mix originates from a new container that is kept out of sight.)

She turns off the TV, aware that Carolyn's show has ended. "Did Prince Henry speak to you today?" she says as she places the light meal down on the glass-topped side table that has the misfortune to match the credenza.

"Maybe," Carolyn says coyly, looking at the tray of food. "But why should I tell you? So you can tell my family how crazy I am? Do they pay you extra to snitch? Well, guess what? I don't care."

"Your family only wants the best for you." Trish sits on a pink brocade wingback chair to Carolyn's side. "They love you so much. And no, I don't get paid 'extra' for anything. I'm only here to look after you."

"Balderdash." She pauses to fume. "The part about how they love me."

"Never did hear that word until I met you. Guessing I never will again."

Unable to keep silent, Carolyn speaks. "I learned that word from Henry's mother, the queen. Yes, he spoke to me today. You know he speaks to me during the commercial breaks, and sometimes, when Lady Gwendolyn looks away, he turns his head and winks at me." She looks so pleased with herself. "Yesterday, he mouthed my name and then licked his lips. It was so seductive. He wants me, and I want him."

"Really?"

"Yes, really. And despite what you all think, Prince Henry *is* coming for me one day. You'll see." Carolyn picks up the cat, and with a small brush from the pocket of her dress, she begins to groom it. Although the feline is faux, I cannot help but feel sorry for it. "As for my family, not another word about them loving me. Fathers who love their children don't leave when their little girls are four, and mothers who love their daughters don't lie and say that their daddies will come back. When they never do. And then take pills and die so they can't come back either."

"Honey," Trish says, pulling at a loose thread at the cuff of the long tee under her top, "from what your aunt and uncle told me, your mama really tried to control her addiction." She rips the loose thread off and stuffs it in her shirt pocket. "And I don't think she lied to you. I think she really believed your father would return some day."

Making a spiteful face, Carolyn sneers at her caregiver. "Well, he didn't, did he?"

Trish leans forward. "Maybe he couldn't. I know you've always believed he didn't want to come back, but maybe he couldn't."

"You think he died? Like she did."

"I honestly don't know. Maybe he hit his head and had amnesia?"

"That's stupid!" Carolyn brushes the cat a bit too harshly and I wince, believing it is in pain.

"If I recall," Trish says with a smile, "didn't Prince Henry have amnesia for an entire season … I mean … year?"

Pursing her mouth oddly, a string of incoherent blathering is forced out until the discernable, "but it's a TV show" is heard.

Trish is heartened. "So, you do know it's not real?"

Gritting her teeth, Carolyn bristles with rage. I hear some very bad words spinning in her head.

"The TV show is scripted," Carolyn says. "But what Henry says to me during some of the commercial breaks is very real."

"I've watched this show with you a hundred times. And I've never seen anything but commercials for coffee, toothpaste, breakfast cereal and the like."

"Because he won't talk to me if anyone is here. He can see me … this room … everything."

"Okay …." Trish, now emboldened, knows she must be prudent with the words she will say next. "Carolyn, why is it that I've never seen this show or these vintage commercials on any TV set anywhere but here?" She hesitates before continuing." Um, my brother-in-law is a sound studio engineer as well as an electrician. So … I asked him for his opinion …."

Putting the small tray on her lap, Carolyn picks up the croissant and takes a huge bite. Purposely being as vulgar as she can, she turns to Trish, chewing with her mouth open.

Surprised, Trish leans back. "Goodness, child, if Prince Henry can really see you, is this the image you want burning his eyeballs?"

"He can't see me when the TV is off, numbskull." Quickly, she chews her food before washing it down with the obscene pink milk. "And what did your brother-in-law say?"

"Well, he thinks that you've had a skilled technician remove the guts of the actual TV and replace it with something that simply replays a television channel from many decades ago ... that you somehow acquired ... um ... by paying out a lot of money."

Noticing some croissant crumbs on her dress, Carolyn angrily brushes them away, not caring that they're now on the seat cushion. "Well, tell your brother-in-law that I think a skilled surgeon removed all of the brains from his head and replaced them with malfunctioning robot parts. So there." She picks up her sandwich and eats as if she hasn't had food in days, finishing it in no time at all.

Trish laughs. "There are days my sister might agree with you."

Finding no humor in the conversation, Carolyn finishes the glass of milk, which leaves a pink mustache on her mouth that she immediately wipes away with the back of her hand before licking it clean.

"Those are not manners befitting a royal household. I did bring you a napkin."

Carolyn smiles devilishly, takes the napkin, and rips it up. "I'm not a royal ... not yet. Don't tell me Henry will never come for me and then at the same time tell me how I should act proper for him. That's called contradiction. It's for the stupid and gullible. Not me."

"Oh, my." Trish stands and looks at the empty tray of food. "I don't think that was enough for you. What else can I get you? Got a box of chocolate-chip cookies in the cupboard. The kind you like ... you know ... that taste homemade."

Carolyn gets up from the sofa and stretches before walking over to look at herself in the mirror. "I suppose so. I just have to make sure I have my girlish figure. For when Prince Henry comes to take me away from this place ... and from you."

Picking up the tray, Trish takes it away while Carolyn amuses herself by trying different poses in the large oval mirror with a frame that thankfully matches the sofa and not the credenza. Grabbing strands of her pink hair with light-brown roots, Carolyn quickly rearranges it in different styles while simultaneously experimenting with an assortment of facial expressions ranging from coquettish to pure-as-the-driven-snow innocence ... and every ghastly visage in-between. It is quite harrowing to witness ... and at the same time, quite curious to even imagine why she equates some hairstyles with some of her more off-putting expressions. Most puzzling is why she thinks her absurd femme-fatale persona would ever put her hair up in a bun. I think of my Ava Elisabeth, who even now, in her sunset years, still has her flowing hair, perfect for the charming temptress she is.

Seven minutes later, Trish dares to reenter the living room with two cookies on a small plate. No, it did not take her long to arrange, but having seen Carolyn expose her breasts in the mirror and laugh seductively as if a man were bearing witness, she deemed it unwise to intervene. What neither of them know is that a man, (me) *did* have the misfortune to catch an eyeful of such unseemly behavior. Still striking poses at the mirror, Carolyn is not ready to sit again.

"Cookies," Trish says, finding no other words for the occasion.

"More milk!"

"Please." Trish mumbles additional words as she walks back into the kitchen to pour more powder into some milk to turn it pink. Upon completing her task, she brings it out to the living room and sets it on the side table. Angered by the lack of a 'please' or 'thank you,' she sits in the chair and says nothing.

"Oh, get over yourself, silly," Carolyn says as she takes her seat again. She reaches for a cookie and consumes it with savagery. Displaying a mouthful of masticated food, she looks at Trish. "Thank you."

"Okay, I'm just going to say it: what the hell is wrong with you today? You're not an easy person on any day of the week, but this afternoon, you're especially vulgar and rude. Are you trying to make me quit? Don't tempt me, Carolyn. I can easily find work elsewhere, and the next person your family hires won't be as nice. And you'll be miserable. Wanna keep testing me?"

Carolyn throws the remaining cookie across the room. It hits a flamingo's backside and crumbles. "You know how vulnerable I am." She looks over at the mess she made. "Whoopsie! Someone had an accident. You'd better go clean it up." Shifting gears, she rides on. "You know I have a fear of abandonment, and you just love exploiting it."

With great reluctance, Trish stands and walks over to the mess. Using a spare napkin in her pocket, she sweeps the pieces into it, then walks into the kitchen for proper disposal. A moment later, she returns to the living room. Giving Carolyn a sidelong look, she sits. "That's the last time I'm tolerating a tantrum or cleaning up any intentional messes. Got it?"

Batting her eyelashes, as if some willing paramour is at her beck and call, she says, "I'd like another cookie, please."

"You know where they are."

"I said: *I'd like another cookie ...* please.'"

"And I said, *"You know where they are.""*

Oh, goodness. There is quite the standoff. Trish is serious about her ultimatum, and Carolyn knows it. Who will budge first? Ah, Trish, of course: the adult in the room.

"I'm not exploiting your fear of abandonment, sweetie. I'm trying to help you. And I think you know that. But if you want a punching bag, ask your aunt and uncle to have your trustee buy one for you. I don't get paid enough for this nonsense, and quite frankly, if they doubled my salary, it would still be insufficient. You treat me with respect, or I'm gone."

Carolyn's mouth opens to spew some ugly words, but she reconsiders and says nothing. Instead, she chooses a pout to display her precious feelings.

"Oh, my. What am I going to do with you?" Trish takes a long pause to ponder the situation. "Look, I don't want to battle it out. I've got my own stuff to deal with ... but I leave it at home when I come to work. However ... that doesn't mean I'm not a human being with feelings ... and limits. Do you understand?"

"Of course. This is the part where I'm supposed to get all weepy and tell you I'm sorry." Carolyn snarls. "Well, guess what. I'm not going to do it. Nope." She crosses her arms defiantly and stares at Trish. I must say: she is very slappable at the moment, and Trish has impressive restraint.

"What's your objective here, Carolyn? To have me quit on the spot? To make me as miserable as you are? What exactly are you hoping to achieve?"

"I'll tell you when I figure it out." (At least she's told a bit of truth here.)

"I'll play along for now, but remember, I get to go home when your nighttime caregiver, Lisa, gets here ... if you haven't scared her off. But know this: I refuse to play childish games with a grown woman *every* day. I didn't tolerate this nonsense from my own daughters, and I won't from you."

"Just go then ... since you hate me so much." Carolyn picks up the faux feline and hugs it to her chest. "Kitty will never leave me."

"No," Trish says with a gentle voice. "Kitty isn't real, so Kitty can never die or go away." She thinks. "But you know, I think even a toy cat has limits."

"That was so mean."

"Not meant to be ... I'm not a mean person. I'm trying ... unsuccessfully ... to help you. Really, Carolyn, I'd love to see you meet real people and establish genuine relationships. Doesn't that sound kind of nice?" She attempts a smile. "Your aunt and uncle want the same thing for you; that's why I'm here. Watching reruns of an old soap opera, expecting some actor to be a prince in real life and come take you away ... is not going to happen. You do understand that

Henry is really an actor, right? He goes by the name Brayton California, which I'm sure is not his given name, God forbid, but for someone who isn't into reality, it's rather fitting you're so fixated on him ... like superglue."

"His name is Prince Henry Stanley Albert Rothschild. That's how my photo is signed." Carolyn nods toward the retina-popping credenza.

"I could sign 'Mickey Mouse' on my photo." Trish sighs in relatable exasperation. "It wouldn't give me a high voice, big round ears, and a tail. I'd still be me."

"Hush, pleb. You tire me."

Commendably, Trish sits and says nothing.

Meanwhile, Carolyn admires the gaudy rings on her left hand. "Trish, when will my gown for the ball be ready? I simply must try it on beforehand. If even a stitch is wrong, it will have to be repaired. I hope you've alerted the dressmakers."

"Lord have mercy," Trish says under her breath. "There is no gown and no ball. And there sure as hell aren't any dressmakers." She stops to check her sanity. "I'm quite sure you know that."

"Was it my ruby gown or the one with the purple sapphire bodice that I chose to wear? Or perhaps that jeweled magenta beauty the queen sent over?"

"You don't remember?"

"No!" Carolyn is angry again. "With all of the balls, and all of the dresses, remembering what I've picked for each one is not as easy as it sounds. Now, which gown did I choose for the upcoming dance?"

"Probably your pink nightgown ... with the bunny rabbits. That's the only one I know anything about, honey."

Popping off the loveseat, leaving poor Kitty behind, Carolyn walks over to her trusted mirror and speaks to it. "Why does this diabolical woman torture me so? I only have one world that makes me happy, and every day of my life, she tries to rip it from my soul and from my consciousness. It's the only place where I have any peace. But she doesn't care. Please … " She breaks into copious tears. "Let me have my happiness. Stop the dream killer. Stop her."

Trish looks upward. "Lord, help me." Getting out of her chair, she walks to Carolyn and throwing every bit of wisdom away, hugs her with intensity. "It's all right, honey. It's all right. Come on, Carolyn. Sit with me."

"No, you're a dream killer." Even with Trish's arms around her, she is defiant and thrashes about while Trish holds her tight. "We won't let you break us up. I'll be his princess. You'll see. I'll never stop waiting for him."

"It's all right, sweetie." Trish gives her a loving squeeze. "Everything's gonna be all right. I'm not here to take anything from you; I only want to give to you. And that's the truth. Let's go have a sit down together. Sound good?"

Carolyn collapses like a folding chair as Trish holds her tight, nearly dragging her to the seating.

"Hurry, Prince Henry." Carolyn weeps. "I'm not the robust lass you first took a shine to. I'm losing my sun-kissed luster."

Looking upward for guidance, Trish says nothing as she manages to place Carolyn on the loveseat and sit by her side. Soon, Carolyn turns on the waterworks.

Twenty minutes have passed, and surely, the princess-to-be must be dehydrated, having relieved herself of every drop of water through her eyes and … ahem … two trips to the pink powder room. Trish's pink scrub top is soaked and stained with Carolyn's unnecessary and brutally heavy makeup. (The bright pink lipstick stains are exceptionally distressing.)

As they sit together, Trish strokes Carolyn's hair with the compassion of a saint. "What do you need, sweetheart? Why do you separate yourself from reality? Why can't you allow a real man to love you? Real friends to laugh with you. A real cat to cuddle with?"

"I don't want to love anyone." Carolyn has apparently located the well of emergency tears in her person and lives to sob again. "And I don't want anyone to love me ... except Prince Henry."

"Because he's not real?" Trish asks. "Right? Which means there's no danger of being hurt or abandoned by him. Isn't that the truth?"

"My parents went away before I could ever know them. And my aunt and uncle never wanted me to live in their house, especially knowing I had a big trust fund and didn't need to. My cousins made fun of me. And so did their friends. That's why I never lived with any of them and why I've been forced to have people like you look out for me. In this stupid place."

"I know all that, sweetheart. But I'm happy to hear about it again. It's important to vent, to get the poison out of your system."

Carolyn rambles on. "Well, if you already know it, because they tell everyone, then you should know better than to say how much they love me. Because hiring people to take care of me isn't love. If they ever let me live in their house ... well maybe."

"I understand. All I can say is that they told me they love you. And they appeared sincere. They interviewed me for hours and checked all of my references before they let me anywhere near you."

"That doesn't mean anything. They did that because they don't want to get sued. They think I'm highly disturbed. Like I might kill someone. They wanted to make sure you're strong enough to handle me and know what you're getting into. Well guess what? I've never killed anyone. Only one lady broke her arm because she went to grab me. That was years ago. I pushed her out of the way, and she fell on the kitchen floor. Her arm kind of hit the tile in a bad way. And it broke."

"Was it a bad injury?"

"Uh ...yeah. I had to get two new tiles put in. Those two with pink alligators on them. They're called 'reptiles.' Ha ha. I thought that was so funny that I didn't even care if they matched the rest of the floor."

"I wondered about that … but I didn't dare ask." Trish shrugs her way out of the stupor she's nearly fallen into. "I was talking about her arm."

"Who cares about her stupid arm? I don't remember. Give me a break."

Oh dear, Trish has no idea how to respond. But luckily, she doesn't need to. Carolyn continues lamenting her life.

"There have been so many caregivers that I've lost count. And not one of them ever stayed in touch when she left. Every one of them pretended to like me. But they were just pathetic money-grubbers. You're nicer. It's almost as if you like me a little or something. You try harder than they did. That's why I want you to hate me. That's why I show you chewed-up food in my mouth. I want you to think I'm disgusting and hate me. Then I can hate you back and never get hurt again."

"I see." Trish smiles uneasily. "I can't say I didn't notice the 'special effort' you put into all of this."

Carolyn giggles. "One lady quit because she despises pink, and she said looking at me and my apartment every day made her sick. And that pink is for little girls and that I needed to grow up." She gets angry as she recalls. "Well, what did she want me to do? Wear black? It's my home. And I don't only wear pink. I wear lots of colors. Golly, I must have one gown in almost every color of the rainbow because I never know how the prince will want me to look. We all have our moods, don't we?"

Defeated, Trish just squeezes Carolyn's hand. "We do, sweetheart." She sneaks a look at the flamingo wall clock and sighs. Nearly two more hours until the end of her shift. Just as she's about to say something to assuage Her Royal Pinkness, the doorbell rings, startling both women.

"Are you expecting anyone?" Trish asks. "You never have company. Ever." She pauses. "Oh, I know. I think it might be Lisa's replacement. She did say she wasn't feeling well when she left this morning. Perhaps the new lady got the time wrong."

Carolyn looks at her quite helplessly. "Maybe my dad has finally come back."

"I'll get the door. You stay here." As Carolyn fiddles with her hair and practices her facial expressions, Trish grabs her small shoulder-strap bag, hoping that the replacement will allow her to escape this lunacy early. She hurries to the door.

For whatever reason, Trish feels a sense of dread and looks out the peephole. She has no idea who the person is, but it is clearly not a fill-in caregiver. With great foreboding, she slowly opens the door. To her right, she sees a haggard man in his mid-to-late seventies. Before she can give him a proper once-over, she chooses to identify him. "You must be Carolyn's father!" She looks upward. "Thank you for answering my prayer. Thank you, Lord. Thank you."

The older man just looks at her. He appears too devitalized to speak.

"You must come in and rest," Trish tells him. "Carolyn has been waiting her whole life to meet you. I know she was only four when you left, and sadly, has no memory of you. Only of your absence. I think you are the cure for what ails her. I truly do." She pauses. "I just hope seeing you won't be too much of a shock for her. Maybe I should talk to her first. Soften the shock, so to speak." She lifts the strap of her purse as it begins to slip down her arm.

"Who is it?" Carolyn calls from the loveseat, hugging the faux feline for comfort.

"Just a moment, honey," Trish tells her. "Please. Be patient for just a few minutes longer. It's all good."

Trish takes a step into the hallway and speaks to the stranger with confidence. "Excuse me, sir. I feel so rude, but Carolyn has never told me your name. You'll forgive me for not knowing it."

"Prince Henry Stanley Albert Rothschild." He barely gets the names out of his mouth.

Taken aback, her eyes move in for closer inspection. Trish sees he's wearing a long jacket … faded purple to the trained eye. A frayed piece of braided gold rope hangs from the right epaulet on his jacket. A pale-gold Mandarin collar of sorts and matching pieces of the same material adorn (and I say that generously) the cuffs. He wears torn black pants and muddy boots.

"Oh, I get it. Someone sent you here. This is some kind of prank." Trish exhales. "I can understand the motivation of whoever sent you, but Carolyn, well, she's not the kind of person to play this kind of joke on. She's um … a very sensitive sort, and I don't know a lot about her past caregivers, but there have been many of them. For how many years, her family wouldn't divulge, though when they hired me, I did ask. I can only tell you she's been through a lot of hurt, and we just try to keep her steady. I hope you can understand. And so, while I do appreciate the humor here … I think … this joke is very inappropriate … dangerous, actually, for someone like Carolyn. Can you understand that?"

"Who is it?" Carolyn calls again.

The man leans against the wall for support. "Ma'am. This is no joke. I am Prince Henry Stanley Albert Rothschild … and I've been trying to find my princess for over fifty years. I've climbed mountains, forded rivers, dug trenches, foraged for food, battled the enemy, lost my horse, dueled with suitors, forgone other lasses, and fought tirelessly with family and friends who did not see the wisdom of my quest. But finally, I'm here. The wait and the journey have been long and arduous. But when I see Lady Carolyn, it will be worth all of my strife and sacrifice. I know she has never stopped waiting for me. I love her, and she loves me." His eyelids flutter as he struggles to stay awake.

At that moment, Lee and Ellie are getting off the elevator and walking toward Carolyn's unit on the way to their apartment.

"I-uh … I don't know what to say to you, Prince whoever you really are. But I don't want this joke to go any further. Carolyn will fall apart if she sees you and hears those words. She is seriously unwell. Don't you understand? I don't know how to get through to you, but let me put it this way: I'm the only one who stands between her and life in a mental health facility. I don't know how much clearer I can be."

He pays no heed to her words. "Ma'am. I am very tired. It took me over fifty years to get here. I was a young man when I set out on this odyssey. I don't know how much clearer *I* can be."

"I want to know who's there!" Carolyn demands, her voice quite loud.

Trish, stymied by the implausible circumstances, is just about to mutter something, when the old man's eyes close, and he slides down the wall.

Lee, witnessing every moment of it, stands still, his eyes glazed over in horror. Putting out his right arm to stop Ellie from proceeding, he can only stare.

"Oh, no," Trish says. "Why me? What in the world do I tell Carolyn?"

"I'll see for myself since you're being a spoilsport."

Hearing Carolyn's voice right behind her, Trish freezes. Stepping over the sleeping form of the questionable prince, she is now on the other side of him, standing against the wall, when Carolyn steps out of her unit into the hallway.

Trish is simultaneously awestruck and terrorized. Carolyn has aged some fifty years. Her gray hair, which nearly touches the floor, has lost its pink coloring, and her face, now rife with crevices aplenty, no longer remembers the rosy cheeks of its youth. Her lips, incongruously alive with bright-pink lipstick, quiver at the sight of the slumbering man on the floor. She wears a tattered pink dressing gown which refuses to give any hint of what it was in a former life. Her hands, with protruding veins, too many liver spots to count, and heavy jeweled rings … reach out for her sleeping prince. Her once-innocent girlish voice now creaks like an old floorboard. "My darling, I always knew you'd come for me. I never lost faith. But they never believed me. Not a soul. Scoundrels and reprobates. Blasphemous naysayers. The whole bloody lot of them."

Trish, taking one last look at him, then at Carolyn, sees a swarm of butterflies circle her head, and then, promptly loses consciousness as she slides down the wall with a thud.

Aghast, Lee grabs his wife by the shoulders. "Oh my God, Ellie. It's contagious. It's the apocalypse. Run!"

She looks at him and rolls her eyes. "Really, Lee? This? Again?"

With no time to spew logic, or the lack of it, Lee grabs her hand and pulls her down the hall.

As if fairy dust has awakened the dozing duo, Trish and the prince open their eyes at the same time. Gasping for breath, Trish pulls herself up, looks again to ensure she isn't hallucinating, then flees for dear life.

"Henry, is that really you?" Carolyn says. "I'm so happy to see you, my darling prince."

"Huh?" the old man replies. "Henry? Oh, yeah. That was my character's name, I think. Sorry, honey. I'm not Henry. I'm Brayton California. Actually, I'm not. My real name is Bob Collins." A weary sigh gives vent to his fatigue. "My agent told me this would be a long gig, but holy shit, this is ridiculous."

Chapter Ten: THIRTY-THREE

Only a few long-time dwellers still inhabit these walls. Oliver Stepworth is one of them. In the early 80s, when this establishment was still a hotel, the unassuming man with the short reddish-brown hair moved into a small room on the second floor, not much bigger than the nearby rooms reserved for staff. Nobody would have noticed him if not for the scowl on his face and the seven suitcases he had in tow. Only movie stars brought that much luggage … and they stayed in luxury suites.

"I barely have room to change my mind in this place," he'd grumble to himself, but living in the hotel was a must for him, so he swapped out the convenience of a larger place he could have afforded elsewhere.

Five years prior to Oliver's residence, he had existed in total contempt of his employment situation — that of a low-level worker in the wardrobe department at a major studio. He longed for an opportunity that offered a creative outlet and one that gave him some control. He loathed the people he worked with: cutter-fitters, designers, wardrobe assistants, artisans, and most of all, his co-workers. He hated being at their level, especially the ones with no aspirations to be greater … and those who acted as if they were.

Working with the lot of them taxed his patience to the core, but the physical work was far more grueling. Sorting shoes, hats, and accessories, taking costumes to be cleaned, running errands, and crippling himself after walking miles through rows of wardrobe every day, did him in. Obsessive-compulsive by nature, memorizing inventory down to shoe and hat sizes for each style, he did a magnificent job, as his nature allowed nothing else. But his wrath grew. Having to kowtow to studio "royalty" with feigned reverence incensed him the most. Yet, it inspired him. He hated being perceived as a nobody and letting others control him. It wasn't long before he vowed to change his situation.

Oliver had never been happy that the studios had no interest in his photographic skills, nor that the actors he admired (and coveted) had little to no interest in him as well. It wasn't long after moving into his second-floor room that he quit his job and became self-employed. Marrying his photography skills and wardrobe expertise, he soon became an undercover paparazzo.

In the beginning, keeping a safe distance from the others in his new trade, he managed to fool people. But as time wore on, it took greater skill. After all, this is not a field where people are not known to one another, and after a while, his disguises became common knowledge. That said, however, Oliver traveled to many locations where he was *not* known, and often, when an unsuspecting celebrity came to the hotel, he was able to transform himself so as not to be recognized. Many he fooled were those he had known from his time at the studio. And yes, there were several for whom he still harbored resentment and distrust, and thereby reveled in the joy of catching them in an ill-timed moment for the world to see.

No one, not even a maintenance worker, was allowed in his room unless he was present and granted permission. Housekeeping was only permitted to pick up and deliver sheets and towels at the door. And to leave a fresh bar of soap every three days. Everything had to be just so. To make sure nobody tried to enter his inner sanctum, Oliver (compulsive and paranoid), would put little slips of paper between the door and the jamb, then memorize their position. When he'd come home to find the paper in the same place, he would feel a sense of peace. One day, after a janitor noticed his strange activity, he shared what he'd seen with the housekeeping staff. Randomly, maybe once a month, someone would move the piece of paper, ever so slightly, just to rattle him, but never enough that Oliver would know for sure it had shifted. Perhaps, had he not carried his resentment from the studio to the hotel staff, or trifled with the janitor after an exchange of unpleasant words, they would have never devised this small prank to play on him.

As things were, a shred of paper, moved even two-sixteenths of an inch would cause Oliver to look askance at it. But it was never enough for him to feel certain that someone had moved it or that it didn't happen by chance. Every time the positioning was off, he would stand at the door and stare at the little piece of paper peeking through. As the staff made sure to never do this more than once a month, Oliver, to preserve his sanity, continued to believe his calculations must have been off but was compulsive enough to record every occurrence in his diary.

As for the staff, when they were lucky enough to happen upon him staring at the door, visibly disconcerted by the slight change in the paper's position, they'd wallow in their glee and mark the occasion on the wall calendar in their break room. After two-and-a-half years had passed, the fun wore off, and the prank died a natural death.

By the time my darling Ava Elisabeth returned from Paris, twenty years later, a stretch of time before Darah bought and transformed the hotel into an apartment house, Oliver's career was waning. He'd made a tidy sum and saved assiduously. He was tired of living in the small room and had decided to move, but when Darah revealed her plan to combine some units, thus creating bigger but fewer spaces, he happily signed a lease for a spacious one-bedroom apartment. Doing so allowed him to retain his dwelling and simultaneously move to a bigger one. A rare feat, indeed. I must add, he drove the construction crew mad, carefully watching them work, but I believe his libido was harder at work than his OCD in those days. I shall not linger in lasciviousness.

Today, Oliver does the odd photography job and is quite content … especially because he no longer has to sneak around in a disguise to do so. Over the years, he has mellowed and become more personable. Still guarded and compulsive, a selective few have managed to gain his trust. Two years ago, he struck up a friendship with Gina, the young woman who lives next door. As for Alejandro, his other neighbor, only pleasantries are exchanged.

One of his favorite people is Timmy, the young man for whom Gina babysits. Together, they sometimes visit, and Oliver entertains them with stories from years gone by.

At the moment, Gina, having glammed herself up for a date, has left Timmy with Oliver for a short time, with the agreement that his mother will pick him up when she finishes work. Now that I have narrated the past, I shall stand here in the present and observe.

Timmy sits next to Oliver on the tufted teal barrel-back sofa and takes a bite out of a shiny red apple. "My mom's chef friend taught me how to make birds out of these. But she won't let me use a knife unless she's watching." He takes another bite. "Too late for this apple. I'm already eating it." He looks around the room and makes a face. "Like I tell my mom. All of these places have the weirdest furniture ever."

"Hollywood Regency. It's a style."

"That's what she called it. She said old things have history. I asked her what that means, and she said like they have stories to tell. But I think old people tell more stories than furniture does. I never heard a chair talk." He laughs.

"It's probably best furniture can't talk, or we'd all be in trouble."

"Mom said older things are more interesting because they have a past. Meaning like stuff has happened to them before."

"That's true. But there are exceptions. You don't have much of a past, Timmy. You're just a kid. But you're still interesting."

Timmy giggles. "How about the man across the hall who pretends to be Santa Claus. He's interesting." He sizes Oliver up. "You're really old … so do you have a past? Are you interesting?"

He laughs. "You tell *me*. Gina always says you ask a lot of questions."

"And you don't answer them."

"How was school today?"

"Okay, I guess. But this kindergarten kid hurt himself on the jungle gym and went around crying that he had a 'hurty knee.' He sounded like such a baby." Timmy takes another bite of his apple. "You have like the cleanest apartment of anyone almost."

"I'm a bit OCD."

"What?"

"Nothing to concern yourself with, Timmy."

"Is that like being a weirdo?"

"Did someone tell you I was a weirdo?"

Timmy realizes he's said too much. "Um … no."

"The old janitor who used to work here? Ace?"

"No … uh … I don't know him. Were you mean to him?" Timmy asks as he fills his mouth with apple.

Oliver gives him a particular stare. "That's not the kind of question you ask someone for no reason." He sits and watches Timmy finish his apple. "You want to throw that core in the garbage?"

"Okay." Timmy gets up.

"Don't get any seeds on the rug."

"I won't." Timmy stands to walk toward the kitchen but looks at the front door instead. "Someone's here. But I don't think it's my mom yet."

"We'll soon find out." Oliver, suspicion on his face, gets up to open the door.

A man in his early sixties, a full head of hair, gray with bits of brown, wearing black rectangular glasses and holding a large bag, smiles as Oliver opens the door.

"Ellmore! I'd completely forgotten you might stop by." He nods to let him know Timmy is there, before the men greet one another as usual.

"Oh," Ellmore says. "Well, I brought you a bag of bagels, cheese, pickles, and some other goodies from the deli."

"You spoil me. Come in." Oliver winks at him. "I love that lavender shirt on you."

"Why I wore it," Ellmore says. "And who do we have here?"

The boy, having properly disposed of the apple core, walks back into the living room. "I'm Timmy. I like to visit Oliver because he's old and says funny stuff. And he has a past."

Ellmore laughs heartily. "You know what? That's the same reason I visit him too."

Timmy giggles. "For real?"

"Oh, definitely." Ellmore takes a seat on the vintage club chair across from the sofa as Oliver takes the bag of food to the kitchen.

"Where do you live, Timmy?"

"In this building. With my mom. It used to be a hotel, but now it's just apartments. They all have weird stuff in them." He whispers. "Weird people too."

"I used to live in a weird place. People called it the Hotel Obscure. Do you know what 'obscure' means?"

"Nope."

"Well, it means 'something that's hard to understand.' That was how people felt about the hotel and the people who lived there. Nobody really knew what else to call it."

"How come you lived there, then?"

From the kitchen, Oliver smiles as he puts the cheese in the dairy compartment on the inside of the refrigerator door. "Timmy asks a lot of questions."

"That's fine with me." Ellmore dusts a speck of something

from his black trousers. He looks at Timmy. "It used to be hard for me to understand myself. So 'the Obscure' was a good fit."

"Were you a weirdo?"

"Still am." Ellmore chuckles. "But I'm a much happier weirdo. I'm just nerdy me. Don't think I'll ever really change."

"What does 'nerdy' mean?" Timmy asks as Oliver walks over to Ellmore and hands him a glass of Sauvignon Blanc.

"You're not having one?" Ellmore asks.

"Promised his mom I'd never take a sip while he's in my care." He smiles. "I'll have one in a bit." He sits on the couch a good distance from Timmy.

"Nerdy means someone who pays too much attention to some things … and maybe not enough to others," Ellmore explains.

"Like what?" Timmy asks.

Ellmore tastes his wine and looks at Oliver. "I like this." He places the glass on the table next to his chair and faces Timmy. "Well, I used to pay too much attention to what I wore. I had a special tie for every day of the week. Sort of like if you wore blue shirts on Mondays, green ones on Tuesdays, and brown on Wednesdays. And you never changed. That would be pretty boring, right?"

"I guess. What other weirdo things did you do?"

Oliver laughs. "Careful, Elm."

"Let's see. Well, for starters, every time I got a new pair of glasses, I picked out round frames that looked exactly like the ones I already had. I never wanted to try anything new. That's why I have rectangular frames now, and some days, I wear round ones. I like to diversify."

"I don't know that word. Or that 'tangular' word either."

"Diversify means to change things up." Ellmore reaches over and takes another sip of his wine. "And my glasses are in the shape of a rectangle. Unlike a square that has four equal sides."

"Oh. Are you and Oliver best friends?"

"I think we are."

"Did you meet him at school?"

"Oh, no. Not that long ago, Timmy. Several years ago. You see, we met at a particular … um … restaurant … and when we started talking, we found out we had some of the same weirdo qualities. Like we were both too particular about how we did certain things. And we both wanted to change our ways … so we thought maybe we could help one another."

"And then one weirdo thing led to another," Oliver whispers under his breath.

Ellmore gives him a look as if to say, "Really now."

"I don't know what you're talking about," Timmy chimes in. "But I think you're both weirdos." He laughs. "But I like weirdos. Most of them."

Just as Ellmore is about to respond, the doorbell rings.

"That's my mom," Timmy says. "I'll get it." He jumps up and runs to the door and opens it. "Hi, Mommy."

"Hi, Timikins!" Darah says, hugging him. She looks at Ellmore. "We've met before. You're Ellmore Badget."

"Junior," he adds.

She extends her hand, and he shakes it. "Darah Gregnut." Such etiquette her aggrieved mother has bestowed on her. At least she has something useful from that woman. "I love your shirt. The last time I saw you, I believe you were wearing apricot."

"Impressive memory," Ellmore says.

"I love dapper men." Darah looks at Oliver. "Thank you for looking after Timmy. I'm a few minutes late. I couldn't get into my office for some reason. Turns out that it was a dirty key."

"What does that mean, Mommy?"

"It means I dropped my keys in the mud when I was inspecting the gardens, and a speck of it dried on the office key … in one of the grooves. Kept me from opening the door. Silly of Mommy, don't you think?"

"And you get mad when I get mud on me."

"Not mad, honey. I just don't like it when you get stains on your good clothes."

"Ellmore used to wear the same color every Monday. Can I wear blue every Monday like he did?"

Ellmore waves his hands in a cross-fan motion. "Oh, no, Timmy. You don't want to do that. Took me a long time to de-weirdo-ize myself. Stay as you are. You're just perfect."

"Let's not go that far." Darah laughs and puts her arm around Timmy. She speaks sweetly to him. "We're going out to dinner with Ava Elisabeth tonight, so we'd better 'hit the road,' as they say."

Timmy smiles. "She's my favorite old person in the whole world. I love her."

A child after my own heart. I feel a camaraderie I never thought would be possible with one so young. What exquisite taste he has. How blessed he is that his mother has such a beautiful friend in my darling Ava Elisabeth ... with whom he is fortunate enough to spend time with. If only such kismet would bless me as well.

"Thank you for everything, Oliver." She smiles at Ellmore. "A true pleasure to see you again. I hope you gentlemen enjoy your evening." She turns to leave, then stops. "Oh, Oliver, I almost forgot." She reaches in her blazer pocket and hands him a tiny piece of paper. "For some bizarre reason, this was stuck in your door. It only has the number 'thirty-three' written on it. I don't know if that means anything to you, but clearly, someone put it there."

He looks at the sliver of paper. Unable to even feign a state of normality, Oliver's face is pale and unmoving — like a bad photograph.

"What's wrong?" Darah asks as she notices Ellmore is baffled as well.

Oliver says nothing.

"Super weirdo," Timmy says to Darah.

She scolds him with a look before speaking. "That's not appropriate. You know what to do."

"Sorry, Oliver," Timmy says, embarrassment hugging him like some ghastly touchy-feely relative he's just met.

Ellmore looks at Oliver, who is still rendered mute as if he's the star of an obnoxious TV commercial for a car dealership that someone has had to silence to preserve their sanity. (Yes, I am overly descriptive at the moment. Sue me.)

"We'd better go. Thank you again, Oliver. And I'm sorry to have inadvertently upset you."

"He'll be just fine," Ellmore says, walking her to the door. "I'll help him sort out whatever's going on."

"Maybe I shouldn't have given that piece of paper to him. But it was stuck in his door and—"

"You did the right thing, Darah." Ellmore smiles at Timmy. "It was superb to make your acquaintance. And please remember, there are lots of colors in this world because we're meant to see them all. Don't ever limit yourself to only a few."

"Okay. I won't. Bye, Ellmore."

"Mommy, what's 'kwaintence'?" Timmy says as the door closes behind him.

Ellmore rushes over to Oliver. "What in the world is wrong?" He guides him to the sofa. "Sit down. Talk to me." Ellmore takes a seat next to him."

Opening the closed fist that holds the piece of paper, Oliver stares. "I can't imagine what thirty-three signifies. And why was the paper stuck in my door like—"

"Like you used to do to reassure yourself nobody had entered your room?"

Oliver looks surprised. He drops the paper onto the coffee table as if it were radioactive.

"That's one of the first things you confided to me. Why do you think I took such an instant liking to you?" Ellmore puts a comforting hand on Oliver's leg. "Do you remember how I told you about my Saturday tie having a stain on it, and how I had to wear my burgundy-and-yellow emergency option? I was very upset, but it turned out to be one of the best days of my life. Oh, how you laughed when I shared that with you."

Too distraught for a stroll down memory lane, Oliver says nothing. Instead, he puts the palms of his hands on either side of his head, as if he is trying to squeeze information out of it.

"My goodness, honey," Ellmore says. "You're driving yourself stark-raving mad."

"It's in my brain … somewhere. The meaning of that loathsome thirty-three. I just have to get it out." Oliver self-ejects from the sofa, hands still on his head, agony distastefully oozing from every orifice. (Well, not literally, but it looks as if it might be. He is a sight.)

Jumping up to console him, Ellmore attempts to guide him back to the sofa. "You've got to calm down."

"I don't want to sit, Elm. I've got to figure this out." He looks at him. "Still think we're so much alike? I'm a Cheshire cat to your shy kitten."

"True. I'll admit, I was a quiet one. Until the day I wore that tie … Oliver … really … calm down."

Oliver stands face to face with him. "Who the hell do you know that *ever* calms down when someone tells them to calm down?"

"That would be nobody." Ellmore walks to the side table and picks up his glass of wine. "Would you like a sip? How about if I pour you a glass of your own now?"

Oliver stomps over to the wine bottle. "Are there any months with thirty-three days in them? Of course not." He takes a cold wine glass from the freezer. "What if I pour thirty-three drops of wine? What will that give me?"

"Not enough for the state you're in."

Still true to his compulsive nature, Oliver pours the perfect amount of wine into his glass, then re-inserts the cork into the bottle. "Maybe there's a secret message on page thirty-three of a book in my library." He leaves the wineglass on the counter and walks over to a small bookcase. He grabs a copy of *Great Expectations*, turns to page thirty-three, and reads the first full sentence he finds. "'All the time Mrs. Joe and Joe were briskly clearing the table for the pie and pudding.'" He groans. "Well, thanks, Chuck. For nothing." Angrily, he puts the book back in the correct slot, then pulls out a copy of *Main Street*. Again, he reads the first thing he sees aloud: "'Why do these stories lie so? They always make the bride's homecoming a bower of roses.'" Another groan of disgust as the book slides back into its place. "Thanks for nothing, Sinclair. Oh, wait. Did people call you 'Sin?' Well, if they didn't, they should have."

Having seen enough lunacy, Ellmore heads to the bookcase and stands in front of it. "Whatever thirty-three means, it's not on page thirty-three of any of these books. And I'm not going to stand here while you curse out the greatest authors of all time. Can't you see this is madness?"

"I think I've figured it out. It's a record speed. LPs were produced at thirty-three revolutions per minute. Maybe it has something to do with that." Oliver frowns. "But what?"

"I think your brain is doing thirty-three rpm … and it's tired. It's begging you to slow down."

Oliver goes to the counter and picks up his wine, then rejoins Ellmore in the living room. "Maybe, it's a warning. What if someone is planning to kill me in thirty-three days … and they're telling me how much time I have left? Perhaps I should set up some hidden cameras. Oh, Lord. I've taken some downright salacious celebrity photos in my day." He pauses to form a defense." Of course, these people put *themselves* in compromising positions for me to discover.

I certainly wasn't responsible for their indiscretions. But a career or two was ruined by my captures. One studio executive and one actress for sure. There could easily be more. What if those has-beens have been waiting thirty-three years to take revenge on me? It's a dish best served cold, you know. That's it, Elm. It all makes sense. Like I said before: I have thirty-three days to live."

"If you don't stop adding two and two and getting thirty-three, you'll only have thirty-three *minutes* left on your clock," Ellmore says with a grin.

"If that was a joke, I'm not amused. My life is being threatened." Oliver takes a sip of wine.

"Of course it was," Ellmore says. "My goodness. It took me fifty-something years to learn that I had a sense of humor … and now you want to relieve me of it."

"You know, if two threes turn to face one another, they resemble an eight. Maybe there's a clue in there somehow. Like an ice skater, who does perfect figure eights, will be the one to do me in. Slash my neck with the sharpened blade of a skate."

Ellmore bursts out laughing. "You're playing with me, right? That's your silliest guess yet."

Oliver puts his wineglass on the coffee table. "Okay, now that I think about it, that one might be a bit on the absurd side."

"I'm glad you see reason."

Oliver begins frantically walking in a circle. "Wait. I'm getting somewhere. It's a message from the universe. It's all falling into place. And you're a part of it. First, Timmy, then you, and then Darah. All of you are accomplices. Ah, very clever. You can't fool me … I remember things … especially words spoken within the past half an hour."

"What in the blazes are you on about?" Ellmore puts his glass next to Oliver's, then sits on the sofa. "In the very shortest of time, you've drained the lifeblood from me."

In some combination of excitement and agitation, Oliver sits next to him. "Okay, hear me out. When Timmy was here, I asked him how school was. He said some kid from kindergarten fell and complained of a 'hurty knee.' That rhymes with thirty-three. Get it?"

"The rhyme yes. The meaning: no. Certainly not."

"Then you come over and start talking with Timmy about whether or not you're a weirdo. And you said you're just 'nerdy me.'"

"Oh, Oliver, really."

"See how that rhymes too?"

"This is insane."

"Then, for the grand finale, Darah says she had a 'dirty key.'" He harumphs victoriously. "Three guests within a half-hour. And each one just so happens to say something to me that rhymes with thirty-three. I'd say that's either a conspiracy, which I doubt, or the universe sending me a message."

"I'm glad you've ruled out the conspiracy angle." Now, let me decipher that 'message.'" Ellmore takes a thin black cloth from his pants pocket, removes his glasses, and cleans them. "It's a coincidence. Nothing more."

Oliver has already moved on to another theory. "You know, it just so happens that the halfway point on Route 66 is in Adrian, Texas. I wonder if the answer lies there."

"Pack your bags, then. And send me a postcard when you get there." Ellmore explodes with laughter again as he puts his glasses back on. "I'm sorry, sweetheart. I'm trying to help you here. But that's downright hysterical."

"I guess that does sound silly. Perhaps I need to drink my wine and calm down a bit."

Ellmore stands. "Splendid idea." He hands Oliver his glass, and after placing it safely in Oliver's hands, picks up his own. "What shall we drink to?"

They clink glasses.

"Figuring out what thirty-three means," says the one-track-minded man.

"You know," Ellmore says, adjusting a cuff link with his free hand, "I'm actually more intrigued as to why the number was left for you in the manner it was."

Oliver hands his glass to Ellmore as he jumps off the couch and runs over to his desk, opens a bottom drawer, and pulls something from it. Taking a sip from his own glass, Ellmore then puts both glasses back on the table as he waits for the next round of tomfoolery.

Rushing back to Ellmore, with an old desk diary in his hands, Oliver sits down. "I think it happened thirty-three times."

"What, pray tell?"

"Thirty-three times that someone moved the paper ever so slightly, leaving me to doubt my sanity. It happened about once a month for just a bit under two-and-a-half years."

"You mean when you put the paper in the door because you were so paranoid someone might enter your room?"

Oliver nods as if he feels ashamed. (But I know he would do it again.)

"I suppose someone might have wanted to mess with your head, had they gotten the drift that your head was already a bit messy to begin with."

"Whose side are you on?" Oliver flips through the pages of the diary, then looks up at Ellmore. "This is all haywire. Someone only moved the paper thirty-two times. I noted the occurrences religiously."

"Forget the exact number for a moment. Did you do anything to deserve it?"

Oliver bows his head in shame. "I might not have been as kind to the staff as I should have."

The doorbell rings, and the two men exchange shocked looks. Who could it be?

Slowly rising from the sofa, Oliver walks to the door. He opens it to find an old man, with scraggly white hair, wearing a brown corduroy jacket and jeans, staring at him. "Ace!"

"You gonna finally let me into your place, Ollie Boy?"

Oliver bristles. "If you promise not to call me 'Ollie Boy' again."

"I reckon that's a fair deal." The old man walks in, surprised to see Ellmore on the sofa. "Hey there, stranger. Ace Flanagan. I janitized here for many a year."

Ellmore stands to greet him. "I'm Ellmore J. Badget, Jr. Oliver's fr—"

"Never did care who loves who or none of that. You don't gotta make up nothing for my ears."

"A relief," Ellmore says as he notices Oliver has rather frozen in place by the door. "Would you care to sit?"

"Nope."

"I'd imagine you have business with Oliver …."

"Nothing you can't hear."

Having now steeled himself for the occasion, whatever it is, Oliver walks over to him. "So, you got your payback … finally. You moved the paper on me thirty-two times, yet you put the number thirty-three on the paper. I'm very precise, so you can't tell me I've got that wrong."

Ace looked around, his eyes taking in everything he'd always been prohibited from seeing. "Nope. Crazy, a neurotic guy like you gets those things right."

"So why thirty-three?"

"That's the number of times I got to drive you a bit more bonkers than you already are. Today being number thirty-three. A crowning achievement, if I do say so. The cherry on top of my hot-fudge sundae."

Oliver glares at him.

"Would you like a drink, Ace?" Ellmore says, trying to break the odd tension.

"No thanks, fella. I'm leaving. Moving out of town. That's why I had to settle the score with Oll … Oliver …before the missus and me take off."

"Is the score settled?" Oliver asks. His dubious visage connotes utter panic.

"Probably," says Ace as he walks to the door and turns the knob. He clicks his tongue. "But ya never know. Sometimes, ya just got to wait 'n' see. Bye now." He closes the door behind him.

"Well, that was different," Ellmore says, walking over to Oliver and putting his arm around him. "A most unusual day, I'd say."

"What he said about waiting, do you think there's something else in store for me? Should I worry? Am I going to have to just wait to see what life brings me?"

"Indeed," Ellmore says, taking his hand as they lower themselves to sit again. "If we're still waiting for something, it's because we feel life. If not … it's all behind us. Whether it be a silly prank from an old man or something completely different and unexpected. Like the two of us meeting." He put his hand on Oliver's. "It's going to be all right. You'll see. We'll be good … you and me. And you have my solemn word; I'll try to always give you something worth waiting for."

Chapter Eleven: LANA COMPTON'S DAUGHTER

As the story goes ... in 1927, somewhere in rural America, a labor-and-delivery nurse told Camilla Compton that her newborn baby girl would grow up to be famous. There was something special in the baby's cry. "Star quality, ma'am. I've never heard anything like it. You'll see that I'm right."

Whether the nurse said that to every new mother, we shall never know. But Camilla took her words as gospel, and from an early age, young Lana, a genuinely talented child, was groomed to make the nurse's prophecy (and the mother's dream) a reality. At eighteen, Lana moved from the sleepy town in which she was born and headed toward the dazzling lights of fame and all that went with it, good and bad.

It would be tedious to expound on all that Lana endured to get a break so young, so I shall cherry-pick the highlights.

Blessed with the ability to sing, dance, and act (and being extraordinarily beautiful), she was discovered by an acting coach who "knew the right people." Lana was a mere nineteen when production began on her first musical. By the age of twenty-one, she was married to the producer who'd made the proper wheels grind forward. She was impressed by his largesse (And yes, I am referring to his generosity), the love he professed, the power he wielded, and the attention he showered on her. She had convinced herself it was true love. But heavy rains, and even more showers ... eventually stop. And droughts can kill much that once bloomed and grew. Ahem.

At thirty-one, Lana put her musical comedy days behind her to become a dramatic actress. After her acclaimed role as an embattled torch singer in *When Love Lived*, her husband, twelve years her senior, began to resent that Lana had achieved a status now greater than his. For nine years, she had been known as his wife, now, he was "Lana Compton's husband." And he loathed it. He convinced himself that his machinations had made Lana a star and never accepted that her talent was the greatest reason for her success. To punish her for having the lion's share of recognition and reward, he strayed.

Devastated by his betrayal, it wasn't long before Lana realized one cannot lose what one never had. She soon found her silver lining. For the first time in her life, Lana fell in love … true love … with her bodyguard.

To best manage her affair, she feigned ignorance of her spouse's cheating as it made her own trysts far easier to arrange.

Having always believed herself to be unable to conceive after so many years and no pregnancies, she took no precautions at all. But oh, how finding love anew can tell a very different tale. And then, three months into her love affair, Lana found herself with child.

She did nothing but worry at first, and pray, hoping an answer would reveal itself, but none did … not one that she recognized as such. After her first trimester, Lana had no choice but to tell her husband. She would have been happy to divorce, but once convinced that divorce would be messier, costlier, and more damaging to her career than she ever imagined (and of course, for him), she agreed to continue swimming in the sea of estrangement. Although it pained her to leave her lover, she knew she could not risk being seen in her condition. Having no other option, Lana returned to the sleepy town where she was born and lived a clandestine life with her sister and family.

During those six months, she struggled over what would become of the child. Unable to even imagine her success being destroyed by an angry husband, and having no idea how to live any other kind of life, she finally accepted her sister's pleadings (and those of her infirm mother) to raise baby Fiona as their own ... and for Lana to ever more be known as an aunt who lived far away and made movies.

For seventeen years, Fiona Almaran lived a happy life, never knowing that thousands of miles away, a gossip rag writer, digging into Lana's past, would soon change her life forever. When news of Lana's secret daughter broke, everyone looked at Fiona differently ... with awe, jealousy, disdain, shock, obsequiousness, and everything imaginable in-between. They liked or disliked her for the same reason: she was Lana Compton's daughter.

Fiona was at odds with everyone. She felt that her family made a fool of her, especially after learning that her older "siblings" knew all along she was not their sister, but their cousin. Why hadn't she been given the right to know who she was? Who was her father anyway? Some bodyguard her mother had an affair with for seven years? Did he care? Did he even know? What was so terrible about her mere existence that would have made "Aunt Lana" lose her career? Her loving family seemed relieved that they no longer had to keep the secret, and, to Fiona, as if they expected long-belated thanks for having taken her in as an infant. With each passing day, she felt their resentment.

Except for one, her friends all treated her differently. After a year of hell, however, this friend, to whom she had confided her despair, asked Fiona if her "mom" might be able to snag a certain movie star's autograph on an 8 x 10 photo for her.

Shattered, she could not fathom how this friend could have been her confidante for an entire year. How could she have understood the depth of her pain, be the *one* person who didn't care that she was Lana Compton's daughter, and then, in the end, reveal herself to be no more than some insidious fraud who'd merely been biding her time in hopes of procuring a signed glossy. On the spot, Fiona (quite uncharacteristically, I might add) articulated the particular orifice where her now-former friend might stash the coveted photo were she ever fortunate enough to obtain one … from someone else. At that moment, Fiona felt more alone than ever.

As for her mother … what a heartbreak. Lana didn't dare come to visit, unable to tolerate the physical and written presence of the tabloids. Instead, Fiona received some tearful phone calls saying how sorry she was. Though Lana cried and cried, when Fiona asked what she would have done differently, Lana could not answer. "I-I don't know, honey," was all she could offer.

Also, the headlines were brutal:

Lana Compton's Love Child Stashed on a Farm in Rural America

Lana Compton's Illegitimate Child Early Product of a Seven-Year Fling-a-Ding-Ding

Married Star Revealed to Have Daughter of Long-Time Indiscretion

He Guarded Her Body All Right: Lana Compton's Love Child Revealed

Undercover Guard … or Under-the-Covers Guard? The Shocking Parentage of Lana Compton's Daughter

"Why Didn't You Want Me, Mommy?" Lana Compton's Child Hidden Away with Family

Lana Compton is a Secret Mommy! Who is the Father? Not Producer Husband!

Lana Compton's Husband Shocked by Her Infidelity So Many Years Ago

Fiona, bashful and reserved by nature, made a bold decision. She would move to the big city to live near her mother. Having grown up in a small town, she knew anonymity would be easier among the masses.

She hated the eyes upon her ... and for what ... being born? It was insane. Although she didn't admit it to herself, she wanted more than anything to live with her mother, to prove to herself she was not discarded trash, but the daughter of a confused woman who now would do everything in her power to make it up to her.

But Lana, accustomed to the spoils of stardom, lived in fear of what would happen should Fiona reside with her.

After Leaving her Daughter on a Farm, Lana Compton Attempts Reconciliation

Mother and Daughter ... Together at Last. Can Lana Compton's Daughter Forgive Her?

Lana Compton's Daughter Moves into Her Mansion ... It's Payback Time!

Fans Demand to Know! Can Lana Compton's Daughter Forgive Mother for Abandonment?

Was Lana Compton's Lover an Alien? Shocking Secret Footage Says Yes!

Lana was imagining headlines every waking hour. They tortured her. But she did not want to abandon Fiona, so she found a guest house for her at a director's mansion: a place where she would have complete privacy and where paparazzi had no access to her … unless she ventured out, of course. Even with this arrangement, the two women did not see one another much, for the paparazzi were never far away.

I shall now state the obvious: a child being born in secret to a famous person is not exceptionally unusual … nor is it worth all of the insane attention given to Lana's situation. As it turns out, Lana's sterile husband was behind the whole sordid mess. It was he who tipped off the reporter and he who kept the not-so-shocking scandal alive. Why? To punish Lana for not remaining true while *he* cheated his adulterous heart out … and more importantly, to achieve a better financial settlement for himself in the divorce. Good-for-nothing trickster. Crafty to the core. Sadly, Lana did not learn of this additional deception until she had to sell her home and watch her career hobble along a lonely road when it once skipped merrily through fields of wildflowers.

Fiona's father, now a married man with three children, wanted no part of his love child as he'd moved far away, and his family knew nothing of his paternity nor of his affair with the married movie star. I have no need to mention him again.

I lied. I do have one more thing to say: Lana would never admit to anyone, most especially herself, that she still loved him. Ironically, he left because he wanted a family, and never forgave Lana for being too ashamed to acknowledge his child. Now, I am truly finished.

After much time passed, the scandal dwindled down to a blip on the radar screen, yet Fiona was still seen as Lana Compton's daughter to those who knew her. Most, of course, introduced her by name, but usually preceded with, "This is Lana Compton's daughter …."

"It's Fiona. Fiona Almaran," she would say. That's when they would nod pleasantly or say, "Of course," but they still saw her as the movie star's shy daughter of far-lesser looks.

Fiona, after being set up in the guest house, was given a car. She traveled quite a distance to attend college in an outlying town where people never thought about film stars and silly scandals. It was a bigger town than the one in which she grew up and offered her the immeasurable bonus of not being known. After six years, she earned a bachelor's degree, then a master's of journalism. All she wanted to do was write non-fiction books and articles from the sanctity of her home. While she was friendly to those she knew, the betrayal of her friend back home never ceased to haunt her. Besides, the only person she really wanted to know was her mother.

During the years she was in school, she and Lana finally developed a relationship. It was not a bad one, but it left Fiona wanting much more, especially as the family who raised her rebuffed her contact attempts, insisting that she had "used them enough for one lifetime." Yes, the child who always thought she belonged was "using" the family.

Meanwhile, Fiona learned how she came to be … and why she'd be wise to accept her father's request to be left alone. She understood that Lana was a mere child when she was pulled into "the business," and that she followed a path laid out for her by many, never really having the opportunity to see who she might have become without so many dictating how she was to live her life.

In the seventh year of their newfound relationship, Lana began to take an interest in Fiona's numerous writing projects, but sadly, she also took an unfortunate interest in enhancements to soothe the pain of personal guilt, a declining career, and fading looks. Fiona tried desperately to help her, but as the years went on, it was clear that Lana had no will to fight her demons. At the age of sixty-two, fourteen years after reuniting with her daughter, she died in her sleep from an overdose. Fiona, traumatized when she discovered her the next day at noon, called the authorities, and the resurrection of tabloid headlines began.

Lana Compton's Tragic Death: Suicide, Overdose, or a Daughter's Revenge?

Lana Compton's Not-So-Secret Daughter Shamed Mother to Death

A Youthful Indiscretion Leads to an Early Death: The Lana Compton Story

How Adultery, Secrecy, and Guilt Killed Lana Compton: A Six-Part Series

Did Lana Compton's Vengeful Daughter Drive Her to Suicide ... or Worse?

Spaceship Spotted Outside of Compton Mansion the Night Before Her Death

Once again, Fiona found reason to retreat, and for the next fourteen years lived in the guest house and wrote articles. She wanted little to do with the outside world. When the property she lived in was sold, for the first time in her life, she had to find lodging on her own.

Where did she end up? Here, of course. Darah had recently taken ownership, and Fiona, who found herself becoming a hermit, thought it healthy to, at the very least, see people from time to time. With the money Lana had left her, she was able to afford a two-bedroom apartment (making one room an office) and gradually emerged (only slightly) from her shell. Often, in the afternoon, she would sit with Ava Elisabeth in the gardens, something she still does, and develop friendly, yet superficial relationships with everyone else.

And now, we are here in the present. Today, my darling wears a flowing green dress, a hand-tooled belt with painted red roses and bright-green leaves around her waist, and, as always, her neck, hands, and ears are adorned with baubles from her former lovers. She sits on the white wicker couch sipping peach iced tea as Fiona walks toward her. It is not often that she wears a smile, but being the recipient of one so contagious, Fiona cannot resist returning it.

"Oh, Ava Elisabeth. Gee, you look pretty today. But then again, you always do. Unlike me who still looks like she's been plowing a field … something I've never done, despite having seen it done more times than I can count."

"You put yourself down, Fiona. You needn't do so. Please, darling, sit."

Without missing a beat, Fiona continues to babble as she sits next to my darling. "It's funny; I was only eighteen when I left my home, but that small-town girl and her lack of sophistication never left me." Fiona frowns. "Even though I left *it* and everything and everyone else behind."

"Not all associations have an indefinite shelf life. And it's especially sad when those whom we call family turn their backs on us." She points to an extra glass of tea. "I ordered this for you, darling. I figured you'd be around today."

Fiona brushes her short brown-and-gray hair out of her face and picks up the glass. "You're always so thoughtful. And you never judge me. Is it any wonder you're the only confidante I have after so many years? I always expect you to ask me why I wear these ugly floral patterns and drab colors … but you never do."

"Do you want to tell me?" Ava Elisabeth puts her glass down and touches Fiona's hand.

"You know, I do. I want to tell you." She smiles awkwardly. "It's rebellion, I suppose. My mother, Lana, always told me to fix myself up a bit, to find a style of dress that suited me, and to wear a bit of makeup to brighten my face. But the more she encouraged me, the more I was determined not to let her remake me in her image. Only now that she's been gone for so many years, I realize she didn't want to do that at all. She only wanted me to look pretty for myself. So my self-esteem wouldn't be so … well … nonexistent. Funny, my mother was as beautiful as you are, but she felt so guilty for everything she'd done that no clothing, jewelry, or hairstyle could ever have made her feel beautiful again." Fiona gulps. "Or give her the incentive to stay alive." She puts her glass down. "Ava Elisabeth, I had a long think last night, and two important things came to mind that I'd like to talk to you about. If you have time."

My darling lets that delightful laugh escape her lips. If I wasn't already so in love with her, this would be the moment I would fall. I've never known any woman to possess so much charm, despite her greed, which pains my very core.

"You can talk to me about anything at all. You know that."

Fiona and Ava Elisabeth stop talking and smile at the gardener who comes by to water the plants in the large pots. He tips his hat and smiles, mumbles something about the Silver Falls Dichondra, then wishes them a good day before leaving.

Picking up her glass, Fiona takes several sips of her tea as if there is something much stronger in the glass that will help to fortify her. "It took me five years to tell you who I was, and when I did, you didn't even bat an eyelash. I understood it was because you are so sensitive to others and so unobtrusive … but it was more than that. You already knew, didn't you?"

"I did. I knew you were Fiona Almaran."

Fiona puts the glass down and puts her hand over her mouth to stop herself from sobbing. "Oh, that's why I love you, Ava Elisabeth. Anyone else would have said, 'You're Lana Compton's daughter' and then followed up with a string of questions." She settles her energy. "How did you know? From the tabloids? You can tell me."

"I knew your mother. We met once in Paris, and several times again when I was stateside. Now that you're asking, I must tell you:

she confided to me about you. And she showed me the photos of you that she carried. I recognized you. And yes, darling, I won't lie and say I didn't see your photo in those vulgar rags at the newsstands. But I would have known you without them."

It is a good thing Fiona does not care for makeup. The way she touches her face in shock would have encouraged the various substances smeared on her face to form the likeness of a deranged circus clown. "Are you serious? Why in the world didn't she tell me that she carried my photo? All the times I accused her of not caring, why wouldn't she have told me that?"

My darling puts a comforting hand on Fiona's again. "Because Lana's remorse was deeper than she could have ever explained or expected you to believe. I'm very sure she didn't think that the act of carrying a photo in her purse would make up for anything at all. So she said nothing."

Fiona sniffles. "How come you didn't tell me you knew? That's some secret to keep all of these years."

My darling leans closer to her. "Because it took so much for you to tell me. How wrong it would have been for me to say I already knew. I was the only person you confided in, and to tell you, I felt, would have been to take that away from you. I hope you can understand. It's not like I didn't want to say anything, but every time I pondered the situation, my mind brought me back to the same place."

"You have some amazing self-control," Fiona says, wiping away her tears. "There's nobody I trust more than you; that's why I want to tell you about a decision I've made."

My darling is quite curious but shows restraint by not too fully exposing her emotion. "And that is?"

Again relying on iced tea for courage, Fiona takes several more sips before putting her glass down. "I've decided to face my fears. I'm going to embrace what I've always run from. I've written for publishers, magazines, and newspapers for more years than I can count now. It finally dawned on me: the most important piece I could ever write would be an article entitled, 'I am Lana Compton's daughter.'" She exhales as her body goes limp in the chair. A moment or two pass. "Yes, it's scary … to write the very headline I've avoided all of my life. But that's exactly what I'm going to do. But I think a multi-part article would be the best."

I see there is something my beauty wishes to say but doesn't dare. I am vexed. I feel my omniscience fading, which I detest, but at this moment, I want to know what is troubling Ava Elisabeth. Fiona doesn't notice the subtleties of her expressions, but being her invisible love for all these many years, there is no detail too minuscule for me to detect.

"What a brave and wonderful idea that is. Lana would be so very proud of you. In fact, I'm sure she's watching over us and knows exactly what you intend to do. What courage you have."

Fiona laughs. "And I didn't need a fake wizard to give it to me."

"Indeed you didn't. Because you know that the greatest gifts are the ones we give ourselves."

Now brimming with confidence, Fiona smiles. "As soon as I go upstairs, I'm going to begin writing … or should I say 'transcribing' it. I think I've actually written the words in my head a hundred times."

Fiona looks away for a second, and I see my darling frown ever so slightly as fear fills her eyes. What could it be?

ONE MONTH LATER

The sun is shining, and Ava Elisabeth takes in the vibrant colors around her. Although the flowers are not in focus, she is just happy to see them. But the reason for her smile is a gift from Darah and Timmy:

a cat harness. Now, my beloved is able to bring her feline inamorato, Mickey, to enjoy afternoons in the garden with her. And yes, I remain envious of the Persian alley cat (I can only be *so* complimentary to the lucky beast) as he sits on her lap and purrs.

Fiona, who has made herself scarce while embarking on her project to publish the piece she once feared to write, has spent almost no time outside.

Today, dressed in black with only a floral headband to acknowledge the existence of color, a letter in her hand, she walks with a sullen countenance toward the pink-and-green-striped umbrella where my darling sits on the white wicker sofa.

"Oh, Fiona! I'm so happy to see you, darling. I know you've been so hard at work, so I didn't want to interrupt, but I'll admit, I was starting to fret a bit." She looks down at the table in front of her. "If I'd known you were coming, I would have ordered a drink for you. But that's still possible. What would you like?"

Fiona bends down to give her a hug, but it is obscenely cursory, and my darling recognizes it as such.

"Something is terribly wrong. Does it have to do with that letter in your hand?"

After the expulsion of a forlorn sigh, Fiona sits, clutching the missive in her hand. "I've been submitting my article to editors for nearly a month. Silly me; I had visions of various publications, all battling for the rights to my story. And of course, being known to these men and women, having written for every one of them, I never imagined that they would all … and I mean *all*…turn me down." She starts to cry but is stingy with her tears.

"Oh, sweetheart." At this moment, it is clear that my darling knew all along this would happen, hence her frown that day. "What did they say?"

"All different things. Let's see: the subject matter wasn't a good fit for the publication, they weren't accepting new pieces at the moment, the material was dated, etcetera etcetera. Then, today, I got this …" She holds up the letter. "… from a woman who has been publishing my work for years. I'll read it to you:

Dear Fiona:

After doing some research, I have learned that your mother was a popular tabloid sensation back in her day … and quite the talented actress as well. After reading your article, and looking through the archives, I understand that the circumstances of your birth, and the subsequent discovery of those circumstances, caused quite a stir for all concerned. I can empathize and see why you would want to share your story after all these years.

But therein lies the problem: after all these years. I'm so sorry to say this, but your mother's last work was some thirty years ago, her best work even longer ago, and her name wouldn't ring a bell with our readers, most of whom are from a younger generation.

Maybe, in the future, if you'd like to rework the slant, perhaps you can resubmit the article as "Fiona Almaran's Mother." As many of our readers know your work, they might get a kick of knowing that your mother used to be famous. Of course, to make it a viable piece, I would ask you to include stories of the celebrities you've met and the ones who she certainly told you stories about … the juicier the better. (Especially those still in the public eye … if possible.)

I can't promise anything, but what I have just described would be far more amenable than what you currently propose.

Sincere best wishes,
Eden

Isn't that the irony of all ironies?"

Mickey becomes restless and jumps to the ground. No doubt, he feels his mother's discomfort and prefers to have all four paws on the ground.

"You're very hurt by all of this." My darling detects the smell of alcohol on Fiona and inwardly winces.

"I'm floored. I thought I was finally giving the world what they wanted … and hey, sorry there, kiddo; you're too late. You know what's clear to me? That I was born to live in the shadows. And come on, nobody would want to read an article called 'Fiona Almaran's Mother.' Eden was only consoling me. She knows damn well I'll never re-submit that article. Especially with ugly celebrity gossip that has nothing to do with anything. No, I'm done trying to sell this piece." She is more liberal with her tears now. "Because I don't want to be told again that my story isn't interesting." Her head drops, and she stares at the lap of her black pants. "I know *my* story isn't very interesting; I get that. But my mother's story, well, it's fascinating. Women of today have far more choices than Lana did way back when. People should know the struggles she went through. And more than anything, they should know her work. She was brilliant." Fiona sniffles. "I still think *When Love Lived* was one of the best films I've ever seen."

"Indeed. She gave quite the powerhouse performance," Ava Elisabeth says as she tugs on Mickey's leash so as not to greet the couple walking down the path. "Here, boy." She smiles as the cat returns to her lap. "A lovely person as well. I was quite fond of her and always wished circumstances had permitted us to have known one another better."

Fiona stands abruptly, startling both Ava Elisabeth and

Mickey. "Forget this stupid article. I'm going to aim bigger. I'll put my story on hold and introduce a whole new generation to Lana Compton. I'll talk to people who knew her work. I'll get quotes from them. Maybe even get a documentary made. I'm going to start immediately."

My darling is quite flummoxed. "Well then, I wish you luck, dear."

"Thanks. I'll see you around." And with that paltry farewell, she hurries toward the building, alive with a new purpose courtesy of some liquid encouragement.

"Oh, Mickey." Frown lines appear on Ava Elisabeth's face. "This is very worrisome. I'm getting a feeling in the pit of my stomach that doesn't make me happy. We both have to hope Fiona will be all right." She lowers her head to one side as if she can hear him speaking to her. "What's that? No, I don't think we'll see much of her anymore, unless by accident. She is quite aware of what I might tell her and doesn't want to hear it." She attempts to laugh. "I'm afraid she wouldn't care much for your opinion either."

FIVE MINUTES LATER

Feeling galvanized after her one-eighty in the garden, a most spirited Fiona enters the lobby, her eyes scanning the large space for possible Lana Compton fans. Seeing a well-dressed older man speaking with the concierge, Fiona waits until he's ready to walk away.

"Excuse me, sir. I know this is very random and out of the blue, but I was wondering if you're familiar with the work of the late, great Lana Compton."

He thinks for a moment as he straightens his tie. "My mother was a big fan. Said the lady could sing and dance like nobody's business. But when Miss Compton left musicals behind to make more serious movies, my mother rarely spoke about her again. I think she thought the world was changing and becoming a less-happy place."

"Oh. I take it your mother has passed."

"No. She's still with us."

Fiona brightens. "I'm Lana Compton's daughter! Do you think she'd like to talk to me?"

"I'm afraid my mother doesn't even know who *I* am anymore, much less your mother. Once in a while, there's a spark of recognition … and in her heart, she knows I'm someone who loves her, but as for remembering Miss Compton, perhaps if she heard her sing, but I don't think she'd have much to say. She lives in a fine facility about an hour from here. I see her as often as I can." He looks at his expensive watch. "I've got to run. My wife is waiting for me. Seems she's always waiting for me." He nods a good-bye, if one can properly do so, and strolls purposefully away toward the elevator banks.

Defeated, but undeterred, Fiona spots an older woman with bright-red hair sitting in the center lobby, peeking out from behind a newspaper. She hurries over to her and takes a seat on the same small couch. "Hello there."

"Hello," comes the skeptical greeting.

"I'm just going to come out and say this because you look like a very cultured woman who's well immersed in the arts."

"Oh, well, I suppose you could say that."

"I'm Lana Compton's daughter. You know, the movie star."

"I certainly know her name. Haven't heard it for years. I never got to see many movies in my youth. My parents were cruel people and didn't think movies were a good use of my time. I saw my share of ballet and opera, but only because attending those performances reflected well on them. To hell with what it did for me."

"I see." Fiona is irritated that the woman still holds the newspaper up. "If you'd like to put the paper down, maybe we can talk."

Her request is ignored. "And now, as fate would have it, my own daughter wants nothing to do with me, and my husband has left me for a slut."

"I'm so sorry."

"Do you have any children?"

"Oh no. I've always been kind of a loner." Fiona grits her teeth. "This is a bit awkward, ma'am, but my mother wore lots of wigs in her movies, and so I've learned a lot about wearing them."

"And your point is …."

"Only that yours is a bit crooked. It's longer on the left."

Millicent slams the paper down and looks at Fiona. "Do you know why I'm even wearing this garish thing? I'll tell you. Because my estranged daughter works here, and this is the only way for me to catch a glimpse of her. I've begged her to reconsider, but she keeps shutting me out. She has no earthly idea what love means."

Fiona sighs. "I don't know much about love either. But I know there aren't any specific rules. Love doesn't always come to you when you want or need it the most. And it's not always what you think it should be. It takes many forms. My college crush, my family, and my mother taught me that much … not intentionally, though. I know that love isn't something you can demand. In fact, the more you feel entitled to it, the less of it you'll have. Kind of funny that it works that way, but it does." She smiles. "Therapy often helps. It can be quite unburdening … not to mention enlightening … to speak with a trained professional who isn't emotionally involved in your life in any way. Maybe something to think about."

The aggrieved one is silent. Without saying a word, she leaves the newspaper on the couch and walks toward the front entrance, the invisible load on her shoulders nearly crushing her. The thoughts in her head, crying out for clarity and begging for validation, remain in great conflict with one another as she pushes her way through the revolving doors.

Ah, such wisdom Fiona has offered, yet, as is true for so many, when it comes to one's own life, sagacity is watered down to such an extent that it is unrecognizable. Undaunted, she gets up and approaches several more of the older residents milling about in the lobby. I see her take a few notes and present her business card to two willing souls.

I am given rare insight into the future.

Fiona, filled with new purpose, will spend her days and nights trying to regenerate (and perhaps rewrite) her mother's life and career as she waits for the world to remember her. The longer she chases this dream, after years of sloughing off the moniker of being "Lana Compton's daughter," the more improbable her chance for success will become. But this is what she will cling to for the rest of her days … until she enables the enhancements to provide her and Lana with a most beautiful reunion.

Chapter Twelve: DREAMERS

It is morning, and I see a man thrashing about in his bed. Where he is … I cannot say precisely. He is not in this building, but he is not far, either. His eyelids are fluttering, and he appears to be waking from a bad dream. Finally, his eyes open, and he stares at the ceiling, terrified. After thirty seconds, he sits up. Sweat is dripping down his face, and he has misplaced the wherewithal to wipe it off. He just stares straight ahead with his lips parted. "What the hell …," he mutters. "What the 'effin hell was that …?"

Fifteen minutes later, he has showered and clothed himself in an old gray sweat suit. Shaving, I shall presume, is of no importance today. At the kitchen table, he reaches for the butter, but as he's placed it slightly too far from reach, he gives up. Instead, he looks at his coffee and dry bagel as if the world has ended and only the three of them are left.

Moments later, another man, clean shaven, attired in pressed jeans and a crisp pale-yellow Oxford shirt, his hair neatly gelled into submission, strides happily into the kitchen, stopping suddenly upon discovering the disturbing apocalyptic simulation at the kitchen table. "What's got you so befuddled, mate? I know it's Saturday and you like to take things more slowly, but I'd wager a sloth could beat you handily in a foot race." He walks over to the coffee pot and pours himself a cup." You've been a bit off all week, but this morning, well, you look more knackered and out of sorts than usual." He pours a bit of cream into his cup, walks to the table, pulls out a chair, and sits. "Wanna tell me about it?"

"Sorry, Jamie. I know I'm not at my best." He makes a second failed attempt to reach the butter.

"Seriously?" Jamie slides the butter over to him. "Need me to put that on your bagel for you too? C'mon, Mark. Talk to me."

Mark picks up the butter knife and then promptly puts it down as if he can't be bothered. He takes a small bite of the dry bagel. Chewing is arduous, and he grimaces until the food is swallowed. "To hell with it." He pushes the plate away.

Jamie slides the plate to his place, takes the bagel half without a missing bite, butters it, and eats.

Mark watches. "You want to drink my coffee too?"

"Got my own." Jamie points to his cup. "This is my coffee. That is your coffee. I'd imagine it's on the cold side, if you've been giving it the same attention as the bagel." He takes a few sips from his own cup. "See, mate? This is how you do it. Lift and drink. Couldn't be easier."

Shooting him a dirty look, Mark takes a sip of his coffee.

"Well done. I knew you had it in you."

"England called last night," Mark says without emotion. "They want you back."

Jamie laughs. "Once more with feeling. You're the easiest flatmate I've ever had, but damned if you aren't the strangest." His face turns serious. "You mentioned a bad dream a few days ago. I'd say you looked rather agitated ... perhaps a bit unraveled, but as we were both on our way to work, I didn't press. Maybe now would be a good time to have a proper chat."

Mark says nothing.

"More dreams?"

"You could say that." Mark finally perks up. "You know, I've made some bad mistakes in my life. I should never have taken that job in London when I found out I was going to be a father, but I did ... and regrets can't change the past. Hey, we were flatmates then, too, so you know how haunted I was with nightmares ... and daymares ...

but these … well, you'll think I'm crazy."

"Already do." Jamie grins. "I took this job in your neck of the woods just so I could continue to witness the lunacy." He laughs. "So you might as well tell all." He waits for a response. "I'm all ears. Tell me about your dreams."

"That's just it, Jamie. They're not *my* dreams."

"Then whose the hell are they?"

"I wish I knew."

"Not mine, I hope. Because I've had some pretty scrummy ones of late, and wouldn't want you poking about ….." He sees the look of fear on Mark's face. "Sorry. I'll stop yakking. And being so insensitive."

Mark takes a sip of his coffee. "This is cold."

Without saying a word, Jamie stands, takes Mark's cup, empties it into the sink, pours him a new cup, and brings it back to the table. "Black. As you like it. Only hot now." He sits again.

"Thanks." Mark takes several sips. "Like I said, they're not *my* dreams. And I know that sounds, like you always say, as if I've lost the plot, but I promise you, I haven't." He thinks. "At least I don't think so."

"I'm listening." Jamie picks up the remainder of the toasted bagel and finishes it.

"Well, at the beginning of the week, I had this dream that I was a woman, having it on with some man. Yeah, yeah, I know where you want to take that, but please don't. There was nothing sensual about it. Even in the dream, I said to myself, 'This doesn't belong to me. Why am I dreaming for and about these people? Who are they?'" He sighs. "Sheesh, Jamie. I've had dreams about women, but never in my forty-six years on this planet did I dream I *was* a woman, much less one I didn't know … having it on with some strange dude."

Jamie presses his lips together, but his eyes are quite talkative.

"Yeah, yeah. I know. You want to tell me *I'm* the strange dude.

I've known you too many years not to hear your thoughts, but please, I'm serious."

"So you didn't know the bloke or the woman?"

"No. I didn't. But it wasn't a dream where I was watching them like some Peeping Tom perv. It was like I *was* her. And trust me, the whole dream was every bit as fucked up as it sounds."

"Blimey!" Jamie exhales his incredulity. "Did this happen on Monday? When I asked you what was wrong and you said I'd never believe you?"

"It did." Mark drinks some more coffee and is now quite animated. "When I woke up Tuesday, it was from a dream where I took my boy to the lake for a father-and-son day in the outdoors. Let me tell you, I felt relieved the craziness was gone. I made a mental note to actually plan a trip soon and happily went off to the office." He pauses. "But then Wednesday came. I dreamed I was the woman again. But this time, she was arguing with a man she called Patrick ... her husband apparently."

"No shagging then, I take it."

"Hell no. But he was on her case big time ... for cheating on him *again* ... and said he wanted a divorce. The fight was super intense. He said he was done forgiving her for something she was never going to stop doing ... and that he never thought her exploits would extend to ... well, he got kind of explicit there. Said she had the morals of a two-bit whore. And that he wasn't going to keep quiet about it. He said he didn't care if her employer, coworkers, friends, family, or neighbors knew because she'd asked for it."

"Whoa ... this is heavy."

"That's an understatement. It was heavy as all get out ... mostly because it was like he was talking to *me* and I was *her.* Mind-boggling stuff. And then, in this dream, I was begging him to forgive me while he flung a slew of accusations at me for things I didn't even know people did to one another."

Jamie speaks cautiously. "Not trying to take the piss out of you, seriously, but in the dream, being her and hearing all of this … did you cry?"

"Not so much. Only a little. I remember feeling vengeful and angry, like I'd be damned if I'd let this bastard destroy my life, though I was aware that I'd done some pretty bad things. But I had a strong sense of entitlement that told me I could do anything I wanted and that didn't deserve consequences that might befit other people. Like I was some kind of special. So hard to describe." He rubs his eyes. "I was alternating between trying to sound reasonable, then cursing at him again. I had an exceptionally foul and creative mouth." He stops to replay the horror. "It was horrendous. More realistic than most dreams. Like I was obsessively reliving something that had already happened … as opposed to conjuring up some fantasy. You know?"

"Did the woman look familiar to you?"

"No! Because I was *her*."

"What?"

"Can you see your face now as you're talking to me?"

"Guess not. Okay, I get it. So how about this Patrick bloke?"

"Zero clue who he is. Nothing remotely familiar about him." He takes some more coffee. "You had an early conference call on Wednesday, so you were gone when I got up and missed hearing the story and seeing my horror-stricken face."

"Well, if it was anything like what I saw a bit ago."

"Today was the worst." Mark finishes his coffee and stands. "This morning, I was her again. And guess what I did?"

"I think I'd better stay seated. What did you do?"

"Handed a wad of cash to some guy in an alley next to an inner-city bar. This time, I couldn't hear the specific words, only loud-ass music coming from the place, but I knew what was going down. And then I saw her husband's lifeless body floating in the air … dripping blood … right past us as we were talking. But I was the only one who could see it."

"Bloody hell. Literally." Jamie takes a moment to absorb the shocking details. "She was putting a hit out on him?"

"Bingo! And I remember feeling like I ... *she* ... didn't feel any remorse. Almost like a weight lifted from my ... *her* shoulders. Then, I was thinking about the guy she was with in the first dream ... and about how ... oh, this is too weird to say."

"How you wanted to shag him again."

"Yeah. Except it was *her* dream. *She* wanted him. Not me. And I was suddenly in this room with a fancy king-sized bed. It was made up nicely, like in some luxury hotel where they put mints on pillows. Except when I looked more closely, I saw there was a sinkhole in the middle of the bed. He was nowhere to be found, but his leather jacket was draped over a nearby chair, so I knew he'd been there. I wanted to check and see if he'd fallen through, as I figured he had, but I was afraid if I got any closer, he'd pull me down there with him and I'd never see the light of day again. It was rather terrifying, actually."

"And that's everything so far?"

"Why? You want more? Like what she wanted to do with him?"

"No, definitely not." Jamie stands. "I'd really like to stay and talk to you about this some more, but Carly and I are spending the day together. Sorry."

"No problem. I remember. Hey, have a good time. But I'm asking you, Jamie, as my friend for these many years, please ... keep this between us."

"Not a word." Jamie walks over and pats Mark on the back. "Have a good day, mate." He pulls a face. "If you can."

Mark walks into the living room and flops onto the couch. His face is very intense. He is clearly ruminating on the dreams. After ten minutes of visible consternation, his expression changes to one of shock and enlightenment. "Oh my God. I know exactly ...." He looks around in a panic. "Where the hell is my phone?"

TWO DAYS LATER

I know not where the previous narrative took place, only that I am back within the confines of my all-too familiar home. I am drawn to a large unit on the fourth floor. There is a den off the living room where a woman named Denise sits at her desk. I believe her to be an architect. In the living room, sitting restlessly at a curved Hollywood Regency piano desk, is a girl, eight, who is finishing up something in a workbook. She stops, erases what she has written, then writes something in its place. Frustrated, she calls to her mother, "How do you spell 'irritate,' Mommy? I wrote it like I spell 'ear' but it doesn't look right."

An angry voice replies. "Damn it, Gracie. How many times do I have to tell you to pick up your dictionary and look it up? You're supposed to learn the meaning *and* the spelling." Denise, a brunette with excessive blonde highlights, gold hoop earrings, and tight clothing, comes marching out of the den and stands by her daughter's chair. "Isn't it funny you should be stuck on the word 'irritate' … being something you do to me *so* well. I should have never agreed to homeschool you. But you had to get yourself thrown out of three schools … and there weren't any left. So abracadabra and all of that … I'm a teacher. I didn't go to architectural school for this low-level nonsense."

This woman is quite the drama queen … and the snob, but my second sight allows me to know that the child was behaving inappropriately in class due to lack of sleep, general agitation, and inability to focus or take direction. Could this be due to a less-than-kind mother? I aim to discover more.

Denise picks a red dictionary from the floor and drops it on the desk. "Look the word up." I must say, she is giving the child quite a menacing look.

Trembling, the child picks up the book and goes to the "E" tab.

"Oh, for f— …." She stops herself from using foul language, but I can intuit with certainty she has done so a multitude of times before. Grabbing the dictionary, Denise looks up the word, then slams the book on the desk with her index finger pointing to 'irritate.' "I want you to write the word twenty-five times. No, make that fifty. And make sure you remember the meaning of it: annoy, make angry. You know, what you do to me every waking hour."

The child takes a page from her mother's playbook. "Oh, well, then you irritate me too, Mommy. Every day. You're a bad teacher. All you do is yell. You yell at Daddy, and you yell at me. And you yell at people on the phone. You say bad words and irritate lots of people." She pauses. "Am I using the word right?"

Denise bites her bottom lip hard before speaking. "Do you have any clue what I've sacrificed for you? This week alone, I've made more mistakes on my designs than I care to admit. I look like a rank amateur. Are you trying to make me lose my job so I'll have more time to waste playing teacher?" She fumes. "Because of you, I got so distracted on a simple design that I left a tree sitting in the middle of a driveway. Do you know how stupid that makes me look?"

Gracie cringes. "Like spelling 'irritate' starting with 'ear?'" She giggles.

"Yes." Denise says, putting her hands on her hips to assert her authority. "That's exactly what it's like. And thanks to you, the other day, I forgot a bedroom window in the master suite, and last week I left the laundry room out of a condo. And guess whose fault that is?"

"Yours."

"No. Not mine. Yours, Gracie." Grabbing her daughter's arm, Denise yanks her up from her chair and drags her over to the pink-

and-purple curved-back sofa. "Sit!"

"Don't talk to me like I'm a dog."

Livid, Denise sits on the sofa with her. "It's no wonder nobody wanted you in their school."

Gracie is bold. "One teacher asked me if my parents were mean to me at home. And I said, 'Not Daddy, never Daddy. But Mommy screams at me … when she's even home.' And the teacher asked what I meant by that, and I told her that when Daddy has to go away for business, that you leave me with a babysitter and sometimes make her stay all night."

Denise is stupefied. "You told the teacher that?" She mumbles some ugly words. "You're a spiteful little brat, Gracie. Even when I'm not with you, I have dreams about you. I'm so upset by everything you do that I have stupid dreams that feel like they don't even belong to me."

"Bad dreams?"

"No. Like I said. Stupid dreams. Like I'm some strange man sitting at a desk and putting numbers into a proposal. Then, picking up a frame with a picture of a woman and a little boy and thinking how much I want to be with them. And then I'm at this lake, sitting with a boy on a big flat rock, just looking around and feeling very peaceful and happy, and wishing the woman in the picture was with us. I can wager a guess what that's about."

Gracie's eyes widen.

"I'll bet that's me, wishing I had a little boy instead of you."

Tears well in Gracie's eyes, but Denise doesn't care.

"I'll bet I'm dreaming I'm a man so I can rid myself of being your mother. Or maybe the woman I'm thinking about is a babysitter who decided to adopt you." She thinks. "Oh, yeah. That makes so much sense." She pauses … most likely to think of another ugly thing to say. "I hate homeschooling you. It's maddening, exhausting, and all you do is complain. God forbid you should thank me. I'm working half days so I can give you my full attention."

Wiping her eyes, Gracie appears angry. "You don't give me your attention. You're always on the phone with someone. And I hear you whispering and making kissy sounds. Gross." She gives her mother an uncompromising stare. "You open a book and tell me, 'read this,' and then you go back to that person who isn't Daddy. You're not like a real teacher. You never explain stuff or anything." She huffs. "I get tired of just reading all day. I want someone to talk to me like a real teacher does."

Denise picks up a throw pillow and punches it. "Really. Then why did you get yourself chucked out of three damn schools, Gracie?"

"Because you ... because you ... yell so much and don't let me sleep, and I can't concentrate, and I get mad at other kids and lots of other stuff. Then the kids talk bad about me, and I get into fights."

The poor pillow takes another right hook to the jaw. "And that's my fault, is it?"

"Yes."

"You're a liar, Gracie. Like just now, you said that you're tired of reading all day. Well, that's a big fat lie that needs to lose some weight. You think? Just last week, what did I do? I'll tell you what I did. I went and collected as many old magazines as I could find. Even asked neighbors for them. Then, I pulled all my company's old annual reports out of the box in my closet. I gave everything to you, along with a pair of scissors and paste. I taught you how to make collages, just like I did when I was your age. Didn't I do that, Gracie?"

"Yeah. I guess."

"Then it would be a lie to say that all you do is read, wouldn't it?"

"I don't know."

"I've told you a million times to learn to think for yourself ... to amuse yourself ... and to learn to be more creative. Because you know what, Gracie? You won't get anywhere in life if you don't have creativity. You'll have to rely on other people to solve every problem for you. And people won't want to do that."

"I *am* creative. Daddy will tell you that. I made a whole storybook for him. With pictures, words, and everything."

"Charming."

"What time is Daddy coming home?"

"He's not."

"What does that mean?"

"It means he's on a long business trip. A forever one. Daddy doesn't like living with you and me anymore, so he'll probably never come home again."

"That's a lie! Daddy likes living with me a lot. He told me I'm his favorite person in the world." Her eyes narrow as she looks at her mother. "But you're not."

Denise stands. "You'll soon find out I'm telling you the truth, you blue-eyed, big-mouthed irritant. Now go back to your desk and finish your spelling workbook. I need to make some calls. And get this through your head: your father is *not* coming home."

FOUR DAYS LATER

I know this much. Just as her mother said, Gracie's father has not come home. Now, as Darah sits with Denise on the couch, Timmy and Gracie are huddled together in corner by her desk, on the floor, playing a game of cards. But alas, Gracie's spirits are down and Timmy notices. As much as the boy is inclined to ask questions, he knows that this is not the time. His mother made a special point on this day to admonish him, "If Gracie wants to tell you something, she will." And of course, Timmy asked why she was making such an unusual statement, but she told him that he would find out later.

"Gracie is quieter than I've ever seen her," Darah says.

Peeved, Denise deigns to answer. She throws an apathetic glance in the direction of the children. "She's with her best friend. Some days, people don't have a lot to say. Like right now, I'm kind of the same way. You know?"

"I see that."

Denise squirms uncomfortably. "So why didn't you just drop Timmy off like you usually do? Why are you hanging around trying to make me uncomfortable? It's not like we're best buds." She pauses. "Hold on. I left my phone in the other room and I need to take this call that's coming in. Not that I need to explain …"

Denise runs into the den. I can see, as can Darah, that she is extremely agitated. Walking in furious circles, she is trying to keep her voice low as she speaks to the caller. Realizing that Darah can see her, and that she is not offering a favorable optic, she ends the call and comes back into the living room.

Darah grimaces. The atmosphere is extraordinarily toxic.

"Work nonsense." Denise takes a seat as if being made to do so. "It's always something with those people. You must know what a bitch it is to deal with people."

Before Denise can respond, the doorbell rings. Sitting in the corner, with hope in her eyes, Gracie looks up.

"I'm not expecting anyone." Denise pushes herself up from the couch as if there is no greater imposition.

Concerned, Darah looks at the children to make sure they are okay.

"What the hell?" Denise screams as she opens the door. "Patrick! How the hell can you be here?"

"Daddy!" Gracie screams as she runs over and throws her arms around him. "I missed you so much."

The tall man in the tailored suit lights up. "I've missed you too, Love Buggy. More than you know." He offers a big smile. "Can you take Timmy in your bedroom while Daddy talks to Mommy?"

"No. I can't, Daddy. I'm afraid if I can't see you that you'll be gone when I come out. Please, don't make me."

Darah observes the interaction with interest.

"What the impossible fuck?" Denise says, staring at Patrick as her eyes bulge out of their sockets.

Patrick looks down at Gracie. "Let's make a deal, sweetie pie. How about if you stay in the room, but you go back over and sit with Timmy? Can you do that for me?"

"Sure, Daddy." The child loosens her grip on him. "I'm so happy to see you. Mommy said you were never coming home again."

"Oh, I'll bet she did," He gives her a kiss on the forehead. "Go on now, honey." He waits until Gracie has taken a seat next to Timmy again. He speaks quite softly. "As you can see, Denise, I'm very much alive and well. No thanks to you."

"I should have killed you myself, you boring piece of self-righteous garbage."

Before he can answer, Mark walks into the apartment, making a path to Darah, who is clearly expecting him.

Timmy looks at Gracie. "That's my daddy. I told you he was real."

"How come I never saw him before?"

Too excited to answer her, Timmy shouts, "Daddy," gets up, and runs into his father's arms.

"How's my boy," Mark says, lifting him into the air. "Heavy. Very heavy."

"Something weird is going on," Timmy says as his father lowers him to the floor. "Isn't it? You never come here … not ever."

Mark furrows his brow. "Can you go over and sit with your friend for a while?"

"How come her dad wants us to sit together too? So we can't hear what grownups are saying? How come you don't want me to know what you're gonna say to Mommy now? How come—"

Mark scruffs up the hair on the top of Timmy's head. "You know, I'd really love for you and Gracie to go into her room right now. That would make your daddy so happy."

Timmy shakes his head. "Nope. She won't go. She's afraid her daddy will disappear again. She already told me five times she's not going where she can't see him."

"Then how about you go back and sit with her. Looks like she's got a pile of something interesting and colorful on her lap. Maybe she'll share it with you."

"Oh, yeah. She's doing some art stuff." He eyes both his parents. "Can we all have dinner together tonight?"

"Absolutely, sweetheart," Darah says. "In fact, I think we're going to be having dinner together a whole lot more."

"Are you getting back together?" He makes a face. "That's a weird question because I don't really remember you being together." He laughs. "I guess you had to be together to make me, right? Were you both naked?"

Darah turns red and looks at Mark. "'How did I get here, Mommy?' That will go down in history as Timmy's first, but not last, awkward question. Also as the *most* awkward question. One I always hoped he'd ask you instead of me."

Blushing, Mark laughs. "Come on, now. Skedaddle, Timbo. We'll talk later."

I now focus on the action at the front door where more ugly words are exchanged between Denise and Patrick, but before completely skewering her husband, she takes a moment to address Mark. "So you're the phantom daddy nobody's ever seen." She now chooses to mimic Darah. "I prefer Timmy to see his father elsewhere. I'm the owner of this place, and it's just easier to keep people out of our business that way." Denise sneers at her. "But you're good with sticking your nose into my business, aren't you, Darah?"

"My personal business is the least of your worries right now."

Highly agitated, it is clear the wheels are turning in Denise's head as she weighs her options. The words "flight risk" come to mind, but before I can offer more extensive commentary, I must report that two men in blue are now at the front door, which nobody has ever thought to close, looking directly at Denise. The burlier of the two speaks.

"Denise Rochelle Castlebury. You are under arrest for Solicitation of Murder. You have the right to remain silent. Anything you say can and will be used against you in a court of law. You have the right to an attorney. If you cannot afford one, one will be provided for you. Do you understand the rights I have just read to you? With these rights in mind, do you wish to speak to me?"

"How the hell is this happening?" she screams.

Mark leaves Darah's side and approaches Denise. "In the interest of keeping her work and personal life separate, my son's mother never told you that the two of us have been employed by the same architectural firm for years. Having different last names, you wouldn't have had reason to connect us if we'd met. But I've heard stories about you, have seen you from afar, and I must say, your colorful language is legendary."

Denise mutters some vile combinations of words that I shall not repeat.

"I don't know how it happened, and I suppose it might mess with my head for the rest of my life, but I had three dreams that weren't mine. They were yours. Yeah, that sounds pretty freakin' crazy, but I did. I imagined your pleasure … um … with some man I can't identify. That was the first dream. Then, I was you again … fighting with *this* man," he says, nodding in Patrick's direction. "And I actually heard you call him by name. 'Patrick.' It was one hell of a brawl."

"What kind of rank bullshit is this, Mr. Timmy's father? What the hell do your dreams have to do with me? Nothing. Absolutely nothing!"

Stalwart in a crisis, Mark continues. "In the third dream, I saw you … standing in an alley near some raucous bar. You were handing a wad of cash to some lowlife and—"

"Shut your mouth. Now!"

"In my dreams, I felt as if I were you. Only I didn't know who you were. About an hour after I woke up, I just kept going over and over it all in my head, trying to make some sense of everything. Then, about an hour after I woke up, it all came together: the language you used … it was so, well, 'colorful,' and I suddenly realized I'd heard you outside of my office one day, dressing down one of my assistants, and you were the woman with the 'legendary mouth' who would never still be employed if she didn't work from home. I just knew that I'd had your dreams, somehow, as far-fetched as it seems, even though no explanation exists. I asked around to find out your husband's first name … and well, that confirmed your identity."

"Oh, really? Well, guess what, asshole? I had your dreams too. You were mumbling incessantly … more like whining … about how you'd never forgive yourself for making 'the worst decision of your life.' Ironically, as you were regretting one bad decision, you were simultaneously making another: cooking the books at the firm. And then you'd look at a photo on your desk and smile. I knew, clear as anything, that you were embezzling for your family to make up for abandoning them." She turns to the officers. "He's a thief. Arrest him."

"I don't know what you saw in your dream, the one that should have been mine, but I was working hard on a proposal, and yeah, as Darah and I have been talking about resolving past hurts and becoming a real family, that's kind of been on my mind. And yes, I look at their photos quite a lot. But 'cooking the books,' nah. First, I'm not in any sort of accounting position, and two, that's just not my nature. I'm just your run-of-the-mill law-abiding citizen. Sorry to disappoint. And you're seriously not one to talk about making bad decisions."

Denise screams at the cops. "You can't arrest me for what this douche bag dreams."

"We're not, ma'am," the slender officer says. "The information provided to us happened to check out. As preposterous as his story sounded, we know not to discount some of the unusual ways we receive tips. We have several psychics who have solved crimes for us in the past. We had more than enough information to locate the 'gentleman' you hired. By the way, he's been apprehended and is willing to testify against you. So, as you can see, in the end, this man was right."

"Let's go, Mrs. Castlebury," the burly officer says.

"This is insane!" Denise screams. "It's absolutely insane. Just because this loser and I work for the same architectural firm, it means nothing. This is someone's idea of a very sick game. Maybe I'm not even awake. In fact, I think right now, I'm having the worst dream of my life. I just don't understand it."

"Ma'am. It's time to go."

"How the hell did this happen? I need to know."

Just as the officers are about to escort Denise out, Gracie comes running toward them, waving a large piece of paper in her hand. "Remember how you told me to be creative, Mommy? I took one of those old reports from your company. I cut Timmy's daddy's head out of one picture, even though I didn't know who he was … and I cut your head out of another. Then I just put your heads on each other's bodies. Cool, huh? She beams with pride, then stares at her mother. There is an eerie chill in the room as the child, just for a moment in time, seems wise … and perhaps cynical … beyond her years. "That's so creative, isn't it, Mommy?"

Chapter Thirteen: LARK

There is an apartment on the third floor that never gets visitors. More precisely, I should say the occupant does not. I do recall, however, the time a kind neighbor brought up a package from the lobby (because it was an unclaimed eyesore), but that was a solid decade ago.

It is late afternoon, and the occupant is reading the casting calls in the entertainment newspaper. Her red knock-off Prada frames are attached to a colorful beaded chain around her neck, and her brown-and-gray hair is partially covered by a red-and-white-polka-dot headband: courtesy of a wardrobe woman who recognized her inner sadness and gifted it to her. Was it really worn by a famous starlet in a 1950s film? Who knows? But she believes it was.

Well-known by most every casting director in town, it is not because she works often or is extraordinarily talented, but because she doesn't, and she isn't. It's because she never stops trying, and thus, her face is a familiar one. She is always cheerful and exudes genuine happiness for the success of others, despite having little of her own. There is also the small matter of her name: Lark, the brainchild of a fourteen-year-old who never gave up being known worldwide by four letters. She always planned to have it legally changed once she was famous ….

When Susan Jones (I suppose I'd wish to be called 'Lark' too), now in her late sixties, was a young girl, like so many millions of other future actors, she knew what she wanted to do the first time she saw a movie on the big screen. More than anything, daydreaming was her salvation … her escape.

Born to a single mother, who Susan always wished had given

her up for adoption, she was never special, nor did she have any family. No siblings, no aunts or uncles, and no father. When she was eleven, she learned that her father was a nameless stranger with whom her mother had stuffed herself into a phone-booth-sized women's toilet at a grungy rock club. In fact, her mother did consider adoption, but she thought having a child might give her a better, more respectable life. Nothing changed: she only became a bad mother who labored under the misconception that if you don't hit your child but merely neglect her, all is right with the world. Her mother never even took care with what to call her. When the nurse at the hospital asked what name should go on the birth certificate, she pointed to the woman's name tag, saw "Susan," and said, "That'll do." Considering everything about the father was unknown, the lack of interest in the child's name was sadly apropos.

At a young age, Susan inquired about her father and was told that he died after a "quick and serious illness." Years later, when she wanted to know how her name (and lack of a middle name) had been decided, her mother spit out the truth like a bitter seed. She not only offered the true story of how Susan was conceived, but also added that she and the sperm donor never even shared first names before … I will not repeat the vulgar way she described their fusing of body parts, but suffice it to say, she took pleasure in laying the truth bare.

Poor Susan was regularly teased and bullied throughout her school years. Mocked for her shabby clothes, unstyled hair, piteous mother, and for living in a trailer park, she sadly avoided friendships … even with those who liked her, not wanting them to be ridiculed for being her friend. She survived the traumatic school years with an I'll-show-them-all attitude, which she considered her secret weapon. She had two real friends. The first one was an 'army brat,' but the relationship lasted only two years when the boy's father was reassigned two thousand miles away. Most of the neighbors at the trailer park were senior citizens, so the only time she saw any children outside of school was when their grandkids came for a visit … with one exception: her next-door neighbor. Julsie, a young woman one year Susan's senior, lived with her grandmother. One of twelve children scattered about the land, she was the only girl Susan ever trusted enough to confide in. Also, Susan felt sorrier for her than she did for herself. The girl had a rough go of it, and Susan believed Julsie was destined to live in the trailer park forever.

From the ninth through to the twelfth grade, Susan worked at a bowling alley down the road, saving every possible cent so she'd be able to leave town as soon as she graduated. And she did. The maternal unit half-heartedly wished her a good life, and the two never spoke again.

And thus, Lark was born. It would be an exercise in mediocrity to detail her less-than-extraordinary existence in her new environment. I will say that she managed to earn a living by working as an extra, clapping enthusiastically in TV show audiences, and sometimes working in a neighbor's food truck when he was shorthanded. For four years, the young Lark attended acting classes, learned the basics, and got to know many who went on to great fame. Most, I shall say, were always kinder to her than her wretched schoolmates ever were. During those busy days of work and school, her free time was taken up memorizing lines for scenes. She thought about Julsie a great deal but never found time to write. Sadly, as she endeavored to scrub her first eighteen years from memory, Julsie was to become collateral damage.

To this day, Lark still earns a living doing much of what she did as a young woman. Auditioning was, and is still, one of her favorite activities. While most would have long given up, she has landed some meager roles over the years. Nothing gave her a bigger thrill than the first time she saw herself on the big screen, followed by her name on the end credits: Angry homeless woman: Lark. The second time was every bit as exciting: Cafeteria lady: Lark. But being known by all and shown kindness that eluded her as a youth, with the occasional small success, is the steam that powers her locomotive.

Is her existence happy … or is it sad … as she waits for a friendly chat or a small, yet cherished acting role? She has thousands of people who call her a friend, yet there is no one whom she sees beyond the audition room, the wrapping of a day's work on set, or the occasional work-related party. Indeed, she is one of the most solitary figures I have ever observed. And while many might think she should want more, which I'm certain is true on a deeper level, Lark works hard to maintain equanimity, to avoid conflict, and to control her life so that little rattles her. It is her survival elixir, and she doses herself with it daily. Life, of course, is never a straight line.

Two years ago, the line moved. She had a dream about Julsie, and upon waking, nostalgia prompted her to write a letter to her friend at the old residence, offering her address and catching her up on the missed years. It was a fairly easy letter to compose, but fear gripped her as she went to mail it. But she did. For a long while, she waited to hear back. There was nothing. Lark always hoped Julsie had received the missive, even if she couldn't, or didn't wish to respond. Even more so, she hoped her old friend had moved on to a happier life.

And now, ten years after someone came to her apartment to deliver a package, two years after she mailed that letter, another person is outside the door, intent on a far more personal encounter.

Lark rises from her favorite piece of furniture in the world: a red-velvet tufted sofa edged with satin fringe. It makes her feel like a movie star. She has two matching chairs nearby, in which she sometimes imagines her famous friends are seated for a lively interaction. One of the chairs, however, is occupied. Seated on a folded red beach towel is her Cairn Terrier, Scruffer McGruffer. He was gifted to her by a production assistant (one of many people who has shown kindness toward a sad soul) whose parents breed the terriers. I am unclear whether "McGruffer" was meant to be a middle name or a surname ... I only know she did not wish him to be Scruffer Jones.

Peering through the peephole, Lark sees a bleached blonde, with ghastly teased hair, who is approximately her age and clad in some mixture of Bohemian attire. The patterns on her skirt are having a knockdown-dragout with her blouse (a lose-lose situation) and the clunky Navajo jewelry appears to weigh as much as a small car. Her violet lipstick matches nothing at all, but Lark, unafraid yet trepidatious, opens the door.

"Hi there." The woman chews mightily on her gum. "Are you Susan? I'm Debbie ... from junior high and high school. It's been over fifty years, but my heart (she pounds her chest) has been begging me to find you again."

Dumbfounded, Lark only stares while Debbie chews.

"I didn't think you'd recognize me. There were a whole lot of Debbies in our class, huh? Debbies, Susans, Cindys, Barbaras, Janets ... names of the day, right? I count seven with my name, and a whole lot of girls had yours." Now self-conscious, she is aware that her incessant mastication is irksome to the ear. "Bet I know what you're thinking: this gum is going to heaven because I'm chewing the hell out of it. Am I right?" Reeking of nicotine, her laughter is unsurprisingly reminiscent of the dry grinding of gears on a dying car.

Lark has no response. Scruffer, who is no longer content to rest in the midst of such an odd occurrence—a visitor—rushes to his mother's side. With a gentle hand motion, she instructs him to be calm and sit.

"Okay, I'll ditch the gum." Debbie reaches into the pocket of a large dirty plaid bag by her side, folds the gum into the corner of a magazine page, and stashes it back into the pocket. "'Done and dusted,' as they say."

Lark is nonplussed. "I don't remember you."

"Oh, yeah, that. I'd kind of be surprised if you did. My hair was kind of dark back in the day … and like I said … there were a lot of Debbies. You don't look like I remember you either. Fifty years. It changes people. Remember how we set our hair every night and slept in those crazy plastic rollers? Anything to look beautiful, right?"

"I never did that." Lark is feeling a bit shaky, and Scruffer, who intuits as much, nuzzles against her leg, his eyes fixed on the intruder.

"Those are some crazy slippers you've got on." Debbie looks down at Lark's red faux-fur red pom-pom slippers. "They match your fancy PJs well."

"It's a velour leisure suit, and I'm going to say good-bye." Lark puts a hand on the door, feeling nauseated as the smell of stale smoke lays claim to her olfactory senses.

"No. Please don't close the door. I'm sorry, Susan. This is just incredibly awkward." She huffs and puffs to illustrate her inner torment. "See, I'm here because I bullied you in school. And the guilt, well, it's been eating me alive for years. I owe you a huge apology. I know I look totally different, but then again, so do you."

Lark takes her hand away from the door. "I can't place you at all. But there were a whole lot of people in the bully club. I've tried to forget about all of them." She bristles internally. "How did you find me, anyway?"

"Oh, your old neighbor gave me your address."

Poor Lark feels those words in her gut. As much as she is glad to know her letter reached Julsie, she is sad that instead of a response, this person whom she cannot and does not wish to recall stands at her door. "I see."

"So will you let me in? Listen, hun, I've been rehearsing this apology for years." She thinks. "And I'm all out of gum … so there's that." She peers into the apartment. "Wowzers! Looks like a movie star lives here." She gulps. "I know; I talk too much. That was part of my problem back in school. If I'd kept my yap shut, a whole lot of people would have been better off."

"Okay. Come in." Lark's tone is not a welcoming one. The people who know her now would not recognize her. Susan's old defenses have come roaring back, and Lark is fearful of where they might take her.

Stone-faced, Lark points to the chair without Scruffer's towel. "You can sit here."

"Oh, boy oh boy. Your red accent wall matches your clothes … and the furniture." The intruder cranes her neck as she sits to see more of Lark's apartment. "That chandelier floor lamp is fabulous. The sconces are to die for. Looks like everything in here is even older than we are, huh?" The wretched laugh follows, quickly turning itself into a hacking cough. She reaches into the pocket of her bag and pulls out a bunch of pamphlets, splaying them on the coffee table before Lark can stop her.

"What are you doing?"

Debbie reels back in stupefaction. "Hun, I just put some folders on your table. Chill, please. These are from the Former Bullies Club. They're filled with stories of people apologizing to those they bullied. One of the stories in there is mine … written for you."

Scruffer jumps off his chair, puts his paws on the table, and pushes the pamphlets to the floor, then playfully slides them around.

Indignation takes hold of the intruder as she angrily picks up the folders. "My God, how is it that you've trained your dog to do that?" She gets down on her knees and picks up the prized pamphlets.

"I didn't teach him that at all. As a matter of fact, I've tried to teach him not to do that. But messing up papers is his thing. I call him my little paper pusher. I can tell you this; what my dog does with paper is far less harmful than messing with someone's self-worth."

"Well, I guess you told *me*!" Debbie sticks the pamphlets back into her wretched carry-all bag (I shudder to imagine what else it might contain) and reclaims her seat. "This really isn't going well.

Maybe a slight do-over?"

"Some things can't be done over." Lark sees Scruffer eyeing her newspaper, so carefully folds it and puts it behind her back for safekeeping. "Back to your chair, boy."

"You're right, Susan. I can't take back what I did in high school. But if it makes you feel better, I've come to sorely regret it."

"Really? How did that come about?"

The intrusive one wiggles her posterior as if she is preparing for a great speech. "Well, as is the catalyst for so many transformations in our lives, I met a man. It was love at first sight and when he asked me out, I thought he simply *had* to be talking to someone else because luck doesn't exactly shadow me, ya know?" She plays with a stretch bracelet made of round turquoise beads. "Damn, I'm so worried 'cause this one bead is cracked and looks like it's going to break in half. You don't have any glue, do you?"

Lark's patience is wearing thin. "No. And if you're that worried you'll lose the bead, take off the bracelet and stow it until you find some glue."

"You snuck a 'stow it' in there. Would I be crazy to think there's a bit of payback in that sentence?"

Lark sighs in disgust. "Yes, you'd be wrong. You know, I don't remember you or any of the other kids who made my life hell. But I know this much: I don't like you any better now."

Debbie puts both palms up in the air. "Whoa … truce. Me and my big mouth. Old habits die hard, and I've yet to put this one fully out of its misery. Please, Susan. I really am a very different person. May I continue?"

"I guess."

Debbie reaches into her bag and pulls out a pack of cigarettes. "You don't mind if I have a smoke to calm my nerves, do you, hun?"

"You're welcome to leave and calm your nerves outside. But no, you can't smoke in here. It's illegal, actually. Even if it wasn't …."

"Ugh." Stuffing the pack back into her bag, she continues. "Well, I was having the loveliest dinner with this man, when what does he share with me? He was bullied in school. I think my expression changed so drastically that he knew I was either a victim or a bully, but I explained that I was a bully-victim. Do you know that term?"

"Someone bullied you, so you took it out on other people to regain your power. Is that right?"

"It is. Oh, Susan, I'm so glad you understand."

Lark's usually cheery face has no sympathy or tolerance. "I was bullied by at least fifty people in the first eighteen years of my life. And I've never said an unkind word to a soul ... a habit I'm coming precariously close to breaking. Moving away and making a better life for myself was how I chose to 'regain my power.' Making another person feel as terrible as I did never crossed my mind. Just the opposite, actually." She fights back the tears she wants no one to see. "Nonetheless, I have my scars. I know what I can handle, and what I can't. I'm a very social hermit ... a hybrid of sorts, but it works for me."

What a brave revelation. Something Lark has never said aloud or even admitted to herself, despite her ritualistic practices. Her hopeful eyes look at the intruder as she longs for validation.

Debbie drops her head. "I was going to tell you my story, but now I realize that it would be wrong to do that. Why should you have any sympathy for someone like me, whose father taunted her every waking hour? Whose older brother joined in on the cruelty just to win his father's approval? Whose mother turned a blind eye because she didn't want her husband to leave her? Who even bullied her daughter on occasion just to get on the bandwagon? I mean, why would you want to hear *that*?"

Lark deliberately exhales several labored breaths. Anger that she hasn't felt for a long time boils inside her. After spending her entire adult life avoiding confrontation, it is encroaching upon her again … in her own home.

Oblivious to Lark's body language, Debbie chews the cuticle on her index finger before prattling on. "Why would you want to hear that when I was fourteen, my brother burst into the bathroom with his friends when I was taking a shower? And that they all saw me naked? And took a photo with *my* Polaroid. Then, they laughed so hard their smiles almost fell off their faces. That was the most humiliating moment of my life … and I had to live it over and over and over again." She sighs dramatically and rips a hangnail from her right thumb with her teeth. "But you don't want to hear how that every boy in school, not to mention several girls, saw that photo? And that my parents thought it was a riot and told me to 'lighten up because we're all naked under our clothes.' They said I should be glad my older brother has such a great sense of humor. Why would you care if that caused me to say a few unkind words to you … when we met in junior high? Actually, truth is, every kid I spoke crap to should have taken the time to find out why … and show *me* some damn sympathy. But no, everyone was too wrapped up in their own petty little feelings to wonder why Debbie was hurting so much." She relives some favorite moments. "So what if I called you a few names? I'll bet your naked photo was never passed around for the world to see, was it?" Now she's is going to town on her left thumb.

Lark gulps in disgust as she pats the empty seat next to her. Hopping off his chair, Scruffer sits next to her. She scratches his neck as she mulls things over. "Are you finished with your 'apology' yet?"

"The more I think about it … say it all out loud … I don't think I owe you one." Her fury settles a bit. "But I've got a big heart, Susan, and some mutual forgiveness would be swell with me. I'm willing to say 'I'm sorry' … but only if you will too. I think that would be very healing for both of us."

Overwhelmed, Lark says nothing.

"I sure could use a smoke," Debbie mumbles as she surveys the apartment. "This looks quite roomy. It's a two-bedroom, yes?"

"I'm very happy here."

"And that's a non-answer. I know one when I hear one."

"What do you want from me?" Lark tries to shake off her unease. "You've made it quite clear that your heart was never 'begging you to find me.' That was a flat-out lie. And if you were abused, I'm truly sorry, but I'm not going to apologize for not acting on something I didn't know one of my abusers was going through. That's a bit much to expect of anyone, much less a teen girl. Furthermore, you're having yet another go at me ... because fifty years of adulthood hasn't done much, if anything, to make you a nicer person. Just the opposite, I'd say. But you have some other motivation for coming here, and I neither know nor care what it is. I just really want you to be on your way. I didn't work this hard to mask my vulnerability to let some stranger retraumatize me. And it kills me to say that, because I've done everything to convince myself that the choices I make are normal. Only they're not. I'm scared to death to let anyone get too close ... or to dream of having any success at all. No, I just live my life trying not to rock my own boat ... afraid that even a splash of real-world water will do me in. That's no way to live ... and it's not a real life ... it's a simulation of one, but it's what I've chosen it to be. I have that right. And you, with your victim bullshit, are not going to destroy me or turn my protective fort into a mound of rubble."

Obsessed with her bracelet, Debbie plays with the cracked bead, then looks up at Lark as if she's just emerged from a trance. "Huh?"

"You didn't even hear a word I've said."

"Okay, Susan. Butcher me! Skewer me! Nail me to the cross! Sorry. This bracelet holds great sentimental value, and I'm just worried."

Lark's patience has excused itself. "Like I said. Take it off until you get some glue. What's so hard about that?" She pauses. "Oh, yeah.

And get out."

"What's *hard* about that is that it was my grandmother's, the only family member I truly loved, and when she gave it to me, on her deathbed, she asked me to never take it off."

"I'm sure she'd be fine with you taking it off for a quick repair."

Scruffer puts his paws on Lark's lap, something he only does when she cries … alone. She knows he is sensing her distress. "Good boy," she murmurs. "Such a good boy."

"That makes sense, getting the bracelet fixed, but I don't know. What if I give it to someone to fix and they lose it? I couldn't bear the loss. It would be like losing my grandmother all over again. I'm so miserable."

"You are."

Debbie, too wrapped up like a ball of yarn, neither hears nor grasps Lark's sarcasm. "It seems the whole world is happier than I am. I passed this couple in the lobby. They were with this young boy. His name was Timmy. He was looking up at his parents, beaming, and telling them how happy he was that they were getting married and they'd be like a real family. Why can't that happen to me?"

"For starters, you're not a six-year-old boy."

"My life has been one disappointment after another. When is it gonna be my turn, huh?"

Lark, I believe, would explode with frustration if biology knew how to engineer the process. "What happened to Mr. Love at First Sight?"

Finally acknowledging Lark is present (in her own apartment), Debbie groans as if she has an intestinal disturbance that no medicine can cure. "How would I know? I never heard from the bastard again. I let him buy me dinner too."

"Were you as enchanting with him as you are with me?"

"Oh no you don't, missy." Debbie, without shame, pulls a pint of Mr. Daniels from her bag of sorts and takes a long swig. Then another one. She stuffs it back from whence it came. "Ain't no way you're going to get revenge by taunting me for losing a man's interest." Again with her teeth, she now rips a cuticle from her middle finger, wincing as she pulls off more than intended. A trickle of blood appears, which she quickly sucks off, repeating the process several times.

Lark, still suffering from the noxious stench of stale smoke, tries to hide her disgust. "I don't want revenge. That would damage *me* more than it would you. It's not in my character. Again, I don't remember you. I thought if we talked, there would be something familiar about you, but there's not. I only let you in here because you were begging me to let you apologize. And after all these years, despite having a bad feeling about my bullies, I thought maybe it would be a good thing for me. Unexpected, not even wanted, but maybe in the long run … good. I didn't follow my own sacred rule: to always trust my gut. (She should have trusted her nose as well, but she dares not say that.) No, I let you in here when every part of me was begging me to slam the door in your face. Because I didn't want to hurt you as I'd been hurt."

"Oh, you poor little spoiled brat. You had it way better than I did. Your parents had money up the wazoo. And your brother was a hunk … a nice one at that. And all those hunky guys were at your house every day. Poor Susan. Taunted for being the poor little rich girl who hung around with losers at school."

"What?"

"You heard me." Debbie's face turns red, and she pulls at her bracelet.

A blank face looks back at her.

"I said, 'you heard me.' You're not very hospitable. You never even offered me a drink."

"Maybe I just knew you'd brought your own bar with you. And for the record, I lived with my inebriated and thankfully often-absent mother in a trailer park. I never had a brother, and the only hunks hanging around were pieces of the cheap ceiling panels that my mother couldn't bother to get fixed."

"Oh, come on, Susie Carmotti. You can't fool me." As she stands, her presence threatening, Scruffer jumps off the couch and snarls.

"Wait! You think I'm Susie Carmotti? From Missouri?"

"Yeah you are."

"I've never been to Missouri, and Susie Carmotti, who is four inches shorter than me, left here ten months ago. She lived next door. Super nice lady. I was so glad she found love and happiness again. Or maybe she knew you were coming and left early to avoid the out-of-town traffic. You know … so she'd be far away by the time you arrived."

"You've got a smart mouth, don't you?" (At least she is finally listening.) "Now that you mention it, she was on the short side." She thinks. "But she would have had fifty years to grow."

Lark leans forward. "Biology lesson. People do not continue to physically grow for fifty years. Healthy people, however, continue to grow emotionally."

Debbie's fingers scratch her greasy scalp. "Hmm … Susie had freckles. You don't have any, and you're not even wearing makeup. So exactly who the hell are you?"

"Someone who is asking you to leave *her* apartment."

Debbie, now livid, continues to tug at her bracelet. "But, um, I just wanted um … "

"I'm sure I'll regret asking you this." Lark blows air through her lips. "Clearly, you didn't make this visit to Susie with any intention of apologizing to her. So what do you really want?"

The human monstrosity squirms and squeals (a vile sound) before responding. "Since you must know, I just got evicted from the room I was renting a month after I lost my cashier job at a local market

… for cursing out some customers who said I smell like smoke. Stupid owner and landlady had both been jonesing to get rid of me; I know it."

"Did the landlady take any mercy on you for losing your job?"

"She gave me three weeks to find a new job, but then she said I wasn't even trying, she had a mortgage to pay, and nobody else would hire me stinking like an ashtray. So just like that: vamoose. Bitch. I was out on my ass and had to sleep in a shelter that first night.

"Next day, I was so distraught, crying my eyes out as I walked through town wondering where I would go. This man stopped me on the street to ask if I was okay. 'Do I look okay?' I told him. Nice guy that he is … took me to the diner for coffee and something to eat. I told him my whole story and how I'd been bullied. He said that he understood … that he related to my pain … and how he never got over his neighbor, Susie Carmotti, turning him down for a date for four years straight. When I told him I knew her from school, and that I'd kind of bullied her for being so 'sparkly, rich, and popular' … like she was shoving my crappy life in my face every day … even though I know now she and the other kids hadn't … he lit up like a fourth-of-July sky. Said he'd just found out she had a big apartment here and that she was super lonely. And said he was pretty sure she'd be real happy to take in an old friend. After we were done talking, he asked me to walk to the bank with him. He took a thousand bucks out of the machine for me to travel here and gave me her address. He said he felt 'good all over' just imagining our happy reunion."

"Oh, yeah, I'm sure he did." Lark rolls her eyes. So, instead of taking that money to rent a new place and start over, you spend your money to travel here from Missouri … just to leech off someone you used to bully fifty years ago? Tell me what part of that I've got wrong."

"He wanted me to come here," the bloodsucker screams. "He gave me the money specifically for the trip. What part about that didn't you get?" Agitated, she tugs at her bracelet. The elastic band snaps and the beads roll off in different directions as she shrieks. "Oh my God. My beads!" She drops to her knees and scrambles to pick them up. She looks at Lark. "I saw three of them roll under your couch."

"I'll get them." Lark gets down and feels around in the darkness. Immediately, she feels the trio of escaped convicts, grabs them, and reluctantly returns them to their captor. While Debbie gathers up the rest, Lark feels something else. She pulls it out. It is a letter. With no time to look at it, she puts it inside her velour jacket.

Now back in her seat, Debbie is moaning. "Well, I found them all. I suppose I'll have no choice but to have this fixed." She smiles at Lark. "So, how about it. You and me. We just met, but oh boy, what a bond we have."

Lark now stands by the chair where Debbie sits. "Up."

"Oh, come on now. You can't be serious."

"Get up. You're leaving. Right now."

"But I don't—"

Reaching to grab her arm, Lark rethinks the touching aspect. "If you're not gone in ten seconds, I'm calling security. Don't test me."

"Do you have Susie's forwarding address?" Debbie asks as she grabs her bag, stands, and walks to the door.

"For you? Certainly not."

"You don't speak for her. You have no right to make decisions for Susie. She might want to see me." Debbie is now sandwiched between Lark and the door.

"I've never been one to speak for other people. Not my nature. But there are exceptions, and if there ever was one … this is it: she would *not* want to see you." Lark motions for her to move as she opens the door and impales Debbie's forehead with eyes of steel. "Go. And for no reason on this earth should you *ever* come back here."

"But …."

And in modern day verbiage, that is exactly where she let the door hit her.

Lark quickly puts the chain lock on and runs to the phone. She calls Darah to relay the incident (and to congratulate her on the engagement) and ensure that her former neighbor's address is never given out to anyone, no matter how desperate or clever their story. That done, she calls Susie, who is thrilled to hear from her and remembers Debbie all too well. After profusely apologizing to Lark and thanking her, she pleads with her to come for a long-weekend visit … and to bring Scruffer. Having never left herself open to anything of the kind, without a thought, Lark agrees. She hangs up the phone with a smile.

As she falls onto the couch, she feels the corner of the letter stab her chest. She'd forgotten all about it. A wave of nausea overwhelms her as she reaches inside her velour jacket for the envelope. Her heart sinks. It is her letter … the one she wrote to Julsie … returned. On the envelope someone has written … deceased on …. Please return to sender. She thinks for a moment. Why does that date sound so familiar? Lark looks at the postmark. Now she remembers. It is the same day she woke from the dream that compelled her to write. In the dream, she saw Julsie, with a big smile, waving at her. Only it was not hello as Lark had understood it to be … it was good-bye. And she was happy and free.

Scruffer sits on the floor and looks up at her with guilty eyes.

"Oh my goodness, boy. My little paper pusher. Those paws of yours hid this away so Mommy wouldn't find it. It's okay, my sweetheart. You did a good thing. You stashed it away so Mommy could find it at just the right time.

Tears fall as she thinks about Julsie. Though her friend never spoke of it, Susan always knew she had some kind of illness that would prevent her from living a real life, and that it would get progressively worse as time went on. That's why she never heard from her, either. How she wishes she had written sooner … and hates that she was right.

The phone rings. "Oh, please tell me that horrible woman hasn't come back and is creating some kind of havoc in the lobby." She picks it up. "Hello?" As Lark listens to the voice, her expression morphs from one of anxiety and fear to radiant joy. The tears flow again, but now for a different purpose. "Really? Everyone thinks I'm perfect for it? Three scenes? Front credits. Two scenes with the star?" The kind soul who has been her 'manager' all these years is ecstatic to give her the happy news. It is the first time Lark has ever gotten a movie role with more than one or two lines … or whose character has had a name, and who will appear with one of the biggest stars in the business. They are pivotal scenes, she is told, and very unlikely to be cut. Being told a script will be sent over to her is perhaps the greatest joy. Such a simple thing, but yet, in all of her years, it was one thing she never waited for … or allowed herself to admit that she did.

A lifetime of fear, building walls, pretense, and constant apprehension reduce her to a limp, fuzzy red mess. But she is happy. She is joyful. Not just for the good news … Susie's invitation to visit and the first real role of her life … but for the bad. Finally, for the last couple of hours, she has lived her life as others do every day. She has faced the unknown and stood up to an intruder who threatened to consume her. Lark is beginning to understand that she did not suddenly change, nor did she just learn to cope. She is as strong and conversely as weak as any other flawed human. She can let down her walls … not all at once … but little by little, and it will be okay. Lark just proved that to herself, for all in a minute's time, she learned of an old friend's death, yet was filled with joy as she understood that friend had found a way to say good-bye to her. Because she is loved.

Chapter Fourteen: THE PSYCHIC

Dell Farmer doesn't like to make plans. It's the best way he knows not to have them fall apart. Instead, he allows life to grab his hand and take him down any road it wishes. At thirty-six, he lives the life of a carefree bachelor. But who is really without cares … without woes … without that which tears one asunder? Certainly not Dell.

He lives in a large one-room apartment on the fourth floor … originally two rooms that became one. Born a fraternal twin, his sister Colleen died a few days after she was born, so the merging of rooms reminds him of what he has always tried to do: live enough life for both of them … as one.

His original name was to be Casen. But when his mother was pregnant, hearing the song "Farmer in the Dell" during a visit to the obstetrician, she amused herself with the thought that she might have a "Dell in the Farmer." After laughing herself silly over such a lowbrow joke, she became rather attached to the name. And thus, Dell was born … Colleen was born … and Colleen died.

There had been so many plans for the twins, and as Dell grew up, he learned more and more how everything was different because his sister died. Having no siblings like most other children did, he wanted someone to blame. Dell also resented his name. Children made fun of it, and when he became an adult, he loathed every person who thought themselves clever to joke about the nursery rhyme as if they were telling him something he was hearing for the first time.

One day, when his mother was putting groceries away, Dell took a stuffed brown bunny, with pink inside its big, floppy ears, out of Colleen's room. It was under several other plush animals in the brightly painted toy box, and he knew his mother would never miss it. (She would have given it to him, but he felt stuffed bunnies weren't for boys.) He named it Collie and spoke to it every day, keeping it hidden under his bed. When he moved out of the house, he took it with him. I wouldn't be surprised if he still had the poor rabbit, but his relationship with it was the one thing he never shared with a soul. Even during the years he was married, he kept "Collie" bundled in a small blanket under the seat of his car.

His other interests as a child were far more out in the open, especially his love for baseball, soccer, and bike riding. One of his favorite indoor activities was pickup sticks. Yes, throwing a handful of colored sticks willy-nilly was a harbinger of how he would live his adult life. It takes no thought or planning to throw sticks, but picking them up one by one without moving another, is exceptionally difficult.

At twenty-three, he married on a whim, divorced three years later, childless, and, while he always held a job, forging a career path was only a vague concern. There have been no goals, no dreams, and no long-term relationships. Women he deemed worthy were not likely to find any prize with Dell.

I shall not languish in the past, especially as my powers of omniscience taunt me with their fading strength. More and more, I cannot see all that I wish to, and that is a burden I must rid myself of. It is maddening to be given a gift only to realize it is being slowly diminished and have no idea whom to curse for the torment I feel.

And so, with only a bit more knowledge of Dell, I stand in his apartment. He is looking at something in the newspaper, but what, I have no idea. He averts his hazel eyes to take in the hideous celery-green-and-orange upholstery on the old Hollywood Regency couch. Two matching chairs complete the Trio of the Damned. To his left, sitting atop an old bookcase, is a vintage Capodimonte lamp with naked cherubs that hold the base of a lamp. Above them frolic creatures in a stream with what appears to be a dolphin and wild reeds.

I do know that Dell finds it grotesque and fascinating. Grotesque because it is … and fascinating because he cannot imagine the mindset of one who thought to put these images together in order to fashion a porcelain lighting fixture. Having seen many of the pieces put out by this factory, he is relieved to know the lamp in his residence is far less hideous than others. The fringed lampshade that crowns it, also garish, resembles an odd hat embroidered with eye-shaped designs. While the lamp demands his attention on a daily basis, he resents the time he spends looking at it and often believes it looks back.

Alas, I resent the time spent describing this lamp, but as Dell is rather obsessed with it, I feel it significant to note.

Eagerly awaiting something, his head makes constant quick turns to look at the mirrored wall clock, another part of the decor that ridicules him. But at this moment, it is the time of day, not the cuts of mirrored glass, that he reflects upon.

It is six o'clock. Like a robot who has been programmed, he stands and walks to the door. Looking through the peephole, he seems strangely content and opens it.

"I didn't even get a chance to ring the bell," the smartly dressed woman in the pale-pink suit says.

"It wasn't necessary. You said you were prompt and would be here at six, and here you are."

She smiles and walks to the chair he would have asked her to sit in.

He follows. "How did you know where I wanted you to sit?"

"I'm psychic. You did hire me for a reading." She extends her hand. "I'm Maxine Evie."

"Dell Farmer. Can I get you anything to drink?"

"I'm well hydrated; no thank you. Shall we both sit now … and begin?"

"Uh … sure."

She crosses her legs as her feet go under the chair. "Why don't you tell me why you wanted to see me?"

"You don't already know that?" Dell asks as he settles onto his seat on the couch.

"I'm a psychic. Not a mind reader. Before I arrived, for some reason, I had a vision of you showing me this chair. But no, I'm not certain why you wanted to see me. I like to have some idea before we begin so I can properly guide my mind and tap into whatever information is meant for you to have."

Dell, nervous, chews his lip before he speaks. "I've never done this before."

She laughs. "That's what most men say before hiring a psychic … or a prostitute."

Now suspicious, Dell isn't sure what he can get away with. "I've never done either. … *really!*"

"I believe you." She chuckles. "What are you hoping to get from our session?"

"Well, uh … I've kind of been a rolling stone my whole life. Like the old song says, you know, wherever I lay my hat is my home. I was born with a twin sister, but she had a congenital heart defect and only lived two days. My parents had decorated the most beautiful nursery for her. A pink zoo of sorts. And they didn't get rid of it because they thought my mother would get pregnant again and hopefully have another girl."

"But that never happened."

"No, it didn't. And the room stayed like that for twelve years, until my mother was able to accept that another child, especially a girl, wasn't in the cards." He swallows the pesky lump in his throat. "Actually, I mean that literally. My mother saw a tarot card reader. She never told me what the woman said, but that's when she got a better grip on reality." He pauses. "Actually, my mother contacting that reader is what gave me the idea to contact *you* … all of these years later."

"I see." She smiles pleasantly. "It must have been hard for everyone to let go of the nursery, not just your mother."

He nods. "It was. But it was good as well. The nursery was like a monument to everything that can go wrong when you plan for something special." He travels into the past to revisit a memory. "I used to envision what Colleen would've looked like. Once, when I was nine, I took my school photos and drew girl's hair on them, just because I wanted to get an idea."

"And did you?"

"Nah. Just realized that I looked bad with long hair while also learning that school photos are a lot more expensive than drawing paper." He looks down. "My mother didn't punish me. She understood. I'm sure she wondered the same thing. She just cried, and I felt horrible."

"There was a major life-changing event after that, yes?"

"How did you know?" He laughs as unease hugs him. "Oh, yeah. Right. Dad thought a change would be good for us. So, he got a new job and we moved to a new home ... not far from here ... where there was no bedroom for Colleen."

"But you felt guilty. As if you'd abandoned your sister, perhaps?"

Dell looks over at the Capodimonte lamp. Imagining that the shade is giving him a dirty look, he resumes partial eye contact with Maxine. "I felt like we'd burned her memory."

With one hand on her lap, the other vertical so she can rest her chin in her hand, Maxine looks thoughtful. "You said, 'burned her memory.' Did you choose that word because of the fire?"

As a ventriloquist would pull the string on a dummy's mouth, that is how I can best describe how Dell's mouth opens. "Yes. Three months after my father started the job, a receptionist left a burning cigarette on her desk before leaving that night, and the place burned down. Or up." Confusion lands on his face. "Never did know if something burns up or down."

"I believe that depends on the something and how—"

Dell smacks his forehead. "Yeah, I know. Not sure why I said that. Nervous."

"So, your father found a new job."

"Yes, he did, but he didn't like it so much. Everything was different in my family. It's like we weren't the same people."

Scratching her chin, Maxine asks, "And what was your biggest takeaway from all of this?"

Dell is surprised by how quickly an answer comes to him. "That plans, especially important ones, lead to disappointment. Colleen, the fancy new job ... I just saw how quickly and how tragically it can all go downhill. Never really put that into words until now, but that's why I'm a rolling stone." He looks around. "This is the most unusual place I've ever rolled to, ya know? I feel like I've got to stay here for some reason or another. But I don't know what I'm waiting for." He bites his lip. "That's why I answered your ad in the newspaper. Let me see what you said." Reaching into his shirt pocket, Dell puts on a pair of brown reading glasses. "I know I circled the ad with my trusty red marker." He takes his newspaper from the coffee table and studiously pores over the classified page. "I can't find it. I know I circled it."

Maxine offers a bright smile. "I know what I wrote, so there's really no reason to read it to me, is there?"

Dell tosses the paper to his side, puts the glasses back into his pocket, and lays the paper down. "I guess not."

"You've had a lot of different jobs in your life, yes?"

"Right. Because I never plan anything, and I don't think things through the way I should. And while I used to believe that was a good thing, I'm changing in that respect." He sighs. "You know a lot about my past, which is a bit unsettling while simultaneously heartening ...

I think … but I'm wondering when you're going to get to my future."

"In order to do that, Dell, I need to make sure that my visions are of you and not someone else. Clearly, I *am* tuning into you, like picking up a signal on an old radio."

His eyes grow wide. "Funny you should say that. I loved the radio as a kid. Used to imagine Colleen was sending me messages through songs."

"And what messages did you get from her?"

"Mostly that she was always with me, even though she had to go away. That I wasn't alone … even though it felt like it. Things like that." He smiles sadly. "Made me feel like we had a connection."

"Do you still feel that way?"

"I do." Dell's vision seems clearer now. "Which is why I answered your ad. I feel like I've screwed up enough of my life. I don't want to live this way anymore. I still have this terrible fear of making big plans, so I thought … you know … maybe I should see if the universe … or whoever makes plans for us … has anything in store for me."

Crossing her arms and leaning back with comfort in the chair, Maxine smiles. "Do you hear yourself, Dell? By contacting me, you *were* making plans … sort of a first step to a happier life. And you're acknowledging the role you need to play in your own destiny."

"I never thought of it like that."

Maxine examines the arms of the chair, looking closely at the hideous embroidery. "I was told that this place had some interesting relics. These chairs are a good deal older than you are."

"Yeah, you could say that. You can also probably say they're uglier than sin, but you're too polite."

"I am polite, but I'm not thinking the chairs are ugly. I'm just wondering why you chose them if *you* think they are."

"Well, when I moved in, the owner, Darah, took me to a storage room with lots of chairs to choose from, but I decided on these because there were two of them."

"Twins. Like you and Colleen."

Again, the ventriloquist has let the dummy's mouth fall open. "Uh, yes. I never couched it in those terms, but I thought two matching chairs, even ugly ones, looked better than ones that were completely different from one another." He pauses. "Hmm. So maybe in a weird way, I was planning."

She nods and smiles. "You work behind a desk now, in a very large building, but you're restless."

"Yes, I do administrative work for a car dealership. Did you already know this about me before you came here?"

Maxine's eyes twinkle. "You only gave me a first name when you called. And that was this morning. No, I didn't know a thing. It's all just coming to me. Very naturally."

"Kind of mind-blowing. Actually, I'm glad you're talking about my past … you've been spot-on with everything … so it kind of makes me feel you'll be the same way seeing my future." He grimaces. "Of course, if you see something not so good, then maybe I'll wish your psychic ability wasn't so great."

"Too many people waste their present lamenting their past and fearing their future," Maxine offers. "It's something I want you to think about. Imagine spending more time on the now and how much happier you'd be." She gives him a knowing look. "Of course, being in the now does require a look backward and forward, in order to put things into perspective. And most of all, if you think ahead without obsessing on the road you'll travel, plans don't have to be the scary things you've turned them into, Dell."

"You're more like a therapist than a psychic, I think."

She laughs heartily. "Oh, perhaps a bit of everything." Her face turns serious. "I know your lack of planning is your way of avoiding their possible destruction, but did you ever think that maybe you're meant to have something even better than you'd hoped for … more wonderful than you'd ever dreamed possible?"

"No." Dell bows his head. "That was an easy answer, but I'm not proud to say that."

"You're honest. That's a good thing."

"I guess. And you're really smart. You also don't look anything like I expected."

She teases him with a laugh. "Oh, and how did you expect me to look? Like a woman with long hair in colorful patchwork clothing ... maybe with a crystal ball in her hand?"

Guilty. "Um, yeah. Something like that. Not with the actual crystal ball, but like someone who would look comfortable with one in front of her."

"I'm afraid that's not me. I'm a bit more traditional ... and then I'm not. We're all a mix of many things, aren't we?"

"Yeah. Very true. So, uh, are we at the part where you look into my future yet?"

"Almost."

"Do you go into some kind of trance for that?"

Maxine laughs. "You have the most charming stereotypes in your head. They're quite endearing."

Feeling a bit embarrassed, his face reddens to illuminate his discomposure. "That's me. I just love to endear."

"You had an early marriage, but she wasn't anyone you wanted to spend a lifetime with, was she? Maybe then, you didn't really want to 'endear,' did you?"

"No. Probably not."

"And you kind of pushed her away so she'd feel the same."

"Yeah. Suppose I did. And you're scary, Maxine. If it's not rude to say that. But I want you to be scary ... in a good way, of course."

"But now, you've recently turned thirty-six, and you'd really like to meet someone."

"How did you know my age?" Dell stiffens as he becomes

suspicious of the stranger.

"Lucky guess. I feel and see a bit of everything. Believe me, Dell, it's a lot easier to guess a person's age than it is to see their past."

His shoulders relax. "That makes sense. It was just weird how you said it so matter-of-factly. And how you knew I just had a birthday."

She responds with a bright smile. "Would you like me to tell you if I see someone out there ... waiting for you?" She thinks. "Whether she knows it or not?"

He exhales in relief. Finally, she is inching closer to the job he hired her to do. "I think I'd like to know that more than anything else, actually."

"It's an important piece of information. To love and be loved is so special ... no matter what form it takes."

"That's true. I'm blessed to have wonderful and accepting parents. I see them every chance I get. For years, they've worried about me, and now, at the ripe old age of thirty-six, I'm finally starting to worry about myself."

"Your parents love you very much. I feel that deeply."

"Yeah ... they do. So, about this possible woman ...."

For the first time, Maxine closes her eyes, as if she is receiving information from someone. "The love of your life is nearby. Very close, actually. But she's in a complicated situation from which she not only doesn't know how to extricate herself, but isn't yet sure that she should. Her woes get more tangled by the day, and now, I fear, they are choking her." She looks at Dell with a seriousness she has yet to display. "You need to understand that the perfect woman may not first appear to you as such. She may be twisted in a ball of twine that needs untangling."

Dell snickers. "Well, I'm not exactly Mr. Perfection, am I? Nobody would ever look at *me* and come to *that* conclusion."

"Who wants perfection? Only a fool, Dell. Being perfect for

another person does not mean one *is* perfect. You know that. I'm only confirming it. You're more insightful than you give yourself credit for." She smiles. "You know that too."

"You've told me a lot, Maxine. But all you've told me about the future is that there's someone nearby who is waiting for me. That's definitely the thing I most want to know, of course, but is that all you see in my future?" He rethinks his statement. "I mean, that's a huge thing, it's what I want most, true love, but I didn't mean to minimize it by saying, 'that's all.'"

"I do know more … much more." A coy smile changes the position of her lips. "But that's all I'm going to tell you. Any more would be too much for you to handle." She shifts in the chair as she prepares to get up.

"I can handle it; really, I can."

She laughs. "No you can't. One thing at a time, Dell. You'll meet her very soon."

"Oh, okay, then. Sounds like you know what you're talking about. We never did discuss how much I owe you."

She stands and goes to the closet as if she's done it a million times before. Opening the door, she turns to her left, bends down, and pulls the stuffed brown bunny out of a box on floor. "I think this belongs to me." Maxine hugs the rabbit to her chest. "It's never too late to love, is it, Collie?"

Rendered mute, Dell can say nothing. Maxine walks over, kisses him on the cheek, affectionately touches his hair … then walks to the door. Quickly pulling it toward her, she leaves and shuts it behind her. Dell immediately opens it, but the hallways are empty. It is a fair distance to both the stairwell or the elevator, and nobody walks, or even runs, that fast.

"Maxine … where are you?" He stands in disbelief, realizing he will never find her. "Totally impossible … I'm dreaming … only I'm not. It really happened." He looks both ways again. "Colleen … oh

… Colleen." The more he pieces together what has happened … and tries to make sense of it all, the more he hyperventilates. Within seconds, he fears that he is spinning out of control and tries to calm himself. He leans against the wall just as Lee is exiting his pet elevator, Darth.

As if his personal radar has clued him in, Lee turns his head and looks down the hall to see Dell, in distress, leaning against the wall next to his apartment door. Feeling this is a personal affront to him, anger rises in his chest as he marches down the hall to confront yet another neighbor who has joined the plot to make him crazy. He's had enough. Resolved to take it no more, Lee is primed for battle.

Meanwhile, Dell's vision has temporarily altered, and he sees everything through a veil of tiny stars, swirling, ever-so-lightly, in the shape of an infinity sign. He sees Lee standing in front of him, but he cannot make out the consternation on his face. He can only say, "My sister was here, and she took her bunny."

Lee drops his briefcase on the carpet. He mocks him. "Your sister was here and took her bunny." He laughs … brutally. "You mean it didn't hop away by itself … to get away from you? Was your sister 'mad as a March hare?' Was the bunny? Are you?" His sarcasm is replaced with rage. "Why are you people fucking with me? Huh? Who put you up to this? My wife? Is she behind it? Are you gaslighting me?" He is screaming now, loud enough to bring Ellie out of their apartment. Spotting Lee and Dell, she runs toward them to break up the commotion.

"Lee, what are you doing?"

Ignoring her, he points a finger at Dell's face. "Go on, man. Do it. Slide down the fucking wall. You know you want to … you know you're going to … I just haven't yet figured out why. Why are you just standing there looking all spazzed out? Is this some kind of wall-sliding foreplay?"

The veil has lifted and Dell is now fully cognizant of the

situation before him. "What are you talking about, dude? I had a shock ... to put it mildly ... and I rested against the wall for a moment? Is that a crime?"

Ellie picks up her husband's briefcase, that was sitting in the middle of the hallway, and leans it against the wall. "Lee, chill, babes. You're not well. This isn't funny anymore. You're losing it ... or maybe it's already gone. Your mind ... in case you don't know what I'm talking about."

"Stay out of it, Ell!" Lee does not look her and keeps his gaze fixated on Dell. "Go on, slide, fool, slide! And don't ask me to help your ass up when you do."

"I'm so sorry," Ellie says to Dell. "My husband really isn't well."

"I'm just fine," Lee snaps. "This is my fight. Stay out of it."

At that moment, Alejandro and Sophia step off the elevator, and Lee's peripheral vision spots them. He turns his head to observe them. "That's Santa Claus. He's a slider too. I don't know about Mrs. Claus ... if that even *is* Mrs. Claus. Maybe she's at the North Pole and Santa's having some fun with a ho ho ho." He watches them as they walk to the door of an empty apartment. "Just heard they're moving to a one-bedroom-with-den from a second-floor studio. Just what I need. Crazy Claus in my midst."

Dell looks sympathetically at Ellie. "Please forgive me. I don't know what I did to upset him. I just had a really shocking thing happen and—"

Ellie puts the palm of her hand up. "You really don't need to apologize or explain anything to me." A smile breaks through. "I've seen you many times before, but we've never met. I'm Ellie."

"Dell Farmer."

"So nice to meet you, Dell. Sorry the circumstances are so ... well, you know."

He is thrilled that she makes no obvious joke about his name and he sees her dark brown eyes looking at him … just long enough to send him a message.

Lee is still blocking his passage away from the wall, refocusing on Dell now that Alejandro and Sophia are out of sight. "Not gonna slide or what?"

"Could you move, please? I just want to go back into my apartment."

"Move, Lee. Let the man open his door." Ellie looks at Dell again. "I'm really sorry."

Lee tenses as his face reddens. "Nothing to be sorry for, Ell. Be quiet. Stop apologizing for me all the time. I'm sick of it."

"And I'm sick of you … everything about you: especially lying about working late and going off to events with your parents because you're too ashamed to take me. Do you think I don't know what you do? Do you think I don't know they're trying harder than ever to get us divorced? Do they have someone picked out for you? Or have you already picked her out for yourself? Whoever she is, I feel sorry for her. And you know what? Tell them they don't have to try anymore. Or be so sneaky. Just send over the papers; I'll sign them. You're not only unwell, but you're a son of a bitch … literally. And the son of a bastard too. You're not the man I thought I fell in love with. We don't even have ups and downs anymore. Only downs. Like in-the-sewer-feeling-miserable kind of downs. I'm sick of being tangled up in this mess of a marriage. I've never tried harder in my life to make anything work. But we were never meant to be. I know that now."

Lee steps back and allows Dell to pass. "Stop yammering about divorce. And quit airing our dirty laundry, Ell."

Astonished, Ellie sees the old woman, the phantom neighbor, standing at her side. Instinctively, she knows no one else can see her. The woman's hair, Country Copper Red, is meticulously combed and styled in a back bun. She looks at Ellie and smiles, cocks her head toward Dell, winks, and smiles again. And she is gone.

"Holy apparition ...."

"What's your problem, Ell. Did you hear what I said? Or didn't you give me the courtesy of even listening? I said: stop blabbing about divorce and airing our dirty laundry in front of other people."

Now fully present again, Ellie snarls at him. "Then maybe don't curse out a neighbor because you think he's gonna slide down a freakin' wall. Ya think, Lee? That's not a bit bonkers to you? Off the wall ... to coin a phrase you can relate to." She looks at Dell. "I'm really sorry. I hope we meet again under better circumstances."

"Me too." Dell can't help but see how beautiful she is ... and how unhappy. He stands a moment longer than necessary to feel the energy between them, then opens his door and walks inside.

He runs to the couch and picks up the newspaper from the coffee table. Taking his glasses out of his shirt pocket again, he puts them on and leafs through every page, but there is no ad circled in red. In fact, his red pen is not even on the table where he is sure he left it. Putting his glasses away for the second time, he walks briskly to the closet and opens it. Reaching down into a box, he pulls out the stuffed rabbit and stares at it in disbelief. "What the ... she took you, Collie. She even knew your name. I know she's been waiting a long time for you." He inspects the toy as if to reassure himself it's not a mirage.

Clutching Collie in his arms, he sits on the couch. "She never even tried to ring the doorbell ... or knock. I just knew she was out there, Collie. And she had hazel eyes, just like mine." He leans back and rests his head against the hideous cushion. After a moment, he looks at the lamp. Oh, how frightening. One of the eye-shaped designs appears to wink at him. That is disturbing to a sane soul like me, but Dell is oddly pacified by it.

He looks at Collie. "I know. Maybe you're still here because she took your twin. All these years, you could have had an invisible twin that I never saw until Colleen appeared. Do you think she grew up in heaven and came down here just to help me? Do you think she's an angel? Or did I just imagine the entire thing?"

The rabbit has no response. Dell glances at the lamp, hoping for enlightenment, but there is only what appears as refuse from a thrift store.

I cannot read his mind at this moment, but it is clear what his smile means, especially now that he speaks aloud … to the rabbit. "Colleen said the right woman was very nearby, but that her woes were tangled. That's the same word Ellie used when she told her husband she was sick of being tangled up in their mess of a marriage. She's the one for me, Collie. I think we both felt it. And I don't care how hokey or cliché that sounds, because sometimes, you just know stuff. You sense it. You see it. And it's more real than anything you've ever known." He sighs. "I'm making a plan right here and now: to wait for her." He looks around the room. "Hope you don't have anywhere to be. I'm going to need some company."

Chapter Fifteen: RUNAWAY GHOST

Poor Karrie is, and has always been, different. Having to introduce herself as "Karrie with a K," is a major sore point, though a minor one in the scheme of things. This sad soul never feels worthy of much. Her older sister, a research scientist at a renowned university, and her younger brother, a neurologist at one of the best hospitals in the world, leaves Karrie embarrassed for being the assistant manager of a small card and gift shop near a popular park. Although she has great pride in her siblings, she never brags about them as doing so only brings on some form of the inevitable question (whether spoken aloud or not): "What happened to *you*?"

When people learn of her accomplished sister and brother, Karrie believes she can see the pity in their smiles and hear the judgment in their thoughts. It is always a punch in the gut. Does it matter whether the source of her pain is real or imagined?

As a child, when the forlorn Karrie (oh, goodness, am I judging too?) would tell her parents they didn't pay much attention to her, they'd scold her for taking the "middle child thing" to heart and declare that she was every bit as important as her siblings, a statement she rarely believed to be true. But somehow, alas, this now thirty-one-year-old woman is confused. She doesn't know if they were in denial or simply lying. All she can do is struggle to find happiness.

The few friends she has find her "sweet but fragile" and delicately try to offer her advice in her pursuit of her "forever man." She has been admonished by men for being "smothering" and by friends for being "too easy." Karrie never seems to follow advice, especially when it is suggested she be "coy" or "aloof," as those traits simply do not fit her. She is always searching for the man who will appreciate her just as she is … finding it exhausting to mold herself into the image others form or want to see (who can do that?), and it is wishful thinking that her qualities will go "mainstream" and be rubberstamped as appropriate and pleasing behavior. Her life, as she sees it, has been an emotionally hardscrabble one, but she is prone to exaggeration and to living in a reality of her own making. She can see a situation as better or worse than it is, but those who know her believe that she rarely assesses accurately.

I shall not list her many foibles nor her past exploits. But, as I observe her in her sixth-floor studio apartment, she is sitting cross-legged on the floor surveying an array of odd items on the low glass-top table, which itself sits on a brass base made to look like knotted rope. In the middle of the table, in this shrine-like chaotic mess, is an antique brass seahorse incense burner, a small bottle of essential oils, and various gems set up in a manner only Karrie understands. The pièce de résistance is a poorly drawn sketch of a thirty-something-year-old man, preserved for eternity in a plastic sleeve with three holes on the left side … handy for those who use loose-leaf binders. Thankfully, the image is not sitting too close to the four fat black candles.

Karrie had been on three "dates" with John (a milestone to make it past the first). They were on the phone, planning their next one, when he screamed during the conversation. The call ended, and Karrie spun out of control in her failed attempt to get him back. As he had been living with friends, she had no address, only the number for a phone now turned off. The next day, a tearful woman called from a restricted number to say that John had been staying with her and her husband, when an iron horse statue, by way of a mischievous cat, fell from a shelf above and crushed his head. He was rushed to the hospital, where three hours later, he died. The cat and the horse are being questioned by police. I jest. I reserve that right.

Having been made aware that John was separated from his wife, thus his temporary living arrangement, Karrie knew she would not be welcome at the funeral, even though she no idea where it would be. Taking her vacation days to weep and wail, she sits on the floor, preparing to contact him by séance. Considering all that transpires in this establishment, a grieving woman's wish to communicate with a dead soul is rather run of the mill, but still worth my time to observe.

The mournful one dabs a bit of the oil on either side of her neck. It has an earthy, heavy musk to it, but its purpose escapes me. Perhaps it merely creates a mood … or maybe … it beckons to spirits long gone to assist in bringing forth those who have just passed. Although Karrie has been advised that recently departed souls are busy with life reviews, and thus make themselves more available at a later date, she dismisses the advice, closes her eyes, and begins. "My beloved John, I bring you gifts from life into death. Please, dearest, make your presence known to me. Commune with me and move in the midst of my deepest love, sensuality, and warmth." (I must say, these are unbefitting words for a man she met in the park, on her lunch break, less than three weeks ago.) She waits but sees nothing exceptional beyond the odd flicker of a flame.

She repeats the chant (loosely suggested to her by a self-proclaimed spiritual guru who bought a sympathy card from her) and now sways her body and lifts her hands upward with an odd grabbing motion … almost as if she intends to pull John from the heavens onto her lap. (That I would like to see.)

The scenery is changing. Karrie opens her eyes and sees an odd mist of sorts swirling through the room. "John, my darling, you heard me. You've come to be with me. I knew death couldn't separate us. When you told me in the motel room that your love was growing with each passing second, I know you meant that only in the purest form. I shouldn't tell you this, but a so-called friend suggested you meant it crudely. Oh, no, not you. How could I not love the man who fell for me on our first meeting … as I did for you. I love you more than I can put into words. And I mean it when I say, 'death will not separate us.'"

I am horrified by the smile on her face. It is frightening. Her lips appear to liquefy and distort as they stretch to her eyes as she recalls her "pleasure" in the economy motel of his choice.

A knock on the door disturbs and angers her, but she considers that John's spirit may be seeking entry in a more traditional manner. For that reason alone, she stands and walks to answer it.

"Hi, Karrie," the pleasant woman in the black pants and Hawaiian shirt says. "I'm Dody, from down the hall. Remember me? Looks like the postman put your mail in my box again. Mush for brains, huh? If it was junk mail, I wouldn't bother you. But it looks like there's a check in here, so I thought I'd personally bring it over." She hands Karrie the mail, smiling. As she waits to be thanked, a swirl of mist that only Karrie can see escapes the apartment.

"Noooooo! John, John … don't leave me, sweetheart." Karrie stares fiercely at Dody. "You let him escape! He's all I have." She throws the envelope into her open apartment, rattles off endearments for the dearly departed, and runs down the hallway. Dody stares in disbelief.

While I say this metaphorically, if eyes could pop out of heads, that is most certainly what Dody's peepers would likely do. Befuddled by Karrie's bizarre behavior and seeing the odd set-up inside, she mumbles "Okay, then" as she closes the door and quickly exits the scene.

Karrie is now halfway down the hallway when she runs into a well-dressed couple. In her hysteria, she nearly headbutts the man.

"Hey, there. Hold steady, lady. I'm not a matador, and you're not a bull. What's the deal here?"

"My boyfriend escaped; I've got to find him."

The couple exchanges eye rolls.

"He escaped?" the woman asks. "From what, honey? Did you

have him in a cage or just locked in your apartment?"

"Neither. He's dead. I had a séance, and he appeared in the form of mist or steam. I can't really describe it, but you know. Like a spirit. Everything was fine until *she* (Karrie gives a dirty look to Dody as she quickly passes) knocked on my door and let him out."

"Whackadoodle … whangdoodle …. flappity-trap doodle," Dody murmurs as she walks away.

The man looks at the woman. "Didn't that just happen to us last week with your mama? She escaped the same way, didn't she?"

The woman nods, playing along. "Sure as heck did." She turns to Karrie. "I feel your pain, honey. It's like a plague or something." She pretends to be mulling over something important. "You know, we were just visiting friends on the third floor, and I saw something very odd moving around. I thought it might be gas, but now that you describe—"

"That must be him!"

As Karrie runs to the stairwell, the man turns to the woman. "Glad you sent her south a few floors."

Karrie clomps her way down the steps and bursts through the third-floor entrance. Panting, she sees Lark and Scruffer entering their apartment after a walk. "Wait!"

Turning around to look, Lark is shocked to see the frenzied woman coming unhinged before her eyes. "Who are you?"

"I'm sorry, but just when you opened your door now, I think my boyfriend got in."

Lark stares. "Did someone from the studio send you here? Is this a joke?" She looks around for cameras. "Who was it? I can take it. I've got a sense of humor."

"This is no joke."

"I literally *just* opened this door. It would be impossible for anyone to have slipped in. I hope you don't mind, but I've got work to do." Again, Lark looks around for any sign that someone is playing a trick on her. Also, after years of bullying, though a long time ago, she can never be too cautious.

Tears stream down Karrie's face, and Lark, accustomed to pain, recognizes it in another. She moans softly. While not in the mood, she is a compassionate soul and cannot stop herself. "What's your name?"

"Karrie. With a K. I live on the sixth floor."

Regret carves its name on Lark's face, but she defies it. "Would you like to come in and talk for a bit? I'm Lark. And this is Scruffer."

Halfway into Lark's apartment, a muffled "thank you" spills from Karrie's lips.

Lark escorts her to the red chair without the towel. "Why don't you sit here?"

Eyeing the couch, Karrie weeps. "Isn't there enough room for both of us on the couch? Chairs make me feel so lonely sometimes. And I've never been lonelier in my life."

Poor Lark, having barely recovered from Debbie's intrusion, realizes she is not as unscathed as she had hoped. "Oh. Okay. But I can only talk to you for a little bit. I'm an actor, and I have lines to learn." Somewhere inside, she waits for a gratifying response, but the weeping stranger hasn't heard her. "I'll get you a glass of water."

While Lark goes to the kitchen, Karrie plops onto the red couch as Scruffer, wary, jumps onto his chair and stares. Meanwhile, Karrie's eyes search the apartment for signs of John in whatever murky form she believes he may be taking.

"Here, have some water." Lark hands her the glass.

Examining the water to ensure he has not converted to liquid, Karrie hydrates herself with one long gulp.

When she is finished, Lark takes the glass, places it down on the coffee table, then sits on the couch, leaving space between them. She does not want to ask the loaded question, but the kind soul inside her cannot refrain. "What's wrong, Karrie?"

"My boyfriend recently died from head trauma. I was having a séance to make contact with him … and after I did the chants a couple of times, he appeared, like in fog or something. I knew right then it was him and that if some stupid neighbor hadn't knocked on the door, he would have materialized. But he got spooked, I think."

Pretending to stroke her face in sympathy, Lark literally pushes her smile down and uses her acting chops to keep the laughter away as she confronts the all-too-real sadness. "I see. I'm sorry for your loss. Had you been together long?"

"Three weeks," Karrie says, unaware that while that is a long time for her, it is a mere second to others. "We'd been together three times too."

"You mean, as in …."

"Yes. Of course. We met in the park twice before … you know, so it's not like we didn't know each other. We must've talked forty-five minutes each time. And it would have been longer, but I had to get back to work. And so did he. He's in construction somewhere."

Lark, with no relatable experience, searches for a kind word or two. "Well, you made the most of your time together."

"My friends, the women I work with, always tell me I'm too easy. But how do you show someone all you have to offer? I mean, you wouldn't go into a store and buy something if you could only see half the product, right? I know because I work in a gift shop."

Trying her delicate best, Lark speaks. "Yes, Karrie. But a human being is not a product to be bought. There's a reason we wrap gifts; they're more fun to open if we have to wait to see what's inside and get to know the wrapping."

The gift analogy strikes a chord with Karrie, but she doesn't wish to acknowledge it. She can only respond with a teary pout.

Genuine sorrow touches Lark. "You sound like you've had a tough life. I have too. I'm twice your age, and I've spent my life purposely getting to know people as superficially as I could … because

I was afraid to let anyone get close. And even though you've been full-on physical with men, ironically, your relationships sound even more superficial than mine. Isn't that odd?"

Karrie does not wear this wisdom well. "Oh, my friends say things like that. But there's nothing superficial about a relationship when you've known each other so intimately."

"What do you know about him?"

"He's dead!" The tears, which never really stopped, are flowing again. "And that he was going to get a divorce; that's why he was living with his friends, and I don't know where to find out anything about him."

"What's his last name?"

"Smith." Karrie fears the retort as she hears the name on her lips.

"Do you think it's possible that John Smith is not his real name?"

"My friend said that. But if lots of people didn't have common names then they wouldn't be common! Hello? So why is it weird his name is John Smith?"

Lark tries on a pair of kid gloves. They fit. "That does make sense, but seeing that he was married, it appears a bit likely that he might not have wanted to tell you his real name. Have you at least thought about it? And if you don't know his name, then how well do you think you knew *him*?"

"Well enough to go look for him, I can't stay here anymore. I'm sorry about your problems, but I have to find my John."

Relieved, Lark stands. "Please … let me walk you out."

"Thanks for the water," Karrie says, hurrying to the door and opening it. As she leaves, Lark closes the door behind her. She smiles. "You know, Scruffs, living in the real world feels very unreal, don't you think?"

Clomping down another set of stairs, Karrie emerges on the

second floor. Alejandro's door is open, as Sophia is leaving to run some errands, and Karrie, spying a whistling steam kettle on the stove, pushes past them, knocks over some cardboard boxes, and runs to the kettle. "Sweetheart!" she says to the rising steam. "Is that you? I'm here now. I found you. It's okay to materialize." She lifts the kettle's lid. "Come out. It's safe now."

I must interject at this point. In many years, I have witnessed much lunacy, but if this moment could be gold plated and win an award, it would take the prize for being the most demented action to ever happen within these walls: rivaled by many, uncontested by none.

Sophia hurries back into the small unit. "Uh, hello there ... Miss Uninvited. Do you know you're in our apartment? Who are you and why are you here? And why are you professing your love to my tea kettle?" She turns off the burner and looks at the mess made by the fallen boxes. "We're in the middle of moving to a larger apartment, and you've just knocked two cartons over because, I suppose, barging into a stranger's apartment wasn't brazen enough for you. Am I right?"

"I'm sorry. I thought my boyfriend was ...." I believe even Karrie can now see herself as Sophia and Alejandro do. "You'd never understand. Don't be angry."

"Who me? I'm not angry." Sophia glances at the two cartons she will have to repack. "Just blowing off steam."

"You're making fun of me. I'm not stupid. I just said, 'you wouldn't understand.' And you don't. Neither of you."

"There's something we can agree on," Alejandro says softly. "Is there someone we can call for you?"

She notices him for the first time. "You look just like Santa Claus. Where am I? No wonder I feel so cold all of a sudden."

"Why don't you let me call someone?" he says in a near whisper.

"You think I'm a nutter, don't you? Well I'm not. I'm just a grieving woman."

"Please sit," Alejandro says. "It's pretty cluttered in here, but that doesn't mean we can't have a chat."

"Hope you don't expect me to sit on your lap, *Santa*."

Alejandro turns red, and his voice darkens. "Perhaps I should leave and let you speak with my wife, Sophia. Woman to woman."

Sophia scolds him with her eyes. She does not wish to be left alone.

"Well," Alejandro says, pointing to his old mustard-yellow club chairs (they will not be making the move), why don't you ladies have a seat, and I'll stand."

Reluctantly, both women sit.

"Can I offer you a cup of tea?" Alejandro asks.

Karrie, like a champagne cork, flies off the chair into a mad rage. "The love of my life could be in there. I know it sounds ridiculous to you, but I saw him emerge in that form when I called him during the séance. I would never drink that tea. It's like spiritual cannibalism or something."

"Oh my Lord," Sophia says. She looks at Alejandro. "I have no idea how to get through to this woman."

Karrie stands and blows out three angry breaths before sitting again. "I'm totally compos mentis, lady. You don't have to 'get through to me.' You have no idea of my pain."

Tears well in Sophia's eyes. "My husband and I lost our infant son many years ago. I was mad with grief, and my family put me in a psychiatric facility where I only became more unstable … because I felt trapped. My pain was the rawest thing I've ever felt in my life. I lost everything, including this dear man, who I've only recently reunited with. So yes, I understand grief to its very core. Stark naked grief … I get it."

Calmed by Sophia's confession, Karrie sits. "Sorry about your son. And um, well, I just found out I'm pregnant."

"Oh, my. That's something. Well, by all means, for the baby's sake and your own, please try to relax. I'm Sophia, by the way. And this is Alejandro."

"Hi." She looks at them both. "I'm Karrie with a K."

Sophia lowers her eyes. "I'm sorry if I sounded insensitive to your pain. When I lost our son, I looked for him in crazy places. Once, I remember being afraid to put my head on a pillow. I was afraid he was underneath, and I'd smother him. He had already been buried, and I knew that, but when we're in such anguish, facts can elude us."

Alejandro, who is sitting on the bed, buries his face in his palms as he recalls the past.

"We had something so special," Karrie says. "He told me I was just what he needed and that it had been a long time for him."

"Since he'd felt such love?"

"Yes, and that he felt so at home inside … with me."

Sophia, feeling uneasy again, smiles pleasantly at Karrie. "You must have many wonderful memories that will comfort you."

"Um … well."

Trying to lighten the despair, Sophia tries again. "Tell me. When did you first know he was the one?"

She is beaming now. "In the park. I was making a mess of my egg-salad sandwich, which I was eating on my lap, and he sat next to me. He said I was the prettiest girl eating an egg-salad sandwich on a park bench he ever saw. Isn't that funny? And so romantic. I laughed so much. I knew right then he was everything I wanted."

"He must have had one hell of a delivery," Alejandro says under his breath.

"Where was your first date?"

Karrie gulps. "Jim's Motor Lodge."

Sophia and Alejandro do not know how to respond.

"I know what it sounds like, but our pull to one another was so magnetic. He said he would explode soon if … well …." She thinks.

"On our first date, he took me to the diner afterward." She giggles. "Guess what I had?"

Sophia gulps. "An egg-salad sandwich?"

"Yes. And when the server brought it to us, we just laughed all over again. It was such a great date." Her face falls. "Oh, I miss my Johnny. I miss him more than anything. I wish we'd gone to the diner on our other two dates, but we thought we had our entire lives in front of us. You know?"

My, this is awkward. Sophia is scrambling to find words ... any words. "Do you have a photo of him?"

"Not a one." And the tears zig and zag down her cheeks. "Only in my mind."

"Are you far along in your pregnancy?"

"Well, I think I conceived the first time we declared our love for one another. So about two weeks, I guess. I'm going to have a boy. I just know it." She looks at Sophia's face. "Oh, I'm so sorry. I didn't mean to upset you."

Sophia offers a brief smile. "It's okay. I've learned to live with our loss. I suppose, after this tragedy, you'll name your son after your father."

"John Smith Junior." Karrie mulls it over. "Unless John was already a junior. Then I guess the baby will be the third or something."

"John Smith," Sophia says through gritted teeth. She looks at Alejandro who can only shrug.

Aware of the interaction, Karrie is angry again. "Some lady named Lark told me she thought it might be a fake name. And obviously, you think so too. Don't lie and say you don't. Like I told *her*, common names are common. Duh. I've got to find him. He's probably swirling around in the lobby looking for me. He won't materialize until he sees me; I just feel it. I shouldn't have stayed here so long." She stands. "I'm going now. And you guys can mock me all you want when I leave. I know you will."

"Oh, no," Alejandro says as he stands. "We see you're in great distress. There's nothing funny about that, as I know from experience. Misfortune and I were introduced at a young age."

"Well, then I feel sorry for her." She hangs her head. "That wasn't nice of me. My aunt Adeline told me once that if you disparage something or someone too often, you may become what you disparage. It's some kind of ancient curse, I think. She was the wisest woman I ever knew; she was like a font of knowledge for stuff regular people are clueless about." She exhales to calm herself." I don't want to become mean. So I take that back. Thanks for letting me sit. My agony is ripping my insides to shreds." More tears. "I'm going."

Before her gracious hosts can utter another word, she is gone.

Overcome with desperation, she roams the lobby. She squints her eyes as if it will help her to locate her beloved. "Where are you, John? Where are you?" Her gaze focuses on a stream of mist that she tells herself is snaking the floor in pursuit of her. She looks down as she walks. "John, if that's you, rise up, darling."

"I ain't John, but it's not a good idea to walk with your head down. Best way to crash with another person … or a wall. Been there done that. Ain't that right, Poodley?"

"Oh, sorry." Karrie looks up but can't take her eyes off the floor. "I've lost him again."

"What's that?"

"Nothing." Karrie pouts. "Nobody understands. Not even your dog."

"Oh, you'd be real surprised what Poodley understands. Smartest darn dog I done ever had."

"Have you had a lot of dogs?"

"Poodley's the first dog I had since before I met my wife, Martha. She didn't like them one bit. Didn't want their dirty paws walkin' on her floors or jumpin' on her furniture. And she had a real thing about dogs on the bed. Made me choose between her and my four-legged friends."

"Oh, that's sad. Couldn't you get her to change her mind?"

"Nopers. Every time I even mentioned wanting a dog, she got real unhappy." Kenny grumbles. "That made two of us."

Karrie sniffles. "I was just telling these people on the second floor how my aunt Adeline always said that if you knock someone or something enough times, you can turn right into the very thing or person you're dissing. I didn't have time to tell them this part, but like you can totally do a switcheroo with the object of your scorn. Yup. My aunt was a mystic, and ignorant people called her all kind of cruel names, but I saw stuff you'd never believe."

Toothpicks could not widen Kenny's eyes more. She has awakened something in his brain.

"I know you're thinking I'm from a screwball family. I can see it in your face. But I've seen proof … even since my aunt died. And she was totally zeroing in on stuff that's invisible to the average person. You can believe it or not. I don't care."

Tongue-tied, Kenny can only look at her, his eyes inadvertently pleading to hear more.

"I work in this gift shop by the park. It was a really long time ago, at least a year, when I saw these people from a psych hospital take this lady out of the bushes. I don't know what happened to her, but people swore she thought she was a dog. Barked like one, did her business like one, and everything. I saw her once, and she didn't seem human at all. It made me think about things my aunt had told me … and I thought that somewhere, the lady's real self might be inside a dog."

"Well, that …."

"I know. It sounds cuckoo to the moon and back. And I'm a very realistic person, so I didn't *really* think that. Just sort of joked to myself. Poor woman. Guess she's still wherever they took her and all."

Dumbstruck, Kenny cannot respond.

"Oh my God," Karrie says, looking toward the revolving doors. "It's John! He's materialized. I've got to go."

Kenny looks down at Poodley. "Don't even think about switching back. Not gonna happen. I like you a whole lot better as a pooch. But it's good knowin' how you got this way. Sure was a head scratcher." He thinks. "Still is, actually."

"John," who is clearly flesh and blood, winces when he sees Karrie rushing toward him.

"You look almost human again."

The dark-haired, unshaven man, in work jeans and boots, can only look at her. "I hear you, Karrie. Wasn't too cool of me to ghost you like I did. That's why I've come by. It's only fair I explain everything." Guilt washes over his stubbly cheeks. "Guess I should start with my name."

"I'm carrying your baby. John Smith, Jr. Oh my God, you look so real."

He blinks. "I am real, Karrie. I didn't die. And what the hell did you just say?"

I must say, if there was ever a moment for Karrie to be at her most foolish, I would designate this point in time for consideration.

"Really? I conjured you up in a séance. I said, 'My beloved John, I bring you gifts from life into death. Please, dearest, make your presence known to me.' And then I saw you manifest as some kind of mist … or steam. Oh, it was some adventure, but I chased you throughout the building until I saw you here, creeping along the lobby floor. And now here you are, fully manifested."

"Karrie. Please. Get a fucking grip. I never died. Do you hear me?"

She touches his arm, then his face. Joy easily triumphs over foolishness. She throws her arms around him as logic covers its face in horror. "Oh, John. I'm so happy. We're going to be a family!"

Delicately, he removes her hands from his shoulders. "Looks

like there's a quiet place in the middle of the lobby. C'mon. Let's go sit down and I'll explain."

Beaming, she follows him to the couch, quite ludicrously expecting a diamond ring to emerge from his side pocket as he falls to one knee. They sit, and her eager eyes soak up every inch of his material being. "You didn't die?" She pauses for a long moment. "Oh, I guess you probably didn't. I feel ridiculous, but …."

"Look, um … my wife and I were separated for the better part of a year … okay. I told you about that. And yeah, I really was staying with friends. Fact, I was about to go get my own place 'cause I was convinced she'd never agree to reconcile. But she did. See, when I was talking to you on the phone, she came into the home and heard me. She got kind of pissed because hearing me planning a date with a woman after I'd just begged her to get back together, so she took a fireplace poker and jabbed me in the side something fierce. Damn that hurt." He touches his side where a hint of pain remains. "That's when you heard me scream bloody murder."

"Oh, no." Karrie's face falls to the ground. It is a very sad sight.

He is eager to finish his story and get this over with. "So the phone went flying out of my hands, and she picked it up and stuck it between her boobs." He is not pleased with the somersaults his stomach is performing. "Anyhow, uh, that very short call you got saying that your boyfriend had died from head trauma; that was my wife. I was standing there. Soon as she ended the call, she deleted your contact information and had my number changed before returning my phone. Long and short of it, Kar, we're together again. And it feels good … real good. Better than ever, actually. The sex is … um … I didn't want to go to your work and talk to you with your friends around, but knowing the name of the store, I called there to see if we could meet in the park, and that's when I found out you'd taken the time off … to grieve for me. Oh, Jesus, Kar."

Her dead eyes look blankly through him. "But I'm preg …

you're going back to your wife?" Reality, the theatrical beast, is now making a grand entrance. "What were you going to say about your name … you know … when you first came through the doors?"

He must think fast. "Oh, uh, just that you'll probably want to call me 'dirtbag' or some other name … instead of John."

"Is your name really John Smith?"

"Sure it is. My parents weren't very clever, were they? Having such a common last name, you'd think they would've picked something a bit more unusual." He stands. "Look, I just had to apologize and set things straight. "Sorry if I got your hopes up. Oh, and speaking of 'getting things up,' as much as I enjoyed you, starved for sex as I was, you might want to hold off a bit with the next guy. Might have a happier ending for you and all. Take care, okay? You deserve a good man, Karrie. See ya." He takes one last look at her. "And again. Sorry. I never meant to hurt you."

And in a flash, Raleigh Evan Langsford is gone, leaving only the dust of "John Smith" in his wake.

Despondent, Karrie stays on the couch and speaks only to herself. "But I had a séance. I did everything right. I called for John over and over … and I know I saw something. I'm sure." She thinks. "Oh my God. I left my door open and candles burning!" She jumps off the couch and runs to the elevators.

Minutes later, standing in front of her apartment, she is grateful to Dody (to whom she owes a great apology) for closing the door. She walks in. The four fat candles provide the only illumination now that the sun has set. But the studio apartment has an ambience quite unlike the one she left behind. Karrie cannot believe her eyes. She looks up and sees the faces of many men, many races, old, young, and in-between. Hair of every color and length … bald heads, beards, mustaches, hats, earrings, tattoos, and even glasses they no longer need. Semi-transparent, they are all calling to her in different languages, their voices merging as they create an otherworldly cacophony:

"Hello. I'm John. Were you calling me?"

"Hola, soy Juan. Te escuche llamarme."

"Salut! C'est moi, Jean. Est-ce que tu m'appellé."

"Ciao, sono Giovanni. Ho sentito il mio nome?"

"Oi, aqui quem fala é o João. Alguém aqui estava me chamando."

"Wer schaut nach mir? Ich höre dauernd meinen Namen. Es ist Johannes."

"Hvem kalder på mig? Hvad foregår der? Det er John."

"Moien, de Jang hei. Hunn ech mäin Numm héieren?

"Ο Γιάννης είμαι. Είμαι εδώ για εσένα."

"اسلام۔ میں یوُحنّا ہوں۔ لگتا ہے کہ آپ کو میری تلاش تھی۔"

"ジョンだよ。誰か呼んだ？ …"

Chapter Sixteen: FADING SUN

Under the pink-and-green umbrella, my queen, Ava Elisabeth, sits in her flowing charcoal dress. Around her neck is a teal-and-gray infinity scarf, and a long silver pendant with an aqua crystal at the end of it … a gift from a Liechtensteiner who boasted of being from the princely family. While I can neither confirm nor disavow his lineage, he was a traveling Lothario who visited Ava Elisabeth's art studio when in Paris and never ceased trying to coax her into whatever sleeping quarters he was presently occupying. I am happy to say that she never gave in, yet she accepted this particular bauble because she found it of great beauty. (I wish she had refused it, but alas, she did not. Thus, it is yet another adornment to taunt me with … another testament to her greed.)

It is a special day in the garden as her dear friend Lone, for the first time in years, is feeling better and able to sit outside. Many months have passed since she had reason to wear her treasured accessories, and today, she enjoys her brown straw cloche hat, wrapped in a tawny hatband accentuated with a gold Etruscan-style hatpin boasting nine small pearls. Sitting next to Ava Elisabeth on the white wicker couch, she feels alive again. Despite the sun, which soon will begin to set, it is a mild day, and Lone is well wrapped in a quilt afghan, a treasured gift from a villager in her former happy life.

Sitting apart from them is Beth, a young woman who now serves as Lone's companion. Absorbed in a classic novel from Lone's bookshelf, she reads while the women talk.

Lone reaches for the handle of the teacup in front of her. Unnerved by the way her shaking hand makes it rattle on the saucer, she pulls it away. "I can't stop thinking about that woman, Millicent—Darah Gregnut's mother. My hand never shook the way it does until she entered my life."

Petting her cherished Mickey, who sits on her lap, the end of his leash wrapped firmly around my darling's wrist, she responds. "You can't allow her get to you, Lone. She's a sad woman who's had little happiness and unwittingly sabotages herself in trying to find some."

"You're one of the sweetest … yet strongest women I've ever known, Avie. And I've never seen you suffer any fool gladly. Yet, that day she impersonated me so boldly and without remorse, then she sat in my apartment while I told her there would be no second chances, you were uncharacteristically quiet. It wasn't like you."

"It's not like me to taunt a sad woman who happens to be the estranged mother of my dear friend."

"They're estranged for a reason, yes?" Now with a steadier hand, Lone picks up the cup of tea and successfully takes a few sips before resting it on the saucer again.

Ava Elisabeth smiles as Mickey licks her hand. "Neither of us have seen her since. Isn't that good enough? You seem almost angry that I didn't have harsh words for her."

Lone sighs. "I felt, for a brief moment, that you didn't have my back. What she did was such an invasion of my privacy, of my being, and you didn't so much as tell her so. You've always been such a gentle creature, but never ever do you let anyone get the better of you … or of anyone you love. You can be fierce when the occasion calls for it; I've seen you in action many times. It's one of the things I admire most about you."

My darling frowns. "So, you think that I failed you … or that I don't love you … because I chose not to tear into a very sad and disturbed woman." She looks into Lone's eyes although her vision doesn't allow her to see them as clearly as she'd like. "I think you've been upset for more than a 'brief moment.' That's quite obvious."

Agitated, Lone shakes her head, then looks down in shame. "I'm an old fool, Avie. Ignore me. I'm lucky enough to have a wonderful companion in Beth, a beautiful relationship with you, and to be outside today. This glorious sun feels like God's warmth on my face, restoring my soul, and yet, I'm rankled by some silly moment in time."

Beth looks up from her novel and sees that Lone appears distressed. "Are you okay, Ms. Aggen? Do you need anything?"

"I'm fine. D.H. Lawrence is far more fascinating than I could ever be. Especially *Sons and Lovers.*"

My beloved laughs. "Don't sell yourself short, Lone."

"I'm fine. What you just witnessed was an abhorrent moment of paranoia and self-pity. It's over." She slaps her hands together. "Now, enough about me. There was something you wanted to share."

Ava Elisabeth looks uneasy. "Well, I did confide once or twice to Darah, but I didn't tell her everything. And now that she and Mark have found their way back together again and are planning a wedding, even though a small one, I can't bear to distract her in any way. Especially not with this."

"You're making me nervous, Avie. Very nervous."

"I think I told you that I was having a visitor … of the spirit kind … at night."

"You did. You said it was Michael." She lowers her eyes. "Tragic that he died such a young death … eighteen was way too young for the two of you to be separated. How certain are you that he's your visitor?"

"Well, before, I suspected it was him. Only now … I'm certain of it."

"Is this a bad thing? To see your soul mate?"

My darling momentarily turns her head. Now she has me as worried as Lone is … only more so, as my love for Ava Elisabeth is deeper than any other soul's could ever be." She speaks softly. "It is not a bad thing. Especially as I can see so clearly when he visits. But it rather amuses me to think of an eighteen-year-old man so in love with a woman well into her eighties. But he says that's my mortal perception. I don't really know how it works, but I suppose he sees me as he knew me." She ponders her words. "And I keep forgetting that souls evolve and grow too. He just hasn't had a physical body to age in; that's all. I let that very important aspect trip me up; I know better."

"You've always been so wise. And don't get me wrong, I'm happy that you see him, Avie. I'm just disturbed by his frequent visits because … well, you know."

"I do believe he is preparing me for a transition."

Lone puts her hand over her mouth. "Oh, no."

"I'm old; you're old. It's all good. It only means that soon we'll be having our chats somewhere besides this beautiful garden. Some place far more wondrous, I'm sure." She pauses. "Well, I can't be sure … it's only an intuition."

Lone wipes away a lone tear. (Who else's tear would she wipe away?) "You have the best intuition of anyone I've ever known."

"Don't fret, my dear. This is a good day. Let's enjoy it."

"It is. It's lovely." Lone looks down the pathway. "Ugh. I spoke too soon."

No, it is not Millicent. It is someone far more loathed: Pandora Beausoleil, a long-washed-up film star who retains the entitlement that she carried with her during her four relevant decades. With her Lauren Bacall lush-curls hairstyle, she strolls in some faux-leopard-trimmed dress for the smart businesswoman, and stops in front of Ava Elisabeth and Lone, annoyed that there is no place for her to sit. She looks at Beth. "You! Helper person. Up!"

Startled, Beth opens her mouth, closes David Herbert Lawrence, then stands. Pandora's eyes, as if they belong to some alien villain from the planet Diabolico, attempt to control her.

"I shouldn't have had to tell you," Pandora says. "Common courtesy, dear."

Just as Lone, who is incensed, is about to tell Beth to ignore her, someone else is approaching who brings the greatest joy.

The gentleman cuts an exquisite figure as he walks. "Drake! Oh, darling. What a wonderful surprise. And look at you ... so handsome and dapper in your executive finery. I had no idea you were coming." Lone turns to Ava Elisabeth. "You arranged this, didn't you? Oh, such a sweet thing to do ... and there I was, scolding you for ... I'm so sorry." She waits for Drake to help her to her feet, and they share a warm embrace.

"I've missed this beautiful smile. And the lady who goes with it." He hugs her again. "You look radiant sitting here in the garden." He smiles. "Guess who's here to take you to dinner?"

"He was going to bring it over," Beth interjects. "But I told him you were up and about." She looks at Ava Elisabeth. "And then a little birdie arranged the rest."

Lone takes a moment to look at each of them. "I'm overjoyed."

"And I couldn't be happier," Drake says. "But I don't want to push things, so I thought the Italian place down the street would be good. We've had enough takeout from there ... long past time we go in person and show them how damn good-looking we are. What do you say?"

"I'd tell you to stop flattering me ... but I'm afraid you might listen."

Drake laughs. "Nah. No worries."

"You're so good to me, Drake. Unless I've died and gone to heaven." Lone's heart is melting ... even as the warm sun fades. No, she has not gone to heaven. But a particular has-been actress, who is seething with jealousy at the handsome, well-dressed man spiriting Lone away, will die and go in the opposite direction if she does not contain her bitterness.

Always outspoken, Lone cannot resist as Pandora watches her. "Oh my, Dora. Your blue eyes were always your trademark. How will anyone recognize you now with them being such a deep shade of green?"

Drake laughs to himself. "Good thing I worked out this morning." He flexes his muscles, knowing Lone will appreciate the show. "Just thinking of all the men I'm going to have to fight off with such a hot chick on my arm … a guy's got to be ready."

"Such silly fawning nonsense," Pandora barks. "And she's no chick."

"You're not the one slipping her arm through mine, are you?" Drake says.

Pandora snarls while simultaneously desiring him.

Lone smiles at Beth and hands her the treasured afghan. "If you will just escort my friend Avie to her suite, then put this away for me, you're free to go home. Thank you for everything. I'll see you in the morning." As Lone and Drake head off, Pandora, a scowl on her face, sits next to Ava Elisabeth, while Beth waits a polite distance away.

"I don't know why you won't allow me in your club." Pandora pouts. "I've been a member of far more exclusive clubs than you ever have."

"I've never required membership to be happy … not anywhere."

"You know what's really audacious?" Pandora's voice grows loud. "The way that frumpy Fiona Almaran looks at me. She's no better than her inebriated mother, whose star faded at such a young age, and I'm very sure she snubs me because Lana and I had a bit of a brawl on the set of—"

Mickey, who had been in purr bliss before Pandora showed up, looks up and hisses.

My darling laughs delightfully. "Really, Mickey, I couldn't have said it better myself." She stands, letting Mickey jump down and feel the ground under his paws. "Sorry, Dora. I don't know how to say this any kindlier, but … I really don't care."

Now standing as well, Pandora stares at her, ignoring the rebuff. "Guess who called me last week? The studio. They're making a film to star five legends who still roam the earth … and I happen to be one of the actresses in consideration. I'm easily the most famous, but that's hardly worth clarifying. Of course, they called to ascertain my interest before developing the project. It's an honor … one that would not have been bestowed on Lana Compton had she stayed sober and alive." Her voice goes into whisper mode. "Her daughter bats for the other team, I hear."

Ava Elisabeth wears disgust on her face. "There you have it, Dora. The studio took you down from the shelf and dusted you off. Isn't that nice? Something positive and uplifting may be happening in your life. You're being remembered, just as you want to be, as you obsess over being. But that's not enough for you. Even this recognition, this possible opportunity … isn't enough to keep you from bashing a dead woman and gossiping about her daughter's sexuality. Not to mention the fact that Fiona is someone I call a friend. What in the world is wrong with you?" My darling is quite peeved. "Perhaps the studio would like *my* input."

"You wouldn't dare!"

Ava Elisabeth loops Mickey's leash around her wrist as he appears overly interested in something moving in a bush. "No, I wouldn't. Because anger, gossip, and revenge are not the sustenance upon which I thrive. To share what I know about you would be akin to giving myself food poisoning." She pauses. "Of course, if I wanted to do it … I would … without hesitation. You're just lucky it's not by bag, as they say."

Pandora is dumbfounded.

"Oh, and by the way," Ava Elisabeth says as she walks toward Beth, who is holding out an arm to escort her, "you should only know what they said about *you*." She winks. "Past tense, darling. Nobody cares anymore."

THIRTY MINUTES LATER

Chevalier Beausoleil, Pandora's white Pomeranian, looks up from the lavender fainting chaise lounge, upon which he is happily settled. He sees that his mistress, who has just burst through the door of her seventh-floor suite, looks as angry as her prized turquoise ceramic Chinese foo dogs who appear to snarl in perpetuity. (Even Chevalier knows that something wicked this way comes.)

She scolds the poor canine. "Merely looking at *moi* is not a proper greeting. But for you, I'll pretend you gaily bounced my way." She walks to the lounge and leans down to kiss the dog. He gives her face an obligatory lick, then closes his eyes. Yes, he knows she's feeling insufferably put upon and has no interest in being wept upon or squeezed for comfort.

"Kerry Blue," Pandora calls. "Where the hell are you?"

The sprightly Irish woman in her late twenties, a dark redhead with a face of freckles, whose father named her after an Irish terrier hoping she would be as spirited and strongheaded as the breed, enters the living room with her arms full of folded lavender towels. "Hello. I was just putting the laundry away."

"Either that or you're doing your best impersonation of a towel rack. I do hope it is the former."

Indeed, Christopher O'Keeffe named his daughter well, though she has long tired of explaining her name. She has been Pandora's personal assistant for eight months, which I can unequivocally state is quite the record. Even the ones who have persevered do not make it past the first trimester.

"Let me put these away, and I'll be right with you." Not waiting for a response, she walks to the garish lavender "room of bath," as Pandora calls it, and places the towels where they belong.

The old movie star, desperate to sit, chooses her purple-and-black-throne chair with the bubble hood. This is not good news for Kerry Blue, who quickly learned that Pandora has not one favorite place, but chooses different spots depending on her mood … and this is the chair no one ever wants to see her in, for every time she occupies it, she takes on the role of Her Majesty the Obnoxious. Behind her, on the wall, are hundreds of framed photographs of Pandora in her heyday. There is not one solo photograph of a friend or co-star … yes, her image is in every last one. At a right angle, over the wall with the faux fireplace, hangs a revolting oil painting which rivals the hideous Gloria Swanson painting in Lee and Ellie's fourth-floor abode. I believe Pandora was trying to emulate Ms. Swanson when she posed for it. Her neck tilts at an unnatural angle … and her eyes, weighed down by false eyelashes, open as if they were fixed that way forever, while her lips part to reveal clenched teeth. Her hands, in a claw-like gesture, touch her throat as she gets ready to utter immortal words that no person in their right mind would wish to hear.

In the flesh, Pandora's back stiffens against the tufted brocade as she prepares to play queen. "Took you long enough. A pet turtle would have returned more quickly."

"Then perhaps you might like to trade me in for one."

"Smart retorts won't get you anywhere. I want a martini."

Kerry Blue wears an insincere smile and stands in place.

"Okay, then … *please!*" the washed-out luminary says, wanting to spit the word out as soon she is finished with it.

While Kerry Blue prepares the martini, this is an appropriate time to share that "Beausoleil" is not, of course, Pandora's true surname. But seeing herself as a "beautiful sun," she chose the French name (along with a new first name) and merged them into something with a musicality far more pleasant than "Pamela Sue Grock."

While Lone Aggen takes pleasure in the small brass sun mirror in her apartment, Pandora enjoys a much larger one in her bedroom. Unlike Lone's, which is hung high like the sun, Pandora's hangs at eye level. Never does a day pass when she does not call upon the mirror to reflect her beauty … over and over again.

"Shaken, not stirred. Two olives." Kerry Blue hands her the requested drink as she places a coaster on the small table next to the royal chair.

"Thank you." She indicates the couch with a nod. "You may sit. Tell me, did Chevalier get his walk?"

Kerry Blue sits, choosing the end of the couch farthest from Pandora. "Of course. We had a lovely walk, and he did …."

"My God. Haven't I told you not to discuss what exits my dog's anal orifice?"

"It's just kind of routine. You know, so you don't have to worry—"

"No bodily function talk. I have other things on my mind." She squints at the young woman. "If you ever get a man, I'd advise you not to make canine excrement a primary topic for discussion. Especially on the first date." She studies Kerry Blue's face. "You're not a pretty girl, but you have a pleasant enough face. You remind me of a perky schoolmate who was the president of the 4H club when I was in junior high. She had that same right-off-the-farm look as you do."

Having learned the art of repelling zingers, Kerry Blue responds with stoicism. "They told me at the agency that you don't want anyone who's really pretty. For obvious reasons. It was a bit insulting, but oddly, I'm a lot more confident in my looks than you are in yours. A photographer I know keeps telling me I have amazing bone structure, and he wants to shoot me."

"As I do now," Pandora mumbles.

"I clean up very well with makeup, but I don't like wearing it much." Kerry Blue looks up. "You've got at least a hundred photos on the wall, and you're heavily made up in every single one."

"Movie stars wear makeup."

"Fiona Almaran told me her mother never wore makeup at home … and loved the freedom of having no more than a good moisturizer on her skin."

"As if I care." Pandora's eyes open wider. "Please don't tell me that you talk to that Fiona person. Because if she can't speak to me, she's not to speak to my assistant. I forbid it. And Lana Compton was an unwell woman whose habits I've never wished to emulate, though I think her daughter does." She takes an angry swill of her drink.

"Yes, I know that Ms. Compton drank heavily and—"

"Hush!" Pandora is now self-conscious of the martini glass in her hand, but not enough so as to put it down. "What were we talking about?"

"My looks. And how I remind you of someone in school from the 4H club."

"Oh … yes. Well, don't despair. There's a pot for every lid."

Kerry Blue is every bit the terrier. "You've had what … three, four lids?"

Unamused, Pandora lays down her glass. "Yes, I had four husbands. You know that. And while that is common knowledge, what I endured in my marriages is not. And I'm not about to share any of it with the likes of you."

"I'm not interested in why your marriages failed."

"You need not phrase it like that." As much as Pandora's ill temper would have her fire Kerry Blue on the spot, she is quite aware that it gets progressively more difficult for the employment agency to find applicants to accept the job of "personal assistant," and that she may have to go days without any help at all. While many do accept the position for the experience of working for an impossible legend (believing they will be able to "handle her"), it is always too unpleasant to continue their situation. Most, however, are fired during a tantrum and are thus deprived of the joy of terminating the relationship at their pleasure. Pandora knows this. She despises the fact that working for her is not a sought-after position, but merely a short-lived one for those, like Kerry Blue who are not faint of heart. More than anything, the idea of having to do her own chores is absolutely abhorrent. Most sadly, aside from her delusions of superiority, she feels, as many do, that kindness is weakness, and thus, she carries on as she does.

"Is there something I can do for you?" Kerry Blue pauses. "I thought that ever since the studio called, you might be excited by the prospect of working again. But you look so unhappy."

"That wretched Ava Elisabeth (I want to smack this woman) and that dreadful Lone Aggen treat me as if I'm dirt under their out-of-fashion shoes. They're together often … and yet, they never think to include me in their exclusive club." She huffs. (Again, with feeling.) "Normally, I wouldn't care, but as you know, I see few people. Of course, it would be an honor for them to enjoy my company, yet they want nothing to do with me. I'm one of the greatest film stars in cinematic history. I have stories to thrill and delight for hours … days, if you will. That hussy, Ava Elisabeth, merely had an art studio in Paris, and pitiful Lone followed her adventurous husband around the globe until he was killed in a small-plane crash. You would think that my experiences would brighten their dull days, but no …."

"I'm sorry you're so lonely."

"Who said I was lonely? Pandora Beausoleil does not get lonely. For a man, perhaps, but not for those pathetic women."

"But you just said …."

"I said they don't wish to include me in their exclusive club; I never said I would accept an invitation if they did." She looks out the window to see the sun has set and imagines Lone laughing in the restaurant with the handsome man who came to take her out.

"Did you make my dinner, Kerry Blue?"

"I did. A cold vegetable platter … with shrimp and cocktail sauce. Exactly as you requested. Shall I get it for you?"

"Not yet. I'm going to take dinner in bed tonight, so I'm asking you to wait until I finish eating. God forbid I should have to take my own tray into the kitchen or have to look at an unclean plate should I wake before you get here in the morning."

"Yes. God forbid." Kerry Blue rises and nods toward Chevalier, who is soundly asleep. "He ate, of course."

Taking the last swill of her martini, Pandora thrusts her arm forward as Kerry Blue, without a word, takes the empty glass and walks into the kitchen.

"Chevalier. *Veins avec ta maman! Maintenant!*"

The dog opens his eyes, yawns, jumps lazily down onto the floor, and stretches. Poor thing knows the drill and follows behind her.

As Chevalier jumps onto the bed, Pandora walks to her sun mirror and takes a good long look at herself. "You may be old, Dora, and I don't care what they say about you, but you're still as bright and glorious as the noonday sun."

A WEEK LATER

"If I hear one more squeak, I'll go mad." Pandora looks at Chevalier, who, without any help from her, has found some joy with a small platypus squeak toy. The dog paws the brightly colored toy close to him, takes it in his mouth, and runs down the hall as the toy squeaks in his mouth, then quickly returns to the living room. As the toy drops from his mouth, he repeats the series of actions.

Today, the "beautiful sun," relaxing in her chaise lounge, looks through old photo albums, which, quite naturally, are filled with her image. Unfortunately, the pleasure of admiring herself is interrupted by Monsieur Chevalier Beausoleil. She addresses him with mild scorn: "You have a basket of toys, but naturally, the quiet ones don't interest you." She thinks. "I'm quite sure you just want to make my hackles rise."

Kerry Blue, who is sitting at a nearby desk paying bills and going through Pandora's mail, contorts her face with disgust, knowing her back is facing her boss. "He's a dog. He's having fun."

Pandora slams the photograph album shut. "Thank you for identifying this animal and elucidating his state of mind. Next you'll be telling me water is wet."

Swiveling around in the wheeled chair, Kerry Blue smiles. "I thought it brought you joy to see Chevalier play."

"If the timing is right, yes. But I've spent a week doing everything I can to prepare for a meeting I've yet to be informed about. Beauty, although natural, is also a business, and getting a manicure, a pedicure, a chemical peel, a massage, an eyebrow arch, and a lip wax, not to mention spending all day in a hair salon, aren't really as exciting as a person like *you* might imagine them to be."

"A person like me?"

"You heard me."

"What about me? In all the time I've worked for you, you've never inquired beyond wanting to know how I got my name. You have no idea if I have siblings, a fella … or a girlfriend for that matter … nothing."

Pandora opens the photo album, but only as a means to avert her eyes from Kerry Blue's. "I know you hail from Ireland."

"But that's—"

Pandora abruptly cuts her off. "You work for me. You have a need to know everything about me that is necessary to perform your duties. I, on the other hand, need to know you are capable and honest. Beyond that, why would I have the remotest interest in your life?"

Kerry Blue shrugs. The words have stung more than she

expected. "Oh, I don't know. Maybe because I'm a nice person, a competent assistant, and you might be even a bit curious. God forbid, as you like to say, you might even care about me. Just a wee bit."

"Oh for ...." Pandora stops herself before uttering an obscenity, but nonetheless, it is heard.

"This will probably shock you, but I have a fella. His name is Dane. He's a microbiologist ... you know, a person who studies microscopic life-forms and processes. He proposed to me last night, and I said yes. Of course. I'm thrilled. I thought you might notice my engagement ring." With great pride, she holds her left hand out, but Pandora refuses to look. "I'm the youngest of five. I have two twin brothers, Keiran and Finn. Kieran manages a large estate in Essex, England ... so hey, you weren't far off on the farm thing, Finn is an attorney in Dublin, and my parents own two bed and breakfasts outside of the city. Been running them for donkey's years. My sister Riley is a photographer in Paris, and my oldest sister, Maeve, lives in London with her husband. I have sixteen cousins, if you can believe that, and they're all over Ireland and Europe.

"I came to this country to be with Dane, and now I have a master's degree in health administration and an engagement ring. But because of his work and the uncertainty of where we might live, I took this job so I wouldn't get bogged down in anything important that would be difficult to extricate myself from.

"On the weekends, Dane and I often go to the beach or take our dog, Darby, to the mountains. You'll never guess what breed he is: a Kerry Blue Terrier. He stays with our neighbor while we're at work. Got the luck of the Irish living next door to a veterinarian with a farm. Hey, there's that farm thing again. I also—"

"ENOUGH! Shut the damn hell up! Seal your Irish trap shut with superglue if need be and don't pry it open again until you are requested to speak. With all of that garbage you just spewed, I find you even less interesting than I did before ... something I didn't think was possible. And in case you didn't hear me the first time: shut up."

Barely able to control her urge to cry, Kerry Blue is 'saved by the bell.' She answers the portable phone on the desk, listens, asks the caller to "please hold," then hands the phone to Pandora as she runs off to the 'room of bath' to cry. Luckily she wears no makeup to work (the agency advises against it) so there are no unwanted substances to wipe from her face. Only tears.

Turning on the faucet, Kerry Blue lets the cold water fill her cupped hands, then gives her face a good splash. Just as she finishes doing so for the second time, she hears a scream that makes Pandora's previous cruel reprimand sound like a whisper. Louder than a male howler monkey in a tree, she bellows so deafeningly that Kerry Blue forgets her own pain and rushes down the hall, into the living room, fearful that Pandora has had a frightful accident.

I shall not repeat the vile and vulgar words that spew forth from Pandora's mouth as she stands, still holding the phone. She is stomping on the purple-and-white carpet while poor Chevalier has run into her "sleeping chamber" (as she prefers to call it) to hide under the bed.

"Those filthy sons of bitches. How dare they set me up for such humiliation. Those lowly pieces of scum … I hope every last one of them gets it up the … anal orifice. How dare they …."

"Please, sit down. I'm afraid you'll fall."

Holding the phone as if it is a gun she wishes to shoot someone with, Pandora pounds the floor as she hurls more expletives.

"Did the studio decide not to use you in the project?"

Stopping in her tracks, Pandora glowers at Kerry Blue. "Do you think, country-bumpkin Irish girl? Do you *think*? Where did you get your first clue?" She runs through the call in her mind. "They had the nerve to tell me that I'm not right for the job … and because there are so few movie buffs left who would know my name … they're going with slightly younger women who are better known and 'less arcane.'"

She bristles. "I am *not* arcane. And who the hell is better known than Pandora Beausoleil? What a fat load of stinking garbage that is!" She stops. "I'll bet that wretched Ava Elisabeth said something. Oh, yes. I'll bet she picked up the phone and made the call of doom. She's a coy one, always pretending to be above the fray, but she's evil to the core. If she had anything to do with this, I'll kill her. If she even *thought* about doing anything to me, I'll destroy her. If she doesn't lose all her sight soon, I'll blind her into darkness and curse her to hell."

She has gone too far now. I stick out my leg to trip her, but nothing happens. (I forget that I am immaterial in every sense.) Still clutching the phone, Pandora storms into her "sleeping chamber" and Kerry Blue follows. Looking into the sun mirror, she is enthralled by her beauty and touches her face with her free hand as she admires herself. "How could they possibly not want *this*? Damn them all."

"You really need to calm down." Poor Kerry Blue. Her words only cause Pandora to spin on her heels with rage. As she does so, the clunky phone flies backwards out of her hands and lands square in the middle of the mirror, smashing it into splinters, shards, and smithereens.

"You wretched woman! Look what you've done. Call management immediately, and get me a new soleil mirror. Now! I cannot bear to be without it. Tell Darah ... or whichever one of her minions you speak with ... that it must be the same soleil mirror I have always had. Don't forget that."

Kerry Blue walks to the phone, which has slid across the floor, and picks it up. "I'll do that." She repeats Pandora's request in an effort to mollify her. "It must be the same soleil mirror that you had." Her kind heart affords Pandora a smile. "Why don't you sit down, and I'll bring you something?" She looks at the floor. "And then I'll clean up the broken glass. Be sure you don't step on it."

Without saying a word, Pandora sits on the bed. As she does, Chevalier darts out from underneath and runs into the living room to hide under whatever piece of furniture he can use for cover.

While Kerry Blue, from the living room, calls to order a replacement, she does her best to block out the piercing scream (resembling that of an angry goat) coming from the bedroom.

TWO DAYS LATER

Being a woman of mighty fortitude, Kerry Blue has yet to quit her job. She stands in the bedroom with Pandora and a maintenance man, Julian, who is adjusting the new mirror that he has just hung.

"Is this a good height, Ms. Beausoleil?"

"It appears to be."

Kerry Blue takes a peek in the mirror and does a doubletake. She has never appeared more radiant or more beautiful. Her eyes and her cheeks have a glow she's never seen before. "Oh, I like this mirror. I don't know what it is, but I never knew I looked this good."

Pandora seethes.

Curious, Julian looks at *his* face. The scars of his youth have disappeared, his eyes glisten, and his thinning hair has thickened. He is mesmerized by his reflection. "Hey, I'm more of a looker than I thought. Ha ha. My wife is a lucky woman." He chuckles. "And I'm gonna make sure she knows it."

"Oh, why don't you fools stop admiring yourselves. Let me look." As Pandora brushes them aside with a hand gesture, she steps to her left and peers into the mirror. She is frozen as she observes the woman who looks vacantly into her once-blue eyes. Now dark olive green, they are hollow and bloodshot. Every line on her face that a surgeon once vanished is now ten times what it would have been had she never sought enhancements. An angry red rash has inflamed her nose and cheeks. Her visage is a virtual field of skin tags, moles, and blackheads. Every vein is visible, and the ones on her forehead have the audacity to protrude. Her once-pouty lips are barely a thin line with a white mustache above them, and the light-brown lush curls are now only thin gray tendrils. Her eyes, sunken and lifeless, torment her, as if asking … begging … one final time, that she do something, anything, to make things all right.

Seeing her bewilderment, Kerry Blue and Julian look into the glass and are astonished to see Pandora as she sees herself. Unable to talk, to whisper, or to complain, the fading sun can only stare.

The two onlookers share their incredulity. "I don't understand," Kerry Blue finally says to Julian. "Didn't you order the soleil mirror?"

Stupefied, he searches his memory. "Uh, yeah. The soul mirror. I found it in an old catalog. Thought it might not be available. Funny thing is, Darah called me into her office for an impromptu meeting, and I never got to order it. But the next day, when I planned to do just that, the catalog was gone. Poof! But then, as magically as it'd disappeared, there was this big ole box sitting on my desk in its place. Had 'Soul Mirror' written right there on the side." He shakes his head. "Funny, I never even heard of one before. No clue how found its way to me. Stephanie, the concierge, said there weren't any deliveries, and besides, my office was locked tight. Always is when I'm doing maintenance calls or gone for the day."

They both look at Pandora, whose expression has not changed. She stands, but there is no breath left in her body.

Julian shakes off a chill. "Um … need anything else?"

"I'm not sure what to do." She reconsiders her dilemma as Chevalier appears by her side, looking at her with desperate eyes. "You know what? We're good. You can go. Thanks, Julian."

"If you're sure …."

"I am. And thanks for all your help. I think Miss Beausoleil got exactly what she deserved. Oh, and no need to close the front door. I'll just grab a few things. We'll be right behind you." She looks at the dog as if to reassure him. "Let's crack on, Chevalier. Shall we?"

The dog did not have to be asked twice. And now they are gone.

Pandora the Petrified still stares. Confession: it is me who "ordered" the mirror. One does not mess with Ava Elisabeth and get away with it.

I am judge and jury.

Chapter Seventeen: HELLO, GOODBYE

I feel powerful having accomplished what I was put here to do. Pandora reaped that which she sowed, and I am deserving of a reward for having encouraged karma to prevail. A promotion of sorts would sit well with me: a restoration of my powers and then some. Full omniscience and the ability to mete out more justice would be a pleasing and apt recompense.

Where shall I go next? I am mildly curious about Lee and Ellie and whether or not they will divorce. It does seem likely, but as they have not personally offended my sensibilities, I take no position either way.

Alejandro and Sophia are settled in their new place where they strive to embrace change. While they are quite in love again, Alejandro, for one, still battles with being undeserving, while Sophia wrestles with chasing away her demons. Yes, positive changes are on the horizon for them, but I'd rather watch paint dry than bear witness as they wait. Fiona Almaran is drinking again, as she waits for her late mother's resurrection of sorts, but I cannot help her. A retired waitress on the third floor (and an owner of many pets) … has taken a shine to Kenny Seymour. Poodley's reaction could prove mildly amusing, depending upon my mood. Karrie has had her first visit with an obstetrician; she has also convinced herself the father will return as her baby grows inside her. I believe she will still be waiting when the child graduates from college. Lark, sweet soul, is having some actor friends over for lunch — a first in her life … a step toward fitting in with the masses. Nice, perhaps ill-advised, but tragically boring.

Ah, I believe my functionality is already being elevated (I know it!), as I feel a pull toward a greater purpose. I must leave those mundane people in my dust as I ascend. Rising upward, I wonder where I am being led as control eludes me. Why am I stopped here on the ninth floor? The room is virtually empty. I see faint images of One, Two, and Three doing exactly what they were when I left them, but this time, I feel no connection to them and do not comprehend why I have been brought here against my will.

All I can see are letters of the alphabet, many times over, floating through the air, dancing in circles, changing directions, and although seemingly innocuous, I feel as though they have a greater purpose. I do not like the sensation in the pit of my stomach. "Am I here for my reward?"

A booming voice breaks out in laughter that rattles me like thunder. "For what would you be rewarded?"

"Who are you?" I demand to know, but the laughter swells, and I feel a decrease where I expected augmentation.

"How do you like being judged?"

I loathe it, but I dare not give this voice the satisfaction of saying so. Only I have no choice; my distress is clear and I believe the evil entity can hear my thoughts.

The laughing voice transforms to one of rage. "You are the judge of no one. You do not know yourself; how can you know others? How can you judge them?"

The letters of my name do not form in front of my eyes, but I see them in my mind's eye. I am Conrad Daniel Beauregard Shintz. "I see it all so clearly now. I am Con Shintz. And now I see the name Ava Elisabeth Rice. 'Elisabeth' disappears and Ava and Rice come together. Avarice. Yes, I am Conscience and she is Avarice. How did it take me so many years to figure out something that was right there the entire time? It doesn't matter. The undisputed fact is that I served in my role flawlessly."

"Wrong! You did nothing of the kind. You have no

conscience. You only see greed in Ava Elisabeth because you have projected your own ... to escape from it."

"No. I am not wrong. She is Avarice. It was there all the time. In her name. It *is* her name. While I have accurately assessed her worst quality, I still love her with everything that I am. I believe I am ready to forgive her for taunting me all these years. Is that why I am here? To offer her my forgiveness and receive hers in return?"

"You insufferable cockwomble. She owes you nothing. *She* is not the greedy one. Your jealousy and denial have concocted this distortion of her character. Do you even know who *you* are?"

"I do. My name proves it. And the middle appellations 'Daniel' and 'Beauregard' have no meaning. They were only put in there to obfuscate my true name ... my calling ... my identity.

"Guess again."

What is happening? The letters in the name D A N I E L appear before me. The A and the E are switching places and now I see D E N I A L.

"Stop this madness!"

Now I see B E A U R E G A R D. The letters fly away, and a rhyming appellation takes their place: N O   R E G A R D.

"Stop this!" The letters now form my first name:

C O N R A D

Before I can react, they change position:

D R   N O C A

"Nooooo!"

The wretched voice bellows at me. "How could you not have known who you were. You were given years after your cowardly death plunge to figure it out. You were given an opportunity to grow, to repudiate your former self by identifying your litany of flaws, to correct them, and to emerge a new man. But your arrogance and entitlement did not die as your body did, Nathaniel Noca. No. They have risen ... bloated and diseased ... only to cling to an old devil who feels himself worthy of reward for the most contemptible behavior."

"But I—"

"QUIET! You built this structure on stolen money obtained in the most heinous ways. How dare you profess to love a woman you have hurt so egregiously? You have stolen her greatest treasure. As if that were not enough, you have hidden behind her, in life and in purgatory. Oh, you do love the woman, in your sick and twisted way, especially as she has been the perfect shield … you have always known she would never have offered you love in return. She despises you … she knows what you have done … though she is still missing key details. Soon, she will know everything. Your secret is no longer safe; it never was. Now, a screen will lower in front of you, and what appears on it is all you will be permitted to see. You will never have any control over anything or anyone again."

I do not understand what is happening. Yes, this ghastly projection screen drops before my eyes. It is blank … no … it is not. My darling Ava Elisabeth appears. She is sitting on her couch, with Lone's quilt afghan around her shoulders and Mickey beside her. On the table in front of her, I see a pitcher filled with some form of drink, five glasses, and a platter of biscuits, cheese, and grapes.

There is a knock at the door, and it opens. Darah enters, walks over to my darling, and sits beside her on the couch. Before Darah can say a word, her eyes are focused on a ceramic bisque figurine on the coffee table. A beautiful angel, with flowing auburn hair, wearing a long pale-blue dress, pours water from a pot into a birdbath, as two white birds wait. The flowers in the angel's hair match those which line the base of the bath, and the angel, and her loving ways, exude a tenderness rarely seen. I recognize it now. It is Ava Elisabeth's cherished angel, the gift from her Grandma Rice, which she left behind the night she fled her childhood home.

"Oh my," Darah says, looking at the angel. "I didn't think you'd ever find this. I only thought she would look after you."

"You know, my darling, that time you took the out-of-town trip, I had the strangest feeling that it had something to do with me. But the self-centeredness of that notion rattled me, and so I let it go … like a feather that flutters in the breeze."

Darah puts her hand to her face, then takes it away again.

"However, shortly after you returned, there was that night, after you had tucked me in, you came out here, to the living room, only to shortly return to my bedroom. I peeked from the covers and could see your figure in the darkness, laying something down on my bureau. Then, thinking I was asleep, you walked over and whispered in my ear, 'Sleep well. And remember your angels are always with you.' At that moment, I knew you had been to see my younger sister, Nora Jaye, and that she had given you my treasured figurine. When I got up the next day, I found my angel exactly where I saw you place her, only in the light of day. She was even more beautiful than I remembered, though quite a bit fuzzier to my eyes, of course. But our reunion was nonetheless as joyful."

"I'm so sorry … do you understand why I came to make that trip, and why Norah Jaye asked me to bring the angel to you?" Darah is nervous. "Do you know who we are to one another?"

Ava Elisabeth speaks in a gentle tone. "I believe that I do, though I am certain there are details I lack. Much of it I had sensed for years. My heart knew, but I thought it was a foolish old woman's wishful thinking. Ours is a story with many parts, Darah. But the angel helped me to put it all together."

"I think I've made some terrible decisions, but I've been trying so hard fix them. But we don't exist in solitude … and while I've tried to do what's best for everyone in my life … I think I've failed on so many levels." Darah is in tears.

"No, darling. I understand why you made the choices you did. They were not of malice, but of preservation and love."

The intrusive floating letters choose this moment to block my view. Damn them.

I see the name before me:

D A R A H   D   G R E G N U T

Blast this phantom speller. I know who this woman is. Ah, but now the letters of Darah's name rearrange:

G R A N D D A U G H T E R

Why did I not know this? My omniscience has been a cruel joke, giving me unnecessary information to lull me into a false sense of security. Yes, I knew it was fading, but now I see … it never really existed. A despicable mirage.

"Can you not see what you have done, Nathaniel?"

"I will not answer to some unidentifiable voice. If I had not done what I had, Darah would not exist. Timmy wouldn't exist. Therefore, I have brought forth love into the world, and I will not accept the blame for anything else."

"You do not justify your misdeeds because the good, the bad, and the unspeakable happen to emerge from them. Ava Elisabeth is not the one of diminishing sight. That has always been you. You were never judge and jury, fool. You were the defendant."

Thank goodness, the wretched voice is momentarily silent, and I can see my darling's suite again.

Darah is still crying. "You know, that day in the lobby when my mother showed up, after six years, I almost spilled everything when we were arguing. Just as I had almost done many times before. But every time, when the truth came to my lips, she'd say something awful, and then I'd be reminded of why I kept it all secret, why I'd kept Timmy secret … and why I should continue to do so." She sighs. "Knowing what happened in her life, I get why she's a walking train wreck, but I didn't want to become one as well. I *don't*. And there was a time, before I learned about you, that I almost lay ruined on the tracks alongside her. But mostly, I was quiet because I didn't want to lose our relationship and all that we share." She takes a moment to compose herself. "I hated depriving my mother of her grandson ... and Timmy of his grandmother ... but I felt that it was just too big of a gamble, most especially for my son. And yes, for me."

Ava Elisabeth reaches over and wipes away Darah's tears. "It's all right, my sweet. It really is all right."

"When my mother reemerged after six years, in such shambles, it occurred to me that I had put up an iron fortress to keep nearly everyone out. That's when I began to think differently about Mark. I still loved him, but the fact that he'd made one bad decision ... to honor his commitment for a dream job in London ... because it was 'only a two-year contract' ... hurt me so deeply. I mean ... I was pregnant with his baby, and he left. Yeah, he flew in when Timmy was born, he visited every chance he got, and he made sure to video chat several days a week. But I was deeply damaged by his actions. No, that didn't mean that we should never be a family again, though for a while, I thought it did. I'd already forever kicked my father out of my life. And unlike my mother, he didn't try to win me back. My mother, no matter how awful she was, *never* stopped trying. But all of my anger with both of them ... coupled with Mark's actions ... just sort of merged into one big grudge. That's when I discovered the proverbial iron fortress I'd skillfully erected."

"I told you, my darling. Everything is okay. You mustn't beat yourself up. You're a wonderful, loving woman."

Darah sniffles, like a child who has just fallen from her bicycle, as she tries to let the consoling words take hold. She glances at the angel, then at the glasses. "Why are there five of these?"

"You'll see."

The two of them sit for many minutes in contemplative silence. There is a knock at the door, only this caller, unlike Darah, does not know to let herself in.

"Perhaps you will open the door for our visitor."

Darah nods, understanding everything, and gets up to do so.

Looking more youthful and beautiful than Darah has ever seen her, Millicent, in a new blue dress, her hair styled in a modern, spray-free, shoulder-length cut, smiles. "I had a feeling you would be here. Don't worry, Darah. I've been doing a lot of soul searching, with the help of a therapist, and I'm more human than monster now. At least I think so, but I guess that's not for me to determine. My therapist says I'm making remarkable progress because I have such a will to do so. I've been seeing her twice a week for several months."

"I begged you for *years* to get therapy." She pauses to let the embarrassment wash over her. "And yes, I should have gotten some myself … and I will. But what made you finally take the plunge?"

"This will sound strange, but I was sitting in the lobby one day, disguised in a ridiculous red wig, when I met this woman who was the daughter of the movie star Lana Compton. When she heard even a bit of my story and saw that I was disguising myself to get a mere glimpse of you, she kindly suggested I seek therapy. I don't know, Darah, but coming from a stranger who I'd never met before, something tweaked in me, and I realized I needed it. Funny thing."

"That actually makes sense, Mother. I think we tend to tune out what we hear too often … hoping … waiting … for things to somehow change … as if by magic. As long as there's not too much work involved on our end."

"Well aren't you the wise one?" Millicent smiles. "I don't know why your friend Ava Elisabeth invited me to her suite, but I'm thrilled to be here." She takes a look at her daughter. "Oh, no. You've been crying."

"Please," my darling says to her visitor as she holds her arms out. "I would love a hug."

Confused but happy for any affection, Millicent walks over to Ava Elisabeth and warmly accepts her embrace. There is so much joy on her face she is nearly unrecognizable.

"Why don't you sit in the chair? Please pour yourself some of this delightful sparkling water and help yourself to any food. Darah will sit next to Mickey and me." She laughs. "No doubt you've figured out Mickey is this handsome feline by my side."

"Oh ... I always wanted a cat. But neither my parents nor Darah's father ...." Millicent stops herself. "No, I won't go backward. I'll just leave that regret in the dustbin of history."

Darah, not saying a word, resumes her seat as Ava Elisabeth continues talking. "Your daughter has something very important to tell you. But, before I ask her to do so, I must tell you *my* story ... one that I have never spoken about to a soul." She swallows her fear. "It has been far too painful to relive, but now, it must be told."

Millicent, who has poured herself a drink, takes a few sips and holds the glass for comfort. "I'm listening."

My darling inhales deeply. "Well, when I was fifteen, I met him for the first time. His name was Michael, and his family had just moved to my town where his father took a job in the local manufacturing plant. That factory was where a good many local people worked, including my father and two uncles. My mother had once been a secretary there; that's how she and my father came to know one another.

"I met Michael at school. I feel old-fashioned telling you that it was love at first sight, but I do believe that kind of love still exists ... as I believed it then. Please understand that while I'm finally ready to tell my story, I still find it necessary to spare some of the impossible details. I'm sure, my darlings, that you can both understand the depth of love that we shared. It was as if we'd always known one another ... our souls destined to be together forever.

"Anyway, back in November of nineteen-forty-two, after an act of Congress, when we were both eighteen, Michael became eligible for the draft. In what seemed like no time at all, he was to leave. All our future plans were ripped to shreds. Devastated, we ran to the next town to be married, and we consummated our union in a cornfield.

Michael's older brother, who was exempt from the draft because of a medical deferment, had their grandparents' wedding rings. When he learned of our marriage, instead of keeping the rings for his own wedded bliss one day, he gave them to Michael. He was very kind."

She reaches inside her dress and pulls out a gold chain with a gold ring on it. "He had mine engraved: 'To Avie … my forever love … wait for me." Tears roll down her tender cheeks. "I have always waited for him, even though he only meant the wait to be as long as his tour of duty. I have never taken this off since he gave it to me; I just no longer wore it on my finger. I always wished to have Michael's ring on this chain as well, but as I never wanted to be found, I made no attempt to contact his family. Besides, it's more than likely the ring was never returned to them.

"There is so much irony here. So many people know me for all the beautiful jewelry I have worn. Yes, it is pretty, but it has never been of any real import. A mere cover-up for a simple ring that was lost to me." She looks down. "But losing my husband, my true love, was my real loss; the ring is merely a symbol of that." She puts her palm up to ask for a pause in time. Finally, she is able to speak again. "I should tell you that I haven't considered myself to be Ava Elisabeth Rice for a very long time. I took Michael's last name, Gary, but I never told a soul."

What is happening! Those vile letters are forming in front of me again.

AVA GARY

A VAGARY

"Do you see how wrong you have been, Cockwomble? Do you even know what a 'vagary' is? It is something that is neither predicted nor explained. That is your precious Ava Elisabeth, not 'avarice,' as you have so incorrectly concluded."

"Shut up. If I need a disembodied talking dictionary, I'll ask for one." I am livid. Meanwhile, Millicent, who still has not put the pieces together, looks into Darah's eyes for some understanding, but Darah is fixed on my darling, awaiting her next words.

"I shall continue. Perhaps five days after Michael's death, with the help of his brother, I got on a Greyhound bus and came out here. I didn't want to grow up in that town … to work in that godforsaken plant … and to imagine the face of my beloved everywhere I looked. I wanted to live in the big city … where the two of us had planned to relocate when he returned from the war. I knew that if I didn't sneak away in the dead of night, my father would have never let me go. Yes, I was a legal adult, but it would have been very ugly and not a scene I wanted to see play out nor one I wished to relive in my memory. My parents, how do I say this most kindly … were 'traditional' and steadfastly 'unbroken' in their beliefs. Nonetheless, I cared for them, and my chosen method of departure, though not preferred, was necessary. More than anything, I hated to leave my sister, Nora Jaye, who was only five at the time, but I had no choice. If my beloved Grandma Rice hadn't died a year before, I don't know what I would have done, but now that I think about it, I believe she would have encouraged me to escape … and even abetted the process. And there is my truth. Perhaps I was selfish, but if I couldn't have Michael, I was going to have my life. And I would always be 'Mrs. Gary,' even if nobody else knew that but me."

"Oh, my," Millicent says. "I can relate to the need to escape … oh, there I go again with my incessant lamentations … as I regularly acknowledge to my therapist." Self-consciously, she looks down. "Please forgive me. Go on, please."

Darah smiles at her mother as if to reward her resolve.

My precious continues. "Michael's brother had given me the tidy sum of money which he had left behind, wrapped in a blue bandanna … just in case such a tragic occasion occurred and necessitated my wanting to leave." She is oozing with love for a mere boy who was undeserving of her. "As soon as I got here, I found a small women's hotel where I lived for two weeks. I didn't look for work immediately, as I wished to first get my bearings in my new environment." She gulps. "But then, I realized I had someone besides myself to worry about. I was simultaneously thrilled and frightened, having no idea how to handle it all, but going back home was never an option. I only knew I would need much more money to care for a baby, so I looked for a job sooner than I had planned. My 'bearings' could wait." She laughs uneasily.

From the look on her face, something is forming in Millicent's brain, but she cannot quite grasp it. She responds by depositing a grape into her mouth … and almost choking on it.

I do not wish to hear what my darling says next.

"You will listen to her, Nathaniel Noca. You will listen to every word she speaks."

How dare this unknown entity invade my thoughts.

Ava Elisabeth is now holding tightly to her wedding ring at the end of the gold chain. "Once I learned of my condition, I thought destiny had blessed me. In no time at all, I found a job working for a doctor … Nathaniel Noca. Soon afterward, I learned that he owned this grand hotel, and I must say, it seemed incongruous with the rather shabby medical practice he ran, but I later learned that his father had refused him an inheritance if he didn't assume a 'proper profession.' I took that at face value, and when the doctor offered me a job and said I could live rent free in the small one-bedroom apartment above the office, well, it was like manna from heaven. I didn't realize I would also live rent free in that vile man's head." (How dare she.)

Darah looks at her mother, and nodding toward the pitcher, only with her eyes, requests a glass of water for Ava Elisabeth, which her mother pours … for Darah as well, which she sits on the coffee table.

My darling smiles in gratitude and takes a small sip before continuing the story I do not wish to hear.

"I thought it only right to tell the doctor I was with child, for he would soon see for himself and might not wish a pregnant widow to work for him. Especially one so young and inexperienced. But he not only said he didn't mind; he assured me he would help with my medical care and that my baby and I would be in 'good hands.'" She shivers in revulsion. I cannot bear this.

Darah, who has a silly habit of covering her face when distressed, does so again.

She takes another few sips of water. "One day, near my due date, not long after the office had closed at six o'clock, my water broke, and I began having intense contractions. In a panic, I called downstairs to tell Dr. Noca, who was going to deliver my baby. He came upstairs, told me I needed a shot for the pain, and that is all I remember until I awoke the next morning. I'd had such a good pregnancy, with so few issues, and now suddenly, this man is sitting by my bed, in my apartment, tearfully telling me that my baby had died, and that without his fast thinking, I would have too. I was completely inconsolable and wished I had died along with her."

Seeing my darling's hand tremble, Darah takes the glass from her and places it down next to her own.

"How chilling. Didn't you ask for any details?" Millicent wants to know as her cerebral matter finally does an honest day's work.

"I was nineteen and so naïve. Also, back in those days, as has continued for a long time in our society, doctors were not to be questioned as one might question them today. And so I believed him, feeling as if my heart had been ripped from my body along with my baby girl."

To feel a part of the conversation, Millicent finds it appropriate to add a small footnote, as if it were one of those pathetic squares of yellow sticky paper that people stick in improper places. "That's harrowing."

"She will soon learn what true evil is, Nathaniel. Do not mock her!"

"I didn't know what to do with myself. I couldn't bear to be in the room where my baby had been born and died. So, when Dr. Noca offered me a grand suite at this hotel, this very one that we're sitting in, I took it. He had it beautifully decorated, and I offered to work for him … because I wanted to pay my way. That was very important to me.

"I lived here for six years. The man's lust for me became intolerable and more off-putting and uncomfortable by the day. When I met this Parisian doctor, Henri, who was here for an extended stay, I couldn't say yes fast enough when he asked me to move to Paris and marry him there." She pauses. "That is a story for another time."

"Oh, you lived in Paris," Millicent says. "Was it wonderful? Like something out of a storybook?"

"It was, but do let me finish here before I lose my nerve." She picks up her glass and fortifies herself with another sip of sparkling water, probably of some fruit flavor, but I no longer have the ability to know such banal things. "I found out, quite a long time after I moved, when my friend Irina visited me in Paris, that on the day I left, Nathaniel threw himself out of my bedroom window and died."

"Oh, my goodness. That's shocking. Because he was so much in love with you?" Millicent wants to know.

"No, darling. That man never understood love. *Never!* Only insatiable greed, lust, cruelty, and other things my lips do not wish to speak."

She is so wrong. I understand love to its very quintessence.

Darah seems alarmed. "Are you okay, Ava Elisabeth? You look very pale all of a sudden. And so weak. Do you want to stop for now? I think maybe you should." She takes the glass from my darling's hands again and sets it down.

She does look very tired. The light in her eyes has dimmed. "I will go on." She stops to catch her diminishing breath. "Irina also told me that she had recently learned, through her mother's neighbor, of this very wealthy couple who had a birthday party, comprised mostly of adults, for their eight-year-old daughter. As if the child's special day was a mere addendum to a cocktail party."

As her mouth drops open in anticipation of what is to come, Millicent puts her drink down as well and stares at my darling. There is a bit of trembling going on. Oh, dear.

"Irina found it unusual," Ava Elisabeth continues, "but what shocked her was when she learned that the child had been born on the same day my baby girl supposedly died, all of those years ago. That curious timing, along with the notorious reputation of my former boss and landlord, Nathaniel Noca, compelled her to dig deeper."

Millicent's unlatched trap allows air to be sucked in like a vacuum. Most unladylike.

"The neighbor, now suspicious of Irina's questions and worried her big mouth would get her in trouble, referred to the couple with a fake name, as I now know, but did let it slip that the woman had tried to have a baby for years. Apparently, no one had ever seen the supposedly pregnant thirty-five-year-old mother for six months. The story was that she had so many difficulties in carrying a child that she found it prudent to live with an aunt, who was also a nurse. And then, like magic, she came back to town with a healthy baby girl. Aside from the perplexing birthday party, which was silly secondhand gossip at best, Irina had no reason to think the child wasn't loved. And she thought it wise to stop asking questions, fearing that if the couple knew someone was making inquiries about their daughter's parentage, they might move away, change their name, and then there would be no chance of finding them ... had I wanted to do so when I learned the story."

Millicent moans in despair (must she be so loud) as Darah puts an arm around her. "Oh, my Lord in heaven. I should have known. It all makes so much sense."

Wanting to offer comfort, Ava Elisabeth is torn as she knows her wretched story must finish first. "When Irina was done telling me what she'd learned, I knew, beyond any doubt, that my baby had never died, and that as soon as I had called him, that sinister man had knocked me out, then delivered and sold my baby to this wealthy couple. I have no idea how anything happened. He had drugged me so heavily.

"Oh, my Lord in heaven" is repeated for all who didn't hear it the first time. Now I see where Darah gets that face-covering gesture from, as Millicent, following her ear-splitting cries of despair, is doing the same, while her eye ducts bring new guests to the overdone cryfest.

"You are seeing the pain you have caused in real time, Nathaniel Noca, and you feel no remorse, no sympathy, no regret of any kind. Is sarcasm all you have to offer?"

I will not respond to this voice. My darling, now in tears and so full of love and empathy, looks into Millicent's eyes for her reaction.

Before she can say a word, the aggrieved one speaks. "I look more like you than those wretched people who never cared for me at all." She weeps, her eyes now glued to Ava Elisabeth's face as if adhered with that dreadful hairspray she once used.

Darah slides over on the couch, taking Mickey on her lap, so that Millicent can position herself next to her newly discovered maternal unit.

"Come to me," Ava Elisabeth says, her arms open and her face full of love. (Why have I been denied such intimacy all these years?)

"I can't believe they bought me," Millicent cries, hurrying to the couch and into her true mother's embrace. "But it all makes sense. No wonder I always felt like a prop: because that's exactly what I was." Her anger rises. "How much did they pay for me?"

Ava Elisabeth pulls the sobbing woman closer while Darah minds her own precious tears. "I don't know."

"A million dollars," Darah says. "And believe me, that was a lot more money in those days than it is today."

My beloved gasps. "Well, that would explain where Nathaniel found the money to fix up this suite for me." (I still resent that she redecorated every inch of it when she returned from Paris. At least no one else ever dared to live here. If they had, I would have killed them. I made that more than clear in my suicide note.)

"I-I don't understand," Millicent says. "Why didn't you come for me?"

Racked with guilt, my darling sighs. "Because over eight years had passed. Irina had no way of knowing the true circumstances, only that *my* daughter was now theirs. The details of the transaction were never discovered. I believed the couple had engaged in an expensive private adoption and that whatever monies paid were for legal fees, and yes, perhaps more for the attorney's eternal discretion. I had no idea that such a sum of money had changed hands."

Millicent turns to Darah. "How in the world do *you* know all of this?"

"Please, dear *daughter* ...." Ava Elisabeth says as Millicent springs a fresh leak at the filial word never once said to her with love before. "Let me finish my story, and you will learn the rest from *your* daughter." The object of all my affections is weakening. "I felt that perhaps I didn't deserve to have you. Foremost in my mind, however, was that you had to be a happy little girl, adopted by people who so desperately wanted a child, who had a beautiful home, and who I sadly assumed must be loving parents. To come and rip you from their arms seemed absolutely sinful and selfish. I did considerate it, though. For weeks on end. But every time, I came to the same conclusion that it would be very wrong, and I must leave you be. I thought it was the most loving thing I could do."

"Oh, how I wish you had! I wish you'd ripped me away from those brutal people. Torn me like a page of lies from the devil's notebook." Millicent, aware of old habits returning, regains her questionable composure and looks at her daughter. "But I suppose if you had, I would have married differently, or not at all, and would never have given birth to Darah."

"You would have been better off, Mother." Oh, now Darah has adopted, pardon the linguistic choice, her mother's self-deprecating drivel. How pitiable.

Millicent consoles her daughter. "It's strange to say this, as these kinds of thoughts are so foreign to me, but no—just as Ava Elisabeth doesn't regret her decision, I can't regret that things happened as they did. Because *you* exist as a result, and we still have time. And now I know how to better use it." She pauses to let an angry thought give birth. "I'm glad your father left me. That woman will take everything he has ... his sanity and his money ... and I won't care." Lovingly, she caresses Darah's hair, happy to be the motherly woman she has never been.

"And whose fault is *that,* Nathaniel?"

My darling looks so weak. She is trying to remain strong.

The voice booms. "Because Ava Elisabeth wants to hear her granddaughter's story. You want to hear that, too, don't you Nathaniel? After all, how can you resist anything that is about *you*?"

Millicent speaks far beyond the desired whisper. "My goodness gracious, Darah. You've known Ava Elisabeth was your grandmother all these years. It's the only thing that makes sense. It's the only reason you would have bought this hotel and become so dear to her." Insert dramatic sigh. "There were so many times I believed you were going to tell me something of great importance. One of them wasn't that long ago. But I screamed such ugly things at you, and no doubt, you chose to hold on to your secret. I never imagined this could be it. I didn't know what you wanted to say, only that I felt fearful of hearing it because I assumed it would show me in a negative light." She sobs. "Because nearly everything said to me was as such. I say this only to clarify, not to go back to my old ways."

Darah squeezes her mother's hand. "I understand; it's okay. Say whatever you need to … and yes, I've known all these years. I'm sorry I didn't tell either one of you. I was afraid of losing the only family I had in Ava Elisabeth." She casts her eyes downward in guilt. "I'm so sorry. That was so selfish of me."

"No. Once again, I'm thinking thoughts and saying words that not too long ago would've been alien to me." Millicent pauses as if to wait for accolades. "I've been a horrible mother to you. If the situation were reversed, I'd have done the same thing. I know it. Now, please, tell me … tell *us* … everything."

"Yes, dear," my darling says. "Please do. I have no idea how you found out, and I really need to put that last piece of this puzzle together before … go on."

"Uh … well …" Darah looks down at the poor cat to give her strength, but he senses his mistress is weakening and has little time for a sympathy nuzzle. He returns to my darling, who tenderly caresses him as he settles on her lap.

"What you are seeing, Nathaniel, is everything these women see. There are no special powers to allow you such knowledge anymore, though you tell yourself there is … and that I am merely a figment of your fertile imagination. But I am not."

I ignore the voice as Darah begins to speak. "When I accepted Mark's proposal, I decided to share these secrets with him. Other than my husband to be, I've never, ever … said a word to anyone. I just want you both to know that."

"You had every right to make your choices. Please, tell us the story, Darah. Your mother and I are eager to hear it."

Looking nervously at the two women, Darah begins. "It all began when I came home from college. I'd just gotten my business degree, and Grandpa had gifted me a car. Actually, he sent me a letter telling me to go to a particular dealership and pick out whatever I wanted. I don't want to sound ungrateful, as I was quite excited, but

I'd hoped he would have wanted to go with me … you know, to make the occasion special … but he was just doing what his friends did for their grandchildren, I suppose. No more, no less."

"No doubt," Millicent says firmly.

"Moving on. As you know, Mother, having grown up with them, and as I have told *you*, Ava Elisabeth, my grandparents had a very large house. I rang the front bell, but there was no answer. Their cars were in the driveway, so I walked around to the back. As my mother well knows, the screened-in sun porch was their favorite place to sit. The windows had green shades that they could pull down when it rained, or at night, when they wanted privacy." She looks at Millicent. "What I'm about to tell you will be awful to hear. Are you sure you wouldn't like a sanitized version?"

"Absolutely, not, Darah. With all the pain in my life, and all the lies I've been told and have told myself, that's the dead last thing I need."

"Okay. I just need to be sure." She looks at both women before continuing.

My darling is still clinging to that ring she wears. How did I never know it was there?

Darah picks up her untouched glass of water, takes a few sips, then rests it back on the table. "Just as I was approaching the screened windows where they could have seen me, I heard Grandpa yelling. He was furious because Grandma had just purchased a very expensive Steinway, and he said he was sick of the way she wasted his money. Then he said, uh, that at least the piano would bring him more pleasure than the child he bought for a million dollars from that 'charlatan doctor.'"

How dare he. I knew medicine very well. Oh, I will listen to what else Darah says, as much as I loathe this story.

"Then he said to Grandma, 'I told you that I wanted to name her Millicent after a great aunt. Ha! I had no great aunt with that name. I paid a million dollars for her and yet she has never been worth even a milli-cent to me. And I knew she never would be.' He then said he was considering the name Penny, but Millicent sounded more 'upper crust.'" Darah turns to her mother, who has a fresh case of the sobs. "Gosh, I'm so sorry. I feel absolutely sick telling you all of this."

"It's okay, Darah. I'm not shocked. He'd told me several times that I was only worth a milli-cent." She pauses. "Funny, with all of my complaints about their treatment of me, I was too embarrassed to share that bit with you. Maybe I was afraid you'd agree." Another painful sigh is emitted. "I just didn't know he'd actually named me Millicent to diminish me from the start. But knowing this is good, because it helps me to realize, as my therapist pointed out, that their dislike for me wasn't because of who I was, but because of who they were." Millicent seems surprised by her own words. "After you found this out, how in the world did you know to search for Ava Elisabeth?"

"Yes, dear. How did you ever find me?"

"Well, about a year after I overheard that conversation, Grandma died suddenly, and then when Grandpa died a year after her and left me all of that money, I had a reason to see his lawyer. I was surprised it wasn't his lifelong attorney, Richard Erstwell, but I learned he had died as well. That got me thinking—Erstwell had to be the one who arranged the sale. I casually asked the current lawyer, the one who executed the will, if Erstwell's secretary, Louisa Montagne, was still alive, as she'd been so nice to me as a child and I would love to see her again. I'd only met her once or twice, but hey, he didn't know that. It didn't take me long to learn that Louisa was physically infirm and living in a nursing home but still of extraordinarily sound mind.

"Nevertheless, I was nervous about visiting her. It felt awkward … kind of creepy and invasive. So, I was surprised … and vastly relieved when she welcomed me with the biggest smile I'd ever seen. When I told her why I was there and what I knew, she said she'd carried the horrible burden of being involved in the crooked adoption all her life and still prayed to God every day to forgive her. Apparently, at the time, she was appalled enough to quit her job, but her husband had just lost his engineering position, and they had three children. As if that wasn't enough reason to stay, Erstwell threatened to destroy her if she ever revealed a thing." Darah pauses. "Great guy to work for, huh? Anyhow, he was very powerful, Louisa needed the job, and so she stayed." Darah stops, plucks, and eats a single grape from the bunch. Like mother, like daughter. "She became very emotional telling me the story, as I am now, but like you, mother, and you ...."— she looks at Ava Elisabeth—"*Grandmother* ... Louisa was hell-bent on finishing, as she told a concerned nurse who came rushing over when she saw how animated her patient was."

"Go on," my darling says.

"Well, Louisa said that after Erstwell died, she went to the son of an associate of his, also an attorney ... and asked him to please find out how Ava Elisabeth was doing. Apparently, she was very concerned ... *Grandmother* ... that in your grief you might have taken your life. But happily, she learned you had lived in Paris all those years, and after forty of them, you'd come back to the hotel Nathaniel once owned ... where you had lived. That was all she told me. We chatted for another hour while I did everything I could to make her feel better. Then I gave her my phone number so we could arrange another visit. And then I left to come here with the high hopes of meeting you."

"But we didn't meet until you bought the place? Did you plan on becoming the owner?"

Darah shakes her head. "Not at all." She pauses again to string more sorry words together. "It's weird. Even though I wasn't sure what you knew, what I really wanted to understand, more than anything, was why you came back here ... to the very place owned by the monster who sold your daughter and told you she'd died. Even if you didn't know he was responsible ... I couldn't imagine this place didn't hold painful memories."

My darling clasps Millicent's hand in hers before responding. "That's the easiest question of all, dear Darah. Aside from that dreadful Nathaniel, who was long gone, there was so much about this place that I simply adored. But more than anything, I came back from Paris and straight to this building, precisely, because I hoped it would help my daughter to find me should she ever know to look." She squeezes the hand that she holds. "That's why I'm here. I've always thought of this building as my private waiting house. I never imagined my granddaughter would buy it and become such a dear friend."

The middle generation is leaking copious tears again. "Oh, Darah. When I think of all the times I berated you for purchasing this place. I said such appalling things. As it turns out, buying this property is the best thing you could have ever done. I'm just sorry that you had to spend every bit of that man's inheritance to do so. That troubles me."

Darah hints at a smile. "But I didn't. Not at all. Nathaniel's brother had died, and his sister, Ruth Tellert, was the sole owner.

The dreaded screen has gone dark again, and the letters are playing with my head. All I can see is my loathsome sister's name.

RUTH TELLERT

I watch as the T at the end of her surname scurries to the front of her given name. Now it is:

TRUTH TELLER

Damn that blasted woman. I deserved all our father's inheritance for the hell he put me through. She and my pathetic brother had no right to it. What inane secrets are hidden in Victor's name?"

"That one is out in the open, Nathaniel. Even a fool like you can figure it out. Your brother lived a happy, loving, and respectable life. Indeed he was a victor. Something you will never be."

I wish that voice would die. I would squeeze the life out of the form it emanates from if only I could locate it.

Millicent has questions. "So how did you end up buying this place?"

"I'd like to know that as well," my darling says.

Millicent reaches over and gives Mickey a scratch on the neck. He is an anomaly to the feline species. So patient. So willing to endure females pawing at him for their own selfish comfort. And just minutes ago, I had given him too much credit for being his own man.

Darah smiles as she sees the joy her mother takes from the cat. "Well, there was just something so lovely and endearing about Ruth. I knew she was Nathaniel's sister, but I had no idea who she was as a person. We sat in her office, and I told her my story. And she told me the horrible saga of her savage brother who'd committed way more heinous crimes than I'd ever imagined. I shouldn't have been shocked, knowing he stole and sold my mother as a baby, but I was." She eyes the grapes, but apparently decides against eating another one. "Ruth was profusely apologetic for what her brother had done. Then, she told me all the wonderful things about the hotel. She did say at one point: 'Ava Elisabeth Rice is the star of this show. Everyone here loves her.' I remember that so clearly. When we finished our conversation, she asked me if she could have my contact information. She said she wanted me to come see her again but asked if she could call me when she was ready. I had no idea what she wanted, but I readily agreed and somehow knew that when we next spoke, I would then learn how to meet you, *Grandmother*."

"Five days later, she phoned. She'd verified all the many details of my story. Also, she knew I had a business background as I'd confessed that I was floundering career-wise, not really knowing if I wanted to go left, right, or upside down. Ruth told me that I deserved to have this hotel, seeing the heartbreak her oldest brother had caused my family, and if I had any interest in owning and running a hotel, or doing something else with this building, she would sell it to me for a fraction of its market value. And so I bought it. And that's it. What

I've just told you both is all I've got. Except …"

"What's that, dearest?" Ava Elisabeth wears sympathy better than her lovely flowing dresses.

"I'm just so overcome with guilt. I've kept the two of you apart for decades."

"I've already told you, Darah," Millicent says. Oh, isn't she the noble one now. "It's okay. I was a very toxic person. I can't imagine how I might have channeled my anger had I known. It probably wouldn't have been pretty. And if you take a close look at all the insane things I've done at my age, imagine the chaos I might have caused when I was far less mature. Despite the awful parents I had, nothing was stopping me from being a better mother to you. No, I preferred to wallow in self-pity at my local pity spa: open twenty-four hours including holidays." She decides a slice of cheddar is in order and plucks one from the platter. "I saw no other recourse than to curse my parents and make you the recipient of my rage. I wanted you to understand every miserable minute of *my* life so you could not only commiserate, but also give me the endless sympathy I thought I deserved … despite how despicably I treated *you*." Remembering her etiquette, she pauses to properly consume the cheese. "By doing things as you did them, although I wasn't a part of anything, you gave this beautiful woman the daughter she was deprived of, and she gave you the mother *you* were deprived of. Knowing that really does make it all so much better. Things work out as they need to."

My darling lovingly touches Millicent's face. "You are being the most wonderful mother. I am so proud of you."

The screen has gone dark again.

"Have you learned anything, Nathaniel? Do you not see that these people are all taking responsibility for circumstances *not* created out of malice or ill will?"

"I see nothing, disembodied voice. My siblings were treated better than I was. I was pushed into a career I didn't want … one that required years of study and sleepless nights, memorization of useless Latin phrases, dissection of dead bodies, endless hours of reading and making rounds, fraternization with fools who actually hungered for these barbaric rituals, and being suffocated by everyone and everything that I so wholly despised. I had so much taken from me … my very soul … and that gave me every right to take it back in any way I saw fit and at every opportunity."

The screen is still dark, yet I see that One, Two, and Three are visible again. One is still playing with a full deck. Ah ha! Now I understand the communication I'm being given. I know exactly why I am here. This hotel, after being converted into an apartment house, has only fifty-one units. *It* is not playing with a full deck. If a physical ninth floor were built and turned into a grand luxury suite, for me, the building would have fifty-two units, and thus be playing with a full deck, and thus, the lost souls in it would be sane again. That is what I have intuited with my genius. I am masterful. I am brilliant. I have solved the great puzzle.

"You are a fool. You have solved nothing. There will never be a ninth floor. It is a space in your head. A place for you to receive messages. One that does not exist in the physical sense. You have learned nothing, Cockwomble. You have been given every opportunity to redeem yourself, and you have spat on every last one. You will pay dearly, but not as dearly as you deserve, for even I am not that cruel."

Thank goodness the voice has gone silent, and the screen again shows me what is going on in my darling's suite. An hour has passed, but nothing much has been missed. I am certain the three of them engaged in sappy, tiresome, female histrionics of which I do not tolerate well.

Darah looks at her grandmother. "I suppose it's obvious who the other two glasses are for. But where are they?"

My darling looks quite pale; the eternal rosiness in her cheeks is no more. "Soon. I expect them any moment." She can barely speak, and the younger generations show great worry on their brows.

Finally, there is another knock at the door. Darah rises and hurries to open it. Seeing Timmy and Mark, as she expected, she whispers to the boy's father, "Please, honey, would you go to apartment 608 and ask Lone Aggen to come here with you. Immediately, if possible. Please tell her its urgent. She'll understand."

Feeling her angst, he goes pale. "Yeah … sure thing. Be back shortly."

"Mark, wait."

"What is it?"

"I didn't want to do it this way, but I have no time to handle things as I imagined. Please, I hate to put you in this spot, but I need you to tell Lone, however briefly, what I shared with you when we got engaged. She needs to know who Ava Elisabeth is to Millicent … and to me."

"I can do that, honey."

"Please tell her I'm sorry. I just thought we had more time."

"I'll be gentle. Don't worry. Go take care of your family; I'll get Lone." As he turns to leave, she ushers Timmy in.

Darah takes his hand. "Come on, Tim. I want to introduce you to some people. First, see this lovely lady here?"

Millicent stands and walks over to greet him.

"Hi, Lovely," Timmy says to Millicent.

Everyone laughs as if the child is remotely amusing.

"This is Timothy Mark, Mother. Your grandson." Darah whispers in her ear, "Being perimenopausal, my pregnancy was almost the shock to me … and of course, to Mark … that Timmy's existence is to you."

"It is, Darah. I never imagined … not in my wildest dreams … that I would ever have a grandchild. Indeed, miracles do exist." She fans herself so as not to faint. (I'd like to see her crumble like a month-old bran muffin surrounded by vulturous flies.)

Oh, how I am tiring of the emotion and the tears. But Millicent is stepping on the gas instead of parking the car and gaining control of herself. At the very least, she could sit in neutral and spare the melodrama.

"This is my mother, honey. You know how Daddy's mommy is your Nana, well, this is your …." She looks at Millicent.

She beams. "Grandma. Please call me *Grandma*." Oh, I cannot bear it. I am reminded of the little Dutch boy of folklore fame who, to save his town from a flood, kept his finger in the leaking dike until he was rescued. Well, unlike the brave little boy, Millicent takes her finger away and lets her tears fill the room. "Oh, Darah, you have a child. I have a grandson. I thought that would never be. This is the most wonderful, bountiful day of my life. Hello, Timmy. I'm thrilled to meet you." She throws her arms around the child and hugs him, not caring that he will be traumatized for life. The brute.

"It's cool to have two grandmothers now."

"Very cool, isn't it?" Her attempt to converse with the adolescent one is preposterous. I doubt she was able to do so *as* a child.

"Timmy," Darah says. "There is something else. Our friend Ava Elisabeth is also your grandmother's mommy. And she is my grandmother, and your great-grandma. Do you understand all of that?"

"She's totally great." Timmy looks very matter-of-factly at his mother. "And I already knew Ava Elisabeth was related. Because I love her so much, and she loves us the same way."

"Oh, dear child," my beloved says, holding out her enfeebled arms. "You are so very wise." He runs into her arms and takes the now-empty space beside her. Why him and not me?

Once she finally releases him, he turns to his mother. "I was gonna ask you if we were like family or something. But everyone tells me I ask too many questions, so I didn't."

Again, they all chortle at the charmless boy.

My darling commands the floor anew, but her voice is shaky. "I love your questions, Timmy. It shows you have a bright and inquisitive mind. It will serve you well in life." She turns to her newly minted daughter. "Millicent, darling, I would love for you to live here. In my suite. I know you have no real home now, and I think this would be the perfect place for you."

"Really? You want me to live here? With you?" She is so happy I expect an abundance of drool to trickle down her chin.

"No, dearest. So that you can live near your family."

"But, I don't under—"

There is a knock at the door, and Mark lets himself in. Lone, who is writhing in anguish, is by his side. She rushes to my darling, who is now cuddling with Timmy who sits in the seat Darah had occupied. Darah stands between her mother and Mark. "Honey, you met Ava Elisabeth many years ago, before Timmy was born, but this is my mother, Millicent Gregnut."

"Millie," she says. "I would like to be called Millie now."

Just as he is about to respond, Ava Elisabeth looks up, still holding the boy, and calls out to Mark in a weakened voice. "So lovely to see you again."

Mark rushes over to her, gives her a kiss, utters some sentimental drivel, then returns to his soon-to-be mother-in-law. "It's very special to finally be meeting you, Millie."

"Please don't say you've heard a lot about me. I couldn't bear …." She nicks another pitiful lamentation in the bud.

He laughs. "I won't. But I *would* like to invite you to our wedding."

The pleasantries are aborted as they all look to the couch and are keenly aware that a painful end is upon them; they can only hold onto one another. The love of my life is about to leave this this earth … this plane of existence. All I want, all that has any meaning to me, is to be by her side. The love I have for her is greater than any of these so-called loved ones carry in their collective heart. As I say these words, the lifeblood is draining from Ava Elisabeth. The water from their useless tears is waist-high; Lone's pitiful wailing will drown anything the others might have to say. In seconds, the child has been elevated to an understanding beyond his years as he sobs and suffocates himself in her bosom.

Lone blubbers into Darah's ear. "Mark is a wonderful man. Thank you for asking him to explain things to me. Yes, a part of me is flabbergasted, yet another feels that everything finally makes sense. I just don't want you worry about the timing. I understand. You see, two nights ago, I begged Avie to take my quilt afghan. I knew the end was near, and I wanted her to have my most treasured possession. Somehow, I believed it would ease her transition. Now, I know that I was also hoping it would ease my grief, by allowing my love to embrace her until it was time. I am so glad everything is out in the open before …"

"I love you all, my family," my darling says. "Love one another as you have loved me and know, no matter how strange the storms and how weary the winds, that I will always love you. Please know that we will be reunited, no matter how much time passes."

The room goes dark, and she is gone. Mickey, still on my darling's lap, lets out an ungodly caterwaul. Timmy, horrorstruck, jumps up and runs into his mother's arms. Within a fraction of a second, a brilliant light shines on my Ava Elisabeth, and an ethereal young man, well-built with dark curly hair and wearing a flannel shirt, smiles and reaches out his hand for her. But it is not the limp hand of the old woman that reaches back. It is that of a young seductress. Eighteen-year-old Ava Elisabeth rises from her discarded body and takes the young man's hand as white sparks burst like a fan made of tiny lights and leave an afterglow of shimmering stars that fill the room with a warmth that could only emanate from her heart.

I have waited two lifetimes for this grand show of love and it is bestowed to the spirit of an adolescent bumpkin from the cornfields. My fury implodes as I reach out to grab my darling Ava Elisabeth, only to be yanked back by a giant claw, perhaps similar to those found in that piteous arcade game that snatches unsuspecting stuffed animals for greedy children to maul and cling to in their sleep. I cannot see it, but feels like the tentacles of a monster. I was certain that this voice was disembodied, but it seems to have grown limbs by which to pull me back from my destiny. "Let her go! She is mine," I call to the flannel-shirted youth who thinks himself a man.

"She was never yours, Cockwomble. You've put on such a grand show of desire that you've fooled yourself."

"Quite, Evil Voice. I have not. I am—"

"Silence. The last act is ending and there will be no curtain call."

Millicent cries as the yokel snatches her mother away. "That's my father! Do you see my father?" She glances at everyone for validation. He's so handsome and he waited so long for her. So very long. And look at how beautiful they are together."

Michael looks around, taking a moment to soak in each person with his transcendental eyes as if to acknowledge every one of them. He takes an extra moment, it seems, to beam in Millicent's direction. Offering one glorious last smile to all, he whisks my beloved into the heavens. I am mere rubble now. She is gone, and only her lifeless body remains … amidst the bounty of stars that are already fading … knowing they have lost all motivation to shine.

I will not dare to describe the tears that threaten to drown out my own. So much despair, and yet, none of these people know how I have suffered through two lifetimes. Damn them all.

Darah rushes to Ava Elisabeth and buries her head on her shoulder. When she finally looks up, she sees the chain around my beloved's neck and very delicately lifts the bottom of it into her hands.

"Oh my goodness. Look, there are two wedding rings here now. He must have left his ring here ... so we'll always know they're together."

The old woman, the one who still breathes between sobs, Lone, is doubled over in grief.

Darah gives her grandmother a kiss and reluctantly gets up to comfort the sobbing one who stands with Millicent. "I know what a huge piece of your heart has broken. I'll always be here for you. I hope you know that." She nods to Mark who is walking a tearful Timmy over to my darling's chaise lounge by the window.

"I will miss her with every breath," Lone says. (Now would be a fine time to prove that.) "We all will. It is such a terrible loss."

"You've known her longest. I understand. What can we do?"

Choked up, Lone walks over to hold Ava Elisabeth and kiss her good-bye, then steps aside so Millicent can do the same. "Time will heal us, Darah. At the very least, it will teach us how to go on until we also must bid farewell." Lone takes Millicent's hand and leads her to the loveseat, at a right angle from the couch, as Darah resumes her seat by my darling, copiously weeping,

Lone looks remorsefully at Millicent. "I'm sorry we got off to such a bad beginning. I had no idea why we resemble one another, but I do now. Avie was my first cousin, you see. We grew up together. When Avie's parents died, long after she'd moved to Paris, she contacted me, along with her sister, Nora Jaye, ... as it was finally safe to do so.

"I don't know how she knew of their deaths, but she had her ways. Of course, Avie didn't know where I was, but my younger cousin did. As it turns out, I was traveling about with my husband, and already being overseas, I arranged to spend a great deal of time in Paris getting to know her again. And then, sadly, here, after my Nigel was killed. As close as we were, she kept some secrets hidden away. She was afraid if people knew we were cousins, they'd pry ... or let secrets slip despite their best intentions. I've no doubt there is more about her

we shall never know. Of course, I knew she and Michael married ...
and that he was killed in the war. I lived only two blocks away from
her growing up."

"Oh, I was wondering ...."

"I never saw such chemistry between two people. If Avie and
Michael hadn't been my role models for love, I never would have
waited to find the right man ... my Nigel. And yes, I knew she wore
her ring on a gold chain. Beyond that ... the rest was the secret to me
that it was to all of you.

Looking at the body her grandmother once inhabited, Darah,
who has heard Lone's words to Millicent, speaks through her tears.
"Even when I told Norah Jaye who I was, she never told me you were
her cousin."

"I'm sure she had been asked to keep that to herself, should
anyone inquire. It's hard to explain. Avie never believed any of us
would betray her; I know that. But as much as she trusted me, you,
and others, she always believed there was only one way to lock away
the things you don't wish a soul to know: say nothing." Lone looks at
her departed cousin, whimpering. "She had an amazing ability to be
open and closed at the same time. And few were any the wiser."

Nodding, Millicent studies Lone's face as if it is something
hanging in an art museum meant to be stared at. "We really do have a
family resemblance."

Asking with her eyes if she can have the seat next to her
cousin, Lone looks at Darah, who gets up and occupies Lone's place
on the loveseat, next to her mother.

Lone takes my darling's pale white hand in hers. "Yes, Avie
and I both resemble our grandfather. That is the likeness between us."
She brushes the hair from my beloved's face as she continues speaking
without looking at her subject. "I'm glad we finally understand one
another, though I'm still curious as to why our first meeting
happened. Or our second."

"It happened because I was crazy and desperate; I'm sorry."

"You were hurting," Lone says with wretched sympathy, looking up at her, then at her departed cousin and friend. "Although it didn't seem as though fortune was smiling on us, at least from my perspective, I believe it was. Maybe so we both could appreciate how you are changing." She looks down at my darling's insentient form and snivels. "The universe has its reasons for so much we don't understand. I will miss you, Avie … in ways that defy words and logic. But I know you arranged to leave this way, so that we would all understand, beyond a shadow of a doubt, that this earth is not our final meeting place. Your wisdom is truly unparalleled."

The aggrieved one looks at her dead mother, feeling the sorrow as it slices through her, then looks at her first cousin once removed. "I'm so sorry I behaved like a deranged woman. I was out of my mind." Now a whimpering simpleton as well (oh, they are loathsome), Millicent looks over at Timmy, smiling. Mark, understanding her desperation to heap affection on his son, stands and allows Millicent to take his place as he walks over to the window. (This is quite a morbid version of 'musical chairs.') In her first official act as a second maternal unit, she sits on the chaise lounge and tries to comfort the boy with useless words as her own tears fall. (If there were any room left on the small lounger, she would no doubt smother the child as a whale would a fish.)

The cat is uttering sounds I have never heard from a feline before. While I'm certain he grieves his mistress, he may also be asking to be saved from the heiress apparent. Oh, how I understand his fear. Poor creature.

Darah speaks to Lone. "I knew she was your very best friend … and I'm so happy to know you are also a cousin. We share so much, but right now, it is the agony of her death that bonds us." She sniffles sans the refinement of requesting a tissue.

"So true, Darah. But Avie would want us all to be okay." She pauses. "We must be joyous knowing that Avie and Michael are together again. Seeing them, I know beyond any doubt that heaven exists and that my Nigel will come for me when it's my time. And I know I'll see my cousin again, and we'll talk for hours as we used to, in a garden more exquisite than the ones we have known. It will all be good. Until that day, I will wait." She looks upward. "Enjoy your splendor, Avie. You always believed it would come."

MOMENTS LATER

Still standing in front of the soleil mirror, "Petrified Pandora" has ceased to exist. Only a hard shell stands in her place; Pandora is out of her suffering. Her mind is now inhabited by one Nathaniel Noca, whose internal screams will never be heard by a soul. Ah, this blistering scab on humanity had said that "no one messes with Ava Elisabeth and gets away with it." He was right. He just never imagined that he was describing his own fate.

He spoke of souls who wait … some for things they cannot name. In all of his judgment, in all of his self-declared wisdom, he never understood that he existed in this waiting house for decades … for the sole purpose of being given an opportunity … at every turn … to recognize himself, to redeem himself, and to make amends. But his egocentricity only festered. Now, for Nathaniel Noca, there is no more time to wait. The universe can be kind … and patient … but even *it* has limits. He never could have escaped his fate, even if his soul had managed to dwell elsewhere. For every house is a waiting house.

When Pandora's body is found and discarded, Nathaniel will inhabit another tortured soul's mind, where his wants, his dreams, and his fears will be greater than he could ever imagine … and his desires will be contradicted in the most insidious and imaginative ways. He will be conscious of every excruciating moment. And this cycle will repeat beyond time for he will never know that a deeper conscience has ruled it shall be so.

THE END

ABOUT THE AUTHOR

LISETTE BRODEY was born and raised in the Philadelphia area. She lived in New York City for ten years and now resides in Los Angeles.

She is the multi-genre author of ten novels and one short story collection. Her books include: *Crooked Moon;*
Squalor, New Mexico; Molly Hacker Is Too Picky!;
The Desert Series (*Mystical High, Desert Star, Drawn Apart*);
Hotel Obscure: A Collection of Short Stories;
Love, Look Away; The Sum of our Sorrows; and
The Waiting House: A Novel in Stories.

She has also published two short stories in an anthology called *Triptych's (Mind's Eye Series, Book 3).*

All of her books are available in both Kindle and paperback.

Website & contact: lisettebrodey.com
Amazon author page: Author.to/lisettebrodey
Twitter: twitter.com/lisettebrodey
Facebook: facebook.com/BrodeyAuthor
Instagram: @ca_lisette
Pinterest: pinterest.com/lisetteca/

www.ingramcontent.com/pod-product-compliance
Lightning Source LLC
Chambersburg PA
CBHW070919260626
47162CB00007B/2732